Simply

Marvelous

Tekla Series

Leigh Jarrett

Published by Steambath Press (self-published)

Paperback 1st edition published April 2012
ISBN-13: 978-1927553091
ISBN-10: 1927553091

Paperback 2nd edition published September 2017
ISBN-13: 978-1927553404

With love to our brothers and sisters in the transgender community.

I hope your journey to wholeness isn't as difficult as Attila's.

Instead, let it be filled with lion-hearted courage, intense love and discovery of self, a lifetime of spiritual celebration, and most importantly, joy—endless, magnificent joy.

For you are perfect and beautiful, and simply marvellous.

Chapter One

Introductions

Mr. Price looked across his desk at the two people sitting in front of him and discreetly sighed to himself. When he'd become the principal of Tekla Senior High some twenty years ago, he never could've anticipated the dilemma he was facing today.

He crossed his arms and leaned back in his chair, trying to decide what the best course of action would be. The school board and the provincial government required that each student complete a mandatory level of physical education to graduate, but as he studied the mother and daughter watching him nervously, he realized that wasn't going to be feasible in this case.

"I think the best thing to do is try and get a doctor's note excusing Annie from physical education," he said. "I'm not sure what your doctor will list as the reason, but I'm sure they'll come up with something." He paused. "Mrs. Luka—"

"Please call me Cynthia."

"Yes, of course," Mr. Price replied. "Cynthia, might I ask how Annie managed to avoid this requirement in the past. This is her final year of high school. Surely this has come up before."

Cynthia rubbed the side of her temple and tried to compose herself. They'd only just moved to the small community five hours in from the west coast of Canada, and she'd been hoping they'd be able to blend in, but apparently, that wasn't going to be the case.

"We've only just moved here," she said. "And up until now Annie has been homeschooled, but he—"

Annie grabbed her mom's arm.

"Mom! Please! She!"

"I'm sorry, Attila ...Annie. I'm trying, all right?" Cynthia took a deep breath. "My ...*daughter* wanted to attend public school for ...*her* final year. God only knows why."

"I want to make some friends," Attila said. "And I want to go to prom like everyone else. I'm all right with who I am."

"But the other kids might not be," Cynthia retorted anxiously.

Mr. Price leaned forward on his desk and caught Attila's eye. "Your mother has a valid point," he said, "but if you hadn't told me, I never would've suspected."

Attila blushed, pleased with himself.

"How do you intend to play this out?" Mr. Price asked Attila.

"I'm not planning on telling anyone." Attila turned to face his mother. "Mom, I'm not stupid. I'll play it safe. No one will ever suspect I'm a guy. I promise."

Cynthia nodded her head in resignation.

"All right," Mr. Price said. "Welcome to Tekla, Annie.

If you have any concerns at all, please come see me."

Attila stood and took Mr. Price's hand in his and gave it a light, delicate handshake. "Thank you. I'll see you tomorrow."

Mr. Price dropped back into his chair as the pair left his office, and reached for his phone. He was going to have to put both vice principals, the police liaison officer, and the counseling office on alert, just in case.

Shaun Desmond shuffled the books around in his backpack, trying to get them to fit, but finally gave up in exasperation. He pulled everything out to start again and gave the backpack a good shake to make sure it was empty. His heart sank painfully as a small, folded note drifted onto the floor.

This had been the longest summer Shaun could ever remember, and even though he was running late, he'd never wanted to go back to school as badly as what he had these past few months. The loneliness of being without his best friend had been the most excruciating experience of his life.

He slumped onto the floor and picked up the note. It was a reminder about a homework assignment from last year, but the writing it contained was as recognizable to Shaun as his own would've been. He ran his fingers over the swooping letters that spelled out Daniel's name and rubbed his sleeve across his face, attempting to wipe away the tears that had escaped.

Daniel had been Shaun's best friend since kindergarten, and they'd planned on rooming together next year at university, but everything had come apart near the end of the last school year. Daniel had always been smaller than the other kids and hadn't been very adept when it came to playing sports, so he'd often been the object of ridicule. But what Daniel lacked in physical strength, he made up with mental acuity. He'd been exceedingly bright and had enjoyed the company of the other like-minded kids in his math and science clubs, and he'd become quite accomplished on the violin. But all of these achievements had only drawn additional negative attention. When he'd been caught making out with one of the guys from his band program, the bullying he'd already been enduring had reached epic and unrelenting proportions. It had become too much for Daniel to handle, and two days before the end of the last school year, he'd hung himself in his room.

Shaun remembered the conversation he'd had with Daniel just moments before he'd taken his life. Daniel had been extremely depressed, but Shaun had thought they'd worked through his emotions for the day. It had become a nightly ritual between them, talking about the events of the day over the phone, trying to gain some perspective on the trials and tribulations of high school, and how things would be different once they headed off to university. They'd ended the conversation with Daniel sounding almost hopeful, but Shaun realized now that Daniel's emotional upturn was because he'd made the decision to end his pain.

The sun streamed in through the torn portion of the drapery that hung haphazardly across Curtis Bantam's bedroom window. He turned away to keep the light from hurting his eyes and rolled directly into a pool of vomit he must've thrown up during the night.

He pushed himself up and looked at it, wondering how the hell he'd managed to throw anything up at all. He'd barely eaten anything in almost three days. Then without warning, his bedroom door flew open and crashed into the wall, making his head scream in agony, but he managed to scurry to the far side of the mattress and drop down onto the floor before his dad entered the room.

Curtis peered across the floor from beneath his bed as the drunken excuse of a man scanned the room looking for him. He breathed a sigh of relief when the threat stumbled back out through the door with the belt he'd been wielding dragging behind him.

He waited for a few minutes until he heard his dad shout something at his mom and fire up his car, and screech out of the driveway. Once everything was quiet, Curtis ventured out of his room into the bathroom to get ready for school.

The mirror above the chipped porcelain sink was cracked and faded with age and neglect, but it had enough surface area left to reflect the image of the stunningly attractive and enduringly innocent face staring into it.

Curtis roughed up his shaggy blond hair and turned his head from side to side trying to see if the swelling below his left eye was going to be visible. His last date of the night had turned rough on him, forcing him to sniff an excessive amount of poppers, even by his standards, while pounding his ass mercilessly.

He'd relaxed into it and let overwhelming nausea from the drugs sweep over him, getting off on the buzzing sensation in his head. He'd been startled back to reality, his body aching, when he was pitched out at the curb, surprisingly close to where the guy had initially picked him up. He figured he must've hit his face when he was dumped from the car, but he wasn't really sure.

Curtis quickly stuffed his hands into his jean pockets and pulled out a fifty-dollar bill. At least the guy had paid him. Maybe he'd even fed him, but he couldn't remember.

Stripping off his clothes, he cringed with every movement; the impact of too many mostly sleepless nights was wearing on him. He turned the shower on and splashed the cold water around his face before he stepped into it. There was nothing like a freezing cold shower to get the blood flowing after working all night.

The doorbell rang, and a commotion instantly erupted in the foyer as the family's five Pomeranians went wild with excitement to see who was at the front door.

Dixie finished the last stroke of mascara and rechecked her appearance in the mirror. She'd added a bright blue streak to her sleek black hair and pushed a new piercing through her lip the night before. It didn't appear to be swollen, and it complemented the new ring she'd added to her nose last week.

The sound of feet pounding up the stairs had her turning toward her bedroom door in anticipation. Her best friend Ming Fujiwara had been away all summer visiting his family in Japan and had only just arrived home that morning in time for school.

Dixie shrieked with laughter as Ming flew in through

her door.

"Oh! My! God!" Ming exclaimed, and leaped at her, tipping her face up to look at him so he could examine what she'd done.

"What do you think?" Dixie asked, posing for him.

"That you're absolutely gorgeous as usual." Ming shoved Dixie over and leaned on her makeup table, studying his own face in the mirror. "What I wouldn't give to have skin like yours. Some girls have all the luck." He gave himself one last look and then sorted through a few earrings strewn about on the table. He decided to change out the ones he was wearing for a pair of hers.

"Your skin is practically flawless," Dixie said and laughed when Ming looked at her suspiciously.

Ming picked up her face powder and brush and tried to lighten up the area just below his jawline, but the powder was about three shades too light. "Says the girl that doesn't have to fight a constant battle against afternoon shadow." He set the powder down in disgust. "Do you have any idea how much time and money I spend each month trying to look fabulous?"

"Whatever you're doing. It's working. You're divine."

"Aren't you just a sweetheart this morning?" Ming wrapped his arm around Dixie and kissed her cheek. "I am so happy to be home again. My relatives do not understand me ...at all."

"Is your Japanese a little rusty?" Dixie grinned, knowing he was referring to something else entirely.

"Hah. Hah. You know exactly what I mean."

Dixie watched as Ming applied some of her light pink

lip-gloss to his lips and started rooting around in the little purse he always carried with him. She sighed with heavy concern as he removed a small vial, tapped some of its contents onto the top of his hand, and snorted it. He repeated the process in the other nostril then reached for a tissue from Dixie's bedside table.

"Now I'm ready to face the first day of what, I pray, is the last school year of my miserable, depressing existence," Ming said and then swooned dramatically. "Unless, of course, the fair and gallant Eric of Quarterback is overcome by my seductive ways and abandons his quest to seek out cheerleading maidens, preferring the loving hands of one, such as myself, that is intimately acquainted with the male form and what it truly desires."

Dixie's eyebrows shot up with amusement, and she snorted. "God, I missed you."

"Little consolation for the broken-hearted, my dear." Ming dabbed at a feigned tear falling from his eye then grinned at Dixie. "At least you appreciate me."

"Always." Dixie stood and reached for Ming's hand with a prayer of her own that this would be the year Ming found true love because he deserved it more than any other person she knew.

Chapter Two

First Day of School

Attila drove into the school parking lot a full thirty minutes before the first of the school buses were scheduled to arrive. A few people were wandering around outside the main doors, but not enough that he felt comfortable leaving the anonymity of his car.

He moved a few of his binders out of the way to retrieve the purse he'd accidentally buried and chastised his carelessness. No self-respecting girl would've abandoned her coveted accessory and organizational tool to such a fate. He popped it open to make sure none of his makeup was broken before placing it neatly in his lap.

The idea of attending public school for his senior year had been a spontaneous one forged partially from his need to connect with other people his own age on an intellectual level, but also fueled by his desire to meet someone and connect on a more primal and physically satisfying level.

Of course, he hadn't told his mother this or she never would've allowed him out of the house, with or without his purse.

Attila was so absorbed by his thoughts that he jumped when someone tapped on his driver side window. He bit his lower lip and blushed at the sight of the lean and attractive guy perched against his car waiting for him to respond.

He turned the key back a notch to restore the power and rolled his window all the way down.

"Can I help you?" Attila asked.

"I'm sure that can be arranged," the guy said as he crouched down, so he was eye level with Attila. "The name's Eric Templeton ...I'm a quarterback."

Attila tucked himself further away from the window, trying to gain some distance between himself and the increasingly familiar Eric, who was now playing with the short blond tendrils of his hair that he'd so meticulously set this morning.

"It's nice to meet you, Eric," he replied and then cleared his throat. "Please don't take this the wrong way, but—"

"What's your name gorgeous?"

"My name?" Attila felt his face flush as his mind scrambled for something substantial to hang on to. The incredibly handsome Eric had just called him gorgeous. He closed his eyes and tried to refocus his thoughts. "Annie ...My name is Annie."

Eric leaned in closer and ran his fingers along Attila's arm, stroking him; all the little hairs rose to attention. "It's been a pleasure meeting you, Annie. Maybe I'll see you around."

Attila waited until Eric had cleared the parking lot and was standing with a group of his friends before he let himself breathe again. It was possible his plan of blending in and discreetly finding himself a boyfriend was ill-conceived, and could just as easily backfire as succeed. Guys like Eric didn't have a sense of humor when it came to finding out he wasn't really a girl.

Especially after they'd hit on him.

The bell for homeroom had already rung by the time Shaun pushed his way through the main doors and into the multi-purpose room. He dropped his backpack and scanned the lists of students' names, looking for his own so he could determine which classroom he should be headed for. His finger passed over the section where Daniel's name would have appeared had he still been alive—and he collapsed onto the floor, grief coursing through his body.

Curtis wasn't a big believer in punctuality, insisting that if you were worth it, people would wait for you. It was an attitude that served him well on the streets but contributed adversely to his already appalling attendance record at school. Luckily, for him, the administration was keenly aware of his less than optimum home environment and they'd always been more than accommodating whenever he was running behind schedule.

He stepped into the vacated multi-purpose room and observed what looked like a crumpled teenaged boy attached to a backpack. Against his better judgment, Curtis strode across the room to investigate and perhaps lend his assistance.

"Hey, you," Curtis said then shoved the non-responsive mass with his foot. "Are you hankering for a bedroll, or what?"

"Leave me alone."

Curtis glanced around the room and briefly considered following the tersely spoken request, but then changed his mind. The guy at his feet looked vaguely familiar.

"What's your name?" he asked, and waited, but there was no response. Curtis tilted his body sideways to get a better look at the guy's face. He'd definitely seen him before. "Hey, aren't you that guy that usually hangs around with that other guy. The little dipshit with the curly black hair?"

"Fuck off!" Shaun spun around and tried to kick Curtis in the shins, missing. "You fucking piece of shit!"

"Whoa. Language there, kemosabe. I'm just trying to help out a fellow cowpoke."

Curtis dropped onto the floor and crossed his legs, but then changed his mind and swung himself onto one hip. He'd had a busy week, and his back door was causing him grief. He was contemplating going back to blow jobs for a while, even though they didn't pay as much until he could figure out a way to make his dates actually use the bottles of lube he chucked at them.

"You're the young gun named Shaun, correct?" Curtis crashed back onto the floor and threw his hands up over his face. "Fuck man. I'm such an idiot." He rolled over onto his stomach and sidled closer to Shaun. "I'm so sorry dude about what I said earlier. About your friend. It didn't click at first."

Shaun closed his eyes and curled himself into a ball.

"Do you want me to call someone?" Curtis asked.

"I just want to be left alone."

"That's all very well, but you're lying in a public area. Sooner or later you're going to be overrun by masses of little varmints." He leaned over and tapped Shaun on the head with his pointer finger. "Or better yet, Mr. Price is going to be called and then you're going to have to explain yourself to him, your parents, and probably a handful of shrinks. Is that what you want?"

Shaun stretched himself out and opened his eyes. "If I say *no*, will you get me out of here?"

"Valiantly, mon cher monsieur."

Shaun laughed and shook his head.

"Why are you helping me?" he asked, curious as to why Tekla's notorious loner was even speaking to him.

Curtis rose to his feet and straightened out a fictitious collar with the dramatic flair of a stage actor, playing at putting on airs.

"Civic duty and all that," he replied.

Then he stopped, his hands dropping to his sides, as his body tensed and his shoulder rolled back at an odd angle, making him twitch. His legs threatened to crumble, but he took a deep breath to relax his mind and then grinned bawdily at Shaun.

Shaun snorted. "What the fuck is wrong with you?"

"Wrong? Who said anything was wrong with me?" Curtis retorted, dramatically extending his hand for Shaun to take, and helped him to his feet. "I take offense at such a suggestion."

"You're Curtis Bantam, right?"

"Depends on who's asking."

Curtis scooped up Shaun's backpack and held the main door open for him to pass through to outside

"I'm asking," Shaun said as he followed Curtis around the back of the school to the covered parking lot. He paused as Curtis opened the passenger door of his car for him. "Where are we going?"

"Well Shaun who's asking, I thought we could take a little drive and get to know each other better."

"That sounds like a cheesy pickup line from a porno flick."

He studied Curtis for a second then grabbed his backpack and slid into the passenger seat. Whatever Curtis had planned was likely to be infinitely more distracting than sitting in school all day.

The guy had a seriously bizarre reputation.

The deafening sound of hundreds of teenagers talking all at once had Attila believing one's ears really could bleed given half a chance. The quiet sound of birdsong and the subtle ting-ting of the little metal spoon his mom used to stir his tea echoed in his mind. But then he reminded himself, this was what he'd signed up for.

He reset his posture and attempted to enjoy his lunch.

All was as it should be until his salad flew onto the floor and the container of cold tea he'd just opened ended up in his lap as a raucous group of rugby players moved to intercept the basketball that had mysteriously been launched into the air.

Attila dropped his hands and breathed deeply to calm his nerves. He gathered his composure and stood, brushing the tea from the front of the dusty pink, tweed skirt he'd only managed to wear once. He looked down at it and sighed, and glanced around as a female voice peered around his shoulder.

"Is it ruined?" the voice asked.

"Possibly. But I might be able to salvage it. I don't think you'll be able to see it once it dries." Attila turned the rest of the way around and studied the girl facing him. She was about five foot nothing, dark of hair, cute as a button, and hugely pregnant.

"You're new here, aren't you?" she asked.

"Yes …how far along are you?" Attila reached out and waited for her to nod her head before laying his hand on her stomach.

"Thirty-six weeks. My name is Candace by the way."

Attila's eyes lit up, and he looked into Candace's face as he felt the baby move against his hand. "That is so amazing."

"You know what would be even more amazing?"

Attila shook his, enthralled.

"I'm sure I can't imagine," he answered.

Candace paused and examined the face staring back at her. She was mesmerized by how the beautifully elegant bone structure and startling blue eyes were unfathomably married to perfectly clear skin, immaculate makeup, and fastidiously coiffed hair. The new girl was absolutely gorgeous.

"What did you say your name was?" she asked.

"I didn't. It's Annie." Attila dipped a small curtsy but caught himself before she noticed. "What would be even more amazing?"

"Having the father of this little bundle man up …and having you tell me how you manage to get your skin so perfect."

"Oh …um. Birth control pills actually."

"I wish I'd known that earlier. It would've saved me a lot of grief all over the place." Candace shifted her body and looked with apparent longing at the bench seating.

"Did you want to sit down?" Attila asked.

"No, if I sit, I'll never get up again." Candace lifted her foot onto the bench and waited for Attila to sit back down. "So your parents are all right with you taking the pill."

Attila dropped his voice to a whisper. "It's just my mom, and she doesn't know. I have a friend that gets them for me." He cringed, sensing someone standing directly behind him.

"What are we talking about?" the person behind Attila asked. "Sounds all clandestine."

"Annie," Candace said. "This is my neighbor Dixie, who has a bad habit of eavesdropping."

Attila slid over as Dixie dropped down onto the bench next to him. But then his attention faltered, drawn elsewhere when Dixie's blatantly gay companion took a seat across from him.

"We were talking about birth control pills," Candace said.

Ming adjusted his scarf then tied it back in a bow.

"Sweetheart," he said. "You should've been talking about those pills a long time before now." He dropped his hands expressively on the table. "I personally can't imagine life without them."

"Yeah until the day your balls shrink, and you can't get it up anymore," Dixie said. "Then where will all the pretty boys be?"

"So aggressive," Ming said and winked at her. He crossed his arms and turned his attention to the person sitting next to her. "What was your name again honey?"

Attila looked up. He'd been deep in thought and hadn't been paying attention. "I'm sorry …it's Annie."

"Is it now?" Ming leaned back and studied Attila intently. "I must say, you are by far the most fascinating creature I've seen around here in a very long time." His concentration broke as the bell rung, and people around them began leaving.

But he wasn't done yet.

"Move it," Dixie said to Ming as she helped Candace with her books. "Mr. Carter turns into such a bitch if we're late."

"Make some kind of excuses for me, would you?" Ming said. "Annie and I have a lot to talk about." He motioned for Attila to sit back down and waved at Dixie, indicating that she needed to take off. Attila waited until the room was empty before speaking.

"What did you want to talk to me about?" he asked.

Ming reached across the table and brushed his fingers across Attila's hand, ending at the perfectly manicured pink fingernails.

"First," he said, "I want to know what your real name is."

"I've told you my name." Attila feigned confusion and

pulled his hand away. "I don't know what you're implying."

Ming stood and walked around to Attila's side of the table, and leaned down, whispering in his ear. "I'm implying that you're a homegrown and exquisitely appointed ladyboy."

Attila shivered.

"Whatever do you mean by that?" he asked.

Attila pressed back against Ming's body as he rose from the bench seat, letting his ass brush across Ming's hips.

He gasped with exhilaration as Ming pinned him there and ran his hand down the front of his skirt.

"I mean there's more to you than meets the eye," Ming said and turned Attila to face him. "There's a guy's change room in the basement that's locked at this time of day." He lifted a key from his pocket and dangled in front of Attila. "Although a few of us have managed to gain special access." He motioned for Attila to follow along and strode off across the room.

Curtis completed the final turn of the hour-long journey and slowed down along a winding street that ran the entire length of the exclusive estate community of *Hillside*. A driveway at the end of the street opened up onto an expansive property overlooking a lake and acres of vineyards. Sprawled along one side was a mansion, the size of which Shaun had never seen before.

"Whose house is this?" Shaun asked, wondering how Curtis would even know someone from this level of society.

"He calls himself Mr. Jenkins, but that's not his real name," Curtis said as he threw his driver side door open.

"What are we doing here?"

"Do you want to make an easy hundred bucks?"

Shaun followed Curtis up the long set of steps and waited while he rang the bell. "What do I have to do?"

"Nothing really." Curtis looked up and smiled as the door opened. They were greeted by a tall, handsome, and obviously wealthy man. Shaun figured he couldn't be more than about thirty and wondered how he'd amassed so much wealth at such a young age. His own father had taken much longer than that to acquire his vast fortune, and it paled in comparison to what he saw here.

"Curtis. What a pleasure to see you," Mr. Jenkins said then looked at Shaun. "I got your message, but you didn't mention you were bringing a friend. Who's this you've brought with you?"

"This is my good buddy, Shaun."

"Is he cool?"

"Of course he's cool, Mr. J."

Curtis took hold of Shaun's arm and pulled him through the front door into the foyer.

"Where do you want me?" Mr. Jenkins asked as he closed the door behind them.

"I'm thinking the lounge," Curtis replied. "That leather ottoman of yours is pretty slick. I love all the attachments."

Shaun pulled sharply on Curtis' sleeve and tucked his face up close to Curtis' ear. "What the fuck are we doing here?"

"Is there a problem?" Mr. Jenkins asked, annoyed.

"No, everything is golden," Curtis replied. "My boy here just needs to take a piss is all. Maybe you could make us something to eat while I attend to him."

Shaun let himself be dragged along to the bathroom situated at the far end of the lounge. Once inside, he dropped down onto the toilet seat as Curtis closed the door.

"All right, here's the deal," Curtis began. "Mr. Jenkins is a long-standing client of mine. He pays really well, but only if he's being watched …if you know what I mean."

"You brought me here so I could watch you?"

Shaun had heard rumors about Curtis' occupation, but he'd always assumed people were making things up because Curtis was a bit of an outcast due to his somewhat unconventional personality.

"Yeah, it's not a big deal," Curtis replied. "You just have to sit there, watch us, and make a hundred bucks. He'll throw in an extra fifty if you jerk off though."

"I can't believe this." Shaun dropped his head. "When I left the house this morning, I was not expecting to spend my afternoon watching two guys have sex."

"Wonders never cease in my world." Curtis lowered his voice. "Hey, you're eighteen, right? I told Mr. Jenkins you were cool, but I thought I'd better check."

Shaun rolled his eyes and nodded his head as Curtis crouched down in front of him.

"So, are you in?" Curtis asked.

"Sure, what the hell. I've got nothing better to do." Shaun rose to his feet and looked at himself in the mirror. He didn't even recognize the guy staring back at him.

"But I'm only looking to make a hundred bucks," he added. "I'm not some fucking pervert. Mr. Jenkins can keep his extra fifty." He followed Curtis out into the lounge.

"How much are you making?"

"A cool grand." Curtis laughed as Shaun's eyes popped open.

"When I'm motivated," he said, nudging Shaun. "I'm very good at what I do. But prepare yourself. We're going to be here a while. I literally have to work my ass off for that kind of money."

Shaun sunk onto the sofa and tried to eat the sandwiches Mr. Jenkins brought in for them, but his mind kept wandering over to the leather ottoman directly in front of him, wondering what kind of deviant behavior he was about to witness.

He was startled from his thoughts when Mr. Jenkins leaned in and offered him a few lines of cocaine. He'd never done anything more ominous than weed but figured he was probably going to need something stronger to get him through the rest of the day. Curtis, who'd already done a few lines, gestured to Shaun that he didn't have to take anything if he didn't want to.

Sighing in resignation, Shaun accepted the mirror from Mr. Jenkins and did the lines. Completely energized, he fell back into the cushions, ready to endure whatever Curtis had in store.

Curtis watched Shaun for a second to make sure he was all right before he flicked some music on and started dancing around, peeling his clothes off for Mr. Jenkins' viewing pleasure.

Attila looked around the change room, noting one of the washroom stalls was already occupied. He listened carefully and grinned. It seemed he and Ming weren't the only ones making use of the dark empty space. He bit his lip in anticipation as Ming moved up behind him and kissed the back of his neck. Attila reached back, raking his fingers through Ming's hair, gasping with exhilaration. He'd never even dreamed his first time would be in a school change room—on the first day of school. He shivered. Truthfully, it was as scary as it was exciting. They hadn't even kissed yet.

The metal reverberated against Attila's chest as Ming slammed him forward, pressing him to the lockers as he reached beneath Attila's skirt, hauling his nylon stockings and thong gaff away.

"Ming …," Attila whispered, unsure.

"Don't worry, baby," Ming reassured. "I won't hurt you."

Attila shut his eyes and sighed with relief when he heard Ming ripping a condom package open with his teeth. He wasn't sure what he would've done if Ming hadn't had one; his desire was pulsing, overtaking him now, demanding to be sated.

He groaned, banging his hands against the metal lockers in ecstasy as Ming eased into him.

"Are you all right, champ?" Curtis leaned over the passenger seat and patted Shaun's face. "We're home safe and sound."

Shaun lifted his head and looked out through the windshield. That was definitely his house they were parked in front of, but he wasn't sure how he was going to make it from where he was, sitting in Curtis' car, to where he wanted to be, curled up in bed.

"You're going to have to help me," he said.

"That might appear a bit odd to the parental units, me traipsing your ass to your room at this hour, don't you think?"

"What time is it?" Shaun asked.

Curtis pulled out his phone and checked. "It's almost ten."

"I thought you said it was going to be an afternoon job."

"That was before you got all crazy and joined in."

Shaun groaned and rolled toward Curtis. He distinctly remembered where everything had gone wrong. When Curtis and Mr. Jenkins had first started going at it, he'd been utterly repulsed but oddly fascinated by what they were doing to each other. After about an hour, Mr. Jenkins had taken a break to use the washroom, leaving Curtis bound to the ottoman poised on all fours, waiting for him to return. Seeing Curtis there, helpless, vulnerable, Shaun's body had done something entirely unexpected.

"I don't know what got into you," Curtis said and then laughed. "Except me and Mr. Jenkins that is. Sweet bottom."

"Fuck off!" A rush of color flooded Shaun's cheeks. "I'm not even fucking gay."

"Yeah, me either. But it's a fucking rush, isn't it?"

Shaun rolled back and pushed the passenger door open. "You're seriously twisted, you know that?" He reached toward the floor, grabbed his backpack, and hauled himself out of the car, slamming the door behind him.

"Do you still need my help?" Curtis asked.

"I don't know." Shaun reached into his pocket and pulled out a roll of twenties, held together by an elastic band. Mr. Jenkins had insisted he receive proper compensation for his services. Apparently, his dignity was only worth about five hundred dollars.

"My parents are asleep already," he said, "and I live around back. Did you want to come in?"

Curtis pushed himself up in his seat and peered out through the open sunroof at Shaun. "I don't know, sport. I've got places to go. People to see. Money to make."

"You're going back out there?" Shaun sighed, deflated, ready to be rejected as Curtis pinched the bridge of his nose. He appeared to be struggling with a decision.

"Tell you what," Curtis said. "I could use a hot shower and some clean clothes before I take off."

"All right." Shaun nodded. "Sounds good."

He turned toward the house and waited for Curtis to catch up before he made his way through a large gate into the backyard of the estate, heading off across the lawn to the pool house he'd moved into just before school started. It was smaller than he would've liked, but it had a decent sized central room including a sofa bed, a massive bathroom, and a small kitchenette. He hadn't moved all of his stuff in yet, but it was starting to look like his own place.

Curtis stepped through the door and looked around.

"This is all yours?" he asked.

"Yeah, my parents figured I needed my own space." Shaun sunk down onto the sofa. "Especially after the thing with Daniel."

"Hey, yeah, I'm really sorry about what I said this morning. I'm sure your friend Daniel wasn't a dipshit."

"Actually, he was." Shaun smiled. "It was part of his charm."

Gazing up at Curtis, he made a decision and dropped his backpack onto the floor, reached for Curtis' hand and pulled him down onto the sofa, pushed him over, and attacked his mouth.

Curtis considered stopping Shaun, to explain that the feelings he was having toward him were a typical reaction for someone who had shared an experience such as the one they'd had that afternoon.

But it was so rare for him to be held by someone who wasn't paying him, he decided against it.

Dixie rolled over and turned on her bedside lamp when she heard a light tapping on her bedroom window. She looked over at the time and exhaled. It was almost two in the morning, and Dixie was seriously considering not letting him in. The last time she'd seen Ming, he'd been in the multi-purpose room with Annie. After that, he'd taken off without letting her know where he was going, and she'd been left to convince Mr. Clark that Ming had indeed planned on coming to class, but that he must've been hindered by unforeseen difficulties. She'd waited for Ming after school, as was her usual routine, but he hadn't materialized or answered her repeated attempts to reach him. She threw back the covers, climbed out of bed, and begrudgingly opened the window.

"Is your phone off?" Ming asked as he jumped into the

room.

"No, I'm screening my calls."

"Are you mad at me?"

Dixie tucked herself back in bed and pulled the covers up around her shoulders. "You abandoned me today."

"With good reason. I made quite the discovery." Ming sat down on Dixie's bed and crossed his legs, waiting for her to bite at his enticing statement, but she remained silent.

"Aren't you going to ask me what it was?" he asked.

"Only if it doesn't involve you getting laid. I'm sick of hearing about your escapades. It's depressing for those of us who actually feel the need to care about the people we sleep with."

"Fine. I'll just leave then." Ming made to stand up but then settled back in. "No, this is too good not to share." He blushed, bit his bottom lip, then sighed. "I think I'm in love."

"Not again." Dixie sat up. "Ming, those jocks are never going to be interested in you. Especially Eric Templeton."

"I'm not interested in jocks anymore. Especially Eric ...who actually had the audacity to hit on my lover this morning."

"Eric hit on your latest love?" Dixie snorted. "Either you've changed camps and started dating cheerleaders, or you're pulling my leg."

"No pulling involved." Ming winked at her. "Just a lot of pushing. An entire afternoon of hot and steamy pushing."

Dixie rolled her eyes.

"All right, who is he?"

"You met him today at lunch." Ming sighed

dramatically and batted his eyelashes. "His name is Attila …and he is an absolute dreamboat of a lover. So soft and innocent."

Dixie crossed her arms and tapped her fingers on her elbows in irritation. "Story time is over. I never met anyone named Attila at lunch today." She moved her feet over and used them to push Ming off the end of her bed. "Those damn drugs you're taking are messing with your head. Now you're hallucinating about sleeping with historical figures. Attila …seriously, Ming."

Ming shrieked, causing Dixie to jump, and doubled over in laughter. He fought to regain his composure, fanning at his face to stop the tears, and finally managed to take a deep breath.

"Oh, sweetie," he said, "that is the funniest thing I've heard in a long time. But I haven't done any drugs since first thing this morning. I didn't need to. Like I said …I'm in love."

Dixie's eyebrows shot up in surprise.

"Nothing?"

"Not a drop, or a sniff, or a swallow all day," Ming answered. "And you did meet him at lunch today. Remember Annie?"

Dixie pressed a hand to her temple, searching her memory for any indicators. Ming had certainly picked up on them quickly.

"Annie's a guy?" she asked finally.

Ming nodded.

"Yes, but you can't tell anyone. He's trying to lay low."

"I think people might get suspicious when the two of

you are hanging all over each other in the hallways."

"I didn't think of that."

"And didn't you say Eric hit on him this morning?"

Ming dropped his head and stared at the floor. "I'm never going to have a proper boyfriend, am I?"

"If by *proper*, you mean one you can parade up and down the hallways of the school. Then, no. Not this one at least." Dixie patted the bed beside her and motioned for Ming to sit down. "Is he really set on keeping the Annie persona?"

"It's who he really is, Dixie."

"What are the chances you could pull off being a straight guy?"

Ming grinned at her. "Slim to none, sugar."

"Then a secret love affair it shall be."

Ming lay down beside Dixie and gazed up at the ceiling. He extended his arm toward it and let Dixie intertwine her fingers with his the way they used to do as kids.

"He really is amazing," he said. "We didn't spend all afternoon fucking. We took off to my house and spent some time just sitting around and talking." He grinned. "And then we went back to fucking. He's strictly a bottom you know. Not that I would've expected anything different. But thank god I'm willing to be versatile in a pinch, or that would've been the end of us right there."

He sighed emphatically. "He would've let me go on fucking him forever. He's an absolutely insatiable nelly bottom. And his blow jobs are to die for …and his rimming—"

Ming looked over at Dixie and smiled. She was watching him with a mixed look of disgust and amusement in her eyes.

"I'm going to shut up now," he said.

Dixie patted Ming's face affectionately and tucked herself into his side, closed her eyes, and drifted back to sleep.

Chapter Three

So Much Has Changed

Kevin Magarey hadn't returned from summer holidays in time to attend the first day, but that was okay with him. He wasn't anxious to return to the school that had stolen one of his best friends from him.

He, Daniel, and Shaun had all grown up on the same street, naturally becoming close over the many years they'd been hanging out. The loss of Daniel had torn his and Shaun's friendship apart, each blaming the other for not being there for him.

Kevin's parents had sent him away over the summer to give him and Shaun a chance to gain some perspective apart from each other in the hope they would come to their senses and reconcile. During his vacation, Kevin had had plenty of time to think and had come to a conclusion, that there wasn't much more either he or Shaun could've done for Daniel. They'd followed all the proper channels. Talking to their parents, Daniel's parents, school counselors, teen depression and suicide hotlines, and even the police liaison officer. None of it had helped. Daniel had made the decision to leave them. Kevin kicked a rock across the street.

During the last week of summer holidays, he'd sent

numerous texts to Shaun, apologizing, but there hadn't been a response from him until three days ago. He pulled the text message up, and read it over, relieved. All seemed to be forgiven. He couldn't wait to see Shaun and go back to some semblance of normal in their lives.

Kevin reached through and unlocked the gate to Shaun's backyard, swearing as his shirt caught on the latch. He had to admit he was jealous of Shaun being allowed to move into his pool house; his own parents would never permit him to move into theirs.

He peered through the glass of the sliding door, but couldn't see Shaun moving around, and the lights weren't on, so he knocked and let himself in. He figured Shaun must've forgotten to set his alarm. Shaun had a bad habit of sleeping in and being late for almost everything. But as Kevin stepped across the room, he could see the bed was empty, so he headed down the hall toward the bathroom. He could hear the water of the shower running, but he could also hear what sounded like someone groaning.

Thinking Shaun had slipped and injured himself in the shower, Kevin ran into the bathroom, straight into what would be forever known as his worst nightmare.

Curtis had ended up spending the night with Shaun, and they'd been attempting to get ready for school when they'd become distracted. At present, Curtis had Shaun pinned up against the glass wall of the shower enclosure and was aggressively rocking him against it with deep, powerful thrusts as he devoured Shaun's mouth. He looked up as he sensed Kevin enter the bathroom, slowed his pace, and set Shaun back on his feet.

"Do you know this guy?" Curtis asked as he pulled Shaun into his arms, clinging to him protectively.

Shaun twisted around and peered out through the opening of the shower enclosure, and felt his stomach drop.

"Kevin," he said. "This is *not* what it looks like."

"I don't know, Shaun," Kevin replied, backing up against the doorframe. He steadied his breathing and ran his hand through his hair in confusion. "It kind of looks like you're letting that guy fuck you."

"All right ...maybe it is what it looks like," said Shaun.

"I think I should go," Curtis said. "Let you two work this out." He cupped Shaun's face in his hands and kissed his lips. "I'll catch up with you at school, sport, all right?"

Shaun kissed him back and nodded.

Kevin guarded his temper as Curtis grabbed a towel and walked out past him. He waited until he heard the door to the pool house close before he turned his attention back to Shaun.

"Please tell me that wasn't Curtis Bantam."

Shaun exhaled loudly as he wrapped a towel around his waist. "If I did that, I'd be lying." He pushed past Kevin into the main room and started pitching through the few articles of clothing he had stored there. He glanced over at the pieces of Curtis' discarded clothing still lying in a pile on the floor, sincerely hoping Curtis had put something on other than a towel before he'd walked through his backyard and out to his car.

Then he smiled. He wouldn't put it past Curtis to drive home in the nude.

"What the fuck happened?" Kevin asked.

"That is a very long story. And I am absolutely positive you wouldn't be interested in hearing any of it." Shaun lifted a shirt out of a box that was set to one side of the room and, figuring it was clean enough, slipped it on over his head. "Short form. I don't know what happened. One minute he was helping me off the floor of the multi-purpose room. Then twenty-four hours later, he was doing that." He indicated toward the bathroom with his hand.

"So, this hasn't been going on all summer?"

Shaun stuffed his feet into his shoes and checked around for his keys before grabbing his backpack.

"God, no," he answered.

"Then you haven't turned gay on me?"

"No." Shaun closed and locked the door after Kevin stepped out through it. "Curtis isn't gay either."

"This isn't about Curtis. I couldn't care less what he does with his dick. Unless he's using it to fuck you."

Shaun bumped Kevin affectionately with his elbow as they walked toward the school. "It's not going to happen again. Curtis and I were doing a few lines last night. Things got a bit crazy, and it spilled over to the morning."

Kevin cringed. "So now you're doing drugs as well as guys?"

"Fuck off! I told you it was a onetime thing."

"But how could you let him do that to you?"

"Because like Curtis says—it's a fucking rush." Shaun slowed down when Kevin came to a complete stop. "What?"

"What is wrong with you?"

Shaun grabbed Kevin's sleeve and started pulling him along. "Who said anything was wrong with me? I take offense at such a suggestion. Straight guys can get off on this stuff too, you know. You should try it sometime."

"Now I know you're fucked in the head."

Shaun shrieked, giddy and relieved, when Kevin pushed him, then ran laughing down the hill as Kevin tried to catch up with him to put him in the inevitable headlock that would precipitate an onslaught of mirthful nuggies unrivaled by any other best friend.

Curtis adjusted the straps of his backpack and threw it down on a table in the multi-purpose room. He took a seat and pretended to be disinterested in who was coming in through the main doors, but his eyes darted around as people passed in front of him, obscuring his view until he finally decided to move his position closer to the door. He slumped down onto the floor in front of one of the posts and pulled his knees up to his chest to wait.

His mind wandered back over the events of the past few hours with Shaun and tried to make sense of them. They'd fucked a few times after they'd arrived back at Shaun's place out of sheer exhilaration from the day, and then they'd fallen asleep. All of that made sense in Curtis' mind. It was when he'd opened his eyes this morning that everything had changed.

Shaun had been propped up watching him sleep when he'd woken up this morning, and the sun had been shining through the window, illuminating the bed and Shaun's startling green eyes as they peered out from beneath the sharp angles of his sleek black hair.

Curtis closed his eyes, remembering what that had felt

like when Shaun had studied his face then descended on him and kissed him.

He shook his head in confusion. The only reasonable explanation for what he was feeling was that Shaun had been the very first person *ever* to make love to him out of pure affection.

There was nothing more to it than that.

He looked up as a pair of shoes stepped into view and he instantly knew he was so far off base with his reasoning that he might as well pack in any hopes of ever seeing the old Curtis Bantam again.

"I've been looking for you," Shaun said.

"I've been right here waiting for you, baby."

Shaun slid down the post beside Curtis and let his shoulder rest against Curtis' arm.

"Did you sort everything out with your friend?" Curtis asked.

"Not really. Kevin thinks I'm not going to be seeing you anymore." Shaun grinned. "I'll break it to him slowly."

Curtis laid his open hand on Shaun's thigh and waited for him to take it. "Slowly is not always a good thing."

Shaun smiled, ignoring Curtis' plea for affection. "Well, in that case, you won't mind if I ask you to move in with me."

"Whoa there, roadrunner!" Curtis turned, looked into Shaun's eyes, and felt his heart melt. "Damn it all to hell."

"I'll clear out a few drawers for you," Shaun said, triumphant, and slapped his hand into Curtis', gripping it tightly in his own. "Now. Let's give these wasters something to talk about."

Curtis beamed at Shaun and attacked his mouth.

The bell had only just rung for lunch, but the multi-purpose room was already filling up fast. Curtis had taken off halfway through the second period to 'take care of some business,' so Shaun had been left to track Kevin down as a lunch companion. He approached Kevin at his locker and waited for him to throw his books into it.

"Have you talked to Candace yet?" he asked Kevin.

Kevin grabbed his lunch and slammed his locker door shut. "Yeah, she phoned me last night. I don't know what she expects me to do. I didn't even want her to keep the fucking thing."

Shaun cringed. Kevin really could be an ass sometimes.

"Are you sure it's yours?" he asked.

"No, I don't. That's the aggravating part. It probably belongs to that fucking wanker, Eric. That guy has got me beat when it comes to banging his way through the female student population."

Shaun pushed Kevin around the corner and tried to direct Kevin's attention away from the people who were staring and whispering as they passed by.

"Maybe we should eat lunch outside today," he suggested, not wanting to subject himself to the ridicule he knew was coming.

"Fuck that," Kevin said. "I heard there's a new girl at the school. She's already caught Eric's eye, so she must be pretty hot."

"Kevin, buddy. Could you do everyone a favor and try

to keep it in your pants for a change?"

"Look who's talking. If I remember correctly, you weren't too far behind me in the polls."

Kevin looked out across the multi-purpose room and spotted the table where their friends were gathered. "Is that her at our table?"

"How the fuck would I know?" Shaun shoved Kevin along so he'd move faster past the other tables, then slid into a seat beside Ming. "I wasn't even here at lunch yesterday."

"Where were you?" Kevin asked.

"I think I can probably guess where he was," Dixie said.

Shaun dropped his head onto his arm as the entire table started whistling and making kissing noises at him.

"Shaun has a boyfriend," Ming said in a singsong voice.

Kevin looked over at Shaun. "I never said anything. I swear."

"You didn't have to," Dixie said. "Half the student body saw them making out this morning."

Shaun moaned softly into his arm.

"And, apparently, that was the noise he was making," Candace said, laughing.

"You said it was a onetime thing," Kevin said to Shaun.

Shaun lifted his head. "I lied."

"Curtis Bantam," Ming said. "I can't say I blame you. That boy must be really skilled by now." He touched Shaun's arm. "We'll talk later. You can fill me in on the details."

Ming looked up across the table when he felt Attila's foot tapping his leg. "Sorry, sweetheart. Shaun here isn't gay. That's why this is such a big deal."

"Can we change the subject?" Shaun pleaded. "How was everyone's summer? I barely saw any of you guys."

"We tried calling," Dixie said. "But, apparently, you were too busy playing with your hot, little boy toy."

Shaun exhaled loudly and dropped his head onto the table.

"Who's your friend, Ming?" Kevin asked.

Attila reached down the table and shook Kevin's hand. "I'm Annie. I didn't catch your name."

"It's Kevin." Kevin rose to his feet and shoved Dixie over so he could sit down beside Attila. "Excuse me, Dix. But I want to make sure Annie is finding her way around the school all right."

"Annie, just ignore him," Candace said. "There's only one thing he wants from you."

"He'd be in for a rude awakening," Ming said under his breath.

Dixie slid down in her seat and kicked Ming hard in the shins, making him shriek and hold his breath.

All heads turned when a commotion erupted from the far end of the room in the form of an energetic blonde girl, dressed all in black, whooping loudly, and leaping and weaving across the room toward their table, and into Attila's arms. She kissed Attila's cheek, noisy as she could manage, then pulled away and started dancing around crazily, spinning and squealing.

"I got transferred!" the girl exclaimed. "I couldn't have my poor little pooky bear out in the big, wide world all by her lonesome."

"You didn't have to do that," Attila said. "I'm fine."

She pouted dramatically at Attila. "Aren't you going to introduce me to *my* new friends?"

Candace burst out laughing.

"Everyone, this is Ed," Attila said and looked at Ming. "Short for Edwina …for real." He groaned as Ed dropped down in his lap. "Ed, this is Ming, Shaun, Candace, Dixie and …Kevin."

Ed looked around the table at the different faces and smiled.

"You've done well, biscuit," she said. "Interesting group dynamics to be sure." She looked over her shoulder at Kevin and sneered at him. "Back off stud muffin. The goods are mine."

Kevin leaped up. "Unfucking believable!"

"Oh, struck out!" Dixie shouted gleefully. "The bases are loaded, but poor Kevin is batting for the wrong team." She turned and winked at Ming, who beamed back at her.

"Has anyone seen Jay?" Candace asked.

"He's just finishing up his tour," Dixie replied. "He should be here by tomorrow."

"Who's Jay?" Ed asked. "Is he a musician?"

"He's a DJ for Tetraforce," Shaun replied.

"No fucking way!" Attila shouted then covered his mouth. "I'm sorry. That just slipped out. I love Tetraforce."

"Not to worry," Ed said. "You've still got the sweetest mouth I know." She patted Attila's face and kissed his lips affectionately.

"Unfucking believable," Kevin repeated and stormed from the room, tossing his lunch into the garbage.

"Didn't he say that already?" Ed asked innocently. "He doesn't think we're together, does he?"

"That would be an honest assumption," Dixie replied.

"Pish-posh. Annie and I are just friends," Ed replied, then jumped when she felt someone touch her on the shoulder. She turned around, ending up eye level with a big silver belt buckle that she tapped lightly with one finger.

"Interesting motif," she said. "It's not every day you see one of these on something other than a mud flap."

"Ed, this is Eric," Attila said.

Ed looked up the length of Eric and climbed off Attila's lap. She circled around Eric and studied his physique, grasping briefly at his biceps. Eric just watched her with fascination.

"What is she doing?" Candace whispered to Shaun.

Shaun shook his head, just as confused as she was.

"He'll do." Ed motioned for Attila and turned back to face Eric. "Have her back by the time lunch break is over or I'll have your balls made into an accessory for that belt of yours."

Ming choked back an objection and watched with horror as Attila followed Eric out through the main doors.

The afternoon sun filtered down through the lower branches of the trees, spinning flashes of light across the forest floor. Attila gazed skywards, studying the remaining patch of blue sky drifting overhead. He turned onto his side and straightened out the blanket beneath him to keep the leaves off his pale yellow designer shorts.

"What are you thinking about?" he asked Eric.

Eric fell onto his back, ran his hands through his hair in frustration, and cupped his head, laughing.

"What?" Attila asked, amused at Eric's evident frustration.

"It's way past the end of lunch hour, and I'm wondering what your friend has planned for my balls."

"She's a little overprotective. But I'm sure your balls are safe."

Eric rolled to face Attila and propped himself up on one elbow. "So, let me get this right. You're not a lesbian, but you're not interested in having sex with me."

"Is that an oddity in your experience?"

"Mm ...I suppose." Eric touched Attila's face and let his fingers drift down Attila's throat and across the neck of his blouse.

Attila stopped Eric's hand as it moved to brush across where his breasts should be. The gel-filled bra was reasonably realistic looking, but it wouldn't pass the scrutiny of an experienced roaming hand.

Eric sighed. "We don't have to go all the way."

"What would you consider to be a fair compromise?"

Attila watched the wheels in Eric's mind grinding slowly. It was a gamble, but Eric was easily the most popular senior in school. If rumors ever started to surface that Annie wasn't really a girl, Eric would be the first to dispel them ...and people would believe him.

Impatient with the delay, Attila pushed Eric over, slid down his body, and undid his belt buckle.

Ming was sitting as inconspicuously as he could in the

hallway across from Attila's locker. He'd popped up onto his feet when the bell had rung for the end of the third period, but now that the hallways were cleared out again, he sunk back onto the floor.

He couldn't understand what was taking Attila so long. He'd considered going out to look for him, fearing Eric had discovered Attila's secret and killed him.

Smacking his head with his hand, Ming reminded himself not to be so fucking dramatic, then checked up and down the hall before reaching into his purse and dispatching a small amount of powdered courage onto the back of his hand. He snorted it as quickly as he could and brushed his hand off on his pants.

He cleared his throat and tried to look as nonchalant as possible when he saw Ed walking toward him.

"Is this Attila's locker?" Ed asked as she pointed to the very one. "He told me it was two twenty, but I can't remember the combo. He said you'd know it. Lucky you were here."

"You know about him?" Ming asked.

"Of course. We've been besties since birth." Ed stood back as Ming opened the locker for her. "Truth be told, we're actually cousins. We practically grew up together." She reached in and grabbed Attila's purse off the hook and pushed the locker closed.

"Do you know where he is?"

Ed checked her cell phone, looking for messages. Finding none, she sent off a text. "He should be finished with Eric soon. Nice little insurance policy that boy is."

"What are you talking about?"

"Standard operating procedure. We've been using it at summer camp for years. Attila sucks off the most influential guy in the group, then he's got himself a built-in guarantee that no one will question his gender."

Ming followed Ed down the hallway in shock. He wandered out through the exterior door she held open for him and headed for his car. As he reached into his pocket, he realized his keys were still back in his locker.

"Are you all right?" Ed asked. "This has got nothing to do with the two of you. He's just protecting himself." She paused, seeing the confusion in Ming's eyes. "Ming, don't let his delicate mannerisms and doe eyes fool you. He's as ruthless as the next guy."

Ming leaned against his car. "I thought we had something special happening between us."

"Come on, Ming. He let you fuck him on the first day of school. Does that sound special to you?" Ed patted Ming on the arm and pushed his face playfully. "I'm just toying with you. He says he likes you. For real. Like really, really likes you."

Ed's phone buzzed, and she wandered off into the parking lot, texting furiously. She looked over every once in a while and smiled at Ming, and then went back to texting. During her final loop, she slowed to a complete stop, mesmerized by something on her phone, and then rose up on her tiptoes to see over the cars.

"Annie's coming," she shouted to Ming.

Ming crossed his arms and pretended not to be interested, but his entire countenance changed when he felt the warm embrace of Attila's arms around his waist.

"Let's get out of here, lover," Attila whispered in his ear. "I need to feel your arms around me."

Eric closed the passenger door of his friend Mike's truck and sedately pulled his seatbelt across his shoulder. He crossed his arms and looked out through the windshield, trying to pretend he had nothing to report. He grinned as Mike shoved him roughly.

"You lucky bastard!" Mike said. "You nailed her, didn't you?" He threw his hands up in dismay. "The second fucking day of school and you've already scored with the new chick."

"Before your imagination runs away on you," Eric said. "She wouldn't let me go all the way."

Mike cocked an eyebrow and frowned.

"And you're admitting to that," he said.

"Yeah. Annie's really interesting." Eric laughed, remembering. "That's why we were out there for so long. We were talking."

"You ...talking."

Eric leaned back against the door and stared at Mike.

"Is that a crime?" he said. "I'm not a complete idiot when it comes to talking to girls, you know?" He paused, recalling their conversation. "You should've heard some of the stuff she was telling me. She is *so* funny." Eric shifted in his seat and smiled. "This is her first time in public school ever. She's been homeschooled from kindergarten right up until now ...and she's brilliant. Like really, really smart."

"Sounds like a match made in heaven." Mike exhaled with exasperation. "So, what did you do with her?"

Eric dropped his head back against the headrest and smiled. "She has an amazing mouth."

"And …"

"She gave me the most incredible blow job I've ever had." Eric rubbed his eyes, smiled and shook his head. "I swear to God. I've never cum so hard in my life."

Mike clapped his hands together and grinned. "Maybe you could introduce me to her tomorrow."

"What?" Eric looked up at Mike. He'd been so caught up in his thoughts that his mind hadn't registered what Mike had said.

"Annie. She's obviously easy. I want to meet her."

Eric reached across the cab, grasped onto Mike's shirt, and practically hauled him out of his seat.

"What the fuck?" Mike yelled as he tried to struggle free.

"Don't you fucking touch her!" Eric stared Mike down then shoved him away. "Just leave her alone."

"All right. Annie is all yours. I get it."

"I don't want anyone talking to her." Eric looked up at Mike and then dropped his gaze. "I think I might actually like her, so tell everyone to give her some space until I work things out."

"No problem, Eric. You're the boss." Mike threw the truck into gear and tore out of the parking lot, wondering what the hell had gotten into Eric, but quickly redirected his attention. They had a lot of beer to buy and very little time to do it before his cousin finished his afternoon shift at the liquor store.

Shaun shifted the contents of his closet, trying to make room for the massive amount of clothing Curtis had dropped off at his house earlier in the evening. He lifted a few pairs of designer jeans and a large handful of couture shirts out of the plastic bag, and hung them up then dug around and pulled out an assortment of brightly colored G-strings and booty shorts.

He burst out laughing.

"What's so funny?" Curtis swooped up behind Shaun and gathered him up in his arms. "Ah, …you've discovered some of the tools of my trade."

Shaun reached back for him and stroked his hair. "Hey, you."

"Sorry, I'm so late getting back."

"Did you get talking to your mom?"

"Briefly. My dad was home, so I had to be quick."

Shaun shivered.

"He would actually beat you?" he asked. "Like for real?"

"Since I was fourteen. My dad is as regular as clockwork when it comes to beatings. Not so much when it comes to working."

"But you don't have a mark on you." Shaun smirked. "And I would know because I've licked every square inch of your body."

Curtis grinned and playfully kissed the back of Shaun's neck. "I've been pretty lucky," he said. "My older brother usually gets the brunt of it. He's a bit of a smart mouth. Plus after the first couple of times, I learned when my dad was likely to show up and made sure I wasn't around for it."

Shaun turned to face him. "Is that why you started hustling?"

"Nah. I needed the money to buy food mostly. And I have a serious clothing addiction." Curtis smiled at Shaun then took Shaun's face in his hands and kissed him. "Enough about me. I have a surprise for you."

"Mm …I like surprises."

"I start my first shift tomorrow."

Shaun snorted and laughed. "You got a job?"

"Yeah. I went on a couple of dates this afternoon, and it felt bizarre fucking around with other guys when I knew you were at home waiting for me. So I talked to an old client of mine, and he got me a job at one of his clubs."

"You did that for me?"

"Yeah, is that weird?"

"No." Shaun grinned. "But what are you doing at this club?" He held his hand over Curtis' mouth. "No, wait. Let me guess." He dropped his hand and let his hips sway smoothly to the music he had playing in the background.

Curtis stepped back and snorted loudly, creasing up as Shaun began stripping his clothes off and tossing them at him.

"Aren't you just the little vixen," he said.

"Bet you didn't know I could dance."

Shaun finished removing the last of his clothing and danced his way back to where Curtis was standing and ran his hands all over his own body, moaning with overwhelming need.

"You're pretty good too," Curtis said, breathing heavy,

matching Shaun's own need.

"Maybe I should get a job," Shaun said as he backed himself up against Curtis' body, grinding his ass into Curtis' hips. "I've heard that business degrees are highly overrated." He reached back, undid Curtis' pants, then turned to face him.

"I've corrupted you, haven't I?" Curtis said.

"Completely." Shaun let his hands slide down Curtis' chest as he sunk to his knees. He was going to spend the rest of the evening showing Curtis exactly how corrupt he'd become.

"You look so different without makeup," Ming said as he stroked Attila's face.

"You're the one that made me take a shower."

"I wanted to make sure there was no 'Eau de Eric' left on you."

Attila pushed himself up in bed and tucked a pillow behind his head. "I'm sorry I didn't check with you first."

"No, it's all right. We've only just met really." Ming sat back and studied Attila's face. "You know. You could almost pass for a guy. That light stubble of yours is adorable."

"God, I hate that." Attila reached up and touched his face. "I guess I'm walking home as a guy tonight."

"You could shave here."

"No, I can't be bothered. I'll be fine." Attila ran his hands into his hair and messed it up. "Do you think I could borrow a pair of jeans and an old t-shirt off your brother?"

Ming swung his feet onto the floor and headed for the

bedroom door. "Sure. He won't mind. I'll be right back."

Attila wandered over to the mirror suspended above Ming's dresser and examined himself. He scowled at his reflection, then dipped his fingers into some hair product and ran it through his short bleach blonde hair, spiking it up in every direction. He smiled, pulled up a chair, and reached for Ming's black eyeliner.

"That's some badass emo stuff you've got going on there," Ming said as he handed Attila the clothes he'd requested, then stepped back in anticipation as Attila completed his look. He laughed aloud when Attila pulled the jeans down slightly off his hips, exposing the top of the boxers he'd picked out for him.

"Do you have a baseball cap?" Attila asked as he sorted through the jewelry on Ming's dresser, picking out a few heavy rings and a thick silver necklace.

Ming threw open a drawer and produced a black and white cap with silver writing. "Will this do?"

"Perfect," Attila said as he slipped it onto his head and winked at himself in the mirror.

"Don't get me wrong. I adore Annie," Ming said as he pulled on a shirt. "But you make one fucking hot guy."

"It's not a bad look really." Attila reached for Ming's hand and pulled him out through the bedroom door and down the stairs to outside. "We could go to a movie together if I dressed like this."

Ming's spirits soared at those words. The fact Attila was willing to dress like a guy to take him out on a date meant he really must have strong feelings for him.

"How do you get to your house from here?" he asked,

looking out at the forest near the end of his street.

"It's straight down that path and then up through the ravine to that escarpment on the other side."

Ming screwed up his eyebrows with concern.

"Maybe your mom should pick you up," he said.

Attila looked at the dark path and tried to decide what was going to get him into the most trouble.

"Yeah, I'd probably get lost down there," he said as he pulled out his cell phone and sent his mom a quick text with Ming's address, praying she wasn't already mad. He'd missed another entire afternoon of school.

Attila cringed at his mom's response. "She's coming to get me." He looked around to find somewhere to sit and wait for her and spotted a large boulder. He motioned for Ming to join him.

"Is she mad?" asked Ming.

"She'll be ramped up to furious once she finds out why I've been missing school." Attila shivered, partially from the cold, but mostly because of the shit he was going to catch from his mom.

"Hey," he said. "Since I look like a guy—" Attila pulled Ming down onto his mouth, enjoying the warmth and taste of him, then licked his lips as he pulled away. "I can kiss you in public."

Ming grabbed Attila's sleeve, panicking when the sound of tires screeching to a stop interrupted them.

"Oh, fuck!" he said anxiously. "Not necessarily."

A pickup truck full of guys pulled up beside them, and the passenger leaned out the window. Ming recognized him. He was one of Eric's friends named Mike.

"What are you boys up to?" Mike asked malevolently.

Attila gathered himself up and tried to determine if he'd seen the passenger or any of the guys in the box of the truck before, then made a mental image of them. This wouldn't be the first time he'd been bullied or beaten up, and he knew the importance of being able to identify his attackers.

He slid off the boulder, pulling Ming with him as the driver of the truck got out and walked toward them.

It was Eric.

Attila took a deep breath. "Hey, how's it going?" he said as he stepped in front of Ming.

Eric turned to his friends and laughed. "Isn't that cute? He's trying to protect his boyfriend."

This, of course, sent Eric's friends into fits of laughter that included pounding loudly on the side of the truck.

"Could I speak to you for a second?" Attila asked Eric, shushing Ming when he tried to interject.

Eric meandered over to Attila and shoved him roughly in the chest, crossed his arms and set his stance.

"Final requests?" he said.

"No, I just wanted to show you something." Attila pulled out his phone and brought up the pictures and videos he'd taken earlier in the day of him and Eric in the bushes.

"Where did you get these?" Eric asked, clearly distressed.

Attila leaned in close and pulled his hat off.

"My sister sent them to me," he replied. "She sent them to a lot of people, including our cousin." He dropped his voice to a whisper. "She told me your pre-cum tastes like cotton candy. Look there. See what my sister's doing with her tongue. So gentle." He sighed and licked his lips, remembering. "I love the taste of cotton candy."

Eric blinked, but kept his eyes on the tiny screen of Attila's phone, mesmerized by the opportunity to re-experience what had transpired that afternoon.

Attila breathed in his ear. "And that little birthmark, barely visible, in the shape of Italy just above your —" He brushed his finger down the front of Eric's shirt and stopped at his belt line, then gazed up into his eyes. "Mm …I'm sure I could find it again," he whispered. "It was quite distinctive."

Eric quickly checked over his shoulder to make sure none of his friends could hear what was being said.

"Annie's your sister?" he asked.

Attila blew air noisily out past his lips in exasperation. Maybe Eric wasn't as bright as what he'd given him credit for. It was a completely insane thing to do, but as Eric had been approaching them, he'd found himself wanting Eric to figure out he was Annie.

Yesterday in class, he and Eric had really hit it off, with Eric touching his arm when speaking to him, and laughing softly in his ear each time he said something even mildly amusing. He'd sensed a suspicion from Eric about his true gender, and he'd dropped a few well-received hints to encourage that suspicion. It didn't look like the revelation was going to strike today, and he didn't want to push too hard, because Ming might figure out what he was up to and go ballistic on him.

"Yes, Annie's my sister," Attila said, straightening up and stuffing the phone back in his pocket.

"Did she say if she likes me?"

"God help us," Ming exclaimed as he leaned against the boulder, determining there wasn't going to be a threat from Eric after all. The boy only had one thing on his mind.

"You'll have to ask her yourself. We don't talk much," Attila said and pulled his hat back on.

"Yeah, my brother and I are like that," Eric replied. "Hey, are you two twins or something?"

Ming snorted in amusement.

"What could possibly have given you that idea?" he asked.

"They kind of look the same, Ming," Eric retorted.

"Fucking brain surgeon in the making," Ming replied under his breath, hoping Eric hadn't heard him. He beamed when Attila leaned in and wrapped him up in his arms.

"Does Annie know you're gay?" Eric asked, waving at his friends to stay in the truck.

"She's my twin sister, but—"

"Right. She would know that then, wouldn't she?" Eric shoved Attila playfully in the shoulder and laughed.

Attila just rolled his eyes.

"What's your name?" Eric asked.

"Attila."

"Annie and Attila. That's pretty funny. The two A's." Eric clapped his hands together and looked around. "Tell you what. We're on our way to a party. Did you want to come?"

"I'm thinking …no," Ming answered bluntly.

"Not you," Eric said to Ming. "I was asking Attila."

Attila turned and faced Ming, and raised his eyebrows in surprise. He sucked at his thumbnail, then looked down at the pink nail polish and smiled, remembering Eric had been holding his hand earlier in the day.

"Maybe. But what am I going to do about this?" Attila asked as he held out his hands so Eric could see his painted nails.

Eric crunched up his face, then crossed his arms in aggravation as the lights started to come on in his mind. He kicked at a few pebbles on the side of the road, turned toward the truck and acknowledged his friends, then turned back again.

"I've got motorcycle gloves in the truck," he replied curtly. "You could borrow them if you like."

Attila batted his eyes at Eric. "Aren't you smart?" he teased. "That settles it then. I'm going to a party."

Ming slid along the surface of the boulder and groaned. For the second time in one day, he watched Attila leave with Eric.

He pushed himself forward and started heading back toward his house, hoping his new boyfriend didn't have a death wish, but thinking maybe there was more to it than that.

The house was more crowded than what Attila had been expecting for a school night, but Eric had explained that the parents of the guy, Nathan, having the party, were only away for one night, so he'd wanted to take advantage of the situation.

Attila pushed through a large gathering of girls, some of which he'd seen at school, and tried to smile at them appropriately, as he completed his trip to the fridge to get a drink. He opened it up and perused the impressive variety of beer, beer, and more beer.

He stumbled when someone bumped up against him.

"Sorry, buddy," Eric said. "Where have you been? I was looking everywhere for you. I've got better stuff in the other room."

"What kind of stuff?" Attila closed the fridge door.

"Just come with me."

Attila followed Eric upstairs and down a hallway toward a closed door at the end.

"I was talking to that friend of yours ...Mike?" Attila said, trying to make conversation to calm his nerves; his instinct to run was screaming at him. "He says you really like my sister."

"Mike needs to learn to keep his mouth shut," Eric replied as he opened the door and motioned for Attila to go in ahead of him.

Attila stepped sideways to peer inside, trying to ascertain whether or not anyone was in the room already. It looked safe enough, and he felt he could trust Eric, but he wasn't naive enough to just step into an unknown.

"Is anyone in there?" he asked Eric.

A burst of giggling preceded a couple of scantily clad girls, who Attila correctly assumed were prostitutes. He allowed himself to be pulled into the room, and dropped down into the plush cushions of a lounge and relaxed. He accepted the joint Eric passed to him, relieved he hadn't been led into a trap.

Attila stretched out, took a long toke, and coughed with amusement as one of the girls pulled his shoes off.

"This is more like it," he said as he passed the joint back to Eric and removed the motorcycle gloves. "Is this an intervention?"

"I just think maybe you don't know what you're missing."

Attila caught Eric's eyes. "I could say the same thing to you." He shifted slightly as one of the girls hauled his pants off. "What could a couple of girls possibly know about the intricacies of the male orgasm and all the pleasurable activities leading to it?"

Eric swallowed and let his eyes dart with brevity to what effect if any the girl was having on Attila, and then refocused his attention back on the girl in his own lap.

Attila tossed off his hat and dropped his head back on the sofa, enjoying the attention, and reached for Eric's hand. He was only mildly surprised when Eric took it. He prided himself on being able to read people, and he'd hit this one dead on.

He rolled his head sideways and looked at Eric.

"It's not the same, is it?" he asked.

"I don't know what you're talking about."

"Eric, I don't have a sister."

"I know. I figured that out for myself." Eric squeezed Attila's hand then released it. "But let's keep that to ourselves."

"Sure." Attila nodded. "Hey, do you really think I'm funny?"

"Attila, please."

"I was just wondering because I already know I'm smart." Attila inhaled sharply and grabbed onto Eric's shoulder. "Fucking hell. Where did you find these two? Piranhas-R-Us?"

Eric laughed aloud, shaking the lounge.

Attila smiled. "You know I can do a much better job than this."

"Keep it to yourself, Attila."

"Right. Sorry." Attila closed his eyes and tried to relax. "I have to say. You surprise me somewhat."

"Why's that?"

"You portray yourself as this dumb jock."

Eric looked at Attila and shoved him playfully. "I am a dumb jock. But thanks for the vote of confidence."

"No, I'm pretty sure a dumb jock would've beaten the crap out of me by now." Attila looked down in his lap and caught the girl's eye. "Sweetheart, yanking on it like that hurts." He brushed her aside and took over the job himself. "I wish I had my purse. I always keep a bottle of lube in it for emergencies."

"Why do you do it?"

Attila moved closer to Eric. "Do what?"

"Dress like a girl."

"Because I am one." Attila motioned for the girl to get her face out of Eric's lap. "Or at least I should've been."

Eric laughed in disbelief. "How can you say you're a girl and be jerking off at the same time?"

"Minor details. I happen to love jerking off." Attila grinned. "Best of both worlds for now I guess."

He caught Eric's eye and tried to gauge Eric's reaction as he reached over and began stroking him.

"Attila …"

"It'll be our little secret. You know you want me to."

Eric closed his eyes and cupped his hands over his face.

"Not a word to anyone, Attila. I mean it."

Attila patted Eric's face assuredly and slid down onto the floor between Eric's legs to take over where the girl had left off. As Eric's need increased, his own desire pulsed fiercely to life, sending him reeling out of control. He released Eric, dropped back, and gripped onto Eric's leg, stroking himself aggressively until his body convulsed and he brought himself through to completion.

Groaning and swearing, he collapsed in Eric's lap.

Eric laughed softly and ruffled Attila's hair. "Better?"

"Much." Attila grinned, let his breathing even out and then took Eric back into his mouth. He caressed him gently at first then repositioned himself so he could make better use of his hands to increase the intensity. Before long, he was reveling in a symphony of low rumbling groans being produced from deep within Eric's chest. He backed off when Eric started calling out to him, then dove back in when Eric grabbed at his shirt with desperate hands, pulling at him to continue. He used the last few seconds to bring Eric to the very brink repeatedly, then he released him, letting the warmth of Eric's climax shower his face and tongue.

Attila licked his lips and kissed the inside of Eric's thigh, then drew Eric back into his mouth, pulling softly on him and enjoying the very last shivers of passion as they left Eric's body.

He jerked around when he heard the door open. And just about choked on his tongue when Kevin walked in.

Kevin leaned across the table and tried to keep his voice down. The librarian had already shushed him twice, but he was too pumped up by the news he was imparting to Jay to contain himself.

"I'm telling you, man," Kevin said excitedly, "this girl is unbelievable, and she loves Tetraforce. You're a shoo-in."

"But you said she's with this Ed person."

"They're like girlfriends or something." Kevin clapped his hands to his head and tried desperately to contain his excitement. "Wouldn't that be fucking hot if you did them both, together?"

"It doesn't usually work like that." Jay laughed and shook his head. "Are you sure she likes guys?"

"Yeah, she gave Eric a blow job in the bushes yesterday during lunch, and then she hooked up with him again at Nathan's party last night. I saw the whole thing."

Jay leaned back in his chair and grinned.

"How much did you see exactly?" he asked.

"Fuck man. I'm telling you. She had his cock in her mouth. Her pants were off and everything. Another two seconds and I would've walked in on them fucking."

"Who are we talking about?" Ming asked as he approached the table. He wasn't in the habit of hanging out with the straight guys when none of the girls were around, but apparently, they were the only people he knew in today's study block.

"This new chick, Annie," Jay said. "Kevin was filling me in on what I've missed the past two days."

"Is this about her giving Eric head in the bushes?" Ming asked.

"Nah, that's old news," Kevin said. "I totally walked in on them at Nathan's party. They were just about to start going at it."

"Them who?"

"Eric and Annie."

Ming tightened his arms around his waist.

"Are you sure it was Annie?" he asked.

"It was a little dark in there, but I would recognize that blonde hair of hers anywhere." Kevin laughed. "And, Ming …not that you would care, but she's got the most luscious little ass I've ever seen."

Ming sunk into a seat. "You saw her ass?"

"Yeah, she was completely starkers from the waist down." Kevin grinned gleefully. "She had her face buried in Eric's lap when I walked in, and she was making the sweetest little noises."

Ming glanced up, catching a glimpse of Attila in the reference section. "Excuse me for a second, boys," he said and pushed up out of his chair.

"Where's he going?" Jay checked over his shoulder and spotted Attila. "Holy fuck! Is that her?"

Kevin leaned sideways in his chair, curious as to what Ming was so choked up about; he couldn't hear what was being said. Then he remembered. Ming had been crushing on Eric for years and explained why he was so upset. He lost interest when Ming pulled Attila around the corner into one of the small study rooms.

"What happened between you and Eric at the party?" Ming asked as he pulled nervously on Attila's sweater.

"What do you mean?"

"Attila, seriously. Don't lie to me." Ming sniffed and dragged his hand across his cheek. "Kevin is going on about seeing you and Eric together last night. And that you had your pants off?"

Attila paced his way around the small room and ran his hands through his hair in exasperation.

"I'm sorry. No one was supposed to find out about that," he replied. "I thought Eric had locked the door, but then Kevin walked in on us just as we were finishing up. Eric talked to Kevin afterward, and he promised to keep his mouth shut."

"So something really did happen?"

"Yeah, Eric hired a couple of hookers to give us blow jobs, but they were useless, so I took over."

Ming shook his head and just stared at him. "Just like that—you took over."

Attila shrugged his shoulders. "Yeah. Just like that."

"Eric let you suck him off …thinking you were a guy?"

"He's a lot more open-minded than you'd think. After the amazing job I gave him in the bushes yesterday, he was willing to overlook the fact I'm a guy."

"But that was Annie in the bushes—"

Ming's mouth dropped open, and he took off into the main area of the library, then came circling back, muttering in disbelief. "Eric knows Annie's a guy. That you and Annie are the same person?"

"He does. But he doesn't want anyone to find out."

"No duh!" Ming scrubbed his hand across his face, trying for the life of him to figure out how Attila had managed to sway Eric in so little time when he'd been trying for years.

Attila leaned back and tried to catch a better glimpse of the table Kevin was sitting at. "Is that Jay?"

"Fuck! You've got to be kidding me." Ming coughed out a gasp. "What kind of sick libido crisis and ultimate death wish are you operating under?"

"What kind of question is that?" Attila paused and watched Ming's eyes wander across his face. "You're the only guy fucking me. And I'm not planning on adding a bunch of straight guys to the roster." He checked around before placing his hand gently on Ming's face. "I only wanted to talk to Jay about his music. That's it."

"And what about Eric?"

"That's over and done with. Eric isn't the least bit interested in guys. The thing at the party was just an intervention gone wrong."

"You promise you won't end up with him again?"

Attila leaned in and whispered softly in his ear. "I promise, lover." He let his lips brush across Ming's cheek as he made his way to Ming's mouth and urgently devoured it.

Chapter Four

From Friendship to Chaos

The driveway to Eric's house was thick with bushes and curved off into a dark thicket before re-emerging at his house. It was getting late, the sun was almost down, and before long, there wouldn't be enough light for anyone making their way on foot to find their way to the house. Perhaps it hadn't been a great idea to invite him.

Eric checked out the living room window to see if Attila was coming into view yet. Attila had called the house from the end of the driveway but was taking longer to make the trek than what Eric had been expecting. He hoped it wasn't because Attila had decided to wear heels, then dismissed the notion, remembering he'd definitely reminded Attila earlier in the day that Mike and a bunch of his other buddies were coming over to watch the hockey game with them, and that it would be better if he left Annie at home.

He rested his head against the cool glass and tried to relax his breathing. After being caught together at Nathan's party, he'd avoided Attila for a few weeks, letting the rumors about him and Annie die down a bit before trying to pick up their friendship again. They'd gotten off to a bizarre start, but he really liked hanging out with Attila. As far as his other friends were concerned, he'd become good friends with both the Luka twins. When they'd questioned him about his encounters with Annie, he'd made it clear that nothing was going on between them, but that they were to keep their hands off her regardless.

He checked the time and decided to call Attila's cell phone to find out what was taking him so long. After ten rings, Attila finally picked up, but Eric could barely make out what he was saying over the booming racket of music in the background.

"Sorry, Eric," Attila said finally, after figuring out who was calling him. "I lost my phone between the seats for a second." A muffled conversation briefly took place in the background and then Attila came back on the line. "I was just about to call you."

"Where are you?" Eric asked.

"I ran into the guys on your driveway. We're making a beer run. Do you want me to pick up anything special for you?"

Before Eric could answer, Attila shrieked then swore loudly.

"What happened?" Eric asked.

"Nothing. Dickhead here just drove over a median." Attila paused as he waited for everyone to pile out of the truck. "I'll just get two cases of whatever I'm getting."

"Hold up, I hate that light shit."

Eric sighed when he realized Attila had hung up on him. He tried to phone him back, but Attila wasn't picking up. He dropped the blinds down and headed into the kitchen to throw some glasses into the freezer and place the inevitable pizza order. He looked over the menu not knowing for sure what Attila would be willing to eat, so he ordered him a couple of different salads. From what Eric had observed after years of dating cheerleaders, it took a lot of effort and restraint to stay that thin. Attila could still dip into the pizza if he wanted, but he wouldn't be forced to fill up on it.

He headed down to the family room when he heard the loud, raucous voices of his friends spilling into the room through the back patio door. It was overtly evident that they'd started drinking as soon as they'd left the liquor store, maybe even before.

"Hey, Eric," Mike said as he tripped over the coffee table, before quickly righting himself. "We're going to let Attila drive from now on. He didn't hit a single fucking thing on the way back." He spun back and high fived Attila.

Eric shook his head and stepped over everyone's legs to get to the remote, and turned the television on. He cringed and swore as an ice cold beer was stuffed into the back of his pants.

"Attila ...what the—"

"Move your beer butt," Attila replied. "I can't see the television."

"Nice, Attila. Thanks," Eric said as he pulled the beer from his pants. He cracked it open and dropped down beside Attila. "How many have you had already?"

"I don't know. Like three. Maybe four."

"Jeez. I'm going to have to peel you off the floor if you keep drinking like that."

"Peel away, baby." Attila laughed and danced his arms around in the air, making Eric roll his eyes.

Eric leaned in closer to Attila's ear. "Please don't get so drunk you start hitting on my friends."

"They know I'm gay, Eric."

"I know that." Eric sighed in exasperation. "Whatever. It's your business."

"That guy Stephen is pretty cute though, don't you think?" Attila leaned forward, caught Stephen's eye, and winked at him.

Eric shoved Attila back against the cushions. "What are you doing? Do you want to get yourself killed?"

"Eric, please. How do you think I lost my phone in the seat of Mike's truck? Young Stephen there was doing his very best to work his hand into the back of my pants undetected."

Eric leaned back and looked at Stephen, and cringed. He hadn't had any idea Stephen was gay, and he'd known him since fifth grade. His anxiety level rose, unsure of the reliability of Attila's recollection when Attila lifted himself out of his seat and approached Stephen. If Attila was wrong, he was going to have to be ready to step in. Stephen was a big guy.

He watched Attila bend down and whisper something in Stephen's ear, and Stephen nod in agreement. Against the reaction of his gut as to what they'd agreed on, Eric sighed with relief.

He leaned back as Attila moved back along the sofa, lay a hand on his shoulder, and bent down to whisper in his ear.

"Stephen is going to show me where the creek is at the back of your property," Attila said. "We'll only be gone a few minutes."

Eric nodded and settled in, and tried to follow what was happening in the game, relieved no one else had noticed the interaction—but he was more distracted than he cared to admit.

He finished his beer, crushed the can, and threw it across the room in aggravation. Attila's habit of running off with every willing guy was beginning to concern him.

The room was reduced to being illuminated by one small light when Eric turned the television off. He looked over his shoulder as Attila emerged from the bathroom. Everyone else had left about an hour ago, but Attila had decided to stay overnight rather than risk taking a ride with one of Eric's drunken friends.

"Are you all right?" Eric asked.

"I think I drank too much."

Attila leaned against the back of the sofa then rolled over it, into the cushions, and lay his head against Eric's shoulder.

"I told you to slow it down."

"Yes, Mom." Reaching his arm across Eric's chest, Attila tucked himself in closer to Eric's side.

"Are you sure you're comfortable?"

"Yes, you're lovely and warm. I think I caught a chill outside." He yawned. "He was worth braving the cold for though. That Stephen is nine inches of well-cut delight."

Eric shivered and tried to clear the image from his

head. Attila had an immensely lousy habit of sharing.

"I don't want to hear about it," he said.

"Not even the nasty bits?" Attila smiled mischievously and poked Eric hard in the ribs, making him squirm.

"Attila, I've warned you before. Don't tickle me."

"But it's so much fun."

Eric cringed when Attila shoved a hand into his armpit and went into full out defense mode when Attila used his other hand to start in on his stomach. He fought unsuccessfully to protect his vulnerable areas while he attempted to pin Attila to the sofa. He eventually managed to gain control, relaxing once Attila was lying quietly beneath him.

"Do you promise to stop?" he asked.

"You're really heavy, Eric," Attila complained. "You're crushing me. Get the fuck off."

"Only if you promise not to tickle me again."

Attila coughed and grinned. "I'll promise. But only if I can tell you what Stephen did to me with his tongue."

"Fuck off, Attila. Don't you dare."

"But he was so good at it." Attila shrieked when Eric jabbed him in the ribs. "All right. Get off. I promise."

Eric looked down at Attila, ignoring his promise of compliance, and studied the subtleties of Attila's eyes. He'd never seen them up close like this before. The depth of blue in them was fascinating.

"Does everyone in your family have blue eyes?" he asked.

Attila shifted slightly, trying to distract himself from reacting physically to the feel of Eric's body pressed to him.

"No, not everyone," he answered.

Eric let his eyes drift across the pink tinge of Attila's cheeks, set startlingly against his porcelain skin, and along the soft contours of his lips. At this distance, Attila really did look like a girl.

"Do you want to kiss me?" Attila asked.

Eric blinked and pulled away, pushing himself further away from Attila's body. "Why would you think that?"

"I don't know. You looked like you wanted to kiss me."

"I've told you before. I don't kiss guys!"

"Fine. My mistake. God." Attila pulled himself off the sofa and headed to the bathroom to get a drink of water. He looked at his eyes in the mirror, mystified, then wandered back to sit beside Eric.

"I'm exhausted," he said. "Where am I sleeping?"

Eric lifted himself off the sofa, reached behind one of the chairs, and pulled out a pillow and a few blankets.

He set them on the sofa and fell down beside them.

"I wanted to talk to you about something," Eric said. He waited while Attila wrapped himself in a blanket and pulled a pillow under his head. "Your relationship with Ming. Is it serious? Because you seem to be with him every time I phone you."

"I suppose it is," Attila replied. "I really like him."

Eric fiddled with the edge of the blanket, unsure how to approach the subject.

"Then why …," he started. "Why the constant stream of these *Stephen incidences*?"

Attila rolled over and pulled a blanket over his head.

"Please don't ask me that," he said.

"Why not?"

"Because I'm a complete fuck up."

Eric rubbed Attila's head through the blanket.

"Attila, you're not a fuck up," he said. "But I don't like seeing you do this to yourself. It's self-destructive …and it's not fair to Ming. Maybe you need to think about sticking to one guy?"

Attila snorted from within his hiding place.

"Where's the fun in that?" he asked.

Eric shoved Attila.

"You didn't *seriously* just say that," he said.

Attila groaned, not liking where this conversation was going. "Is that what you want me to do?" He peered out from beneath the blanket and searched Eric's face. "Go steady with Ming?"

"I want you to be happy. And if Ming does that for you, I think you should consider dropping the charade and be a couple."

Attila pulled the blanket back over his head and considered what Eric was suggesting. Monogamy really wasn't his thing, but it was of ultimate importance to him that Eric respect him, and it didn't sound like his current behavior was working in his favor in that regard. Besides, Ming had been on his case recently, saying he was willing to forfeit his perceived sexual preference if it meant he could hold and kiss him in public.

He would have to talk to Ming tomorrow about making their relationship official.

Shaun swung his locker shut and grinned at Curtis. His

boyfriend was actually going to stick around for lunch and meet his friends.

"Are you sure you're up for this?" he asked Curtis.

Curtis dropped his head and laughed. "No, but I'm going to have to meet them sooner or later. May as well be today."

"At least we won't be the main topic of conversation."

"Yeah, can you believe that? Ming with a chick."

Shaun held his hand out for Curtis' and gripped it tight in his own as they made their way down the hallway.

"Maybe there's something in the water," he said.

"Kind of like a—" Curtis paused and looked at the faces staring up at them, letting his gaze fall on Ming and Annie, who were cuddled together sharing their lunch.

He shook his head.

"Oh …now that's just wrong," he said.

"Welcome to the crazy table, Curtis," Candace said. "Sit down and join the insanity. Everyone's welcome. The freakier and more messed up the better."

"Then I should fit right in," said Curtis as he slid into a seat beside Shaun. He leaned in close to Shaun and bumped him with his shoulder. "Hey, where's that friend of yours …Kevin?"

"He's not speaking to us anymore," Dixie said as she rested against the table. "Sorry. I've got big ears." She clapped her hands together dramatically and placed them on the table in front of Curtis. "So, Curtis Bantam, tell us …are you really a hooker?"

Ed shrieked and started drumming her feet on the floor.

"Oh my god, Pookie, I love our friends," she said then threw her crumpled napkin at Attila's head.

"Curtis has a proper job now," Shaun said and smirked.

Ming set his sandwich down. "Yes, I heard about that from a friend of mine." He brushed the crumbs off his fingers. "He says you're good." He grinned, glad he was going to be able to direct the attention away from himself and Attila for a moment.

"I don't know about you," he continued, "but I always find those booty shorts ride up on me. I suppose that's what the customers are paying to see though. My friend says you have a really nice ass."

"The number of times I've heard that," Curtis replied. "I should get a t-shirt made up." He bumped Shaun with his shoulder. "What do you think? We could both get one. Your ass is definitely nicer than mine is. Yours is so firm ...and tastes so musky and—"

"Whoa ...way too much information," Dixie said, covering her ears. "I'm sorry I brought up this line of questioning."

"That'll learn ya." Curtis winked at Dixie and bit into his apple.

Shaun pressed his forehead against Curtis' shoulder and shivered as Curtis' hand drifted up along the inside of his thigh.

"You're so bad," he whispered.

Curtis kissed Shaun's head. "Only because you're so fucking hot. I can't wait to get you home so I can throw you on the bed and—"

"Enough!" Dixie banged on the table. "I'm sorry. No one will ever mention the hooker, go-go dancer thing again."

Candace shot up out of her seat, gripping fiercely to Ed's arm—making Ed scream in surprise.

"What's the matter, honey?" Attila asked as he reached for Candace.

"I think my water just broke."

Ed peeled Candace's fingers from her arm, scooted away, and lifted her feet off the floor.

"Fucking hell," she said. "I'm not dealing with that."

Attila opened Candace's bag and pulled out her cell phone, quickly scanning through it, looking for her parents' number.

"Who should I be calling?" asked Attila.

"No one. I'm on my own." Candace cringed and gripped the table. "Could someone please get me to the hospital? Now!"

Attila moved aside when the curtain was pulled around Candace's bed, confused as to what was happening, and what role Candace was expecting him to play. She'd insisted that she wanted him to stay with her, stating he was the only real girlfriend she had at the moment. Apparently, her best friend, Clare, had moved away during the summer. When Attila had asked her about her parents, he'd discovered they were away on holidays.

He looked up as a nurse held back the curtain.

"Are you going to be acting as Candace's birthing coach?" the nurse asked as she motioned for Attila to join her at Candace's bedside.

"Candace?" Attila asked nervously.

"Please, Annie. I need you. I can't do this by myself."

"I don't know what to do."

"We'll walk you through it," the nurse said. "The most important thing is to make sure mom stays hydrated and as comfortable and relaxed as possible."

"Don't you have people to do that sort of thing?" Attila asked then gasped when Candace grabbed onto his hand and pulled him closer. He cringed, witnessing intense pain cross Candace's face, and turned to the nurse to find out what he needed to do.

Eric rushed down the hall toward the maternity ward, then slowed, slightly taken aback when he saw the group of Candace's friends huddled around the coffee machine. He reluctantly stepped up behind them and cleared his throat.

"How's she doing?" he asked.

"Took you long enough." Dixie pushed past him to sit down.

"I just heard," Eric said. "I got here as quick as I could."

Ming tapped him lightly on the chest. "I knew it was yours."

"We don't know that for sure," Eric replied. "But it could be, so I want to be here for her."

"Like I said," Dixie said. "Took you long enough."

"Guys, please stop busting my balls," Eric said. "How's she doing? Has the baby been born yet?"

"She's been in there for about six hours already," Shaun replied, wanting to cut Eric some slack. It could just as easily be his.

"Seven," Ed corrected. "I've been counting the seconds. If it weren't for Annie, I wouldn't even be here. I hate hospitals."

Eric's face creased up in confusion. "Annie's here?"

"Yeah," Ed said. "She's in with Candace. I think they were on their way to the birthing tub." She grinned mischievously. "I hear the birthing coach has to get into the tub with the mom."

"Which way do I go?" Eric asked, frantically surveying the hallways, attempting to determine the way to the tub room.

Shaun lifted a finger and pointed out the direction, sending Ed into hysterics as Eric sped away.

Attila stood at the edge of the tub, gripping it tightly as the nurse helped Candace to undress. He felt the flush rise in his face as he attempted to shield his eyes, not wanting this to be his introduction to the female form. He took a deep breath, realizing he needed to stay strong for Candace, and looked up.

He felt his heart stir; she looked absolutely radiant.

"Did you bring a bathing suit?" the nurse asked him.

Attila shuddered nervously, shaking his head. "I hadn't realized I'd be going swimming today."

"That's all right. Some people prefer to support mom from outside the tub."

Attila let out the breath he'd been holding.

"That would definitely be me," he said, feeling a shiver of relief run through his body, but the tension ramped right back up when the nurse directed him toward where he should be positioning himself, and what he should be doing to provide relief for Candace.

He was considering making a run for the door when he heard Candace scream out in pain. He immediately lost his inhibitions and set to work helping her, and after some time passed, Attila actually began to enjoy the connection he was feeling with Candace and was sinking into the rhythm of the holds and massaging motions when a nurse tapped on the door and poked her head in.

"How are we doing in here?" she asked.

"She's doing great," Attila replied. "The doctor just checked her, and she's at nine and a half centimeters already."

"It shouldn't be too much longer then." The nurse caught Attila's attention. "And how are you doing?"

"I'm ecstatic. This has been the most amazing experience." Attila smiled brightly at her. "I'm thinking of changing my career choice. I'd love to work here."

"We'd be happy to have someone as enthusiastic as you." The nurse let her hands rest on her hips. "There's someone out here named Eric. He says he might be the dad." She waited for a response. "Do you want him to come in, Candace?"

Candace clenched her teeth and nodded her head, grasping viciously to Attila's arm as another contraction started.

The light crackled to life in the dank little space that was the only washroom for the six women packed into Candace's hospital room. Attila looked at himself in the mirror and used a washcloth to clean away the remaining makeup from his face. The tub room, being hot and steamy, had melted most of it away already.

Attila turned his head from side to side, trying to evaluate the growth of stubble on his face. He dropped the cloth when he heard a light knock on the door.

"Who is it?" he asked.

"It's me," a muffled voice replied.

Attila rolled his eyes and opened the door to let Eric in.

"I wasn't sure what to get," Eric said. "Your mom helped." He lifted a pair of jeans and a black t-shirt from the duffle bag he was carrying. "I tried to pick out something girly, but she insisted."

"My mother is in serious denial," Attila said as he picked through the bag, pulling out a pair of pink, silk panties and a matching padded bra.

Eric grinned. "I managed to scoop those when she wasn't looking. You said you were soaked through to the skin."

"Thanks. I appreciate your effort."

"It's the least I could do. You were amazing in there with Candace. I can't thank you enough for being there for her."

"It was definitely an experience."

Attila began peeling off the wet layers of clothes and handing them to Eric to put in the extra plastic bag he'd brought with him.

"I wondered how you managed that," Eric said.

"What?" Attila asked as he threw the final stocking into the bag.

"Hiding your …like that. What is that thing?" Eric held the bag out and let Attila drop the last item of his clothing into it.

"It's called a gaff." Attila turned toward the toilet and relieved himself after what felt like days without a washroom break. After shaking himself off, he peered into the bag of clean clothes.

"She didn't give you one, did she?" he asked.

"Sorry. I didn't know to ask."

"It's not your fault." Attila sighed and looked at himself in the mirror again, trying to determine which direction he was leaning, and decided to shave. After finishing, he turned back to face Eric, propping his naked body against the edge of the sink.

"Do you want to grab a beer?" he asked.

"Only if you put some clothes on."

"Always so fussy." Attila motioned for the underwear and bra and slipped them on, adjusting the position of the gel inserts.

Eric looked at the overall effect and cringed.

"Don't you like me in pink?" Attila pulled on the jeans Eric handed to him. "You picked them out."

"I was imagining them on a girl's body at the time."

"Now that's a pity." Attila slipped the shirt on over his head and looked around, sliding his feet into the canvas shoes that had fallen onto the floor. "I guess that's me."

He snapped his fingers theatrically. "Dressed in two seconds flat. Something to be said for that."

"Is that you ready then?"

"Just a second." Attila rechecked his appearance in the mirror and used a handful of water to smooth out his hair. Without product, it wasn't sitting right.

"Can we go now? Candace was falling asleep when I came in here. She'll want to say goodbye before we go."

"Has everyone else gone home?"

"It's almost midnight ...so, yeah." Eric opened the door and waited for Attila to exit, then turned off the light.

"Hey there, Mommy," Attila said to Candace as he touched her face, waking her up. "We're going to go."

Candace smiled up at him. "Annie, you look so good without makeup. You've got such beautiful eyes."

"You're delirious from childbirth." Attila grinned and leaned over, and kissed Candace on the forehead.

"Annie, I'm glad we talked about what happened with Eric."

"Yeah, well. I tend to run on when I'm nervous." Attila winked at Candace and took one of her hands in his. "You were amazing today. Thank you for sharing that with me."

Eric stepped in and brushed his hand across Candace's hair.

"You did good today, kid," he said. "I'll be back in the morning to pick you up." He leaned down and kissed her cheek. "I'm going to be there for you, all right?"

Candace wiped a stream of tears from her face and nodded her head in grateful agreement.

"We'll let you get some sleep," Attila said, "so we can head out and get really, really drunk." He high fived Eric and bumped him with his hip. "I'm feeling strangely energized. Let's go dancing."

Candace shrieked in amusement and clamped her hand over her mouth, not wanting to wake up the other women in her room. She motioned for them to leave and blew a kiss to Eric, and rolled over, no longer able to keep her eyes open.

Eric sat, sipping on his drink, not sure of what to make of the club that Attila had taken him to. He was used to going to sports bars or neighborhood pubs for beer and cheap chicken wings. He'd never actually set foot in a nightclub before. Looking out at the dance floor, he tucked his face into his hand, laughing at the spectacle unfolding. Attila had found someone of his *persuasion* to dance with, and he was having an absolute blast with him.

Setting his glass down, Eric called the server over for another round. As far as he was concerned, he was a new father and more than deserved another drink.

Attila spun around on the dance floor and leaped up onto the area containing their table, and leaned on it, smiling at Eric.

"So, are you going to dance with me, or what?" he asked.

"I don't dance."

"God, you straight guys are so boring." Attila sighed and slid into his seat. "Dancing is like a precursor to sex. You get to check out the other person's agility and fluidity before taking the plunge."

"Did you and Ming dance first?"

"No. Dancing is overrated. We went straight to

fucking."

Eric shook his head and grinned.

"Hell," Attila said. "We didn't even bother with the talking bit. That doesn't make me a slut, does it?"

"Did you know his name?"

Attila tapped his lips in thought. "Nope. I don't think so."

"You're a slut."

"Hm …so be it." Attila grinned happily, enjoying the banter.

Eric shifted over and slid the round of shots he'd ordered closer to Attila. He picked one up and waited for Attila to do the same.

"To Candace and the baby," Eric said then threw back the shot and picked up another one. "And to my friend Attila."

He nodded to Attila, saluting him with the shot. "Today you did something very few men would have the balls for."

Eric waited for Attila then threw back the shot. His hand slammed back onto the table, reaching for the next.

"Wait," Attila said, then paused gathering his thoughts.

"This one's for you, Eric," he said. "For witnessing a lifestyle, absolutely unfathomable to you, and being there for me anyway."

Both shots went back.

Eric smacked his glass back down on the table, swooning.

"I think I'm sufficiently drunk now," he slurred.

"Goodie," Attila sang. "Now you'll dance with me."

Attila reached for Eric's hand and hauled him onto the dance floor. He backed himself up against Eric's body and moved with him to the music, fighting the temptation to push Eric's boundaries, opting to enjoy their friendship instead. But when he felt Eric run his hands down onto his hips and pull him closer, grinding against him, breathing heavily in his ear—all bets were off.

Eric cleared the crap off the backseat of his truck, pitching everything onto the floor, and sat back as Attila climbed through the space between the two front seats and stripped off his clothes. The last thing Eric remembered was an image of Attila rising and falling on top of him, rolling his head back in ecstasy.

Curtis ducked into his locker as Eric stormed past, pitching juniors aside in his wake. Everyone knew Eric was a bit of a hothead, but Curtis was curious as to what had pissed him off to this extent. He got his answer when Annie skittered down the hallway trying to keep up with Eric's tremendous stride in her high heels.

Always up for a good bit of gossip, Curtis ran to catch up with them. He was further intrigued when they flew into the guy's washroom, and followed after them, pushing past the guys Eric was throwing out. He waited in the entrance, just out of sight, and tried to keep his breathing quiet.

"I'm so sorry, Eric," Attila began. "Please. I didn't do it

to hurt you. I honestly thought you wanted to."

"You took advantage of me," Eric replied. "I was drunk, and you took advantage of me." He spun against one of the stalls and drove his fist into it, making Attila jump.

"Eric …please."

"Girls don't do shit like that, Attila. That's a guy thing."

"Please don't call me Attila at school." Attila turned on the water in the sink and splashed some of it around his face, trying to calm himself. "Someone might hear you."

"Fine …Annie." Eric sighed and dropped his voice. "You knew I wasn't interested in fucking around with guys, and you went ahead and tricked me into it anyway, didn't you?"

"I thought you'd changed your mind." Attila turned the water off and looked at the mess he'd made of his mascara. "You came on to me when we were dancing. You held me against you."

"I was drunk!" Eric raced at Attila, making him shriek. "You look and act like a girl. A really fucking, hot girl. What did you expect?" He bashed his hand against the wall and paced around the room. "I thought we were friends."

"We are friends. But sometimes the lines get blurry with us."

"Attila, what happened last night, can't ever happen again."

"But it wasn't so bad, was it?" Attila approached Eric, cautiously, and lay his hand on Eric's arm. "You really liked it." He cringed when Eric glared at him. "I'm sorry, but you did."

"I don't like guys that way." Eric held up his hand as

Attila made to interject. "I don't fuck guys. I just don't."

"But, Eric...."

"Attila, you need to stop this before anyone else gets hurt. I know it's not what you want, but you're not a girl, and you need to find a better way to deal with that."

"I know ...and I will, I promise." Attila gripped his hands together and held them to his lips. "Eric, please. I don't want to lose you as a friend. You have to forgive me."

Eric shook his head in resignation. "Fuck. I'm starting to think I should've beaten the crap out of you when I had the chance." He shoved Attila affectionately and pulled him into his arms, burying his face in Attila's neck. "Now I'm stuck with you."

Curtis slid along the wall and pried the door open, slipping silently out of the washroom and into the hallway. He phoned Shaun and told him to come find him.

The whispering hushed to complete silence when Ming and Ed entered the usually vacant counseling office. Curtis leaned back into the plush leather sofa and pulled Shaun into his arms.

"Hey, guys," Curtis said. "What's up?"

"You two were whispering fast and furious," Ed replied. "Making steamy plans for the weekend perhaps?"

"No, we're staying home," Shaun said.

"I still can't believe that," Ming said. "You guys moving in together after one night of fucking each other's brains out."

"It wasn't like that." Curtis kissed Shaun on the cheek. "Our souls connected and wouldn't let go. We had to move in with each other."

"That is so adorable," Ed said and turned to Ming. "Which reminds me. Where is your adorable little love muffin?"

"I haven't seen her since the first period," Ming answered.

"You might want to try the guy's washroom on the second floor by the art department," Curtis suggested.

"And why would that be?" Ming stepped forward and placed his hands on his hips, ready to defend his boyfriend.

"Annie and Eric were having a fight in there," Curtis replied and then stopped, deciding to hold his tongue.

"You might want to talk to him, Ming," Shaun said. "We've been friends for a long time. I don't want to see you get hurt."

"Why would I want to talk to Eric?" Ming asked.

Shaun snorted. "I wasn't talking about Eric."

"Jigs up, ass bandit," Curtis said. "We know about Attila. And Shaun is right. You really need to talk to him. He's going to bring this school down around our heads if you don't rein him in."

"Fucking hell," Ed said as she sunk into a chair by the door. "This is why I wanted to be here. That fucking cousin of mine is a raging, loose cannon queer." She pulled out her phone, started texting, then set it in her lap to wait for a reply.

"What did he do this time?" Ming asked Shaun.

"It's pretty bad," Shaun replied. "Even for him."

Ming looked at Curtis. "What did he do?"

"I'm sorry, Ming," Curtis said. "He slept with Eric."

Curtis gripped onto Shaun's hand and watched Ming wander out through the door, wondering if he'd done the right thing by telling Ming the truth; it had just slipped out.

Ed dropped her head into her hand and rubbed aggressively at her face. She read over a text she'd received from Attila while he'd been in the nursery with Candace's baby, stating he was falling in love. She'd assumed Attila meant with Ming. Now she realized she'd been mistaken. It had been Eric all along. It had always been Eric. Would always be Eric.

Shaun climbed into bed, noting how crisp and clean the sheets felt. His mom had cleaned up for them this week and done all their laundry. She'd said surprisingly little about Curtis' choice of undergarments. Of course, she didn't know he and Curtis were together as a couple. She'd assumed Curtis needed a place to stay and her son had selflessly opened his home to him. Curtis' history and family issues were notorious throughout the neighborhood, and she was pleased Shaun had felt inclined to help Curtis out by letting him live there, and she'd made a special point of telling him.

"You look guilty of something," Curtis said as he dropped down onto the bed.

Shaun motioned for him to come closer so he could lay his head on Curtis' chest. "I feel bad about lying to my parents."

"Do you want to go talk to them?" Curtis brushed his fingers through Shaun's hair and tucked it neatly behind his ear. "I told my mom exactly what was going on."

"How did she take it?"

"She hit me in the head with her frying pan." Curtis grinned and then squirmed when Shaun poked him in the ribs.

"What are we doing, exactly?" Shaun asked.

"Hell if I know."

"I don't think my parents would accept that as an answer."

Curtis bent down, kissed Shaun's head and turned Shaun's face up to look at him. "That's the only one I have, lover."

Shaun rolled his eyes and fell back into his pillow.

"I have something for you," Curtis said and rolled toward the edge of the mattress, reaching under the bed. He pulled out a single, long-stemmed red rose with a small note attached and held it out for Shaun to take.

Shaun sat straight up. "You got this for me?"

"Yeah, I paid money and everything." Curtis smiled as Shaun took it. "I could've just taken it. No one watches those flower cases, but I wanted it to be special. It didn't seem right to steal it."

"It's beautiful. Thank you." Shaun held Curtis' face and gently kissed his lips, then turned his attention back to the flower and removed the note. "What's this?"

"Read it." Curtis held his breath and rubbed Shaun's leg nervously with his hand, waiting for him to open the envelope and remove the card he'd so painstakingly dictated to the sales clerk, wanting just the right sentiment. He felt as if his heart was rising in his throat as Shaun's eyes scanned over what was written there.

The relief in Curtis' eyes flooded the room when Shaun burst into tears and pulled him into his arms.

Attila hauled the covers up over his head when he heard Ed tapping on his bedroom door.

"Go away!" he shouted.

"I'm coming in," Ed said, then tried to open the door, but Attila had pushed his dresser up in front of it, and it wasn't budging.

"Leave me alone."

"You can't lock yourself up in here forever. Everyone's wondering what happened to you. And poor Ming was absolutely distraught when I told him you weren't coming back to school."

"It's the only logical solution." Attila brushed his hands through his hair and looked up at the ceiling, then rolled to face the door.

"So, exactly who knows about Eric and me?" he asked.

"Just Curtis and Shaun …and Ming told Dixie."

"Great. That's just perfect." Attila's eyes creased up with concern. "Has anyone said anything to Eric?"

"No. I told everyone to keep their yaps shut." Ed pushed on the door again to see if she could get the dresser to shift. "No one is going to say anything to Eric. And no one else is going to find out. Why don't you come back to school?"

"I don't think that's a good idea."

"Ming is willing to forgive you."

Attila sighed heavily. "I really wish he wouldn't do that."

Throwing the covers off, he crossed the room and attempted to move the dresser. "Has Eric said anything to you about my leaving school?" He shuffled the dresser sideways, leaving enough of a gap to open the door so Ed could squeeze through.

"Why don't you talk to him yourself?" Ed asked.

"I lost his number when I threw my phone at Curtis' head."

"That's the worst excuse I've ever heard."

Ed peered in through the door and seeing that the dresser was mostly out of the way, gave the door a good shove. She looked up as Attila threw himself back on the bed.

"Whoa, morning shadow much," she said as she dropped down beside Attila. "You should get cleaned up, and we'll head out for a while. Your mom says you don't have to leave until morning."

"Maybe I shouldn't go to that stupid boarding school."

Ed clapped her hands together with excitement.

"I knew you'd come around," she said.

"But I'm worried about Candace finding out. She and Eric are together now, and they're trying to set things up for the baby and everything. I don't want to mess that up for them."

"It'll be fine. No one is going to talk."

Attila threw his hands over his face and sighed. "I'll give Ming a call tonight and tell him the good news."

Pulling himself off the bed, Attila stretched out his shoulders, letting the tension of the past few days fall away.

"I'm so happy again." Ed held Attila's face and gave

him an affectionate kiss on the forehead. "I'm going to raid your kitchen while you have a shower. I haven't had lunch yet. You better look like a girl by the time I get back, or I'm not taking you anywhere."

Attila smiled. "Yes, Mom. One girl coming right up."

After stripping off his pajamas, Attila started the shower, stepping into the soothing warmth. He was going to take his time and enjoy it. Ed wouldn't mind amusing herself in front of the television. He should have plenty of time to do himself up right.

As the shower began to run cold, he reluctantly shut it off and grabbed a towel, wrapping it around his waist. He pulled open a drawer and started rooting around for a new razor, but his mom had removed them all from his bathroom again. In exasperation, he headed for the main bathroom to steal them back ...and ran straight into Candace, who'd been waiting out in the hallway.

"Oh, I'm sorry," Candace said. "I was looking for Annie. The front door was unlocked."

"She was here, but she went out somewhere," Attila replied and then tried to slip past Candace to get back into his bedroom.

"You must be her brother Attila."

Attila shrugged and nodded.

"That would be me," he said.

"You hang out quite a bit with Eric and his friends."

Attila leaned against the doorframe and tried to set his stance as masculine as possible. "Yeah, we watch sports ...and drink beer ...and stuff."

Candace peered past Attila's shoulder into the

bedroom, wondering why he was in what was obviously Annie's room.

"What school do you go to?" she asked.

"None," Attila answered. "I'm homeschooled."

"Did you know Annie is leaving Tekla?"

"Yeah, she mentioned that." Attila cleared his throat and scratched at his chest, cringing as he realized his nails were excessively long for a guy. He crossed his arms to hide them.

"Is that why you're looking for her?" he asked.

"No, I'm looking for her because I just heard from someone that she slept with Eric."

Attila coughed and almost choked.

"That can't be right," he said. "Annie wouldn't do that. Whoever said that must've been mistaken."

"Annie's boyfriend Ming said it. I overheard him talking to his friend Dixie. Apparently, one of our friends Curtis heard Eric and Annie arguing about it." She sniffed loudly and tried to contain her emotions. "Eric denies it of course."

"You told Eric you overheard people talking about it?" Attila covered his mouth, panicking. "No one was supposed to find out."

He inhaled sharply as a few tears escaped.

"Eric must be so upset," Attila said. "Is he all right?"

Candace was about to answer, but paused, studying Attila's face further, taking in all the little details. Her eyes gradually expanded as she pieced everything together.

"You? Oh, my god! It was you!"

Clinging to the banister, Candace spun around as Ed

raced up the stairs, completely out of breath.

"I'm sorry, Pookie," Ed said. "I didn't hear her come in."

Attila sunk to his knees and leaned against the wall.

"I don't know what to say, Candace," he said. "I didn't mean for all this to happen. I'm so sorry."

"You're …a guy?" Candace said, her face dropping in shock. "Annie is a fucking guy?"

"I never meant to hurt anyone." Attila reached for Candace, imploring her with his eyes. "I know you're mad, but please don't tell anyone about Eric and me. It doesn't have to go any further than our friends." His breath caught as he began to sob. His only thoughts were of Eric. "Please, I'm begging you. It would destroy Eric if anyone else found out he'd slept with me."

"You fucking freak!" Candace tore away from Attila's grasp and paced off down the hallway, then came storming back and slapped Attila hard across the face. "Don't you ever come back. If you do, I will tell the entire school what you are—and every detail of what you've done."

Ed jumped back as Candace pushed past her and ran down the stairs, slamming the door on her way out.

Curtis threw the last of his clothes into a bag and checked the time on his phone. Shaun would be home from school soon, and he wanted to make sure he was gone before then.

He looked down at the note he'd roughly pieced together explaining why he was leaving and broke down. His interference had pulled Shaun's friends apart in astronomical proportions. He never wanted anything like that to be his fault again.

Curtis set the note down and picked up the card Shaun had kept from the flower he'd given him, and looked it over. The words contained in it expressed his love for Shaun. They still rang true. That was why he had to leave. He was no good for someone as pure and innocent as Shaun.

Scrubbing his face, Curtis looked around the room, across the bed they'd shared, and bolted from the pool house.

It was for the best.

Chapter Five

Seven Years Later

The lecture hall in the furthest corner of the university's business department was only about half full, and Shaun was beginning to wonder if he'd made a wise choice by continuing with his education, completing the final year of his MBA. Quantitative Decision Making did not sound like something he'd have much interest in. He looked around the theater seating and made his way up the stairs all the way to the back, and took a seat.

He'd just transferred to Dalhousie University located on the east coast of Canada. It was a long way from home, but his girlfriend Deirdre had been offered a job she couldn't pass up, and they'd needed the money, so they'd moved.

Somehow, Shaun's parents had found out what had been going on between him and Curtis, and they'd frozen his trust fund money, promising to release it once he finished university and married Deirdre. The lack of money had put a severe dent in Shaun's normally lavish lifestyle, but it hadn't been as horrendous as he'd thought it would be. He and Deirdre had pieced together a nice life together so far.

Shaun looked around the room trying to see if there were any familiar faces. He'd made a point of going to a few campus parties before classes started so he wouldn't feel out of the loop.

He waved down toward the teaching platform when he saw a couple of guys he'd met a few nights before.

They ran up the stairs toward him.

"Hey. Shaun, right?" one of them said.

"Yeah." Shaun shook his head and laughed. "I'm sorry. I'm horrible with names."

"I'm Rowan. And this egghead is Bram."

Rowan laughed as Bram shoved him.

"We're waiting on a friend of ours," Bram said as he looked around. "A big stupid guy whose grades defy logic."

"Do you guys want to sit here?" Shaun asked. "I'll move down a few seats." He waited for them to nod then gathered up his stuff and moved a few seats over. He settled his things and glanced up as the guys started shouting at someone at the front of the hall.

Shaun's eyebrows shot up in surprise.

It was Eric.

Eric sprinted up the steps and high fived Rowan and Bram. Then his eyes fell on Shaun.

"Wow! Blast from the past," Eric said and reached for Shaun's hand to shake it before taking a seat.

"You guys know each other?" Bram asked. "We thought Shaun was a stray."

"Yeah," Eric said. "We went to high school together."

"Cool," Rowan said as he rose to his feet, tapping Bram furiously on the shoulder. "Look, there she is." He pointed down to a slim young woman with long, straight red hair dressed in a flowing pink blouse, sleek gray pencil skirt, and three-inch heels.

"Who is that?" asked Eric, intrigued.

"Her name is Shannon," Rowan replied. "She was in two of my classes last term. She's gorgeous …and she's brilliant."

"I've seen her around campus," Bram said. "Isn't she seeing that teacher's aide, Simon, over in the science department?"

"Yeah, she was, but word has it they broke up over the summer," Rowan replied. "I'm thinking of making my move."

"Why on earth would a girl like that be interested in a guy like you?" Bram asked. "She's got too much class to date a Neanderthal." He leaned out past Rowan to speak to Shaun. "Why don't you ask her out? You've got that whole dark and handsome, steamy model thing going on."

"I don't think my girlfriend would approve," Shaun replied, laughing.

Eric pushed Bram back into his seat, and out of the way.

"You have a girlfriend?" Eric asked Shaun.

"Yeah, her name is Deirdre." Shaun tapped his pen on the seat in front of him. "We've been seeing each other for about five years now. She was offered a great job out here, so we moved."

"I thought you'd be working for your dad while you were going to school, interning, and stuff?"

"We had a bit of a falling out a few years ago …high

school to be exact." Shaun nodded when Eric gave him a knowing look. "He's been making things difficult for me since then. Apparently, I have to earn back his respect."

"Bummer." Eric sat back in his seat and then leaned forward again. "Did you stay in touch with Curtis at all?"

Shaun dropped his head. "No, I haven't heard from Curtis since the day he took off on me."

"Would you be interested in seeing him?" Eric asked.

"Of course. Curtis was my best friend."

"The reason I ask is ...I think I saw him in town the other day."

Shaun looked up. "You saw Curtis? Here?"

"Yeah, he was going into that gay club down on Thirty-Fifth." Eric stopped when Rowan and Bram both looked at him in surprise. "What? I was driving past on my way to the grocery store. Is that a crime?" He redirected his attention back to Shaun. "Maybe you should go check it out. See if it's him."

Shaun sunk back into his seat and flipped his binder open as the professor started the lecture. He tried to concentrate on what was being said, but the entirety of his mind was elsewhere.

Shannon discreetly popped her compact open and pretended to be checking her makeup, but was in truth checking out the row of young men sitting at the very back of the lecture hall. She clicked the compact closed and brushed a fingertip down the bridge of her nose, thinking life really did have an interesting way of messing with you. She closed her binder when the professor called the end of class and proceeded to feign clumsiness by dumping the contents of her purse onto the floor. Unfortunately, the wrong group of men came to her aide, and she watched the ones she was interested in walk out the door. She fretted briefly over the missed opportunity and picked up the rest of her things. She would catch up with them later in the student union pub. It was the first day of classes, and guys like that always ended up at the pub after first day.

Deirdre finished washing the last of the dishes and began putting each piece away as Shaun dried them.

"Maybe he was having a bad day," Shaun suggested.

"I don't know, Shaun. I think the guy is just an ass." Deirdre set the last plate in the cupboard and closed the door. "I'm glad I don't have to work with him every day. That man would drive me insane. His wife must be a saint."

"Proof that there's someone for everyone." Shaun grinned.

"So, what time do you think you'll be back tonight? I have an early start tomorrow."

"I'm thinking no later than eleven. The guys and I are just going to hit the pub and play a few rounds of pool."

"Pretty freaky about that friend of yours, Eric, isn't it?"

"We weren't really friends, but I knew him well enough." Shaun folded the tea towel and hung it on the hook beside the fridge. "He's an all right guy. It should be fun catching up."

"I won't wait up," Deirdre said and then kissed him. "Could you take the garbage out on your way?" She smiled. "Love you."

Shaun laughed softly. "Love you too. See you later."

After grabbing the garbage, Shaun headed out the door and down the stairs to his car. He tossed the bag into the bin and slid into the driver's seat of his battered, tired Camry. He paused for a second, thinking about the likelihood it was actually Curtis. Couldn't be. He started the engine and arrived at the pub just as Bram was piling out of his truck with Eric and Rowan in tow.

"I wasn't sure if the wife was going to let you out of the house tonight," Rowan teased Shaun. "Being a school night and all."

"We're not married, jackass," Shaun replied. "I can do what I want ...for now." Then he laughed, prompting a punch in the arm and a nuggie from Bram.

"Don't be getting yourself tied down," Bram said. "A wife and kids is a serious detriment when it comes to picking up chicks."

Eric roared with laughter and clapped Bram roughly on the shoulder as he pushed the group of them through the doors of the pub. They headed straight for the bar and leaned against it, waiting to place their orders. Once they'd thrown back a few shots, they contented themselves with beer and turned back around to view what was happening throughout the pub.

"It's pretty busy in here tonight," Rowan commented. "It might be difficult to get a pool table."

"What the heck is going on over there?" Eric said. "I can't even see that table." He patted Shaun on the arm and motioned for the guys to follow him across the room.

They pushed past a few of the guys hovering intently

and soon discovered what, or more precisely whom, was causing the sudden interest in pool.

Shannon looked down the table and lined up her next shot, leaning forward just enough to let the onlookers on the other side of the table catch a glimpse down her top. She took the shot and stood to watch the balls sink into the pockets she'd intended.

She reached for her drink and upon seeing it empty raised her eyebrows at the closest male, smiling as he ran off to get her a refill. The next shot she wanted to take wasn't going to place her where she wanted to be standing, so she re-evaluated the table and decided on the next best thing. She walked around the edge, letting her hips swing just enough to ensure all eyes were trained on her.

She came to a stop directly across from the young men she'd spotted in class today. She pursed her lips in concentration and then leaned forward, lifting her eyes momentarily to confirm they were watching. She dipped down further to give them the full view straight through to the little diamond gracing her taut, sleek midriff, took the shot, smiled at them, and soaked in their reaction.

All four men laughed, in shock, pounding each other in jubilation at what they'd just seen.

Rowan clutched at his chest in false cardiac arrest and stumbled back toward the bar, hauling his friends with him. "Have you *ever* seen tits like that before?"

"I'm going to have a boner all week thinking about those perfect little rosebuds of hers," Bram said. "Fucking unbelievable."

"And fucking untouchable," Eric added. "She is way

out of our league." He laughed. "I think I need another drink after that."

Shaun pushed through to wave the bartender down. "I'll buy the next round. What is everyone having?"

Absolute silence.

Shaun turned back toward the guys.

Shannon extended her hand to Shaun as his friends stepped back to let her pass.

"Hi, I'm Shannon," she purred.

"Um ...Shaun." Shaun took her hand but wasn't quite sure what to do with it, so he kissed it and let it drop.

"Do you want to grab a booth?" Shannon asked.

Shaun looked past her to his friends, who were nodding their heads furiously to do whatever she asked.

"Sure," he said then checked over his shoulder toward the bar.

"Would you like a drink?" he asked.

Shannon looked over at the bartender and nodded at him.

"He'll send something over for us," she said. "Come sit." She directed Shaun toward a booth at the back of the pub and waited for the occupants to vacate the space for her before sitting down.

"People here seem to know you," said Shaun.

"I was dating a TA for a couple of years. It comes with some privileges. We split recently though."

"Yeah, I heard."

"Did you now?" Shannon smiled when she saw Shaun blushing. "It's all right. Dating on campus is like dating in a bubble. Everyone knows your business." She tapped him on the wrist then left her hand there. "Are you seeing someone?"

"Um …yeah." Shaun pressed his lips together and dropped his eyes, only looking up when the bartender brought two martinis over for them. He was slightly embarrassed to see they were pink and shoulder checked to find his friends laughing.

"And who is this lucky person?" Shannon asked.

"Her name is Deirdre." Shaun tentatively took a sip of the drink. He really needed the alcohol regardless of its color. "We met a few years ago back home."

"And where is home?"

"The west coast. Inland."

"Me too. Perhaps we've crossed paths before."

Shaun grinned. "No, I think I would remember that."

"Yes, I'm sure I would've remembered you as well." Shannon glanced up toward Shaun's friends and winked at them, sending them into a chorus of groans. "Who have you got with you this evening? Not the furry ones, but the young man in jeans."

Shaun smirked at Shannon's reference toward Rowan and Bram. They really did need to think about shaving their beards off.

"That's Eric," he said. "We went to high school together."

"What's his story?" Shannon pointed at Eric and motioned for him to approach the table. "Is he attached?"

"Not as far as I know."

Shannon smiled seductively at Eric as he took a seat across from her. "My, my, but aren't you just simply marvelous."

"Um …thanks," said Eric, not quite sure what to do with a compliment like that.

Shannon turned her attention back to Shaun. "Thank you, Shaun. I'll see you in class tomorrow."

Shaun walked away from the table practically in stitches as he joined Rowan and Bram at the bar. He leaned against it and caught his breath, wiping mirthful tears from his eyes.

"Oh, my god," he said. "I feel sorry for Eric." He sighed heavily then hiccupped, sending himself into more fits of laughter. "That woman is one serious predator."

"I'd be prey for her any day," Rowan replied.

"Apparently, you're too furry," Shaun said then snorted, almost falling off his stool.

"Did she say that?" Bram asked.

Shaun nodded his head, unable to speak without losing it.

"That's it," Rowan said. "I'm shaving as soon as I get home."

"Wait! Wait, look," Bram said, yanking on Rowan's sleeve. "They're leaving already."

Shaun righted himself and watched Eric being led to the door of the pub. Unable to contain himself, he waved at Eric dramatically while the other two made stupid grunting and kissing noises.

"Oh, that was absolutely priceless," Shaun said. "I think I've had enough for one night. I'm going to head home."

"Yeah, us too. Seeing Shannon's tits was the highlight

of my evening," Bram said. "I'm going to go home and dream about them. We'll see you tomorrow."

Shaun waited until Bram and Rowan pulled out of the parking lot before climbing into his car. He slammed the door and rested his head back against the seat. It was only nine, and he'd told Deirdre he'd be home by eleven. That gave him two hours.

He turned the engine over and eased out of the parking lot, turning down the road that would take him to Thirty-Fifth Street.

Eric fell back on the bed, completely blown away by what he'd just experienced. In all his years of sleeping around, he'd never fucked anyone as skilled and adventurous as Shannon. His mind spun, thinking back to some of the things they'd done together, and some of the hidden places Shannon had taken him to.

He stretched out totally exhausted and watched Shannon fix her hair in the mirror. She was the most beautiful creature he'd ever laid eyes on. Every contour of her, absolute perfection. His body shivered with the memory of the taste of her skin.

He was about to get out of bed to head home, thinking Shannon didn't seem like the cuddling type, when she surprised him by climbing back into bed, pulling herself up alongside him and resting her head on his chest.

"What are you thinking about?" she asked.

"You mostly. And how I'd like to see you again."

"Mm, …we'll see." Shannon ran her hand across Eric's chest and down onto his stomach, smiling when he jumped.

"You're ticklish."

"A little." Eric grinned. "Actually, a lot."

She winked at Eric then positioned herself on top of him and started kissing her way down Eric's body, licking and biting at his skin and writhing with anticipation.

Eric threw his head back in exhilaration as she took him in and pulled at him gently with her mouth until he felt his need increasing to a new, unprecedented height. She released him, and Eric grasped onto her hips as she lifted herself back up his body and lowered herself down onto him. His heart raced at what she was doing. He wasn't in the habit of having anal sex after what had happened with Attila, but he was going to make an exception.

Shannon swore quietly as she drew Eric all the way in.

Eric's heart shuddered with excitement as she rode him sweetly, rocking her hips, her startling blue eyes gazing down at him and sending his mind reeling as he crested deep within her.

Shannon threw her flaming red hair back and pulled it off to one side before lowering herself to Eric's ear.

"You still taste like cotton candy," she said.

Shaun pulled into the parking lot and checked to make sure no one was around before getting out of his car and making a run for the door of the club. He stepped inside and kept his eyes averted as he paid his cover charge, then snuck around to the tables in the shadows near the back of the room. He tucked himself into the corner and ordered a row of shots when the waiter came by.

The guy on stage at the moment was doing his best to

entertain the small crowd of men, but they were becoming bored with his lackluster performance and were heading to the bar to replenish their drinks instead. Shaun sighed, annoyed, when a weather-beaten old biker wandered over to his table and sat down.

"I'm working. So fuck off," Shaun said.

"I'll pay a hundred fifty."

Shaun threw back a shot and shook his head.

"Two fifty. Not a penny less," he said then raised his eyes, smiling seductively to tempt him. "I usually don't go for less than three hundred. But I'm feeling generous."

"Fuck you!" Biker guy threw his chair back and stormed away.

Shaun grinned. "Not on your budget." He threw back the next two shots and reclined in his chair, trying to relax. He'd *dated* for a bit after Curtis left, trying to erase the pain that Curtis' departure had left, but he'd stopped when he met Deirdre, thinking moving forward was the answer to his anguish.

He threw back another shot as he thought about her. Even though they were close, he'd never shared that part of his life with Deirdre, and he had no plans of ever doing so because it was still a big part of who he was. He'd tried to remain faithful to her, but there'd been more than a few occasions when he'd sought out male company over the years. Each time returning to her feeling absolutely guilt-ridden and disgusted with his cowardice. It was an existence that he couldn't see himself continuing.

He looked up when the spotlights and strobes sprung to life, and the music cranked up to dance club proportions.

Shaun knew everything was going to be right in his world again when the performer entered the main stage. He grabbed his drink and worked his way down to the stage seating, and took a seat, front and center.

It didn't take long for Curtis to spot Shaun sitting there grinning at him. He winked at Shaun as he gyrated to his knees, encouraging the men crowding the stage to tuck their money into his sparkling silver G-string. He made a special point of giving Shaun a private dance, only carrying on to the other patrons after Shaun added his own money and smacked Curtis' ass.

Shaun fell back into his chair, barely able to contain himself. His emotions eventually spilled over, and he had to make his way to the washroom to compose himself. He leaned against the counter, splashing cold water on his face, trying to comprehend how the events of the day had led to this point.

The sound of the door opening behind him had Shaun peering up into the mirror and running into the arms of the only person who'd ever made him feel whole.

Eric shoved Shannon away from his body and scrambled to the other side of the bed, falling onto the floor.

"What did you just say?" he asked as he righted himself, needing clarification on something that just couldn't be true.

Shannon crawled to the edge of the bed and lay down on her stomach, propping her head up with one hand.

"I said …you still taste like cotton candy."

"Why would you say that?"

"Because it's one of the things I remember about you."

Eric backed himself up against the dresser and grabbed his shirt off the floor, covering himself. He studied Shannon's features, looking for any similarities, but his heart was pounding so hard, he was having difficulty focusing. He took a deep breath, attempting to clear his head.

Then, she smiled at him.

He would've recognized that smile anywhere.

The recess at the back of the washroom wasn't as dark as what Shaun would've preferred, but he was in no state to argue its lack of privacy as Curtis rocked him hard against the cold brick wall, his legs wrapped around Curtis' waist, forcing the abrasive surface to blister the skin of his ass.

He folded his arms tighter around Curtis' neck, moaning and crying out in pain as he took what Curtis had been carrying for him.

Wanting only to please him.

Have him love him again.

Curtis drew Shaun closer to him, grasping, desperate, as he shuddered deep within him. Heaving, he took Shaun's mouth, whispering his apologies for being so rough with him.

"It's all right," Shaun said as Curtis set him down.

"No, it's not all right." Curtis looked around and spotted Shaun's shirt. "Here, let me help you with this." He picked it up, allowing Shaun to put it on, but then began doing up the buttons for him.

Shaun tried to push Curtis' hands away.

"Curtis ...don't. I can do it."

"No ...I shouldn't have taken you like that." Curtis turned on his heel and slammed a hand against the cold wall.

"It wasn't right," he said. "I'm sorry."

"I'm fine. Stop apologizing."

Curtis turned and studied Shaun's face, and felt his heart melt.

"Were you ever going to come back for me?" Shaun asked as he finished with his belt and began checking his hair in the mirror.

"I thought about it every day."

"I waited for you. I even kept your card." Shaun pulled out his wallet and slipped his fingers in behind his driver's license. He removed the card and glanced down at the worn print. He'd spent hours brushing his fingers over those words.

"Can I see it?" Curtis asked, unsure as Shaun handed it to him. His eyes wandered over the card and then up to Shaun's face watching him; Shaun's expression was just as it had been that first morning they'd woken up together — the day his life had changed.

"I don't know what I was thinking," Curtis said.

"Right ...," Shaun said then snatched the card back, stuffed it into his wallet, and turned to leave, prompting a puzzled expression from Curtis that quickly turned to panic.

"No! That's not what I meant!" Curtis shouted, stopping Shaun and pulling him into his arms. He nestled his face in the curve of Shaun's neck. "I don't know what I was thinking when I left you that day. Not the words written on that card."

"So …do you still love me?" Shaun asked.

Curtis stepped back and held Shaun's face. "Of course I do. I could never stop loving you."

"So, you still want to be with me?" Shaun sighed and let a few tears stream down his cheek. "You still want me."

"Infinitely. But …do you still want me?"

Shaun tossed his head and looked out from beneath the cascade of hair shielding his eyes, and nodded his head.

The last seven years of agony had finally come to an end.

Eric opened his eyes and studied the ones staring back at him.

There was no denying it.

They were definitely his.

"Attila …what the fuck?"

"I'm sorry, Eric."

"You're sorry? And when have I heard that before?"

"Really, Eric. I was going to say something after class today, but you took off so fast. And then after seeing you …" Attila brushed at a few tears as they rolled down his face. "I'm sorry. I'm still a complete fuck up. I can't help myself." He rose to his feet and headed for the bathroom, pressing the door closed behind him.

He pulled it back open a sliver and peered out.

"I'll transfer out as soon as I can," Attila said. "And I won't tell anyone about this. I promise." He blew Eric a kiss and then lowered his gaze. "Could you flip the lock on your way out?"

"Hold on," Eric said, his face pinched in confusion. "You can't just use me and dismiss me like that."

Attila shrugged.

"So, what do you want me to say?" he asked.

"I don't know. I haven't seen you in seven years."

"I'm sure you've survived fine without me." Attila pushed the door closed, but then popped it open again. "It was nice to see you again though after all these years."

"Attila," Eric started then sighed. Some things about Attila hadn't changed at all. He was still so disconnected, treating people like objects as if their feelings were inconsequential.

"Please don't treat me like I meant nothing to you," Eric said.

"I'm not. I just don't know what you want from me."

"I don't want anything from you. We were friends." Eric scrubbed his hair in irritation. "We were good friends. I want to spend some time talking to you."

Attila exhaled in resignation but stayed where he was peering out from behind the door.

"Fine …talk," he said.

Eric wrinkled his nose, not sure where to start.

"Does anyone else know about you?"

Attila almost slammed the door shut, but he resisted.

"That's what you want to talk about?"

"I just spent the last two hours fucking you, so yeah."

Attila pulled the door open wider and leaned against the frame. "The last surgery of my gender reassignment was three years ago. I was able to change my birth certificate and everything after that, so as far as anyone else is concerned, I've always been a girl."

He shifted and picked at the faded paint of the door.

"So," he added. "No one will ever find out you slept with a guy in high school."

"That's not why I asked," Eric said.

"I know. I'm sorry."

"You've done a lot with your face as well."

"A little here and there."

Eric pulled himself up off the floor and wandered across the room, slowing as he approached Attila. "You look so different."

"That was the idea."

"Attila. Why did you leave Tekla?"

"I didn't want anyone else finding out I was a guy."

"Why not? Most people would've been relieved to know Ming hadn't lost his mind."

Attila couldn't contain a thin smile.

"Ming wasn't the issue," he said.

"What was?"

"Candace was going to tell everyone about us."

"Why would you care about that?"

"That's a stupid question."

Eric stepped forward and propped himself against the doorframe, keeping Attila from retreating again.

"Why is that a stupid question?" he asked Attila.

"Eric. Can we not do this?" Attila stepped back into the bathroom and tried to close the door, but Eric's foot was in the way—and his notorious temper had suddenly flared up.

"Answer me, Attila!" Eric bellowed, banging his fists against the door. "Why the fuck did you care so much?"

Attila almost lost his balance, tripping backward.

"Dammit, Eric," he said. "Now you're scaring me."

Eric pushed hard on the door, making Attila slide back against the sink. "Good. Because for years I've been asking myself *why*. *Why* did Attila entice me into the backseat of my truck?"

Attila blew a strand of hair away that had landed on his lips.

"I told you," he said. "I thought you wanted to fuck me."

"So, I was just another fuck to you?"

"No, of course not. But it didn't mean anything."

Eric's hands curled into fists.

"It didn't mean anything?"

"That's what I said …nothing."

"I don't believe you. Tell me what really happened that night."

Eric clenched his teeth, waiting for an answer, as he continued his efforts to contain his frustration.

"I want to know why you did it," he said.

"I don't know."

Eric slammed his hand into the wall by the medicine cabinet, sending a multitude of pill bottles in every direction.

Attila screamed and covered his face. "I don't know."

"Bullshit!"

Attila slid to the floor, protecting his head, and tucked his knees up in front of his body. "Eric, please don't hurt me.

I'm so sorry."

"Attila!" Eric shouted. "For the last fucking time! Why?"

"I just wanted to be with you," Attila whispered.

Attila cringed and pulled himself tighter as Eric lunged forward, ripping the shower rod from the wall. He shrieked when the shower curtain brushed past his leg but opened his eyes to peer through his arms. Eric was leaning against the wall watching him intently but seemed to have calmed down significantly.

"We were good friends," Attila continued. "But I felt so much more for you than that." He closed his eyes again.

Eric sunk down onto his knees at Attila's feet and settled his hands on Attila's shoulders.

"What?" he asked. "Tell me what you felt."

Attila shook his head.

"I can't."

"Attila, please. I need to hear you say it."

"It was all so confusing." Attila looked up, tentative. "Eric, I was madly in love with you …and I didn't know what to do with it. I knew you didn't feel the same way about me. When you held me on the dance floor that night …I imagined that maybe you loved me too. I desperately needed to feel that love moving within me."

Eric sighed and slid down onto the floor beside Attila.

"That's all I needed to know," he said.

"Why?"

"Because deep down, I knew you didn't put me through all that crap because you were trying to destroy me. Ming tried to convince me otherwise. But I didn't believe him." Eric crossed his arms and looked at Attila. "You should've told me who you were today."

"I know, but I wanted you to hold me one last time before I told you …before I completely repulsed you."

"God, Attila. You could never repulse me." Eric checked behind him and brushed Attila's hair to one side so he could put his arm around him. "Piss me off maybe, but not repulse me."

"You're just saying that."

"No, I'm not. I mean it. You're special to me."

Attila leaned his head against Eric's shoulder, taking in the comforting scent of him. "Well, it's nice to hear you say that at least." He reached over tentatively, and slipped his hand into Eric's, basking in the responding embrace.

"I've missed you," he said.

Eric exhaled as the tension left his body. "What am I going to do with you, Attila?" He shoved Attila playfully. "I swear I should've beaten the crap out of you when I had the chance. Now I'm really stuck with you."

Attila pulled back and stared at him. "You don't want me to leave the university?"

"No. I want you to start hanging out with me and give the rest of the men around here a break. You're seriously scary with that whole seduction routine of yours."

"You liked that, did you?"

"I'd be lying if I said I didn't."

"What about the rest of it? Was the sex good?"

Eric's eyebrows shot up in surprise. "You're not seriously asking me that."

"Too soon?"

"No, I was thinking more in terms of the sounds I was making. The number of times I came …stuff like that." Eric grinned and pulled Attila closer. "It was amazing. You were amazing. You always have been amazing to me."

"Now, I'm totally confused."

"Attila. I never would've had a problem having sex with you as a person. It was the fact you were a guy that turned me off."

Attila sat straight up and set his face with anticipation.

"So, you're all right with this?" he asked as he looked down at himself and ran a hand across his bare stomach.

"I think I'm all right with it." Eric's eyes wandered along the gentle curve of Attila's face, prompting him to lean in and give Attila a soft kiss on the cheek. He lifted his hand to Attila's chin and turned his face toward him so he could study his eyes.

"Fuck, Attila," he whispered.

Eric breathed across Attila's lips then took his mouth, letting himself explore the depth of his emotions. As he pulled away, he watched Attila's reaction and smiled at what he saw. "Yeah, I'm definitely all right with it," he said and lifted himself to his feet.

He held out his hand for Attila to take. "Come back to bed. We have some catching up to do."

The lecture hall had even fewer people in it than the day before. Eric looked up toward the back row and spotted Rowan and Bram waving furiously at him. He grinned and took the steps two at a time to reach them.

Eric was absolutely beaming by the time he sat down.

"Oh, now that is one happy man," Bram said, slamming his hand on Eric's back. "Look at that face, Rowan. Our boy here had himself a wild and crazy night."

Rowan crossed his arms. "I should be mad at you. I spotted her first." He shoved Eric's head playfully and laughed. "But I'm more interested in hearing every hot and juicy detail than I am in holding a grudge."

"She was unbelievable," Eric said. "I'm absolutely exhausted."

"That's it?" Bram asked. "That's all you're giving us?"

"We need something more explicit than that," Rowan added. "Is the rest of her body as hot as her tits?"

Eric grinned. "Even more so."

Rowan and Bram groaned, holding their chests, but then scrambled to look respectable when they saw who was making their way up the stairs to the back row.

"Hey, baby," Attila said as he slid into the seat next to Eric. He'd toned his outfit down a little this morning, opting for more of a campus look that consisted of skin-tight blue jeans, a white t-shirt with a plunging neckline, and a ponytail. The exception had been the mahogany colored, knee-high leather boots with three-inch heels. There were some things he wasn't willing to compromise on. He had a reputation to uphold.

"You look amazing," Eric said.

"Aren't you sweet?" Attila held Eric's face and gave him a long sensuous kiss, then leaned forward in his seat. "Are you going to introduce me to your friends?"

"Yeah," Eric replied. "This is Rowan ...and Bram." He paused and smiled. The two were staring at Attila open-mouthed, in utter shock. "And this is Shannon. As you already know."

"Hey, guys. Nice to meet you," Attila said then looked around. "Where's Shaun?"

"He's running a bit late," Rowan replied after regaining his speech. "Something about bumping into an old friend last night."

"There he is." Bram stood up and tried unsuccessfully to motion discreetly toward Eric's visitor. As Shaun approached the back row, Eric asked Bram and Rowan to move down so Shaun could sit down between himself and Shannon, then changed his mind and asked them to move even further down the row, out of earshot.

Shaun set his books down, guarded, and reluctantly took a seat between Eric and Shannon.

"Hey, Shannon," he said.

"How are you this morning, Shaun?" Attila asked.

"Great. What's going on?"

"I have no idea." Attila looked at Eric. "Care to enlighten us?"

"Was it Curtis?" Eric asked, anxious to hear the answer.

"You went looking for Curtis?" Attila asked. "How did you find out he was working down—" He came to a startling stop when he realized Shaun was staring at him.

"Did you tell her about Curtis?" Shaun asked Eric.

"It may have slipped out last night."

"Thanks a lot, Eric," Shaun replied. "Maybe I should tell her about Annie."

"Who's Annie?" Attila asked, trying to recover from his slip up.

"A girl I knew in high school," Eric replied. "I'll tell you about her later." He turned back to Shaun. "Was it him?"

"Yeah, it was him."

"And? What happened?"

Shaun lowered his eyes and sighed, not certain if he was excited, or just bloody overwhelmed.

"What always inevitably happens when Curtis and I are together," he answered.

"You didn't," Attila said. "What about your girlfriend?"

"How much did you tell her?" Shaun said, glaring at Eric in incredulous shock. "Maybe I should tell everyone about Attila."

"Calm down, Shaun," replied Eric. "Shannon was already aware of this stuff between you and Curtis. Do you remember that gawky, ginger-haired girl that lived around the corner from me?"

"No, I don't."

"I used to hang out with her when I was a kid."

"I don't remember," Shaun said. "What grade was this?"

"Five," Eric said at the same time as Attila said *six*.

"Grades five and six at Watson Elementary," Attila said. "I moved away after that, but I kept in contact with a few people."

"Like who?" Shaun asked.

"Oh …um …Candace and Dixie mostly."

"Small world, isn't it?" Eric concluded, reaching over and clapping Shaun on the back. "So, what's happening with Curtis?"

"I don't know." Shaun paused and tried to reorganize

his thoughts. "It's like I can't help myself when I'm with him. I'm drawn to him like some sort of crack addict."

"The sex must be really good," Attila said then held up his hands in defense as they both stared at him. "What? I've been hooked on people because of incredible sex before."

Attila glanced at the people turning in their seats, and then down at the professor staring up at him. "I said that way too loud, didn't I?" He slid down in his seat a little and lowered his voice.

"Sometimes that's the way it is between guys," he added, much quieter this time. "It's a physical craving your body knows can only be satisfied by one person." He looked past Shaun at Eric and smiled. "Of course, sometimes, that same person can mean so much more to you than that."

"Great," Shaun said. "Now I'm getting gay sex advice from a girl. How much stranger could my day become?"

"The sky's the limit on such things, Shaun," Eric replied, smirking. That had indeed been the way it had gone yesterday.

Deirdre arrived home to find Shaun knee deep in boxes that he'd pulled from their storage unit. Most of the contents of those boxes were strewn across the floor except for two pictures Shaun was holding in hands. "What are you looking for?"

"School pictures from elementary school."

"Did you find them?" Deirdre stepped closer and took the pictures Shaun held out to her. "Which one are you?"

Shaun leaned in and pointed himself out in both pictures.

"You were so cute. Look how tiny you were." She peered intently at the pictures. "Who were you friends with?"

"That's Eric. The guy I told you about at school. And there he is again in this picture." Shaun took the pictures back. "Watson Elementary was a tiny school. There was only one grade five and one grade six class. And there is no ginger-haired girl in either one of these pictures."

"I don't understand the significance."

"Eric's new girlfriend, Shannon. They both claim she went to Watson in those grades."

"Maybe she missed picture day two years in a row."

"No, I don't remember her at all. Look at how few kids there are in these classes. I would remember her."

"Why would they lie to you about something like that?"

"I don't know." Shaun paused in thought. "I'd like to invite them over for dinner tomorrow night and see what I can find out."

"Shaun, maybe you should just drop it. I'm sure they have their reasons for fabricating something like that."

"Yeah, you're probably right." Shaun set the pictures back in the box and started cleaning up, but then sunk onto the sofa. "No, there's something not right," he said. "There's something about her that is so familiar. But I can't place her. It's going to drive me crazy until I figure it out."

"All right, but I hope spaghetti works for you because we're running short on funds again and I've only got ground beef left in the freezer." Deirdre set her hand on Shaun's shoulder, but he was too deep in thought to acknowledge her.

Eric leaned back in his chair and reached for Attila's hand, grasping it tightly in his own. They'd spent another incredible night together, and their close friendship had rekindled itself where they'd left off, but better. He'd never felt as comfortable with anyone as what he did with Attila, and being able to hold him and make love to him was more than he ever could've hoped for.

"That was an amazing dinner, Deirdre, thank you," he said.

"I'm just sorry I didn't know about Shannon's dietary restrictions. I should've asked," Deirdre replied, secretly wishing she had the willpower to lay off the carbs.

"That's all right," Attila said. "The salad was lovely. And it's the company that really matters anyway, isn't it?"

"I think we should take this into the living room," Shaun said. "Eric, do you want to help me get some coffee ready while these ladies relax?"

Eric agreed, rising to his feet, and kissed Attila on the lips, winked at him, and then headed into the kitchen after Shaun.

Shaun set the stack of dirty plates down on the counter and turned to face Eric with his arms crossed.

"All right, fess up," he said. "Who is Shannon really?"

Eric checked over his shoulder to make sure Deirdre and Attila were seated in the living room. "What are you talking about?"

"She's not in any of the pictures."

"What pictures?"

"The school pictures. Shannon did not go to Watson Elementary. But I know her from somewhere. I just can't place her. Where do I know her from?"

"Shaun, you need to drop this."

"I can't. It's going to drive me insane." Shaun pulled the coffee pot out and began filling it with water. "Maybe it's her eyes. There aren't too many people around with eyes that color."

Eric scrubbed at his chin, wishing Shaun would change the subject. "Shaun, please just leave it alone."

"The last person I knew with eyes that color was Annie …or Attila …whatever." Shaun turned from the sink, his body numbing from every extremity, and the handle of the coffee pot slipped from his grasp, smashing onto the hard ceramic tiles. He sunk onto the floor in disbelief, only looking up when Attila squatted down beside him to make sure he was all right. He reached up and placed his hand on Attila's face, studying it.

"Oh, my god," he said. "It really is you."

"Shaun, darling!" Attila said. "I think maybe you've had too much to drink." He leaned in as if to give Shaun a hand up, but whispered in his ear instead. "Please keep this to yourself."

"But …does Eric know?" Shaun whispered in reply.

"Does Eric know what?" Deirdre asked as she helped Shaun to his feet. "Shannon, could you grab me the broom from that cupboard? I don't want us tracking this glass throughout the place."

Attila nodded and headed for the cupboard Deirdre had pointed out but kept listening to hear what was going to be said next. He honestly didn't mind if Shaun found out who he was, but he wasn't sure how Eric felt about Shaun knowing.

"Yes, Shaun," Eric replied. "I know exactly who Shannon is."

"What are we talking about?" Deirdre asked as she took the broom from Attila's hands and started sweeping up.

"Shannon is a good buddy of mine from high school," Eric said as he pulled Attila into his arms. He backed Attila up against his body and wrapped his arms around Attila's waist, kissing the back of Attila's neck as he sought the comforting familiarity of him.

Shaun stood and stared dumbfounded.

"Well, mystery solved then," Deirdre said as she dumped the glass in the garbage and began fussing around looking for a different coffee pot to use.

"Shannon moved away partway through the school year without even saying goodbye to me." Eric paused and held Attila tighter. "I don't think he had any idea what that did to me. How much I missed hanging out with him."

Deirdre popped her head up from behind one of the cupboard doors and looked over at Eric and Attila. He and him?

"I didn't know," Attila said as he turned to face Eric.

"Why didn't you call me? We could've talked about it."

"I thought you wouldn't want to talk to me." Attila brushed his hand across Eric's face and tucked a few tendrils of hair behind his ear. "After everything that happened between us, I didn't think you'd ever want to speak to a screwed up guy like me again."

"Attila, you couldn't have been more wrong."

"All right," Deirdre said with irritation. "Someone needs to fill me in on what the hell is going on around here."

Shaun covered his mouth and exhaled, joyful tears streaming from his eyes to coat his cheeks. Everything truly was right again. Curtis …now Attila and Eric. He grinned. He was back in a world where he actually belonged, and where he wanted to be.

Chapter Six

Definition of Love

Shaun tripped over a pair of shoes in the hallway as he tried to reach the phone in the kitchen. He was running late as usual, but he wasn't too concerned. He'd already finished the paper that was due and only needed to make sure it was in before the end of class.

He lifted the receiver of the phone, but there was only a dial tone; he'd been too slow getting to it. His pulse surged as his cell phone sprung to life, playing the ring tone he'd assigned to Curtis. But it was all the way back in the bedroom. He sprinted down the hallway almost clipping his hip on the dresser and fell onto the bed, answering the call; but once again, he was too late.

He'd been seeing a lot of Curtis since the night he'd surprised him at the club, making his way down there at least four times a week. Sometimes they would stay and use the dressing room to fuck around in, and sometimes, if Curtis finished work early, they would head out to Curtis' trailer. Either way, he always came home feeling sated, but longing for their next meeting.

Groaning, Shaun rolled off the bed when he heard someone knocking at the door. The rent was due, and once again, they were running short of money. He'd considered going on a few *dates* to make up the difference, but he couldn't think of a logical explanation that would satisfy Deirdre as to where the extra money had come from, and he didn't feel right about keeping something like that from Curtis. Whenever he and Curtis brought an extra guy into the mix, it was always together, and never for money. Curtis wouldn't have approved of him hustling.

He reluctantly opened the door.

"Hey, sport." Curtis pushed his way into the apartment. "You should learn to answer your phone."

"Stop. You can't be here," Shaun said tersely.

Curtis wandered into the living room and looked around, picking up the different decorative items scattered about the room. He lit a cigarette and walked into the kitchen, checking out the fridge and a few of the cupboards, lifting this and that to inspect it.

"Do you live with someone?" he asked.

"Curtis, seriously. You can't be here."

"I wanted to see where you lived. You always come to see me, and I thought it was high time for me to come see you." Curtis crushed out his cigarette in a small antique candy dish. "I got your address from a charming young lady at the university. Hope you don't mind, but I wanted to surprise you." He turned and smiled at Shaun. "Your place is pretty nice. Kind of girly though with all the kitschy stuff. Are you sure you're not living with someone?"

"I never said I wasn't."

Curtis dropped down onto the sofa. "No, I suppose you didn't, did you, Tonto?" He sighed and relaxed into the cushions.

"What's her name?" he asked.

"Deirdre. We met about five years ago. She's the reason I ended up out here. She got an excellent job."

"A job. Like a real job?"

"Curtis ...don't."

"Hey, I'm just trying to scope out the competition."

"She's not your competition," Shaun replied.

"Oh ...am I too late? Did she win the horse race already?"

Shaun grinned, disregarding his anxiety about Curtis being there. Deirdre wasn't due to come home for hours. He threw himself on top of Curtis and took his mouth, letting his hands work the buttons of Curtis' pants open. He bit at Curtis' chin then sat up, stripping his own shirt off over his head.

"I'll take that as a big fat *no*," Curtis said.

"And I'll take you any way I can get you."

Shaun lifted himself off the sofa, allowing his hips to rotate seductively as he raised his arms up over his head and danced to the music in his head. He bit his lower lip, winked at Curtis, and gyrated back toward him using a sequence he'd seen the performers at the club doing. He ended up straddling Curtis' hips, thrusting his own upwards, and moaning softly in anticipation.

"I swear," Curtis said. "You could put those other boys at the club to shame. You are so fucking hot."

"Maybe you could get me a job there."

"I could."

Shaun stopped what he was doing. "Seriously?"

"Yeah, you're really good. And Charles, the guy who owns the place, is looking to increase his audience base by adding some *boy on boy* action." He ran his hands up Shaun's chest, across his shoulders, and down his arms. "It would pay really well."

"Doing what? Dancing together?"

"No, we'd be in the *members only* area of the club, so we'd be doing a bit more than dancing."

"We'd be fucking on stage?"

"Essentially, yeah." Curtis pulled Shaun closer to him and began licking long lines across Shaun's chest and circling his nipples, sucking on them gently and savoring the enticing taste of his skin.

"Do you think we'd be really hot together?" Shaun asked.

Curtis sat back and looked up at him. "Fuck, yeah."

"All right, I'm game." Shaun kissed Curtis with finality. "It sounds like a lot of fun." He leaped off Curtis' lap and stripped the rest of his clothing off, letting his body undulate and sway seductively once he was done.

Curtis licked his lips, watching Shaun suck a finger into his mouth then thrust it into himself, grinding and groaning dramatically.

As Shaun increased the tempo and force of his thrusts, Curtis barely managed to remove his own pants before his mind exploded with images of what he and Shaun would be doing on stage.

The sun was streaming through the windows across Attila's face, waking him up. He rolled over and smiled when he saw Eric's sleeping form beside him. He moved closer, touching the softness of Eric's skin and gently kissed his chest, waking him up.

"Good morning," Eric said.

"It is, now that I get to wake up with you every day."

"You don't think we rushed into things. Moving in together?"

"Rushing is what Curtis and Shaun did back in high school."

Eric grinned and then laughed. "True. But their souls intertwined and connected …or something."

Attila wrinkled up his nose in thought, disregarding the bizarre complexities of Curtis and Shaun's love affair.

"Question," he said. "Curiosity really."

Eric rolled to face him.

"When we're together," Attila continued. "At school, or when we're hanging out. Do you think of me as a guy or a girl?"

"Attila, regardless of the packaging, you're definitely a guy. A seriously gay guy, but a guy nonetheless."

"What about when we're having sex?"

Eric cleared his throat. "That one is more difficult."

"Try."

"Well, my body is definitely fooled into thinking you're a girl. I think you'll attest to that …but when I look into your eyes or hear your voice, taste your skin, or feel you holding me. I know exactly who you are."

"Does that turn you off?"

"I think I'll let you be the judge of that."

Eric pulled Attila into his arms and took Attila's mouth

with the utmost of passion, diving into the fervent warmth there. His pulse raced as Attila began making the sweet sounds of desire that always drove him to distraction, and he gasped with exhilaration as Attila's hands began their quest for intimacy, starting at his shoulders and working their way down his body.

Attila let his hands sweep across the smooth contours of Eric's back all the way down to his thighs. He closed his eyes and enjoyed the soothing sounds of Eric's arousal and the endearing knowledge that the man he'd desired for so many years was finally in his arms, fully aware of who and what he was.

He gazed up at the ceiling and let the tears stream down his cheeks as Eric slid into him, sighing softly with joy, but secretly wanting so much more from his lover. He held Eric tight to his body as he rocked him, ardent with desire, and tried to smile through the tears when Eric pulled away to gaze down at him.

"Hey, Attila," Eric said as he slowed. "What's wrong?"

"I'm just a bit emotional." Attila exhaled and fanned at his eyes with his hands. "It's been a crazy few weeks with you."

"It's been an amazing few weeks."

Attila pinched his face up and started crying again.

"I'm sorry," he said. "I don't know what's wrong with me. Those fucking hormones I take mess me up sometimes."

"Are you sure that's it? There's nothing else bothering you."

Attila shook his head.

Eric brushed delicate fingers across Attila's lips and studied his eyes, trying to determine what was really bothering him.

"Are you still in love with me?" he asked.

Attila sighed heavily. "More than you can possibly imagine."

"Why don't you ever tell me you love me?"

"It's hard for me to admit something like that to you ...and to myself. Even with my new packaging, you're right. I'm still the same guy. And I've always been a bit of a player."

Attila shut his eyes and shook his head. He shifted over as Eric climbed off his body.

"I'm sorry," he said.

"What are you sorry about?"

"Nothing." Attila turned his face away from Eric, staring toward the window. "Let's not do this."

"Attila, what is it?"

"I don't know." Attila sighed. "I guess ...I'm just sorry I'll never be the type of woman you want me to be."

"How do you know what kind of woman I want?"

"I know you want children, Eric. I saw the way you looked at Candace's baby when you thought it was yours."

"Don't do this to yourself." Eric lifted one of Attila's hands and gently kissed his fingers. "Look at what you've achieved. You're an intelligent, warm, and incredibly beautiful woman." He touched Attila's chin, encouraging him to turn back to face him, caught Attila's gaze, and felt his heart being drawn into his eyes.

"You're perfect just the way you are," he said. "I can't

imagine being with anyone else." He leaned over kissing Attila's uncertain lips. There was so much doubt there. "I'm in love with you, Attila, and I think I probably have been for a very long time."

Attila's face flushed with emotion, not fully believing Eric, but he reached out toward Eric, inviting him back into them. It was possible the man he loved …loved him back. After all these years.

The floor outside the dining room door was covered in construction dust, and it was finding its way into every other room in the house. It would've been preferential to move out while the kitchen was being renovated, but his partner Seth had insisted it wasn't necessary to go to the extra bother.

Ming was not thrilled with the arrangement at all, and he was at his wit's end trying to keep the dust from getting into his bedroom and onto the clothing in his precious wardrobe.

The sound of the noisy generator finally relented as the workday drew to an end, allowing Ming to breathe easier after what had been an extremely stressful day. He reset the cold cloth across his eyes and prayed the aspirin would start working soon.

He'd met Seth at a party a few months after high school graduation, and they'd been together ever since. Seth was a good twenty years older than he was, but they had a relationship that worked well for them both. Ming played the role of the willing and dutiful wife, and in return, Seth provided him with an expensive home, closets of extravagant clothing, and a steady flow of cash that allowed Ming to explore his own interests at his leisure.

Frustrated, Ming groaned at his own incompetence when he heard Seth come in through the front door; he'd forgotten to order dinner, once again. His oversight was going to put Seth in a lousy mood for the rest of the evening. He considered feigning a stroke to avoid the inevitable lecture about his responsibilities but decided it would probably make things worse, as he'd be forced to spend hours in the emergency room. The last time he'd done something like that, it had ended up being downright embarrassing.

"Ming?" Seth said as he stepped into the room. "It's almost seven. Where's dinner?"

Ming rolled himself off the sofa and put on his best smile. "I thought we could go out for dinner tonight." He strolled toward Seth and traced his hand seductively across Seth's chest. "The dust in here isn't very conducive to an intimate meal."

"You forgot to order dinner again, didn't you?" Seth sighed. "Ming, what on earth do you do all day that you can't even manage to organize something for me to eat when I get home?"

"The day got away on me. I have a vicious headache."

"Another one? That's every day this week." Seth pulled Ming into his arms. "Did you take something for it?" He kissed the top of Ming's head and lifted Ming's face up to look at him.

"Yeah, but it's not really helping," Ming replied.

Seth kissed Ming's lips. "Tell you what. You've wanted

to visit your friend Dixie for a while now. Why don't I get you away from this construction zone for a few days?"

"That would be absolutely glorious." Ming ran his hands up Seth's chest and started undoing the buttons of his shirt. "Thank you. I think I'm feeling better already." He winked at Seth and began pulling him down the hall toward their bedroom. "Why don't you come with me and I'll show you."

"What about dinner?" Seth grinned.

"I thought we could start with dessert."

Ming set to work reminding Seth of why he kept him around. If there was anything of worth he'd taken away from his time with Attila, it was the art of seduction and the corresponding ability to drive men to absolute, mind-shattering distraction.

Shaun recounted the stack of fifty-dollar bills and put them in the envelope with the others. He checked to make sure Deirdre wasn't making her way down the hall before he slid the envelope back under their mattress. He pushed it in as far as it would go.

He'd finally figured out a way to bring more money into the house without Deirdre asking too many questions, and he was pretty proud of the fact it also doubled as an alibi regarding where he went four nights a week until all hours of the morning. He'd told Deirdre that he'd secured a job as a bartender down at the campus pub and she'd bought it.

There was one major fault in his plan. Shaun was bringing in far more money performing at the club than he could possibly make as a bartender, so he'd begun hiding some of the money under their mattress until he could get to the bank and set up a separate bank account.

Shaun lifted his backpack off the hook on the back of the door and rooted through it, chastising himself for accidentally stuffing one of his work outfits into it the night before. He pulled the colorful strip of spandex out and looked at it briefly, trying to decide if he was going to need it tonight or not. He and Curtis had worked out a new routine during the week, and the plan was to use it tonight if the owner of the club, Charles, could get the shower hooked up in time. It was Friday night, and the crowd would be looking for something new from their favorite *boy on boy* couple.

He balled up the G-string and zipped it into the front pouch of his backpack. He would need to remember to throw it into Curtis' bag so Curtis could take it to the laundromat for him.

"Are you going to be leaving soon?" Deirdre asked as she poked her head into the bedroom.

"Yeah, I'm just putting together some things before I go."

"Do you think you'll be late again tonight?"

"More than likely." Shaun kissed Deirdre's forehead. "Don't wait up for me." He hoisted his backpack onto his shoulder and without giving it a second thought, headed off to work. He knew he should be feeling guilty, lying to Deidre, and cheating on her.

But it was Curtis.

Bram turned up the radio in his truck and reclined his seat. The parking lot was pitch-black, so there was little chance they'd been seen by anyone.

He looked over at Rowan. "This is stupid."

"Cheryl is positive it's Shaun."

"She's only caught brief glimpses of someone who looks like Shaun going into that club. It could be anyone." Bram held up his hands as Rowan made to object. "I know. Eric told Shaun he saw his friend down here. But even if it is Shaun's friend, why would Shaun head down here to see him practically every night of the week?"

"Maybe they're more than friends."

"Don't be ridiculous. Shaun?" Bram sighed. "I think we should just ask him. I really don't want to go in there." He sat up and strained to see across the road. "Holy fuck! There he is."

"See. It's Shaun."

"What do you think he's doing all the way down here?"

"I don't know." Rowan scratched at his head. "Hey, wait. I bet he's working as a bartender." He laughed with relief. "He told me he did a bartender's course over the summer so he could get a job to help pay for school. That's why he's down here."

"You're just remembering that now?" Bram smacked Rowan in the head. "And here you had me worried that our little Shaun was one of the queers that frequent that place."

"Strange place to be working though," Rowan said.

"Maybe that friend of his got him the job."

"Yeah, probably. Let's get out of here."

"Hold on a second." Bram grinned mischievously.

"Opportunity knocks. How freaked out would Shaun be if we sidled up to the bar like a couple of fags?"

"Interesting idea." Rowan tapped his finger on his lips in feigned contemplation. "I think I like it." He beamed and clapped his hands together in anticipation.

"Only one problem though," Bram said.

"What's that?"

"We have to actually go in there."

"We'll just head straight for the bar and avoid looking around. It can't be that bad. It'll be an adventure."

"All right." Bram threw his door open and hauled himself out of the truck. "Here goes nothing." He ran with Rowan to the door, not wanting anyone to spot them going into the club. After getting past the bouncer, they moved down a long hallway into the main area. The music was already cranked up, and the dance floor was rolling in bodies undulating to the sound of the thrumming bass.

Bram stood and watched for a second, but then Rowan spotted the bar at the back of the club, grabbed hold of Bram's arm, and hauled him toward it.

"What do you want to drink?" Rowan asked Bram.

"I don't want to stick around long enough for a drink."

"Well, too bad. I'm thirsty."

Rowan paid for two beers and scanned along the length of the bar looking for Shaun. "I don't see him."

"I do." Bram pointed toward a short bar on the other side of the room. He grabbed his beer from Rowan's hand and shoved him toward the back of the room so they'd be out of sight. They slid into some seats and watched Shaun climb up onto the bar and dance his way along its length, rocking his hips to the music, wearing barely there, skin-tight, white booty shorts.

"He's pretty good," Rowan said. "Don't you think?"

"Would you shut up?" Bram shoved Rowan roughly then cringed. Shaun was lowering himself onto the bar and stretching out, thrusting his hips in time with the music as the men surrounding him tucked money into his shorts, and ran their hands over his body, squeezing, touching....

"All right, that's a bit much," Rowan said. "I'll give you that."

Bram threw back the rest of his beer, completely fixated on what Shaun was doing. "Why the hell is he doing this?"

"Maybe he and Deirdre are having money problems."

"Enough to do this?"

Rowan's head snapped up, scanning the space when he heard a shrill whistle coming from the other side of the room.

"Jeez, that's fucking loud," he said as he looked around, trying to see if he could spot Shaun's enthusiastic fan. Then he punched Bram in the arm. "Is that Shannon?"

"Where?" Bram stood up to get a better look around and sunk back into his seat when he saw Attila dancing around and whistling at Shaun, encouraging him. "Yeah, that's her all right."

"What's she doing here?"

"Apparently, she's cheering Shaun on."

"The things you learn about people by simply leaving the comfort of your dorm." Rowan grinned. "I think our strapping young Shaun is going to be awfully busy finishing our term papers. Blackmail is such a sweet thing."

The volume of the music lowered slightly, and Shaun leaped down off the bar and headed out through a door beside the stage.

"It looks like he's taking a break," Bram said and stood up. "We should get out of here before he sees us." He motioned for Rowan to get up and move faster so they could get past the throng of men moving toward the stage, but ended up being swept along with them instead, and away from Rowan.

The volume of the music rose back up again, and a few spotlights came on, lighting up the stage.

"Looks like he's not done yet!" Rowan shouted as he pushed his way through the crowd to get standing beside Bram again. He whistled and joined in singing along to the music, finding the energy of the men around him to be contagious.

"Can you stop that?" Bram said. "You're embarrassing me."

"Loosen up, Bram. This place is a riot!"

"Hey, guys," Attila said as he stepped up behind them. "I didn't know straight boys were into this kind of thing."

"We're not. I was just goofing around," Rowan replied. "What are you doing here?"

"I come here all the time. Home away from home and all that. Are you here to see Shaun?"

"Not exactly," Bram said, looking toward the stage as Shaun began his routine. He stepped aside when a large, muscle-bound biker dressed all in leathers pushed past him.

"Hey, Attila!" the biker said. "How's the most beautiful man I know?" He pulled Attila into his arms, squeezing him, and pounding him on the back. "I've been on the road for a few weeks. I missed seeing your gorgeous face. What's new with you?"

"I've been keeping busy, Bubba," Attila said. "I have a new boyfriend."

"Well, he's a lucky man to have found a guy like you," Bubba replied then winked and strode off into the crowd.

Attila glanced over at Bram and Rowan, who were staring at him blankly, and smiled. He'd recently revealed to Eric that there were more than a few people who knew he wasn't a girl. Eric had been upset at first because he'd lied to him about it, but then Eric had surprised him by saying he felt it was important for Attila to stay connected with the gay community, as a man, and he'd forgiven him. They hadn't gotten around to discussing the possibility of spillage into the straight community though.

Bram wrinkled up his brow and turned back toward the stage.

"Who's the other guy?" Rowan asked as Curtis entered the stage and turned on the shower at its center.

"That's Curtis," Attila said. "Shaun's high school sweetheart."

Attila watched for their reactions, thinking their entire bizarre group of friends may as well be hung in entirety today.

He released a shrill whistle as Shaun and Curtis stepped into the shower and started dancing and making out with each other to the music. Bram, horrified, spun around, and shoved his way out through the crowd, headed for the door.

Rowan watched him leave and shrugged his shoulders.

"He's no fun at all," he said to Attila, then turned back and started shouting and whistling along with the crowd. He lost his enthusiasm when Shaun danced the shorts he was wearing off his body and used his teeth to remove Curtis'.

"Are you sure you want to stay?" Attila asked Rowan.

"Why …what are they going to do?"

"Just a bit of dancing. The real show happens in the other room, but …" Attila laid his hands on Rowan's shoulders and turned his entire body away from the stage. "Sweetheart, you're going to have nightmares if you keep watching this."

Rowan attempted to twist around to see what was happening, but Attila held him fast, and then the lights went out on the stage.

"There. All safe to look again." Attila patted Rowan on the head and led him toward the bar, being mindful to avoid the men checking Rowan out. "Would you be a dear and buy me a drink? I'm parched from all that whistling."

"Sure," Rowan replied. "But what happens now?"

"Now, all the people with loads of money go into the other room while the rest of us stay out here." Attila glanced up and waved when he spotted Eric making his way across the club.

"Hey, baby," Eric said to Attila and kissed him, then looked at Rowan. "Where's your other half?" he asked

Rowan.

"He took off running when Shaun danced his shorts off."

"I find that so odd," Attila said. "Shaun has such a nice ass."

"Hey, I'm with Bram on this one," Eric said as he glanced around the room. "So, are the guys finished for the night?"

"No, they're not done yet," Attila replied. "They just went into the showroom a few minutes ago." He carefully took the drink Rowan handed to him and smiled; it was a pink martini.

"Sorry I got here so late, but I'm not going to lie," Eric said. "Watching Shaun grinding on Curtis isn't high on my priority list."

"You never know until you try," Attila said and winked at him. "Shaun said they'd be in the showroom for about thirty minutes tonight and then they'll come out and have a drink with us."

"Thirty minutes!" Eric laughed sharply.

"Eric, darling," Attila said. "We're talking about Curtis Bantam. Thirty minutes is a walk in the park for that boy."

"I was more concerned about Shaun's ass."

"I suspect Shaun's tight little ass has seen more dick than most girls named Jane. He'll be fine."

Rowan took a sip of his drink and shook his head, thinking he really needed to get out more. The world was more of an insanely diverse place than he ever could've imagined, and extended far beyond the mundane walls of the student union pub.

He watched the dance floor for a few songs, and then nodded at Eric and let himself be led into a reserved booth at the back of the club. He set his drink down on the table and leaned forward to get Attila's attention.

"So, you're actually a guy?" he said.

Attila held out his hand. "Attila Luka. Nice to finally meet you properly, Rowan." He shook Rowan's hand and nudged Eric.

"What?" Eric said, kissing Attila's shoulder. "I don't care who knows. You know that."

"I wasn't sure," Attila replied. "Bubba there attacked me with the beautiful man routine, and I didn't know what to do."

"It's fine," Eric said and leaned toward Rowan. "Attila and I were buddies in high school."

Rowan scrubbed his hand across his face. "And you didn't recognize him?"

"I recognize him now when I look at him," Eric replied. "But he looks quite different from what he did back then."

Attila smiled at Eric and reached for his hand. He lifted it to his lips, kissed it, and held it against his cheek.

"I have a million questions," Rowan said. "All of which are completely inappropriate."

Attila laid a hand on Rowan's, laughing. "Sweetheart, look at where you are. Trust me. There is very little that is inappropriate in this place." He motioned for Rowan to lean closer. "I had a complete sex change, so I'm all girl bits now …top to bottom."

Rowan looked at Eric, and Eric grinned bawdily at him, nodding his head, then creased up laughing when

Rowan turned pale.

Eric reached across the table and patted Rowan's shoulder, then stood up and started shouting, clapping, and whistling as Shaun and Curtis made their way over to the table.

Curtis bowed theatrically and smirked, wrapping his arm around Shaun as he fell into a seat, pulling Shaun into his lap. "Ah, show business," he said. "Makes a man really fucking thirsty. My boy here drained me dry." He snapped his fingers at the bartender and signaled for what they wanted.

Shaun nudged Curtis hard in the ribs.

"What?" Curtis said. "You did. You took it like a champ."

"This is Rowan," Shaun said as he pointed across the table. "He's in one of my classes at school."

Curtis leaned forward and shook Rowan's hand.

"Nice to meet you, Rowboat," he said and then grinned. "Judging by the look on your face, I would surmise that you didn't have a fucking clue what my lover got up to in his spare time."

"That would be completely correct," Rowan answered.

"Well then, we're even, because I have no fucking clue what he gets up to at that school of yours."

Rowan snorted in amusement and downed the rest of his drink. When he looked up, Curtis was watching him intently.

"But see, here's the thing, Sailboat," Curtis continued. "You wandered into this club, all accidental like. Am I right?"

"Yeah, Bram and I thought Shaun was bartending here."

Curtis looked around. "Who's bran muffin?"

"He's another guy from school," Shaun said and dropped his gaze, realizing everyone at the university was probably going to hear about what he'd been doing at the club, including the nature of his relationship with Curtis. It wasn't the end of the world, but he'd been hoping to keep it a secret for a while longer.

"Hm ...strange names these friends of yours have." Curtis kissed Shaun on the cheek and then caught Rowan's attention. "My good man of the sea, I'm sure you'll agree that this club is a wee bit off the nautical chart for most respectable scholars."

Rowan nodded his head.

"Stellar," Curtis said. "Now, frequent flyers to this fine establishment are aware that it would be considered impolite to recognize one of the pilots while off the tarmac." He reached forward and touched Rowan on the hand, keeping his eyes trained on his face. "Do you understand what I'm saying?"

"You don't want me to tell anyone about Shaun," Rowan said.

Curtis clapped his hands together in mock enthusiasm.

"Would you look at that?" he shouted. "That school is pumping out little thinkers after all." He drummed his hands on the table and then slammed them down in front of Rowan. "One last thing before I forget. Be sure to update corn muffin. Or I'll have to go looking for him myself."

Curtis winked at Rowan. "And there's no guarantee I'll remember to change out of these clothes when I hit the campus dorms to find him ...or you, for that matter."

Shaun grinned and rested his head against Curtis' face.

"Hey, sport," Curtis said. "Who loves you?"

"You do."

"And who wants you?"

Shaun laughed and blushed. "You do."

"And how much do I want you?" Curtis traced his fingers across Shaun's lips and gazed into his eyes.

"Infinitely."

Shaun tucked his head into the curve of Curtis' neck and whispered something to him.

"Right then." Curtis jumped up, dumping Shaun to his feet. "Apparently, I have more work to do to satisfy this young man." He saluted everyone at the table. "Thank you all for *coming*. Oh, no wait ...that was me." He scooped Shaun up in arms, making Shaun shriek with surprise and start laughing. "*Come* again soon. No, that's going to be me too. Now, I'm really fucking confused."

Everyone at the table watched Curtis carry Shaun out through the door toward the dressing rooms, mumbling about who was going to be *coming* next, or if they should even *come* at all.

"What the fuck was that?" Rowan asked lightheartedly.

"That was a seriously tweaked out Curtis Bantam," Attila said and leaned into Eric's side. "As a friend of ours in high school once said. Welcome to the crazy table. Sit down and join the insanity. Everyone's welcome. The freakier and more messed up the better."

Shaun rubbed his eyes and yawned as he tried to curl himself back into Curtis' chest, but the hard edge of the bed was mangling his pillow so severely, he couldn't get comfortable.

"What's wrong?" Curtis asked and sat up. He looked down at Shaun fighting with his pillow and smiled. "Here, sport, let me help you with that." He waited for Shaun to move over then he rearranged the bedding. He pulled Shaun back into his arms and cradled Shaun's head in against his chest.

"You were amazing tonight, sweet cheeks," Curtis said.

"Yeah, it felt good, but we need to talk to Charles about heating that water a bit more." He laughed. "Any colder and I won't be able to find your winky."

"That would be absolutely tragic, never mind embarrassing."

Shaun rolled over slightly, looking for his phone. "What time do you think it is?"

Curtis reached up and moved the curtain covering the cracked and dingy window of his trailer to one side. "It's getting light out."

Shaun sighed in exasperation. "I don't want to go home."

"Why don't you just stay here then?"

"I can't. I have to get back to Deirdre."

"Why?"

"I live there with her, remember?"

"That doesn't mean you have to keep going back

there." Curtis shifted himself over and turned to face Shaun. "Shaun, do you love me?" he asked as he used his finger to trace the arch of Shaun's eyebrows and then his lips. "I tell you all the time how much I love you. But you've never said it back."

"I love being with you." Shaun smiled.

"But do you love me?"

Shaun covered his face with his hands. "I don't know. When I'm around you, my head gets all fuzzy, and all I can think about is making you happy." He paused. "I love pleasing you. And I love knowing that you want me. And that you love me."

Curtis pushed himself back and stared at Shaun. "But you don't love me? Do you love Deirdre?"

Shaun gripped his hair tight in curled fists, his brow dipping in confusion. "No, it's not like that."

"What's it like?"

"I'm supposed to be with her like that …you know?"

"No, I don't know. I've never done what I'm supposed to."

"Curtis, stop. You're confusing me."

"Shaun?" Curtis began, then paused, scrubbing at his chin, not sure if he wanted to explore Shaun's confusion further. Something was lurking there that could change things. He could feel it in his gut. "Do you know why I love you?"

"Of course. You love me because you want me."

"No, Shaun. I love you because you're an incredible person." Curtis blinked with concern as a frightening realization swept through his mind. "I want you because I love you. Not the other way around. Love doesn't work like that, Shaun."

"That can't be right." Shaun lowered his eyes in confusion and tried to sort through what Curtis had just told him. "Mr. Jenkins said he wanted me—" He scratched his nose. "But you're right. He never said he loved me." He looked up at Curtis and shook his head with determination. "No. He must've loved me."

Curtis shifted further away from Shaun.

"Mr. Jenkins wasn't in love with you," he said.

"Then why did he want me?"

"Holy fuck, Shaun. That's messed up." Curtis threw the blanket off and climbed away from the bed, and began pacing the length of the trailer. "You and me …it's only been about sex? When I say I love you, you think it's because I want you? And that's it?"

Shaun tucked himself up and covered his head with the blanket, trying not to panic at Curtis' sudden change in mood.

"Curtis? Please don't be angry. What did I do?"

"Shaun, I think you need to leave." Curtis pulled the blanket off Shaun and shoved him with his foot. When Shaun didn't move Curtis hauled Shaun to his feet and pushed him toward the door of the trailer then scurried around, picking up Shaun's clothes and throwing them at him. Shaun clutched the clothes against his body and cringed by the door.

"Why are you doing this?" Shaun shuddered as a wave of terror pulsed through to his core. "What did I do wrong?" He gasped and fought to catch his breath, trying to figure out what had gone so horribly wrong. "I was good. I let you love me. Please, don't be mad at me. I can be better. I promise. I'll be better from now on, Curtis. I will. I can make you happy." He trembled and cried out, breaking down in tears.

"Shaun, stop it!"

"Stop it? You stop it! Why are you being so mean to me?" Shaun sobbed and gripped at his stomach. "Don't you love me anymore?" He dropped to his knees and reached out for Curtis. "Please, Curtis. I can be better. I promise. I can make you want me. I can. Then you'll love me again."

"Jeez, Shaun, you need help." Curtis pulled Shaun back onto his feet and into his arms, and held him. He kissed Shaun's head and let his lips linger there.

"We never should've gone to see Mr. Jenkins," he whispered.

"But I liked Mr. Jenkins."

Curtis stepped back and held Shaun's face. "No, Shaun. No, you didn't. Don't you remember?" He searched Shaun's eyes and felt his heart break at what he was seeing. "Oh my god. I didn't realize you were so fragile. What have I done to you?"

"You didn't do anything to me." Shaun blinked at him. "It must've been me, Curtis. What did I do wrong?"

"You didn't do anything wrong, sweetheart."

"Then why are you crying?"

"Because you need help, baby."

Shaun sighed with relief, not fully understanding, but recognizing Curtis wasn't mad at him anymore.

"Are you going to help me?" he asked.

"With my dying breath." Curtis held Shaun tighter and looked around, trying to remember which of the compartments held the key to the safe in the floor of his trailer. It was going to take every bit of money he'd ever saved to set this right.

Chapter Seven

The Search

Curtis flipped through the paperwork and shoved his hand through his hair. His anxiety beginning to get the better of him. Something he needed to watch out for; the last thing he needed was his condition putting him under scrutiny. He searched his pockets. He'd left the little pills he used to calm himself back in the trailer.

He just needed to focus, but there were a lot of questions on the admissions form that he wasn't able to make out. Some of the words and terms were things he'd never seen before, and he was having trouble sounding them out.

He scanned through the pages again, trying to determine which sections he could get away with fabricating the information on and sighed with exasperation; he didn't even know when Shaun's birthday was.

"Is everything all right, Mr. Bantam?"

Curtis looked up into the eyes of the admissions clerk.

"I'm sorry, but I don't know a lot of this stuff," he replied. "I have Shaun's wallet, but he doesn't have much in it. He likes to travel light." Curtis handed the wallet to the clerk and watched as she flipped through the contents. He'd already removed every piece of identification that could be used to trace Shaun back to his family. This was none of their business.

"Does he have any family we could contact?"

"No." Curtis shook his head. "I'm all he has." He stared out the window of the waiting room at the vast sheets of rain drumming a symphony against its hard surface. They'd driven for three days through the pouring rain to get to *Cedar Creek Psychiatric Center*. He'd phoned a few different places, but this had been the only one with an empty bed available.

Curtis tried to tune out the rain; the sound of it would forever remind him of their agonizing trip halfway across the country. He closed his eyes as his heart twisted, remembering Shaun's constant chatter about wanting to be better so he would want him, and how he would make him love him again. It had taken every ounce of his strength to keep from crying out and driving his truck and trailer over the sheerest cliff he could find, just to end the pain.

He'd finally succumbed to the strain of the emotional exhaustion and given Shaun a sedative. The peace had been both welcome and heartbreakingly painful.

A voice broke his thoughts.

"Mr. Bantam?"

Curtis wiped the tears from his face and pulled himself out of the waiting room chair. He approached the doctor who had called him and tried to keep his body from shaking too violently.

"I'm Dr. Scorcy." The doctor stepped aside to let Curtis

through the door into his office. "I'll be Shaun's primary physician should he decide to stay with us." He sat down behind his desk and motioned for Curtis to take a seat.

"Can you help him?" Curtis asked, his anxiety now threatening to take over his body. He steadied his breathing, but realistically, there was nothing he could do to stop it.

"I'll know more after I've spoken to him again, but I'm curious as to how he arrived here in your care." Dr. Scorcy crossed his arms. "He was pretty heavily sedated when you brought him in."

"He's all right now though, isn't he?" Curtis folded his arms in his lap then unfolded them. He rubbed his nose, twitched, and began scratching at his arms. "I only gave him a little, so he would stop. He needed to stop."

"Stop what?"

"He just kept going on and on." Curtis held his breath as the tingle in his face began creeping down his arm.

"Mr. Bantam, what is your association with Shaun?"

"It's Curtis."

Curtis twitched, letting his shoulder rotate back in its socket as he tried to erase the image of the only Mr. Bantam he'd ever known. His mom had contacted him a few weeks back to tell him his father had died in a car accident. *That* Mr. Bantam had been driving home drunk and had been killed instantly when he'd hit a power pole. Curtis considered the swiftness of his death to be cosmically unfair considering what he'd put him and his brother through as children. He would've been happier if his father had suffered a slow, agonizing death.

He looked up at Dr. Scorcy, sufficiently distracted by the image of his father. "Shaun and I have been together since high school. He doesn't have any other family."

"No parents?"

"Not that I'm aware of."

"Which high school was that?"

"Just a school—"

"There isn't anyone who will be looking for Shaun."

"Nope slope. Just me." Curtis placed his hands on his knees and tried to hold them from bouncing up and down.

Dr. Scorcy dropped his eyebrows and examined the young man seated in front of him. He was remarkably attractive, in a boyish sort of way, with thick blond hair and shy, but seductive blue eyes. He was also completely unkempt and clearly disturbed, mentally.

He watched how Curtis' eyes darted around the room and how his body shifted nervously in his chair, trying to get comfortable in an environment that was obviously foreign and extremely frightening to him. Dr. Scorcy wondered what type of environment would provide a feeling of security to someone like Curtis.

He flipped open the admissions folder and read over what Curtis had managed to fill out and what the clerk had gleaned from Shaun's mostly empty wallet. There wasn't enough information there for them to track down who Shaun was or where he'd come from. He briefly considered phoning the authorities.

"Curtis," Dr. Scorcy said. "You do realize this is a private clinic, don't you? You have to pay for Shaun to stay here."

Curtis nodded his head, not sure how much this was going to cost him. "I can pay," he said as he started rooting around in the large duffel bag he'd hauled into the room with him. He lifted out a few stacks of grubby twenty dollar bills wrapped in paper and elastic bands and set them on the doctor's desk.

Dr. Scorcy looked down at the mess of twenties in front of him.

"The fee for the center is thirty thousand a month," he said and felt his breathing constrict as he saw a streak of anguish cross Curtis' face.

"How long does he have to stay?" Curtis asked.

"At least two months. I wish we could help you."

"No, I can pay." Curtis hauled the bag off the floor and dropped it onto the desk. "There's almost sixty thousand in there. I'm only about five hundred short." He looked at Dr. Scorcy pleadingly. "But I can easily make that much if I work all night. I could bring it to you tomorrow." He sunk down onto his knees. "Please, you have to help him. He means everything to me."

Curtis left the psychiatric center with the empty duffel bag slung over his shoulder. He turned and started walking backward as he scanned the windows of the building looking for Shaun.

Dr. Scorcy had told him that for the first two weeks, he wouldn't be able to visit Shaun because they needed to separate him from the outside world until they could determine what had precipitated Shaun's psychiatric condition. After that, he could visit Shaun every weekend.

He stopped walking and stared up at the building, fascinated by how a structure as mundane and unassuming as this one could hold the key to Shaun's happiness. He just hoped Shaun's happiness would include a place for him.

Curtis turned and made a run for his trailer. He'd hidden it a good three kilometers into the forest that surrounded the psychiatric center. He didn't want to be too far away, just in case Shaun needed him. As he ran, the fresh air invigorated him, and he smiled for the first time in days. He was going to enjoy a decent night's sleep tonight knowing Shaun was somewhere safe. He wasn't even going to have to work tonight. Dr. Scorcy had waived the last five hundred dollars owing.

Attila pulled open the door and let Deidre into his and Eric's apartment, and followed her down the hallway to the living room where Eric was waiting for them.

"I'm sorry, guys," Deirdre said. "But when he didn't come home again this morning, I didn't know who else to turn to."

"No, that's fine, sweetheart," said Attila.

"Eric said the two of you saw him a few nights ago?"

"Yes, we did." Attila looked at Eric and raised his eyebrows, looking for some guidance.

Eric just shrugged his shoulders.

"Where did you see him?" Deirdre asked, her voice laced heavily with concern.

"At work. We saw Shaun at work," Eric said and then motioned for Attila to go along with it.

"Yes, that's right," Attila agreed. "He was working very

hard."

"But I asked down at the pub, and they say he's never worked there," Deidre said. "Where did you see him working?"

Attila sighed, resigned. "Down at the gay club on Thirty-Fifth."

"What the hell is he doing working there?"

"Curtis got him a job," Eric replied. "He's been working there for a few months now."

"Who's Curtis?"

"A friend of ours from high school," answered Attila.

"Then we need to talk to this Curtis." Deirdre looked from Attila to Eric and back again. "Maybe he knows something."

"Deirdre, honey," Attila said. "I called the club after Eric hung up the phone with you. Curtis' truck and trailer are gone."

"I don't understand."

Eric rolled his head back and looked up at the ceiling. He did not want to be doing this, but there was no point in keeping secrets. Shaun and Curtis had definitely run off together.

"Shaun and Curtis. They were a couple back in high school," he said. "It was pretty serious. They were living together." He studied Deirdre's face. She hadn't known. "I'm sorry he never told you."

Deirdre just shook her head and shut her eyes. "That can't be right," she said. "You must be mistaken. Shaun isn't interested in guys. He's not gay. I would know."

"Deirdre, honey," Attila said. "There are a lot of people

out there that swing both ways. Shaun and Curtis were definitely together. Everyone at school knew. They didn't exactly hide it." He paused. This next bit was going to hurt. But she deserved to know.

"They started seeing each other again a few months ago," he added.

Deirdre looked up. "They've been seeing each other?" She shivered as the realization of why Shaun often didn't show up until morning sunk in. "Has Shaun been sleeping with him?"

Attila nodded his head, confirming her suspicion.

"So, you both knew about this?" Deirdre said. "And you perpetuated his affair with this guy? Knowing I was at home waiting for him?" She glared at Eric and then at Attila. "You just hung out with him and his boyfriend like I didn't matter."

"It wasn't like that," Eric said.

"I'm sorry, sweetie," Attila added. "It was none of our business. We didn't want to interfere in your affairs."

"More like you wanted to protect your own kind," Deirdre said. "All you perverse freaks have to stick together, don't you? Because no one else will have you."

"Hold on, Deirdre. That's uncalled for," Eric said, rising to his feet. "We're just as worried about Shaun as you are."

"And you, Eric. You're even worse." Deirdre continued, glaring at Eric as she shot up on to her feet. "Fucking an abomination like that—" She pointed at Attila. "And pretending he's a girl."

"That's enough, Deirdre!" Eric crossed the room to take Attila into his arms. "I know damn well Attila isn't a girl, but he's a human being for fuck's sake! Try to think before you speak!"

Eric held Attila tighter and whispered assurances to him, letting the mascara-streaked tears falling from Attila's eyes stain his shirt.

"You're fucking deviants! The whole lot of you!"

Deirdre grabbed her purse and pulled out a thick envelope.

"I don't know what the fuck Shaun was doing down at that club," she said. "And I'm sure I don't want to know because he was certainly making a lot of money doing it." She threw the envelope down on the coffee table. "I found this under the mattress. There's about ten thousand dollars in there."

Deirdre stormed across the room and then turned back on them. "If you do find Shaun, tell him he can take that money and shove it up his ass. He should be used to that."

Attila cringed as Deirdre slammed the door on her way out.

Eric looked over at the envelope and felt his stomach drop. If Curtis and Shaun had run away together and Shaun had been a willing participant, why hadn't he retrieved his money?

"What are you thinking?" Attila asked, observing the worry in Eric's eyes.

"I think Curtis might've kidnapped Shaun."

Ming made his way down through the last set of doors separating the airline passengers from the waiting area and spotted Dixie jumping up and down excitedly, waving her arms around.

He ran toward her.

"I can't believe you're really here!" Dixie shrieked.

Ming wrapped Dixie up in his arms and spun her around, then kissed her cheek and set her back on her feet. "I'm sorry it took so long for me to come see you."

"I guess Seth keeps you pretty busy."

Ming coyly dropped his gaze. "The man does tend to have a voracious appetite." He looked up again and smiled. "Not that I'm complaining ...but enough about me. What's new since I talked to you?" He slipped his hand into Dixie's and pulled her along to the luggage kiosk to wait for his bags.

"I got a strange phone call this morning ...from Eric."

"Eric of Quarterback? Seriously?"

"Yeah. It had to do with Shaun. They're both finishing up their master's degrees in business at the same university."

"Eric is in university? Now I know there's something wrong with the education system in this country." Ming reached out, grabbed his first bag, and set it at their feet.

"Is this your only bag?"

Ming raised his eyebrows at Dixie, making her laugh.

"What did Eric want?" he asked.

"He was wondering if I'd heard from Shaun."

"Why?"

"He's gone missing." Dixie stepped back as Ming set another bag on the ground. "Apparently, Shaun ran into Curtis a few months back, and they started seeing each other again."

"Well, that's a good thing. Shaun was devastated when Curtis took off. They were great together."

"No, see that's the thing." Dixie moved even further away as Ming set yet another bag on the ground. "I think we're going to need a cart." She scanned the area and grabbed the nearest cart, and helped Ming pile his growing mountain of bags onto it. He'd pulled another one off the conveyor belt in her brief absence.

"I thought there was a restriction on how many bags you could take on the plane," she said.

"That only applies to some people." Ming paused briefly, double-checking to make sure he wasn't leaving one of his bags behind. "Please tell me you have a car. Taxi drivers are never impressed when I show up anywhere with this many bags."

"Go figure." Dixie leaned into the cart and started pushing it toward the door. "My car is out here."

"So, what's the thing with Curtis and Shaun?"

"Right. Eric said Curtis had been asking Shaun to move in with him ...but Shaun kept refusing because of his girlfriend."

"Shaun has a girlfriend?"

"For five years. They were planning on getting married once Shaun finished school." Dixie approached the car and unlocked the trunk, crossing her arms as she waited for Ming to hoist at least one bag in before helping him with the rest. He'd always had a bad habit of expecting people to wait on him.

"Does Eric think Curtis did something to him?" Ming asked.

"He thinks Curtis kidnapped Shaun."

"Kidnapped him? That's a stretch even for Curtis."

"Maybe not. Eric was telling me Curtis' bizarre behavior has been escalating recently. Especially with all the drugs he takes."

Ming slid into the passenger seat, his face creased with lines of concern. "I suppose Curtis was bound to crack eventually. I hope Shaun is all right."

"There's one other thing, Ming." Dixie placed her hand on Ming's leg to catch his attention. "I debated whether or not to tell you this, but I think you deserve to know."

"Know what?"

"Eric is living with someone. And I'm sorry, baby ...but it's Attila."

Ming's head snapped up. "What?"

"His name is Shannon now ...I mean *her* name."

"Her?" Ming implored Dixie with his eyes. "He didn't, did he?"

"Yeah, he did. About three years ago."

"Like completely?" Ming dropped his head into his hands when Dixie nodded at him, attempting to quell the nausea rising in his chest.

"But he was so beautiful," he said. "So fucking perfect."

"It's what he wanted ...but I don't understand it either."

"How long has he been with Eric?"

"Just a few months. They met up at the university."

"That must've been a shocker for Eric."

Dixie laughed. "That's for sure." She smiled, brushing Ming's leg affectionately. "Eric told me Attila had some significant work done to his face as well and he didn't recognize him at first, but get this ... Attila seduced Eric into his bed, and didn't tell him who he was until after Eric had been fucking him for hours."

"God ...some things never change." Ming smiled. "How's Attila doing?"

"He's doing great. He sounds happy."

"You talked to him?"

"For a few minutes. He says he misses you."

Ming exhaled and brushed at a few tears running down his cheeks. "I loved him so much."

"I know you did, honey. I know you did." Dixie reached over and gave Ming a hug. Her prayers of Ming finding his true love in their senior year of high school had been granted, but unfortunately, she hadn't included a prayer for that person to love Ming back.

Curtis sat patiently in the waiting room pretending to read through the magazines. One of the things he'd learned about being illiterate was that it was essential to keep people fooled by pretending to read stuff. Otherwise, they were likely to catch on.

This was the third weekend in a row that he'd attempted to see Shaun. After the initial two weeks were up, he'd arrived at the center with a bouquet of flowers in hand only to be told he wouldn't be permitted to see Shaun that day. The following week it had been the same thing. Shaun was making significant progress, but he wasn't ready to see visitors yet.

He brushed out the creases in the paper surrounding

the bouquet of flowers he'd brought with him today, concerned they were going to start to wilt if he was kept waiting much longer. He straightened up as Dr. Scorcy came out of his office.

"Curtis, could I see you in my office please?"

Curtis glanced around and picked up the shopping bag he'd brought with him. He'd been working a lot to keep his mind occupied and had accumulated a fair amount of money again, so he'd gone shopping to buy Shaun some new clothes.

He followed Dr. Scorcy into his office and took a seat.

"When can I see Shaun?" he asked.

"That's what I wanted to talk to you about. I'm not entirely sure yet." Dr. Scorcy sat down behind his desk and leaned back, trying to look as non-threatening as possible, but kept his finger near the emergency button just in case Curtis became violent. He'd seen it too many times before and wasn't about to be caught out.

"Why not?" Curtis crossed his legs and set the flowers in his lap. He could sense Dr. Scorcy's fear and wasn't about to fulfill his expectations. He needed to see Shaun, and Dr. Scorcy was the only way through the locked doors of Shaun's ward.

"We uncovered some unusual things while working with Shaun. Things that involve you." Dr. Scorcy relaxed. It didn't appear as though Curtis was going to be a threat after all. He sat back up and studied Curtis; he'd undergone an amazing transformation since he'd first met him. Curtis had cleaned himself up and looked as if he'd stepped straight off the pages of an exclusive men's fashion magazine. He sighed in frustration. Curtis' skill set and stunningly seductive good looks were obviously in high demand in their small community.

"Do you remember a Mr. Jenkins?" Dr. Scorcy asked.

"Yeah, I think that date was what started all this with Shaun." Curtis cast his eyes downward, trying to avoid Dr. Scorcy's scrutiny, not wanting to be judged too harshly. "Shaun had just lost his best friend to suicide not even three months before that. I wasn't thinking. I never should've taken him with me that day."

"So, Mr. Jenkins is a real person?"

Curtis nodded his head,

"He was a long-time client of mine," he said. "He always paid double if I brought someone to watch."

"Watch what? You having sex with him?" Dr. Scorcy watched Curtis nod his head. "How long have you been doing this, Curtis?"

"Since I was fourteen." Curtis looked up wondering why Dr. Scorcy was suddenly interested in him. "I only did it because I was hungry. I always got my dates to feed me before they fucked me."

He rubbed aggressively at his nose and then crossed his arms.

"Did they pay you money as well?" asked Dr. Scorcy.

Curtis' eyes flew open in surprise. "Yeah, of course, they did. I don't let random guys fuck me for free. I'm not some kind of sex maniac."

"I never suggested you were."

"Good." Curtis twitched nervously, trying to think of what to say next. "I was careful with my money." He straightened up his posture, attempting to appear put together. "I hid the extra cash I didn't use for food and clothing, and stuff. Kind of like one of those savings accounts you hear people talking about. I was going to buy a place of my own someday. That was the dream. To own my own place and never have to worry about being beaten up by some stupid drunk in the middle of the night."

"Who beat you?"

"My fucking pathetic excuse of a father." Curtis tucked his thumb into his mouth and started chewing on his nail. Then dropped his hand into his lap, and began picking at the stem of one of the flowers. A thorn caught his thumb, breaking his thoughts and bringing him back to the conversation.

"What has this got to do with Shaun?" he asked. "When can I see him?"

"I still haven't decided that yet." Dr. Scorcy's gut twisted as Curtis appeared to fold in on himself. It was like witnessing a person's soul collapsing. "What did you do with all that money? Did you manage to finally buy your own place?"

Curtis stared at him with incredulous shock. "No, I gave it all to you ...to help Shaun."

Dr. Scorcy shook his head and had to pinch the bridge of his nose to stop his emotions from escaping.

"You really love him, don't you?" he asked.

"More than my own life, Dr. Scorcy."

"Tell me this. If you love Shaun so much, why did you coerce him into performing sex acts on the stage of that club the two of you were working at?"

Curtis shifted in his seat.

"He wanted to. I didn't make him," he said and then smiled knowingly. "Shaun is a bit of an exhibitionist without any encouragement from me. And he's an incorrigible nymphomaniac. The idea of getting paid to have sex with me at work was a huge enticement for him." Curtis swallowed, immersed in his own thoughts. Had he done it again? Screwed Shaun up further.

"Is what we did at the club part of why Shaun is so sick?" he asked.

"Surprisingly, no." Dr. Scorcy leaned forward on his desk. "Everything seems to stem from this Mr. Jenkins figure."

"I tried to stop him."

"Stop who?"

"Mr. Jenkins. He caught on quick that Shaun was a virgin, and he really wanted to fuck him. I tried to convince him to leave Shaun alone, but he wouldn't listen." Curtis cracked his knuckles, first laying the flowers in his lap, thinking back to what had happened that day. "Mr. Jenkins is an extremely violent man when he gets angry. I couldn't push him too hard, or he might've hurt Shaun even worse than what he did."

"Did he rape Shaun in your opinion?"

"Repeatedly. I couldn't watch after a while. The expression on Shaun's face is something I'll never get out of my mind." Curtis closed his eyes, not wanting to remember. "Shaun thought he was enjoying it somehow, or that he should've been." He sniffed back the emotions as he thought about the look fixed on Shaun's face that day; he'd been smiling almost maniacally through the sheets of tears that were coating his face.

"What happened after that?" Dr. Scorcy asked.

"I finally convinced Mr. Jenkins to let me have a turn so he could watch Shaun and me together." Curtis dropped his head into his hands as a wash of tears flooded his eyes. "I was much gentler with Shaun, whispering in his ear that he was all right now. That he was with me. And that I would never hurt him."

"How did he respond?"

Curtis' body shook as he remembered.

"He kissed me," he said, "then he said thank you, and that he'd be good from now on."

A small sound of anguish escaped Curtis' chest, and his body began to heave sporadically as he sobbed. "I thought he meant he was going to be all right," he said. "That's not what he meant, is it?"

"No, it wasn't." Dr. Scorcy ran his fingers along the edge of his desk, pleased to have been correct about his theory concerning Shaun and his obsessive dependence on Curtis. Shaun's recollection of that day had been extraordinarily sketchy and disjointed, and at times he hadn't been sure if Mr. Jenkins was a real person or someone Shaun's mind had conjured up to bury an even more disturbing memory.

"Somewhere in Shaun's mind, he thinks you saved him that day," Dr. Scorcy said. "After that, your approval became of ultimate importance to him. He would've done anything for you."

"He would've too." Curtis nodded in agreement. "I had

no idea it was because he was sick. I thought it was because he loved me."

Curtis held his stomach as it pulled viciously at him. "I would've got him help sooner if I'd known."

Dr. Scorcy stood up from his desk. "Curtis, I'm going to give you a few minutes to collect yourself and then I think it would be all right if you saw Shaun. He's been asking for you." He smiled. "He's been asking for you a lot."

Curtis lifted his head and tried to catch his breath. "He has? Are you sure? I thought you said he was making progress."

"Shaun is feeling much better. He's responding well to therapy, and he's working through what happened to him that day, and I think he's moving past it quite well."

"And he still wants to see me?"

Dr. Scorcy motioned for Curtis to follow him out through his office door. "I think Shaun has something he wants to tell you."

Kevin set the phone down and breathed a sigh of relief. He'd finally found the *John Doe* he was looking for. When Dixie had phoned him looking for his help, he'd been reluctant at first. He and Shaun hadn't exactly ended their friendship on good terms.

He flipped through the file he'd started on Shaun and then closed it over. He hadn't used too much of his time or police resources. He didn't think the chief would even notice he'd been neglecting his other cases files.

Resigned, Kevin looked over the list of phone numbers Dixie had given him of people he should contact after he'd located Shaun. None of them were people he ever thought he'd talk to again. Except for Candace. He'd been thinking about her recently, wondering how their daughter, Brittany, was doing. She would be six and a half years old now, but he hadn't seen her since her fifth birthday. Candace lived halfway across the country, and she had a new boyfriend. Two things Kevin didn't have time to deal with.

He picked up the phone and dialed the first number on the list. He was surprised when a soft, female voice picked up the phone.

"This is Constable Magarey," he said. "I was hoping to speak with Eric Templeton. Is he available?"

"Kevin?"

"Yes. Who's this?"

"Oh …um. It's Annie."

Kevin held the phone away from his ear and stared down at the sheet of paper in front of him. Dixie hadn't mentioned that Eric and Annie were together.

"Annie, it's so nice to hear your voice," he said "So, you and Eric. I wasn't expecting that."

"Yes, well. We bumped into each other at the university here, and the rest is, as you say …history." Attila looked around the room for a place to sit down but settled against the kitchen counter instead. "How have you been?"

"I keep busy with my work mostly. It was always a dream of mine to work in law enforcement."

"That's good you enjoy your work. So many people don't. So, have you had any luck locating Shaun?"

"Yeah, actually I did." Kevin flipped the folder back

open. "He's been under the care of a psychiatrist for the past month at a private facility called the *Cedar Creek Psychiatric Center*. It's a small exclusive place in southern Ontario ...very remote."

"Why on earth is he there?"

"Apparently, Curtis checked him in."

"I would've thought it would be the other way around."

Kevin laughed. He'd thought the same thing.

"Did they say what was wrong with him?" Attila asked. "The last time I saw him, he seemed fine to me. A little clingy when it came to Curtis, but he was always that way."

"They wouldn't tell me anything. There are confidentiality regulations that even I can't get past."

"Well, at least we know he's safe." Attila lifted a tissue out of the box and dabbed at his face. "I never thought for a second that Curtis would hurt him. He loves Shaun too much."

Kevin refocused his attention away from Shaun and his unconventional relationship with Curtis, and leaned back in his chair, throwing his feet onto his desk. "So, you and Eric finally got things sorted out." He grinned. "I have to say I was quite jealous of him back in the day."

"Were you really?"

"A hot girl like you, completely blowing me off for a tool like Eric. It was hard on the ego." Kevin sat back up in his chair. "Are you and Eric coming to Mexico over spring break?"

"I'm sorry. Why would we do that?"

"Ming is putting together some kind of reunion. I thought he would've called you about it."

Attila bit at his bottom lip then cleared the guilt from his mind.

"Things didn't end well between Ming and me," he said.

"Yeah, that's right. You left Tekla after you broke up with him. You know, I never understood the whole thing between you and Ming. That boy has been gay for as long as I can remember."

"Those were strange times at Tekla."

"That's for sure." Kevin paused. "Hey, would you mind doing me a big favor?"

"Sure. What do you need?"

"I was supposed to call Deirdre and Candace when I found Shaun, but I still have to phone Dixie back, and as it is my chief is going to have a fit when he sees all these long distance charges."

"That's all right. Eric will be home soon. I'll get him to call them for you. And maybe we'll see you in Mexico."

Kevin laughed. "Now that is something I can look forward to."

Shaun pulled on the last sock and stood up to look at himself in the mirror. He hadn't seen Curtis in over a month, and he was really nervous about speaking to him. He'd had to continually remind himself that they'd had plenty of normal conversations that didn't revolve around their act at the club, who they'd fucked, how they'd fucked them, or who they were planning on fucking next. He hoped they wouldn't be stuck for things to say to each other.

He checked his appearance one more time and took a deep breath before opening the door of his room.

His face lit up when he saw Curtis waiting in the corridor, and he couldn't help himself. He rushed at him and leaped into his arms.

"Hey, sport!" Curtis said, pulling Shaun closer, wanting to breathe in the familiar scent of him.

Momentarily sated, he stepped back and held Shaun out at arm's length so he could look at him. "You look good, baby."

Shaun leaped back up at Curtis, attacking his mouth, and pushing him up against the wall. He was gasping for breath and laughing when he finally pulled away.

"I missed you so much," Shaun said.

Curtis chuckled. "I can see that." He looked up and down the corridor and picked up the shopping bag and the flowers Shaun had knocked from his hands. "Maybe we should take this into your room before I get you kicked out of here."

Shaun smiled and pushed him through the door.

"Are those for me?" he asked when he spotted the flowers. He accepted them from Curtis while winking at him and yanked the lid off his water container, carefully placing the flowers in it. "They're beautiful. Thank you."

"I bought you some new clothes. All the best labels." Curtis opened the bag, pulled out a couple pairs of jeans and a few shirts and sweaters and set them on the bed. He folded the bag in half, nervous, not sure if Shaun was going to like what he'd picked out. They didn't exactly have the same taste in clothes.

"Thanks, Curtis. I'll be the best-dressed guy in the place." Shaun reached for him, taking the bag from his grasp, and tossing it onto the pillows. Then he held both of Curtis' hands in his, guiding them both to take a seat on his bed. "Thank you for everything you've done. I'm not supposed to, but I know what you gave up for me to be here."

Curtis looked up and studied Shaun's eyes, and smiled. "You look like you're feeling better."

"I am. I really am." Shaun grinned, squirming with excitement. "I am so thrilled to see you. You have no idea how badly I've wanted to see you."

"Shaun, you can't be like that with me anymore, or they won't let you out of here. They'll have you transferred to a public facility." Curtis' brow creased with anxiety. "Dr. Scorcy told me you're moving past all the dependency issues."

"That's the amazing thing, Curtis." Shaun jumped to his feet. "I feel like I've moved past it. I couldn't give a rat's ass what you think of me or what I can do to please you." He creased up laughing. "All right, maybe that's not entirely true, but only because I was able to strip away everything and uncover my true feelings for you."

Curtis sat up straighter and reached for Shaun's hands, forcing him to stop leaping about and sit down for a second. "Have you talked to Dr. Scorcy about this?"

Shaun nodded his head.

"What did he say?" Curtis asked.

"He says that although much of our relationship was

being dictated by my illness, there was an element of reality developing below the surface."

"Meaning what, Shaun?"

"Meaning, I love you, Curtis. I really, truly love you."

Curtis' heart began beating rapidly, precipitating a rush of emotion that completely overcame him. He fell back on the bed and pulled Shaun into his arms, burying his face deep into Shaun's hair as he tried to inhale him into his body; he couldn't get close enough to him at that moment. The shattering reality of his wildest dreams coming true had permeated his soul. "I love you too, baby." He kissed Shaun's head.

Shaun grunted happily, content, but had to release Curtis when he heard a light knock at the door. "Oops," he said. "We're not supposed to have the door closed." He reluctantly rolled off the bed and opened the door, smiling and nodding at the nurse that had interrupted them.

Curtis waved at the nurse and sat back up, grinning bawdily at her until she turned and walked away.

Shaun snorted in amusement.

"So, I guess this isn't a conjugal visit?" Curtis said and smiled. "I suppose that's too much to ask from a classy joint like this." He patted the spot beside him and wrapped his arm around Shaun's shoulder when he sat down.

"I talked to Dr. Scorcy about that," Shaun said, "but he says the administration is being weird because we're two guys."

"No worries. I'm just glad to see you feeling better." Curtis brushed his fingers along Shaun's lips. "Although, I would gladly pay more money if it meant I could feel your body against mine again. I've been dreaming about it every night."

He took Shaun's mouth and then deepened the kiss, moaning with exhilaration as Shaun's hands sought to find a way into his clothing. He was attempting to control himself, but his need fired up fiercely when he felt the warm touch of Shaun's fingers running down into the back of his pants.

He groaned in frustration when he heard someone clear their throat from the direction of the doorway.

"Oh, hey, Dr. Scorcy," Shaun said, and then brushed the moisture off his lips.

"Shaun, we talked about this," Dr. Scorcy said.

"We were just kissing."

"I think our definitions of *kissing* may vary slightly."

"I can't help it." Shaun sighed. "He's so fucking hot."

The sound of a few nurses sniggering out in the corridor had Curtis smiling with amusement. He'd already caused quite the stir when he'd arrived today, sending many members of the clinic's staff scurrying around so they could get a better look at him. He glanced at Dr. Scorcy and raised his eyebrows at him.

"You said that physical contact with Curtis wouldn't hinder my progress," Shaun said. "You said it. I heard you."

"But it hasn't been decided whether or not you'll be permitted this type of visit with Curtis."

"Everyone else is permitted. It isn't fair."

"I agree with you, Shaun, but my hands are tied."

"My boyfriend paid a lot of money for me to be here." Shaun started rocking back and forth to some music in his head, and then stood up and danced his way around the room. "And personally, I think we deserve the same rights as the straight couples."

Shaun peeled his shirt off over his head, swaying his hips seductively and rotating his body around the room, feeling the excitement build as Curtis watched him. "You know this is only going to end one way." He gyrated toward Curtis, licking his lips and moaning, then checked over his shoulder as he continued dancing, to address Dr. Scorcy. "It's your choice whether the door is open or closed because Curtis and I really don't care if we have an audience. In fact …I get off on having people watch us."

"Yes, I'm painfully aware of that." Dr. Scorcy studied the two men, marveling at the stunning contrast in their appearance. He sighed in resignation. "In the interest of sheltering the other patients, I'm going to turn a blind eye, but try to keep the noise down." He shut the door, cringing when Curtis began whistling and making raucous sexual noises at Shaun. He would just have to ask his staff to avoid this particular wing of the unit for a while.

Shaun grinned and fell into Curtis' lap and took his mouth aggressively, reveling in Curtis' passionate response. He pulled back and held Curtis' face in his hands. "I'm so fucking horny."

"Aren't you always?" Curtis kissed Shaun briefly and stroked his cheek, and then set Shaun aside so he could peel his clothes off. "I get the feeling from Dr. Scorcy that you've been misbehaving."

"I found a few hot guys willing to fuck me raw on a regular basis, but sometimes we aren't as discreet as what

Dr. Scorcy would prefer." Shaun removed his pants then pushed Curtis over, straddling his hips as he began stroking him.

"How hot?" Curtis asked.

Shaun's eyes flashed with excitement. "Fucking hot. But none as hot as you. We can track them down later if you're interested."

Curtis gazed down the length of his body as Shaun repositioned himself, arching his body up to meet his lover, euphoric to be with Shaun, his only love once more.

He closed his eyes and let the desire wash over him.

Chapter Eight

Reunion

Dixie put the last of the groceries they'd picked up after leaving the airport in the cupboard. She opened the fridge and checked the temperature. The last thing she needed was a large group of people suffering from food poisoning. She threw it shut again and wandered over to one of the open breezeway windows, admiring the expansive stretch of sand rimming miles of gloriously blue and seemingly untainted ocean through the massive window.

Laughing in amusement, Dixie turned, excited, as a string of colorful obscenities erupted from the front hall of the elaborate villa Ming had rented for the two-week long, Mexican reunion.

"What did you do, Ming?" she asked.

"I dropped this fucking bag on my foot."

"Oh, poor baby. Someone made you carry your own bags." Dixie grinned. "Where's Seth?"

"He's back at the car grabbing the rest of my stuff."

"That poor man. I don't know how he puts up with you." Dixie reached for Ming's apparently unruly bag and hauled it up the stairs for him. "Did you hear back from Candace?"

"Last I heard she was still trying to resolve her passport issues." Ming unzipped the first of the many bags that were already in the room and started hanging things in the closet. "She's going to be a few days late."

"Is she planning on bringing Brittany?"

"No, she's going to leave her with her grandma. Which is unfortunate, because Kevin was looking forward to seeing her."

"I keep telling him he needs to get off his lazy ass and fly out to see her more often."

Seth stepped into the room and heaved two bags onto the bed.

"That's the last of it," he said. "If you don't look fucking hot for the entire two weeks we're here, I'm going to be sorely disappointed, and you'll have to carry your own bags back home."

"Don't worry, sweetheart." Ming let his hand drift over one of the bags. "I won't disappoint you." He winked at him. "I have lots of secrets in here that will make you very, very happy."

Dixie rolled her eyes.

"I'm going to finish unpacking my stuff," she said. "Can you guys listen for the door? Jay's plane was supposed to have landed about an hour ago. He should be here any minute."

"We've got it." Ming encouraged Seth toward the door. "Be a dear and listen out for Jay. I have to get changed."

Seth nodded his agreement, content with his momentary submission, and headed back downstairs as requested. He'd just reached the bottom step when he heard someone knock at the door. He opened it expecting to meet the world famous disc jockey Ming had been telling him about, but instead found himself face to face with one of the most alluring women he'd ever encountered.

"Hi," Attila said. "I hope we have the right place. We're looking for Dixie and Ming." He looked back over his shoulder when Eric stepped up behind him with their bags.

"You've got the right place," Seth replied, and reached out for Attila's hand, lifting it to his lips. "I'm Seth Richmond. It's such a pleasure to meet you…?"

"Shannon," Attila replied and winked mischievously at Seth, then motioned over to Eric. "And this is my boyfriend, Eric."

Seth nodded at Eric without actually making eye contact. His attention was fully trained on Attila.

Attila smiled sweetly. "May we come in?"

"Oh. Yes, of course. I'm sorry." Seth stepped back out of the way to let them pass. "Ming didn't mention you."

"I did so, darling," Ming said as he hung over the banister at the top of the steps. "This is the friend I was telling you about. The one you're not supposed to *out* to anyone."

"Hey, Ming," Attila said as he looked up the stairs, but Ming sighed quietly and redirected his gaze away from where Attila and Eric were standing together.

"Hey, Attila," he replied finally under his breath.

Seth spun back around. "You're Attila?"

"Guilty." Attila raised his hand and brushed past Seth, patting him condescendingly on the cheek as he made his way into the living room. He wandered up to the large windows and starred out at the ocean. "The view is amazing. Come see, Eric."

"Wow, that's something else," Eric agreed as he stepped up behind Attila and wrapped him up in his arms, letting his chin rest on Attila's shoulder. "I can't wait to see you out there in that little bikini of yours." He kissed Attila on the cheek and turned back toward the room when he heard the shrill shrieking sound coming from Dixie as she rushed down the stairs toward them.

"Oh, my god, Attila! It's so good to see you …and you too, Eric, of course." Dixie grasped both of Attila's hands and stood back to examine him. "Eric was right. You're absolutely gorgeous!" She pulled Attila into her arms. "You look so different. I wouldn't have recognized you. Are you happy with everything?"

"It was quite the ordeal." Attila stepped back and held Dixie's face. "But I'm finally comfortable in my own skin."

"It's so incredible what they can do now …," Dixie replied as she took Attila's hand and led him away to show where he and Eric would be staying. She'd picked out a ground floor bedroom with unrestricted views of the ocean.

Ming sighed, numbed by the sight of Attila not looking anything like the image he'd been carrying around with him and headed back to his room, leaving Seth and Eric standing in the living room staring at each other. They were both relieved when someone knocked on the door.

Jay adjusted the bag on his shoulder and stared up at the massive mahogany door, waiting for someone to open it. He smirked as the girl to the left of him leaned in and kissed him on the cheek.

"What's up, Cindy?" he said.

"I hope your friends know how to have a good time," Cindy replied, then pulled at Jay's arm when the girl to the right of him giggled and whispered something in his ear.

"Tawny, baby. You can't be doing stuff like that," Jay said and then wrapped his arm around her. "I told you this was important to me, and you promised to behave."

"And you told me you were going to leave that slut Cindy at home," Tawny said and glared past Jay's shoulder at the other girl. "I was hoping to have you all to myself."

"Who are you calling a slut," Cindy said as she flipped the finger at Tawny behind Jay's back. "You? You fucking skank."

"Now girls, I've told you before," Jay said. "You start fighting like that, and I'm going to have to—"

"Hey," Eric said, extending a hand after opening the door. "Jay Parker, right?"

Jay slid his sunglasses down the bridge of his nose and peered at Eric. "Do I know you?"

"Eric Templeton. We went to Tekla together."

"Right." Jay hovered a finger, pointing at him. "Eric. You were one of those football guys, weren't you?" He pushed past Eric and stood in the middle of the front hall. "Is Kevin here yet?"

"No, there's just—"

Jay waved his hand at Eric in irritation. "I'm sure I'll find out soon enough." He dropped his bag on the floor and looked around, nodding at Eric. "Take this to my room, would you?"

Eric looked over at Seth, but Seth just shrugged his shoulders.

"Jay! Baby!" Dixie shrieked as she bounced into the room and threw herself into Jay's arms.

"Hey, Dixie cup!" Jay scooped Dixie into his arms and spun her in a small circle, sending his girls into a panic as they tried to keep from being knocked over. "How's tricks with my favorite girl?"

"Fabulous," Dixie squealed excitedly. "You would not believe who I ran into the other day. Do you remember that certifiable groupie named Lauren?" She raised her eyebrows as she spotted the girls pressed against the walls. "Jay, do these ladies have names or do I have to guess?"

"Sorry, sweetheart," Jay said. "This here is …Cindy, and this is." He snapped his fingers in thought. "Tawny. This is Tawny."

Dixie smirked. "So, you're close then?" She bumped him with her hip. "Soulmates du jour?"

Jay grinned at her and pulled her back into his arms. "I miss you little Dix. You were the best road manager a guy could ever have." He stopped, distracted, peering over Dixie's shoulder at someone behind her. "Well, hello there," he said.

Dixie turned around and smiled at Attila.

"Jay, close your mouth," she said. "This is Eric's girlfriend, Shannon. And she is completely off limits."

Jay looked over at Eric with a new appreciation.

"Sorry, I blew you off there, dude," he said to Eric, and then redirected his attention back on to Attila.

Attila clenched his teeth and cast his gaze downward,

his legs trembling beneath him. He'd assumed Jay would be too busy touring to make a trip to Mexico to hang out with a bunch of his old high school friends. That would've been preferential.

The last time he'd seen Jay was a good two years after graduation when he'd only just begun the process of transitional surgery. He'd run into Jay and a group of his music buddies at the underground nightclub he'd been frequenting for months. It was an accepting space for him to hang out, even meet a few guys, but the clientele there made it entirely off the beaten track for someone like Jay, and he'd been stunned to see him there.

Of course, Jay had recognized him immediately, calling him Annie and trying to get close to him, believing he was the hot girl from high school he hadn't managed to bag. Attila remembered the deep, sinking feeling he'd had in his gut when Jay and his buddies had manhandled him out of the club and into Jay's waiting limo.

"Hey, are you all right?" Eric lowered himself down a bit and tried to catch Attila's attention. He brushed Attila's shoulders with his fingers then pulled him into his arms. "What's the matter?"

"I'm just really tired," Attila lied.

"Then let's go lie down. I could use a nap myself." Eric smiled at him. "Come on." He touched Attila's nose. "I'll make you some tea, and we can fall asleep to the sound of the ocean."

"That sounds wonderful." Attila stroked Eric's face and tried his best to smile at him. He let Eric lead him away.

"That guy has all the luck," Jay said. "Except for that

psycho Annie chick that blew him back in high school." He laughed and sneered, shaking his head.

"Fuck," he added. "What a freak of nature she turned out to be."

"What are you talking about?" Dixie took Jay's arm and led him into the living room to sit down. She motioned for Seth to take the girls down the hall to the room they'd be sharing with Jay.

"I ran into Annie at a club about four or five years ago," Jay said. "She was out on the dance floor grinding with some guy, so I worked my way in there to see if I could get a little action." He leaned closer to Dixie. "Except as it turns out ...*she* is not a she." He sat straight up and looked at her. "I swear to God, Dix. I took her out to the limo, and she had the most amazing round luscious tits, but when I ran my hand up under her skirt—" He shook his head with disgust. "She had a fucking dick between her legs."

Dixie's eyebrows dipped down with concern.

"What happened after that?" she asked.

"I got the fuck out of there." Jay laughed. "But a bunch of my buddies thought it would be a riot to fuck her anyway."

"They didn't though, right?" Dixie stood, taking took note of the fact Eric had re-entered the kitchen and was starting a kettle to make Attila's tea. This was going to go south, fast, no matter what Jay said next. Eric was leaning against the counter, listening.

"Fuck yeah," Jay said, his voice heavy with revulsion and obscene amusement. "I could hear that freak Annie squealing like a greedy little whore all the way down the fucking street. She loved every ass pounding second of it."

Dixie was quick to her feet.

"Jay, I think you should leave!" Dixie shouted as she raced to intercept an out for blood, raging Eric storming his way toward the living room—but he knocked her aside.

Dixie screamed for someone to help.

Seth was the first to rush into the room but wasn't sure how to stop what was unfolding. Eric had launched himself, fists flying, at Jay, pounding Jay in the face.

He was about to phone the police when Eric reluctantly pulled himself off Jay of his own accord and dropped onto the sofa.

"What the fuck is wrong with you, man?" Jay yelled as he tried to stem the flow of blood coming from his nose. "I didn't realize you actually had a thing for that freak back in high school." He brushed his sleeve across his face, disgusted with the mess the blood was making of his clothes.

Eric dropped his head and tried to bring his escalating temper under control. He knew how much it scared Attila when he lost it.

"His name is Attila," he said. "And don't you ever call him a freak again." He looked up at Jay. "Or I *will* fucking kill you."

"Ha! So you *did* have a thing for that he-she abomination."

"Jay, I'm warning you …Attila is not an abomination."

"Whatever." Jay shook his head and spat on the floor, trying to clear some of the blood from his mouth. "Fucking unbelievable. Goddamn faggots everywhere I turn these days."

Dixie pulled herself up off the floor. "Jay—what your friends did to Attila that night …that wasn't right. You know that, right?"

"What difference does it make?" Jay said. "That freak—" He glared at Eric, challenging him, "is probably long gone by now. Lying dead in a fucking ditch somewhere."

Attila stepped out from the hallway and leaned against the fridge. "You lied," he said and closed his eyes, "about what really happened, Jay. You lied about what happened in the limo."

"And how the fuck would you know that?" Jay said. "Stay out of this and go back to your fucking room, you stupid bitch."

Eric bolted from his seat and pinned Jay against the wall.

"Apologize!" he warned. "Right now!"

"Eric, let him go." Attila folded his arms protectively around his hips and made his way into the living room. "He's not worth it. He's just an arrogant little shit that doesn't know one end from the other."

"What did he do to you?" Eric asked Attila through clenched teeth. "Tell me so I can kill him. What did Jay do to you?"

"I didn't do anything to her!" Jay shouted, struggling in Eric's grasp. "What the fuck is wrong with you? Both of you are seriously fucked in the head!"

Attila laid his hand on Eric's shoulder and brushed it with his thumb to calm him. "Let me handle this. Please."

Jay smirked as Eric backed away, and grinned as Attila

wandered up to him and ran his hand across Jay's chest.

"Jay, sweetheart," Attila began as he stepped in close to him. "Look into my eyes and tell me what you see." He blinked, watching Jay for any sign of recognition—but there was none.

"I don't know what I'm looking for," Jay said.

"That's because you never bothered to look me in the eyes when you saw me at school or any other time we ran into each other," Attila said. "You see, most people ...they recognize me because of my eyes. But not you ...and you know why that is?"

Jake shook his head.

"Because you were always too busy looking at my tits," Attila replied, then pressed Jay closer to the wall.

"What the fuck are you talking about?" Jay asked. "I don't even know you."

"You know me, Jay. Think hard." Attila leaned in closer and breathed across Jay's lips. "Last time you saw me, I was thrown over the bar of that fancy limo of yours, and you were fucking me up the ass while your friends pounded on the doors, shouting for you to let them in to get a piece of me."

Jay's body tensed as something familiar about the voice he was hearing registered with him.

"Oh—" Attila said. "So, you do remember me?"

"Whoa ...now, hold up, Annie. I didn't mean anything by it."

"But you did mean something by it. You thought it was exciting fucking a tranny, didn't you?" Attila pushed Jay hard against the wall. "But we never finished. You booted me out before I'd even had my turn." He leaned in close and licked a long line up the side of Jay's face. "Maybe I should fuck you right here, lover. Would you like that? If I fucked you?"

Attila shoved Jay into the wall and then released him. He turned away, but then spun back and plowed his fist into Jay's face.

"That's for raping me, you bastard!" Attila screamed, then took another swing at Jay's face, sending him to the floor. "And that's for thinking I actually enjoyed your pathetic excuse for a dick!"

"Jay," Seth said. "I'm going to offer you a head start before I phone the authorities." He looked up toward the balcony area Ming was currently occupying. "You're not welcome here, and I think it's safe to say you're no longer one of my husband's friends."

Ming waved at Seth and blew him a kiss. They weren't actually married, although they'd talked about it. Regardless, it was nice to hear Seth call him husband. He watched Attila reach for Eric, seeking his support. But despite what must've been an excruciating encounter for Attila to revisit, there was incredible strength radiating from Attila's eyes. Some things would always remain constant with Attila—he was a survivor.

Dixie covered her face and exhaled, hardened against her and Jay's history, and tried to compose herself. She'd always known Jay, and his buddies got into trouble whenever they went out on the town unattended, but she hadn't realized just how disgusting and violent some of their actions had been.

She sunk onto a stool in the kitchen and attempted to calm herself as Seth removed Jay and his girls from the house.

Attila gripped onto Eric's arm, his body shaking uncontrollably, as he leaned against the wall just outside their bedroom. He took a deep breath, but his mind was still reeling from the pain of the memory he'd worked so hard to bury.

"What do you need me to do?" asked Eric.

"Just give me a minute."

"Should I be calling someone?" Eric brushed the hair from Attila's eyes and tucked it affectionately behind his ear.

"No, I'll be all right." Attila pushed Eric's hand away and entered the bedroom, collapsing onto the bed while Eric closed the door.

"When Jay found me," he said. "I'd been living as a transsexual for about a year. I was used to dealing with clueless, straight guys wandering into the club and coming on to me. But he caught me completely off guard—because I knew him. I ended up in a bad situation I couldn't get out of."

Eric sat down on the side of the bed in silence.

"I didn't tell you," Attila continued, "because I knew it would upset you. And I honestly didn't think I'd ever see him again."

"I'm just glad you're all right." Eric motioned for Attila's injured hand and smiled. "It looks like we're both going to have bloody knuckles for the next few days." He kissed the swelling, reddened skin. "I want you to know that you can tell me anything." He looked into Attila's eyes. "Nothing could change the way I feel about you. You're an extraordinary guy, Attila."

Eric climbed onto the bed and lowered Attila into the bedding.

"And you're an incredible woman," he said. "But it's you in here—" He touched Attila's chest, letting his finger trace an outline of Attila's heart. "—that I love."

"Stop," Attila said, allowing a small smile to surface. "You're making me blush."

Eric licked at his lips, unsure.

"You were right …that night," he said. "I did want to kiss you."

Attila wrinkled his brow in confusion.

"What night was that?"

"At my house. The hockey game. The *Stephen incident*?"

"Oh, that night." Attila grinned. "I knew you wanted to."

"I was so lost in the crystal, blue depths of your eyes …I *would've* kissed you if you hadn't asked me if I wanted to."

Attila reached up and touched Eric's face.

"I wish I hadn't been so scared of you back then," Eric said.

"You were scared of me?"

"Yeah," Eric replied then laid a kiss on Attila's lips. "Whenever we hung out, you did stuff to my insides that I couldn't make go away. Given time, I think things might've changed between us."

"Like physical things?" Attila asked, intrigued.

Eric shook his head and exhaled. "Maybe. I don't know. It's possible you could've worn me down eventually."

Attila wrinkled up his nose in thought, making Eric eye Attila cautiously. He'd seen that look before.

"What's going on in that devious mind of yours?" Eric asked.

"I'm thinking after our nap, we need to experiment along this theme." Attila grinned when Eric looked at him anxiously. "Don't worry. I'll be gentle." He kissed Eric and held his face. "I just want to push your boundaries a little in the interest of science."

Seth closed the door behind him and leaned against it as he watched Ming standing motionless, staring out the window. He approached and laid his hands on Ming's shoulders.

"Did that fight in the living room upset you?" he asked.

Ming nodded his head.

"Well, he's gone now," Seth said. "He won't be coming back."

"Thank you." Ming lifted one of Seth's hands to his cheek and brushed it against his face, finding comfort in its warmth.

"Did I ever tell you I was in love once?" Ming asked Seth.

"No, you didn't." Seth removed his hand from Ming's grasp and used it to wrap Ming up in his arms. "Did you want to tell me?"

Ming nodded.

"Where did you meet him?" Seth asked.

"I met him during my final year of high school at Tekla. He was new at the school. And he was beautiful." Ming smiled, remembering seeing Attila for the very first time, and knowing immediately that there was something special about him. "We ended up fucking in the change room on the first day."

"Sounds meaningful." Seth grinned.

Ming laughed and pulled Seth's arms tighter around him.

"Then what happened?" Seth asked.

"We spent the next few weeks skipping a lot of school and just hanging out ...I totally fell for him."

"Did he feel the same way?"

"No, he was in love with someone else." Ming sighed. "Someone I assumed was completely unattainable. I thought that once he figured that out, I would have him all to myself."

"But that's not what happened."

"No. When Attila figured out he couldn't have the guy he wanted, he took off, and I never heard from him again."

"I'm sorry he hurt you like that." Seth kissed the back of Ming's head and breathed in the comforting scent he so enjoyed waking up to each morning. "So, exactly what was so unattainable about this other guy?"

Ming grinned. "He was a straight football player."

"Oh, wow. Your lover was setting his sights high."

"Yes, he was." Ming paused. "And he finally achieved them."

"What? He ended up with the football player?"

Ming turned himself to face Seth, wrapped his arms around Seth's waist, and buried his face in Seth's chest.

"He's downstairs with him right now," he said, then his breath caught, and the tears he'd been holding all morning spilled out, soaking his face and the front of Seth's designer shirt.

"Gay or straight ...a prostate gland is a prostate gland." Attila sighed heavily and let his hands rest on his hips. "There's nothing to be embarrassed about. So, you liked it ...big deal."

"I did not!" Eric shouted from behind the bathroom door.

"I have a sheet full of cum that says differently."

"Attila, please." Eric dropped his head against the glass shower enclosure and let the hot water run down his back, praying he could rinse away the humiliation he was feeling.

Attila tapped lightly on the door.

"This is a ridiculous thing to be arguing about," he said. "It is a well-documented fact that manual stimulation of the prostate gland can lead to orgasm. Baby, just think of it as a boy's g-spot."

Attila jumped back as the door flew open.

"A boy's g-spot?" Eric said. "Seriously, Attila?"

Attila grinned at Eric and planted a noisy kiss on his lips.

"Do you like my bikini?" he asked, hoping to release Eric from his embarrassment by changing the subject.

He spun around for Eric to see, and positioned himself in a quick succession of seductive poses that soon had both him and Eric cracking up. Attila grabbed his sun hat and used it to fan the mirthful tears from his eyes as he pulled the bedroom door open.

"That wasn't quite the reaction I was hoping for," he said.

"We'll re-evaluate later." Eric attempted to tie the strings on his swim shorts as he followed Attila down the hall but gave up in frustration. "I hate these stupid things."

Attila looked back and motioned for Eric to head into the kitchen so he could help him. "We should grab something to drink before we head outside. It looks scorching out there." He pulled on one side of the ties in Eric's swim shorts, expecting the other side to move, but it didn't, so he undid the plastic clip and tried to rethread everything back through it, except now the original tie wasn't budging—and then the clip fell off onto the floor.

"Well, that's really fucking stupid," he exclaimed with annoyance.

Eric smirked happily.

"Maybe you just need to find its g-spot," he said.

Attila shrieked with amusement, slapped his hands on Eric's face, and kissed him soundly.

"You are so adorable," he said then pushed Eric up against the fridge and took his mouth more urgently, his emotions swelling as he felt Eric's response begin to press against his body.

"And you are such a bad boy," Eric said when Attila finally released him. "I outta spank you."

"All right, back it up people," Ming said as he pushed past them. "Some of us actually want to use the kitchen for its intended purpose. You have a room. Go use it. Save the rest of us from having to see you two making out every five seconds."

Attila stepped away from Eric, patting his arm, and tried to get Ming's attention.

"Yeah, I'm going to head outside," Eric responded to Attila's prompt. He ran his hand down Attila's arm. "I'll see you in a bit. Take your time."

Attila smiled at him. "Thanks, sugar."

Ming groaned, anxious about the impending conversation, and pretended to be looking for something extremely elusive in one of the cupboards as Eric slipped out through the patio doors.

"Ming?" Attila said and waited. "You've been hiding in your room since I arrived. I think we need to talk."

Ming slammed the cupboard door shut.

"Oh, so now you want to talk?" he retorted. "What happened to talking before you ripped my beating heart from my chest, threw it on the ground, and stomped all over it?"

Attila's eyes rimmed with tears as Ming's words sunk in, his heart stumbling through a few beats.

"That's what you did," Ming continued. "You danced around and let the love I had for you drain into the soil at your feet."

"I didn't know," Attila said as pain scattered patterns across Ming's face. "I'm sorry, Ming. I didn't know."

"How could you *not* know?" Ming slid from the counter he'd been perched upon, landing barefoot on the floor.

"How could you not know how much I loved you?" he asked Attila. "We spent every fucking day together. How could you *not* know something like that?" Ming swiped away a trail of tears staining his cheeks with a brusque hand.

Attila lowered his head, utterly incapable of producing a single excuse that would explain why he'd been oblivious to Ming's feelings. He'd really liked Ming back in high school, even considering the possibility he was falling in love with him, but he'd pushed his feelings for Ming aside, holding on to the faint hope that Eric might someday look at him differently.

"I wasn't paying attention," Attila said. "I was arrogant, and I was shallow. You deserved *so* much better than me."

"I didn't want better than you …I wanted you."

Ming held his stomach and tipped forward as the anguish flowed through him, making his head swim. He sunk down onto the floor and attempted to twist his body away when Attila sat down beside him. He eventually gave in and let Attila wrap him up in his arms.

Holding Ming as he sobbed, Attila looked up to where Seth was leaning against the railing of the balcony — but had to look away. There was no sympathy being afforded to him there. Ming was in pain and Seth was feeling it straight through to his bones.

He re-adjusted Ming in his arms so he could rest his face against Ming's head. He whispered a continuous string of how sorry he was until Ming finally started to breathe easier.

Attila pulled back when he felt Ming laughing.

"What's so funny?" he asked.

"I don't know," Ming replied. "I don't know if I should be laughing or crying." He looked up at Attila and smiled. "The guy I fell in love with isn't a guy anymore. You're a fucking girl."

"I always was, Ming. You know that."

"I know. We talked about the whole surgery thing and everything …but I didn't think you'd actually do it." Ming sat straight up. "I for one loved your body."

Attila shrugged his shoulders.

"Ming, you wouldn't have been happy with me long term, and you know it," he said. "You need a strong man who can throw you over the sofa cushions and fuck your ass from now till Sunday."

"And that wouldn't have been you," Ming said.

"No, that definitely wouldn't have been me." Attila rubbed Ming's shoulder affectionately and helped him to his feet.

"I can't believe you're with Eric." Ming elbowed Attila. "After all that effort, you finally got him into your bed."

"Eric has always meant so much more to me than that," Attila replied, then paused. "I know it's hard for you to understand, Ming, but Eric was my best friend when I was at Tekla."

"What about us? What were we doing?"

Attila shivered and exhaled, seeing that Seth was still watching them. "We were lovers. I loved you in my own way, but we didn't exactly have much in common." He glanced over and could see Eric watching anxiously through the window from his spot on the lounge chair he'd occupied while he was waiting.

He smiled at Eric reassuringly and waved at him.

"Go on then," Ming said. "Go to him. And tell him he's one lucky guy to have found someone like you."

"Thank you, Ming." Attila touched Ming's face, then hurried over to the patio door and slipped out, making his way over to where Eric was sitting before his legs gave out.

The shock of Ming's admission unsettling him.

"Is everything all good between you and Ming?" Eric asked.

"I think so—" Attila bit his lip, looking out at the ocean as he clung to Eric's chair for support. "Ming told me he was in love with me back in high school."

Eric let his hand slide up and down the length of Attila's leg, marveling at the smoothness of his skin.

"You didn't know?" he asked.

"No. I had no idea." Attila looked down at Eric. "I was so busy getting fucked by every guy I could get my ass around, I wasn't paying any attention to Ming or what he might be feeling. I was horrible to him."

"Don't be too hard on yourself." Eric kissed Attila's leg and looked up at him. "That's not who you are anymore."

Attila furrowed his brow.

"But that's the thing," he said. "I am. I did the same thing to my last boyfriend. That's why he broke up with me last summer."

Eric lowered his eyes and reached for Attila's hand. He kissed each of Attila's fingers then smiled up at him.

"Let's see that bikini of yours out in the water," he said.

"Don't you want to talk about what I just said?"

"No, actually. I don't." Eric slipped his hand into Attila's and led him out onto the beach. "I said you could tell me anything and it wouldn't change how I felt about you."

"But, Eric...."

"No, Attila." Eric stopped and studied him. "That was then. And this—" He touched Attila's chest and then touched his own. "This between us ...is now. And it's different." He brushed his thumb across Attila's lip and kissed him. "This is you and me. Together. Right now. And that's all that matters to me."

Attila watched Eric's eyes studying him.

"You're right," he said. "I love you so much. I would never do anything to hurt you."

"I know you wouldn't." Eric raised his hand to shield his eyes from the sun and peered down the beach.

"Hey," he said. "Is that Shaun down there?"

Attila scanned the beach, trying to see who Eric was referring to. But just as he caught sight of him, the figure in question was lifted up into the arms of another guy, run down the length of the beach, and thrown into the water. Both men were wearing sleek black thongs on their tanned and toned bodies.

"Yeah, that's definitely Shaun and Curtis," Attila said. "No one else would dare run around on the beach wearing one of those."

Eric waved his arms until Curtis spotted them, then laughed with genuine happiness when Curtis went to retrieve Shaun from the water and ended up being pulled in with him.

They looked happy together.

Shaun and Curtis ran most of the way up the beach with their hands clasped, but Shaun leaped ahead in a final sprint, leaving Curtis behind, to reach Eric and Attila first.

"Hey, guys," Shaun said as he hugged each of them in turn. "I'm so sorry we scared you guys by taking off like we did."

"Is everything all right now?" Attila asked.

Shaun beamed at him. "Everything is perfect. I couldn't be happier. Truly …I couldn't." He bounced up and down, attempting to still his tongue, but couldn't contain himself.

He held out his hand for Attila to see.

Attila grasped his hand and looked up in shock.

"You guys got married?" he asked Shaun.

"As soon as Shaun was discharged," Curtis answered. "We headed into town and tied the old knot."

"Oh, I see," Attila said, then dropped Shaun's hand. He twisted his hair into a bun, securing it with a few pins to keep it from blowing in his face, then crossed his arms.

"Attila," Eric said, "they're in love. They have every right to get married if they want to." He touched Attila on the shoulder, but Attila pulled away and headed for the water's edge.

Eric turned back to Curtis and Shaun.

"Congratulations, guys," he said, shaking both their hands. "From both of us …really." He stepped back and clasped his hands together. "I'm sorry about Attila. He's had a rough day."

"Is the *ring ding*, Ming giving her grief?" Curtis asked.

"No, I think he and Ming have worked everything out." Eric scrubbed his face, concerned, as he watched Attila standing motionless in the water watching the waves come in.

"Maybe the ring less the ding is the quandary?" Shaun said, making Curtis laugh at the use of his speaking style. He took Curtis' hand and used it to spin himself around under Curtis' arm.

"Perchance, my fair swashbuckler," Curtis replied.

"What are you two on about?" Eric asked, completely lost.

Shaun sighed and directed Curtis toward the villa.

"Eric, sweetheart," he said. "I love you to death, but there are times when you're as thick as a brick."

Kevin threw his bag onto the bed and dropped down beside it, stretching himself out. It had been a long flight, and he needed to rest for a while before he subjected himself to the rigors of reacquainting himself with people he'd effectively abandoned during his final year of high school. He wouldn't have even considered coming along to the reunion if Dixie hadn't insisted.

He'd run into Dixie a couple of years back while he was away on business. They'd been staying in contact ever since. It was a long distance relationship that suited his lifestyle perfectly. His job kept him extremely busy, and he had very little leisure time. Whereas Dixie worked from home and was almost always available. Whenever he had a spare moment, he could phone her, and more often than not, she would be there to answer his call.

The shrieking and laughing coming from the living room had Kevin groaning. He was going to have to head out there before someone was sent in to get him. Dixie had let him in, so she'd probably informed everyone he'd arrived by now. It wouldn't be long before his peace was interrupted.

As he entered the living room, the familiar sound of Shaun's voice hollering at him brought a smile to his face.

"Hey, Shaun," Kevin said as Shaun flew at him. Rough hands messed up his hair, prompting Kevin to put Shaun in a headlock and nuggie him while Curtis watched quietly from the sofa.

"Constable Kevin Magarey," Curtis said disdainfully then waited until Kevin released Shaun. "It's been a long time."

"Yes, it has." Kevin reached for Curtis' outstretched hand and shook it. "You had everyone worried there for a while."

"Did I really? Well, my first—" Curtis looked at Shaun and smiled, and motioned for him to sit down beside him.

Kevin stood patiently, waiting for Curtis to continue. He hated the little mind games Curtis played with people, and he wasn't about to give him the satisfaction of thinking he was becoming flustered by the delay in his response. He scratched his head and gazed around the room, trying to look interested in the decor.

"—my first and only priority was Shaun," Curtis continued, grinning inwardly. He'd definitely irritated Kevin. "I would never do anything to hurt him. You should know that."

Kevin raised his eyebrows. He hadn't expected Curtis to answer in complete, cohesive sentences. He mustn't have found a decent drug dealer in Mexico yet.

"I never thought you'd hurt him," he replied. "But it would've been nice if you'd told someone where you were taking him."

Curtis leaned back and crossed his arms. "But see ...I didn't want anyone to know where Shaun was. He was getting the help he needed, and I didn't think it was prudent for his family or friends to find out what he'd been through."

Kevin blinked his eyes, then his brow furrowed.

"Why?" he asked. "What happened?"

"Like I said," replied Curtis. "No one else needed to know."

Shaun laid his hand on Curtis' leg and leaned in, kissing his cheek. He smiled when Curtis turned to face him, enthralled by his concern, unfounded as it was. He didn't mind.

He looked around the room, spotting Dixie and Ming, and redirected his attention on to Kevin.

"The first day back at Tekla, graduating year. I was raped," Shaun said. "Repeatedly. Over a long period of time."

Shaun dropped his gaze to the floor when he heard Dixie gasp, but then looked up, encouraged to continue when he caught a glimpse of Eric and Attila hovering in the kitchen, watching him intently, their warmth toward him evident.

"The whole thing was my fault," Curtis said. "I never

should've taken Shaun with me that day." He wrapped an arm around Shaun's shoulders and held him as tight as he could. He still couldn't believe Shaun loved him after everything he'd put him through. He'd been so surprised by Shaun's suggestion of marriage that he'd immediately gone to Dr. Scorcy to find out if Shaun had been showing any signs of regression. Dr. Scorcy had assured him that whatever Shaun was feeling could be trusted as real and true.

"The guy was a friend of Curtis'," Shaun said, then he paused while he waited for Dixie and Ming to take a seat. He took a deep breath and kissed the thumb of Curtis' hand before continuing.

"I was just supposed to watch. And I did for the first hour," he continued. "But then the guy took a break and went off to the bathroom. He left Curtis tied to the ottoman …and he looked so vulnerable all trussed up and gagged like that."

"What the fuck were you—" Dixie exclaimed, but Ming shushed her from continuing.

Shaun closed his eyes as he remembered what he'd done next.

"I'd never thought of the renowned *Curtis Bantam* as being vulnerable before …and it fascinated me."

He opened his eyes and shook his head.

"Shaun," Attila said. "You don't have to do this."

Kevin looked up at Attila and did a double take. The last he'd heard, Eric was supposed to be bringing Annie with him. The redhead was definitely easy on the eyes, but he'd been looking forward to seeing the girl that had caused so much scandal and excitement in high school.

"I just wanted to taste his skin," Shaun continued. "But it was so soft and warm beneath my lips. I couldn't stop myself."

Attila tucked closer to Eric and reached for his hand.

"I was in no state to object." Curtis rolled back into the cushions and smiled. "He was so sweet and gentle." He paused, remembering. "I had no way of knowing my friend would react the way he did when he walked back into that room and saw Shaun fucking me."

Kevin cringed and turned away, and headed for the kitchen to pour a glass of water. He held it against his head briefly, letting the cooling effect calm his rapidly developing headache.

He downed the entire glass, set it in the sink, and poured another one, with ice, for Shaun.

"Thanks, Kevin," Shaun said as he took the glass from him.

"Were there drugs involved?" Kevin asked.

Curtis snorted loudly and took a sip of the water Shaun offered him. "It was a minimum four-hour date." He smirked. "Were there drugs? What the fuck do you think?"

"Did any money change hands?"

Shaun raised his eyebrows in unison with Curtis. He looked at Curtis, and they both shrugged their shoulders.

"I don't know what you're talking about," Shaun replied innocently.

Kevin rolled his eyes in aggravation. "Guys, please. I'm not going to bust you."

"Bust us for what?" Curtis asked. "I can't even

remember what we were discussing." He stood and helped Shaun to his feet.

"My mind is an absolute blank," Shaun added. "I must be tired. The last thing I remember is running down the beach."

"I think we should go lie down." Curtis waved over at Ming. "I parked my trailer out front. Hope that's all right."

"You drove down?" Ming asked.

"Of course," Shaun said. "We left about a month ago. You'd be amazed how much money you can make between home and here."

He looked at Kevin. "I mean friends. You can make a lot of *friends* on the road."

Kevin just rubbed his eyes, shaking his head.

"Thanks for the offer of a room, by the way, Ming," Curtis said. "But Shaun and I are more comfortable around our own stuff. So, we'll just stay out in the trailer, if that's all right."

Ming nodded his head and waved them away. He watched them go out through the front door and released the breath he'd been holding. "Well, I can't say I'm upset to hear they want to room elsewhere," he said. "What a fucked up couple they turned out to be ...not that I'm surprised."

"Easy, Ming," Eric said. "Don't be throwing stones."

"Curtis, I get ...but Shaun?" Dixie added. "That's the same future trust fund brat that used to complain about how the pool house he was living in was too small at two thousand square feet."

Ming laughed. "Now he's living in a trailer, hustling for a living, married to Curtis freakin' Bantam."

Attila leaned over and whispered something to Eric, and then they both moved out of the kitchen.

"We're going to hang out with Curtis and Shaun for a little while," Eric said. "We've got a lot to catch up on."

"Oh, my god. I'm so sorry," Dixie said. "I completely forgot you guys are friends with them."

"That's all right," Attila replied and headed toward the door. "We'll see you guys in a bit. Perhaps in time for dinner."

Ming leaped up and intercepted them before they stepped out through the open doorway.

"I'm so sorry about that little repartee," he said. "I'm sure once we get talking to them a bit more they won't seem so strange."

Attila snorted in amusement and reached for Eric's arm.

"We'll see you later, Ming." Eric closed the door behind them and sighed in exasperation. "Did the fact Shaun just told them he was raped in high school escape them somehow?"

"I think they were more focused on the visual of Curtis tied to the ottoman and how it bolstered and reinforced their prejudices against him, and subsequently …Shaun."

"Typical."

Eric tapped on Curtis' trailer door and smirked happily when he heard a crash and a colorful string of obscenities.

Curtis popped the door open, completely naked.

"Hey, guys," he said and stepped back. "Come on in."

"Thanks, Curtis," Eric said. "The air was getting a bit

stuffy inside the villa. Hope you don't mind."

"Mi Casa es Su Casa, buddy," Curtis replied. "You know that."

Eric climbed up the steps and had to duck his head to make his way into the back of the trailer. He let Attila pass by him and climbed onto the bed area that doubled as the trailer's only seating, making himself comfortable beside Shaun who was only draped in a thin sheet. Eric had to smile. If someone had told him a year ago that the closest group of friends he'd ever had would turn out to be a transgender woman and a couple of male go-go dancers with a serious aversion to clothing, he would've thought they were insane.

"Can I get you two a drink?" Curtis asked.

"Have you got any tequila?" Attila replied, hopeful.

"Have I got tequila?" Curtis grinned. "We're in fucking tequila country. Of course, I have tequila." He pulled open a cabinet and lifted down a large bottle and four shot glasses. He filled each of them and threw his own back in unison with everyone else. He repeated the process three more times before screwing the lid back on the bottle and setting it on the windowsill.

"That feels much better," Eric said and stretched out, yawning. He reached over and shoved Shaun's head playfully. "So, how are you really feeling, psycho?"

"I still have some lingering nightmares," Shaun answered. "But I'm doing really well, thanks to Curtis."

"That must've cost you a fortune," Attila said to Curtis.

"It was worth it." Curtis smiled across the bed at Shaun. "Money comes and goes, but love like ours …that only comes around once in a lifetime."

"So, who asked who?" Attila inquired, curious to know more about the course of their nuptials.

Shaun beamed. "That would be me."

"So, the mental patient asked the mental person to marry him," Eric teased. "You could make a movie out of that." He shrieked and tried to duck as Shaun swung a pillow at his head.

Curtis chuckled, remembering. "Well, I'm glad he did, because I never would've been able to work up the courage to ask him."

"You?" Attila replied in disbelief. "Curtis, I've rarely met anyone as confident as you."

"It's different when I'm around Shaun. He makes me weak in the knees," Curtis admitted, then winked at Shaun.

"I know the feeling," Eric said. "Even back in high school, Attila did strange things to my insides."

Attila blew a kiss across the bed to Eric.

"You liked him back then?" Shaun said to Eric and then punched Eric hard in the arm. "Oh, my god! I knew it! You knew Attila was a guy when he sucked you off at Nathan's party!"

Eric's face flushed and he nodded his head.

"Now the truth comes out." Curtis rubbed his hands together, gleeful. "So, tell me, Eric. Were you actually mad at Shannon for seducing you into the back of your truck?"

"I didn't seduce him," Attila said. "I thought he wanted to."

"Did you want to fuck him?" Shaun asked Eric.

"No, of course not," Eric replied. "I'd told him a

thousand times over that I didn't fuck guys."

"Interesting," Curtis said and tapped at his chin. "So, this subject had come up before between the two of you."

"I don't know what came over me," Attila interjected demurely.

Curtis looked at Attila. "You are one naughty girl."

"I try to be good." Attila fluttered his eyelashes in feigned modesty and then cast his eyes downwards, taking note of the fact that Curtis was absentmindedly stroking himself into an erection beneath the thin sheet. He swallowed, aroused, and licked his lips. Then caught himself on and looked away. He redirected his attention toward Eric and smiled.

Eric laughed under his breath and raised his eyebrows.

"I think maybe we're interrupting something," he said to Attila and made to get up. "We'll catch you guys later."

Shaun touched Eric's arm. "You don't have to go yet. We'd like you and Attila to stay for a while longer."

Curtis bumped Attila with his elbow and caught his eye. "Do you want some of this?" He pulled the sheet back, his hand firmly stroking, and then let his dick go, encouraging it to sway.

"No—" Attila took a deep breath. "I'm fine. Thank you for the offer though, Curtis."

"We're both clean," Shaun said. "We've been tested recently. Curtis is absolutely fastidious about safety."

"That wasn't actually my initial concern," Attila replied.

"Attila," Eric said, almost whispering. "You're practically drooling over there." He ran his hand around the back of his neck and rotated his head. "It's Curtis. I'd be all right with it."

Attila pinched up his face in confusion.

"That's not something we've ever talked about before, Eric," he said. "Being with other people like that."

Eric leaned forward and touched Attila's foot. "I'm not talking about other people. I'm talking about Curtis and Shaun. They're our best friends."

Shaun blinked, partially from shock, but mostly in anticipation. He nodded discreetly to Curtis and then ran his hand down Eric's arm, and leaned in to kiss his shoulder.

"Hang on, Shaun," Eric said, pulling his arm away. "I wasn't talking about me. I was talking about Attila. I'm not gay. He is."

"Pity." Shaun pouted at Eric and sighed dramatically. "Let me know if you change your mind." He looked across the bed and smiled; Curtis and Attila had already started making out.

Eric turned his attention back to Attila and found himself watching Curtis' aggressive, greedy mouth attacking Attila's, seemingly in an attempt to consume him. He was momentarily stunned, but then became unexpectedly aroused by Attila's urgent response to Curtis, and he felt his gut twisting with anticipation when Attila released Curtis' mouth and shuffled down the bed to take Curtis' full erection deep into his throat.

Despite his best efforts, the sound of enjoyment coming from Curtis and Attila caused Eric's own need to respond. He reached out and ran his hand down Attila's leg, prompting Attila to drop Curtis from his mouth.

Attila wiped his hand across his lips and smiled at Eric. "Are you all right, baby?"

Eric nodded his head and motioned for Attila to come to him so he could kiss him. His desire surged as he took in the taste of another man on Attila's lips and he dove deeper, trying to capture what Attila had experienced. He finally released him and quivered with excitement as Attila pursued Curtis again.

"Fucking hell!" Curtis threw his head back and laughed. "You're one lucky bastard, Eric." He groaned and then inhaled sharply as shivers ran down his body. "No offense, Shaun. But Shannon's mouth is fucking brilliant."

"None taken," Shaun said as he moved closer to Eric. He let his hand drift up Eric's leg, and after visually challenging him for a second, began rubbing Eric's obvious erection through the thin material of his swim shorts. Emboldened by Eric's acceptance of his touch, Shaun moved in closer and kissed and licked at Eric's neck, then breathed softly in his ear. When Eric didn't object to his advances, he slipped his hand into Eric's swim shorts and was rewarded by the sound of Eric breathing heavier.

"Shaun …," Eric said, then promptly forgot what he was going to say; he was fixated on what Attila was doing to Curtis. His breath escaped in short gasps, and he closed his eyes as Shaun hauled his swim shorts off his hips. Eric's face flushed, embarrassed, fearing the future regret of his acceptance, but he found himself unable to object, to stop what was happening, when Shaun slipped between his legs and took him into his mouth, and began pulling at him.

He tried to relax and think of something else other than the fact a guy he'd known since kindergarten was sucking on his cock, but he couldn't get past it; his arousal was waning. He laid his hand on Shaun's back and nudged him to get his attention.

Shaun stopped what he was doing and looked up. "Not working for you, is it?"

"I'm sorry, buddy. It's not you. You're really good, but we used to play in little league together. I just can't."

"No problem." Shaun crawled back up, retaking his place beside Eric and leaned into his shoulder. "We can just sit and watch them. Maybe jerk off a little." He settled in to watch Curtis and Attila but then changed his mind and dug a few wriggling fingers into Eric's stomach. Eric of course reacted, and Shaun threw Eric into a headlock when Eric squirmed to get away.

"Don't." Eric gasped. "Don't you fucking tickle me."

"Still ticklish, are you?" Shaun adjusted his hold on Eric and used what leverage he had to haul Eric down on top of him.

Eric laughed. "Nice wrestling move."

"Mm …I thought so," Shaun replied, then wrapped his legs around Eric's waist, trapping Eric as he tried to get up.

"Shaun, what are you doing?"

"Trying another tactic." Shaun ran his hands over the smooth surface of Eric's bare shoulders and down his back to his ass and pulled Eric tight against his body. He began a slow thrusting of his hips, rubbing their bodies against each other, and moaned with exhilaration as their cocks began to harden against each other.

"How does that feel?" Shaun asked.

"Fucking strange, Shaun." Eric grinned. "But in a good way."

"Ah …progress." Shaun pulled Eric tighter to his body, and his mind shrieked with excitement as Eric devoured his mouth.

Attila looked over his shoulder at Eric, who was now fully involved with Shaun and felt his heart skip slightly, wishing Eric had been as open to experimentation back in high school as what he was now …with Shaun. He frowned and turned back to Curtis.

"Don't take it personally," Curtis said as he watched Eric and Shaun together. "Eric has grown a lot since he met you, and even more so since you started seeing each other." Then he undid the tie on Attila's bikini top and threw it off to one side. "The important thing to remember is that he loves *you*."

Curtis sat back, admiring Attila's body. "That is fucking amazing." He reached out, pinching at Attila's nipples and then motioned for Attila to move closer so he could take one into his mouth. He played the hard nub with his tongue and then sucked on it, letting it pop noisily from his mouth when he was done.

"They're a lot more fun than a padded bra," Attila said.

"That's for sure. What about down here?" Curtis asked as he untied the strings that held Attila's bikini bottom together. "My tongue would love to give you a little more attention."

"I don't know, Curtis," Attila whispered as he held the bikini bottom from falling away. "It isn't completely right.

Eric doesn't ...he never wants—I mean, I never ..."

Curtis brushed Attila's thighs affectionately with his hands and studied his face. "Shannon, anything that is part of who you are on the outside will always be perfect in my eyes, because you're important to me, and I know who you are on the inside ...in your heart." He leaned in and kissed Attila on the lips. "But if you want me to stop, that's fine. I'm not going to pressure you."

Attila rose up onto his knees, despite the anxiety rolling through him, and allowed Curtis to pull the bikini bottom away, prepared to cover himself again and retreat. But there were no sounds of displeasure coming from Curtis. He gripped Curtis' shoulders and dropped his head back, sighing as Curtis' tongue began probing the recesses of his newfound femininity. His heart thundered with the joy of absolute acceptance when Curtis pushed him over onto his back, growling with desire, and increased his ardent demands; his arms wrapping around Attila's thighs, hauling Attila closer as his tongue stroked Attila's warm, pink creases and sought to discover new depths of pleasure for him.

Reaching out for Eric's hand, Attila gripped it tightly, catching and holding Eric's eye. He brushed his other hand through Curtis' hair and responded to each increasing attempt until he couldn't hold back any longer. He arched his hips and let the thrill of a climactic shiver roll through his body, sighing happily when Eric smiled at him. Then Curtis turned him onto his stomach and started kissing and sucking at his shoulders, making him shriek with delight.

Eric watched as Curtis stretched out on Attila's back,

tucked his face into Attila's neck and grasped both of Attila's hands in his own, gathering him protectively under his body

"What do you want, sweetheart?" Curtis said. "Front or back?"

Eric mouthed the word *back* at the same time as Attila said it, knowing it was his preference. Even with the changes in his body, Eric was constantly reminded that Attila still responded like a guy—a guy that sought his fulfillment from men. Attila had argued with him about it when he'd brought it up, denying any credibility to what Eric was seeing, and defending his decision, that the gender reassignment had aligned him with his true gender.

He pinched his eyes shut, and tried to block out the sound of Attila swearing, and groaning with pleasure, as Curtis entered him.

"What do you want to do, Eric?" Shaun asked as he squirmed out from under Eric and rolled onto his hands and knees, crawling forward along the bed. He looked back along the length of his body at Eric and tried to judge what Eric's decision would be. He swayed his hips from side to side, offering himself, sighing and caressing his hole in an attempt to entice Eric.

"I can't, Shaun." Eric rubbed his hand across his face, not sure what to do. His desire was tempting him to take Shaun up on his offer, but he couldn't bring himself to do it.

"All right," Shaun replied then reached for the bottle of lube Curtis had just thrown over to him. He dispensed some into his hand and began stroking himself, letting his chest heave and drop as his need increased. He nodded over at Curtis to let him know he was ready for him, and turned his body, ready for Curtis to make the switch from Attila to himself, but then shook his head discreetly when he saw Eric was watching him intently.

Shaun sat back on his haunches and then rolled onto his back.

"Do you want to talk about it?" he asked Eric.

Eric lay down beside Shaun and draped his hands over his face. He let them fall when he sensed movement beside him. He had to slide closer to Shaun when Curtis shoved him with his foot to get him to move out of the way. He rolled over to face Shaun.

"I want to understand what Attila sees in it," he replied.

"You can't do that without trying it," Shaun said, his attention focused more on what was happening behind Eric. Then he licked his lips and returned to Eric, blinking with fascination at the turmoil creasing Eric's features.

"There's nothing else like it," he continued. "Having someone possess you so completely, feeling them move inside you like that ...the energy, the power, the passion ...it is the most amazing rush." He lifted Eric's hand, guiding him to touch him, to try again. Eventually, Shaun was able to release Eric's hand and relax as Eric continued of his own accord. He closed his eyes and let the tension in his body rise and fall, each time closer to completion. He thought it would be a good first step for Eric to finish him.

Shaun gasped, and his eyes flew open, his breath shuddering out of his body in surprise when he felt Eric's mouth close down around his cock. He looked away and steadied his breathing so as not to spook him, but reached over and touched Curtis' arm.

Curtis turned toward Shaun and almost laughed aloud. He leaned closer to Attila and whispered something in his ear, prompting him to look up, whereby Attila immediately pushed Curtis off him so he could make his way over to Eric.

Attila touched Eric's shoulder, and then held Eric's face when he released Shaun and sat back, breathing heavily.

"You don't have to do this for me," Attila said.

"I want to," Eric replied then kissed Attila and pulled him close to his body. "I want to experience what makes you so happy."

"Sweetheart, it doesn't work that way." Attila brushed his hand along Eric's face and studied his eyes, and smiled. "I know you love me, and I appreciate you valorous effort to understand me, but there are going to be some things that remain a mystery to you."

Shaun shifted around, annoyed. Someone was tapping on the door. "I'll get it." He slid off the bed, pulled the curtain across, obscuring the scene unfolding, and tugged on a robe, then struggled with the latch and threw the door open.

"Oh hey," Ming said. "I was just wondering if I could talk to Eric for a second. It's important."

"He's extremely occupied at the moment," Curtis shouted from beyond the curtain. "Extremely."

Shaun grinned at Ming. "Apparently, Eric is occupied. Is there anything I could offer you to make your visit with us more memorable?" He sat down on the top step and attempted to wrap his robe around his knees, to keep Ming from sneaking a peek.

"Perhaps a soda or a good old fashioned blow job?" he added, but then, a loud groaning sound erupted from the curtained area followed by some soft whispering. Shaun laughed and clasped his hands together. "I'll be damned. He did it."

Ming pushed on Shaun's shoulder and tried to get past him, but Shaun shoved him back down the stairs.

"What the fuck, Ming?" Shaun said.

"What's going on in there?" Ming shouted into the camper.

"None of your fucking business," Curtis replied, whipping the curtain aside, glaring at Ming. Then threw it closed again.

Ming had seen enough in that brief second of the curtain being drawn to start a cycle of twisting panic and confusion. He might've misinterpreted what he'd just seen, but all three of them had definitely been naked, and Eric had been straddling Attila's reclined body, kissing him. He sunk down onto the bottom step. His eyes hadn't been deceiving him. Curtis had been positioned behind Eric, and he'd been gripping onto Eric's hips as he thrust into him.

Ming's head snapped up when Shaun patted him on the back.

"I need to get back to these guys, or I'll miss my turn," Shaun said but then paused before he got up. "Ming, sweetheart, you need to understand something. Eric and Attila mean everything to Curtis and me." He smirked when it looked as if Ming was about to faint. He'd never liked the guy, the make-up and preening, and cutting remarks. Always swooning over Eric like a disgusting, little lovesick faggot. Shaun spat past Ming onto the sand. He'd love to see Ming curled up on it—bloody, beaten and crying for mercy.

Shaun shoved Ming away from the door, making him stumble.

"In Eric's mind," he said, "he needed to experience this for Attila. I know it must seem strange to you, but Eric did it because he really loves Attila and would go to any lengths to keep him."

Shaun paused for effect.

"Something you weren't able to do," he said, sneering. "If you'd been able to keep Attila satisfied, he wouldn't have needed to run around behind your back, screwing every guy he could get his hands on, including Eric."

Seth sat back with his drink and tried to follow the conversation between Dixie and Kevin, but there was too much of their history steering the current topic for him to understand what they were talking about. He sighed with relief when Ming walked in through the front door but was soon on his feet when it appeared as though Ming was about to break down in tears.

He raced up the stairs as Ming headed for their bedroom, only just managing to get his foot in the door before Ming would've slammed and locked it.

"Ming. What's wrong now?"

"My life sucks." Ming released his hold on the door and

let Seth into the bedroom. "And Shaun is a lying, self-righteous prick."

"I'm starting to think this holiday with your so-called friends wasn't such a great idea." Seth dropped down into a chair and crossed his legs. "So far, I've had to throw one guy out because he's essentially a violent sex offender. Another one, the self-righteous prick, was institutionalized because he was raped in high school ...but for some reason he's in love with and married to the person who deliberately led him to said rapist ...never mind that said husband, according to detective numbnuts down there, is a raving lunatic and they make a living by prostituting themselves?"

He stopped and took a deep breath. "The football player is a complete testosterone-fueled hothead, and his boyfriend—" Seth held up his hands as Ming made to interject. "I'm sorry, Ming. I know you were in love with him, but that Attila is seriously dangerous. He's got Eric wrapped so tightly around his little finger that he could get Eric to do absolutely anything."

Ming groaned and leaned his head against the window.

"What now?" Seth asked with exasperation.

Ming banged his head on the glass a few times. "Did I ever tell you I had a serious crush on a football player?"

"Ming.... No." Seth dropped his face into his hand. "Is that why you wanted to go out to the trailer? So you could talk to Eric?"

"I thought it would be good to clear the air." Ming sighed. "Let all my past obsessions go. To start anew."

"And? What did he say?"

"I didn't get a chance to talk to Eric. He was too busy making out with Attila while Curtis fucked him up the ass."

Seth stared at Ming in silence.

"Say something." Ming turned back toward the window.

"I'm at a complete loss." Seth paused, his mind reeling with the absurdity of recent events. "Other than the fact that aside from Dixie and to some degree Kevin, your friends are fucking insane." He scrubbed his face anxiously with his hands. "I'm losing faith in humanity. Who isn't here yet?"

"Candace. She had a baby with Kevin back in high school."

"Good, that's not too unusual nowadays."

"Except everyone thought it was Eric's, including Eric because Candace had a tendency to sleep around. And Attila helped to deliver the baby during a time when Candace thought Attila was Annie." Ming paused. "Oh …and that was also the night Attila tricked Eric into fucking him." He looked at Seth. "That's why Attila broke up with me and quit school."

Seth exhaled the breath he'd been holding.

"All right," he said. "Who else?"

"Just Ed and Timothy."

"Please tell me they're a normal gay couple."

"No, Ed is short for Edwina. She's Attila's cousin."

"God, no!" Seth ran his hands through his hair in exasperation. "Then please tell me she's completely sane in comparison to Attila."

Ming shook his head *no* and smiled.

"She's really nice though, in a quirky way," he said. "A little bit excitable, but she means well."

Seth rose from his chair and crossed the room to stand beside Ming. "Do you think I'm too old for you?"

Ming turned and straightened out Seth's rumpled collar and ran his hands down Seth's chest. "Where's that coming from?"

"Your friends. They're so different from anything I've ever experienced before."

"They're different from anything *anyone* has ever experienced before. It has nothing to do with your age."

Seth cupped Ming's face in his hands. "Good, because you've done something to me. Something I never expected, or even knew I wanted." He continued when Ming looked at him expectantly, waiting for him to clarify what he meant. "My whole life I've only ever wanted one thing. To be rich and successful."

"Well, you certainly managed that."

"Funny thing though." Seth smiled. "It wasn't until I met you that I was able to enjoy any of it."

Ming bit his lip in thought and confusion.

"You like watching me shop?" he said.

Seth laughed and pulled Ming into his arms. He held him tight then leaned back so he could look into Ming's eyes.

"No, silly," he said. "I'm in love with you. I never thought I'd meet someone I wanted to share my life with, but here you are—" He lowered his gaze. "I know you don't feel the same way about me, but maybe over time you can grow to love me."

Ming rested his head against Seth's chest and tried to come up with the words for how he felt. He wrapped his arms around Seth's waist and turned his head so he could hear Seth's heart beating.

It was thrumming rapidly and nervously beneath the surface, waiting for him to respond.

"You're right," Ming said. "You've provided me with everything a boy could ever want …but I'm not in love with you." He held on tighter as he felt Seth's body tense. "Just a second. I'm not finished." He lifted his head and kissed the spot on Seth's chest just above his heart. "I do, however, love you. It's not the same as what you're feeling. I love you. But I'm not in love with you."

Ming looked up at Seth. "Do you understand what I'm saying?"

Seth nodded his head. "Do you still want to marry me?"

"Of course I do." Ming stepped back and held both of Seth's hands. "What on earth would I do without you? And I'm not talking about the money?" He lifted Seth's hands to his lips. "You're my best friend. You get me, even when I don't."

"So, you don't mind marrying an old fogey like me."

Ming smiled mischievously. "Well now, that all depends. Having a best friend is great, but if we get married I expect to be fucked on a regular basis, or I'm going to get a little testy."

"That won't be a problem," Seth said as he tucked his hands under Ming's shirt and pulled it off over his head. He bent down and started licking and kissing at the skin of

Ming's neck, savoring the sweet taste of the body butter Ming caressed himself with each day, then slipped down and deftly untied the silk house pants Ming was wearing, letting them drop to the floor.

He stood up as Ming stepped out of them.

"I seem to have lost my clothing somehow." Ming ran his hands seductively over his own body and sighed softly as his fingers brushed across his smooth, warm skin. He turned toward the balcony door, slid it open, and stepped out onto it, shaking his hair out as the evening wind swept across him. Then leaned back against the railing, and looked up at the sky; the stars were just starting to twinkle into view.

"That's a pity about your clothes," Seth said. "What are you going to do about it?" He sat down on the bed and watched Ming spin his body along the perimeter of the balcony, and felt his desire rise each time Ming stopped at a bar in the railing and used it to undulate his body close to the ground and then back up again. Ming's ability to drive him to the very edge of distraction without even touching him was one of the many things he loved about him.

"I shall have to make the most of it." Ming worked his way along until he was next to a long marble bench that looked out over the ocean. He climbed up onto it and stretched out on his stomach, checking to make sure Seth was still watching. He looked out across the beach. They were on the second floor, but there were still a few people wandering around that would be able to see the bench if they looked up. Ming decided he didn't care if anyone saw him. As long as they didn't call the authorities. He needed to erase the image of Eric and Attila together in the camper.

He rolled onto his back, immersing himself in the moment, and began stroking himself. As his need increased, Ming thrust his hips into the air, his body writhing across the cool marble until his mind began to blur. He arched his back, pushing hard into his hand and let the euphoria sweep over him as he continued to build to his cresting point, stroking and thrusting increasingly faster, desperate to reach his goal. His heart hammered in his ears as he looked up at the darkening night sky and released himself, the warm drops of exhilaration showering his face and chest, mixing with the mess of tears leaving streaks down his cheeks. There'd be no forgetting what he'd seen. There'd be no forgetting Attila.

Ming slipped off the marble bench back onto the balcony when someone below on the beach started clapping and whistling. He peered over the edge to see who it was.

"Hey, Ming!" Ed jumped up and down on the sand, waving her arms around. "We've been knocking like crazy. No wonder you didn't hear us." She shoved the tall guy poised sedately beside her in the arm. "What did I tell you, Timmy, old boy?" She laughed and redirected her attention back to Ming. "I told him, my friend, Ming, is one crazy sex kitten. But he didn't believe me."

Tim nodded his head at Ming and waved.

"I stand corrected," he said. "Can you let us in? I really have to piss, and Eddie won't let me defile the beach for some reason." He grinned sardonically. "I think you managed to though. I know I had to step back." He creased up, no longer able to contain his amusement. "That's quite the range you've got on that thing."

Ming groaned with embarrassment and motioned for them to head to the back patio door. He used a towel to wipe off and pulled his house pants back on, and kissed Seth on the shoulder.

"We'll have to continue this later," he said.

Seth laughed and smacked Ming's ass as Ming headed toward the door. "I sure the hell hope so."

Ming sped down the stairs to open the door for Ed and her boyfriend, wondering where the hell everyone else had gone.

Chapter Nine

Truth

Eric shoved Shaun and covered his head in frustration at the turn of events. He'd been certain things would've worked out differently.

"No! Are you fucking kidding me?" he shouted.

"I know. Did you see that?" Shaun replied. "He was so close. But that last fucking turn got him again."

He slammed his hands together with exuberance, pleased that Eric had suggested hanging out with him to watch motocross racing in his room. They didn't have a television in the trailer, and Curtis hated any kind of sports, so it was rare that he had an opportunity to sit around and enjoy them with someone.

Curtis had headed out to look into some real estate, and Attila had gone with him to keep him on track, leaving Shaun and Eric on their own for the afternoon. Shaun's trust fund money had finally been released after much contention from his parents, and he and Curtis had decided to use the money to buy a small nightclub in Mexico. Shaun had looked at a few places with Curtis already, but he didn't want to get overly involved until a club was secured, and then he would step in and organize the actual running of the business. He was glad Attila had taken his place today because the possibility was always there that Curtis would sign something he didn't understand; he still stubbornly refused to admit he couldn't read half of what was put in front of him.

Eric changed the channel and hit the mute button. "There's a baseball game starting in about twenty minutes. Did you want to stick around?"

"Sure. But do you mind if I crash until then? Your bed is way more comfortable than the old thing in our trailer." Shaun flopped down and pulled a pillow under his head. "I think Curtis and I are going to take Ming up on his offer of that room. It would be nice to get a proper night's sleep for a change." He rolled back, poised on his hip, and looked at Eric. "You'll wake me in time?"

"Yeah, sure. Just throw me that other pillow, would you?"

Eric took the pillow Shaun handed him, tucked it behind his head, and flicked through the channels until he found the one that would have the game he was waiting for. He deactivated the mute button on the remote and turned the volume down, wanting to hear when the game started, and closed his eyes. He and Attila had stayed up late the night before, talking about their future plans, and he was feeling the effects of the mostly sleepless night.

He opened his eyes again and yawned, confused as to when he'd rolled on to his side. He peered over his shoulder at the television. There was a golf tournament on. Disoriented, Eric reached for the bedside table in search of his phone to see what time it was but was impeded by a heavy arm draped across his waist. He looked down at it and noted the wedding ring.

He rolled back and shoved Shaun with his elbow.

"Shaun, wake up."

"What?" Shaun opened his eyes and squinted at the brightness shining in through the doorway of the bathroom due to the sun moving its way around to that side of the house. He pulled his arm off Eric and rolled over to face the other way. "Sorry. Force of habit. I always end up hanging all over Curtis at some point."

"Yeah, Attila does the same thing." Eric looked at the bedside table, but couldn't see his phone. "What time is it?"

Shaun reached for his phone and checked it. "Three thirty." He looked at the television, expecting to see the baseball game in progress. "Did we miss the game?"

"Yeah, I fell asleep. You don't want to watch golf, do you?"

"No, I can't stand golf. I'd rather go back to sleep if that's all right with you. Curtis said he'd be back at five." Shaun stuffed the pillow further under his head, keeping his back to Eric, and sighed with contentment as he allowed himself to fall back asleep.

Eric lay back down and rolled over to face Shaun, too tired to get up and close the bathroom door to keep the sun from shining in his eyes. The steady rise and fall of Shaun's sleeping form caught his attention, and his eyes wandered, intrigued by the gentle curve of Shaun's neck and the length of his tanned arm poised like a picture frame over his broad muscular back.

He tentatively reached out and let his fingers brush

along the soft indent between Shaun's shoulder blades, marveling at the warmth of his bare skin, and felt Shaun shiver at his touch. His body responded with a surge of urgency, prompting him to move closer and let the scent of Shaun's skin fill his senses until he couldn't resist tasting him.

He hadn't been able to remove the memory of what they'd shared in the trailer, their bodies fitting against and inside each other as if they'd been designed to do so.

Eric's mouth closed down on the nape of Shaun's neck, and he pulled him closer, pressing him firmly against his own body. His mind went blank, and his body took over when Shaun sighed and reached back for him, forcing Eric's hips to thrust willingly against Shaun's ass, sending his need escalating.

His tongue took the taste of Shaun's fervent, charged skin into his mouth as he caressed his way along Shaun's spine, lingering as each seductive tremor glimmered through Shaun's body, only pausing briefly to vanquish the swimsuit that was impeding his progress. He let his hands glide up Shaun's back as he dove deeper, thrilling in the sounds of passion escaping from Shaun's throat as he savored the soft recesses of Shaun's willing desire.

Drifting back up along Shaun's body, Eric brushed his lips against Shaun's skin, and lowered himself down, breathing heavily. He kissed the smooth angle of Shaun's jaw and groaned in anticipation as Shaun shifted slightly and thrust his body into the bedding, his ass rising and falling, desperate to draw Eric into him.

Shaun shoved the pillow away and gripped the bed

sheets, quaking with need as Eric struggled to remove his own swimsuit. He tucked his head and let the mattress muffle his ecstasy-induced obscenities as Eric pushed into him, held him down, and began rocking him intensely, the power of Eric's hips forcing him increasingly further into the depths of the bedding.

He cried out as Eric's strong arms encircled him, crushing his already skewed reality, and held his breath until the final crest shuddered through Eric's body only moments after his own.

As he lay quietly, Shaun used the silence to try to ascertain what Eric was going through, emotionally, above him. He closed his eyes when he heard Eric begin to weep quietly, and struggled to release one of trapped his arms in an attempt to comfort him.

Freeing one, Shaun reached back and ran his hand through Eric's hair, relieved when Eric grasped it and clung to it.

"Do you want to talk about it?" Shaun asked, then rolled over and took a deep gasping breath when Eric climbed off and stretched out beside him. Eric was a much larger man than Curtis, and the extra weight had been a bit constricting.

Eric shook his head and shuddered as a sob escaped. He looked at Shaun staring at him, concern in his eyes, and felt his need surge again. He closed his eyes and tried to redirect his attention.

Shaun caught the uncertainty and desire wash across Eric's face as he studied him, and wasn't sure what, if anything, he should do about it. His body was telling him to pursue his impulse, but his heart and mind were undecided. All his reservations vanished when Eric reached for him, overwhelmed him, and proceeded to caress his mouth and body into an absolute wave of submission.

The fresh cool of the air conditioning inside the villa was a relief after spending an entire afternoon in an overheated car with an obese, sweaty real estate agent that insisted on smoking a continuous string of cigarettes. Of course, the whole experience wouldn't have been as irritating if they'd actually managed to find a club that suited Curtis' bizarre but specific needs. Attila couldn't wait to have a shower and wash away the heat of the day and pass out for a few hours with Eric, but when he stepped into their room, he found Eric hauling the sheets off their bed and gathering the entire mess of bedding into a rushed, unruly ball.

"Hey, baby," Attila said, smiling tentatively when Eric looked up at him. "Did you have an accident?"

"I was watching a baseball game," Eric replied, gripping the bedding tight against his chest. He shifted uncomfortably. "I spilled beer and chips everywhere." He avoided making eye contact as he pushed past Attila. "I'm going to throw these in the wash."

"All right," Attila said. "Did you grab a new set already?"

Eric turned back. "Yeah, there's a new set on the chair, but you don't …you don't need to put them on. I'll be back in a second."

Attila reached for Eric but relinquished his attempt

when Eric turned and hurried off down the hallway. He tossed his purse beside the bed, sat down on the edge of the mattress, and leaned back, inhaled deeply and closed his eyes, only opening them again when he heard someone step into the doorway.

"Shannon ...where's Eric?" Curtis asked, cautious, noting Attila's demeanor. Something was up.

"He's washing all the bedding," Attila replied. "Sheets, pillowcases, blankets—everything. He *says* he spilled beer on them."

"Really." Curtis stepped into the room and crossed his arms. "Hardly. That's not the smell of beer."

Attila dropped his gaze and nodded his head.

"Who do you think it was?" Curtis asked as he sat down beside Attila and put his arm around Attila's shoulders, waiting for him to make the first suggestion.

"It wouldn't have been Dixie—" Attila said, then shuddered and tried to quell the anxiety rising in his throat. "Or Edwina."

"Are you thinking it was Shaun?"

"Who else could it be?" Attila rested his head against Curtis' shoulder. "Eric has been spending a lot of time with him."

"Shannon, sweetheart," Curtis said. "Before you jump to any conclusions, let me talk to Shaun. If he was with Eric this afternoon, I have a hard time believing Eric would be open to anything more than wanking off to a few porno videos. What happened the other night was just a bit of experimentation." He kissed Attila's head, dismissively. "Eric loves you."

"Yeah, you're probably right." Attila sighed, unconvinced. "But why didn't he just say so. I don't mind if he was just jacking off with Shaun. But honestly …having to change all the bedding like that?" He shook his head. "How much jizz are we talking about?"

"Fuck, I don't know." Curtis stood up. "I'm going to go find Shaun. Hopefully, he'll be able to clear this up."

Curtis stood in the doorway and watched Attila fuss nervously with the hem of his skirt. He sincerely hoped Eric hadn't crossed the line and started fucking Shaun on his own time. He wouldn't put it past Shaun to do something like that; the boy was unstoppable. But he and Attila had been having some fairly serious discussions recently when Shaun and Eric were off rough housing and throwing a football around on the beach. It was becoming increasingly evident to him that Attila wasn't happy in his new body, and was regretting his decision to undergo the gender reassignment surgery, especially since, despite the physical changes, Eric still considered and treated Attila like a guy.

Turning away, Curtis headed toward the basement where the laundry room was located. Shaun hadn't been in the trailer, and he wasn't anywhere else in the house. He knew Shaun all too well. If he and Eric had hooked up earlier in the afternoon, and there was no other form of additional release available, Shaun would be wherever Eric was, looking for more.

He stood outside the door and listened, but could only hear the sound of the washing machine, so he tried the door.

It was locked.

Undeterred, Curtis fished some wire from his pocket that he kept for that specific purpose, and squatted down to work the lock. He soon had it unlocked and slipped into the space.

The basement, for the most part, was unfinished and appeared to run the entire length of the villa. Curtis stepped around the furnace area and peered into the darkness beyond. He could hear faint sounds coming from the far end; sounds as familiar to him as his own breath. He briefly considered turning back and opening a conversation with Shaun when he emerged, but in the interest of knowing the full truth, he needed to see the extent to which Eric had strayed.

Curtis kept close to the wall as he moved closer to where he could clearly hear the two of them. He felt his heart heave with sympathy for Attila at what his experience was telling him he would find happening around the corner.

He pulled in a deep breath and stepped out from where he was standing.

Eric was seated on a large crate that had been pushed up against the wall, and his arms were wrapped securely around Shaun's body as Shaun sat astride him rocking his hips to pull Eric's cock in as he devoured Eric's mouth, his ass clenching and releasing.

Curtis knocked loudly on the ductwork and received some satisfaction when Eric shot up, dumping Shaun onto the floor.

"Fuck, Curtis," Shaun said as he pulled himself to his feet. "What are you doing sneaking around down here?"

"Trying to determine what the two of you were up to this afternoon," Curtis replied. "Mystery solved."

Eric grabbed at the swim shorts pooled at his feet and pulled them back up around his waist.

"How did you know we were up to something?" he asked.

Curtis stuffed his hands into the pockets of his pants and paused, deep in thought, trying to figure out what if anything he should tell Attila. He redirected his attention back to Eric, deciding he needed to determine where Eric's head was at before making any decisions.

"For starters, Eric," he began. "Your sudden interest in doing laundry was a tad suspect. Secondly, your room smells like a fucking bathhouse. Did it not occur to you to open a few windows and air the place out before Shannon came back?"

Eric ran an anxious hand through his hair.

"Attila knows?" he asked.

"She knows you were having sex while she was out," Curtis replied. "And she suspects it was with Shaun." He leaned against the wall. "What the fuck were the two of you thinking? Shaun I can understand. He'll fuck anything. But you, Eric ...why?"

Eric sank down onto the floor and did his best to support his head in one hand. "I don't know what happened. One minute I was watching Shaun sleep, and then the next—"

"Oh no, you don't," Curtis said and stepped closer to where Eric was seated on the floor. "You can only use that kind of excuse once, Eric. And today ...today wasn't a one time, *Oops, I slipped into your ass* type of affair. You've been fucking my husband all afternoon. And now, here you are at it again."

Eric closed his eyes and tried to organize his thoughts. He knew Curtis wasn't upset about him fucking Shaun. They had an open relationship that way. Curtis was upset with him for betraying Attila's trust. He was overtly aware that Curtis and Attila had become closer over the past few days since they'd slept together, and it was a development that had been playing heavily on his mind, making him question things.

"What about you and Attila?" Eric asked Curtis.

"This isn't about Shannon and me," Curtis replied curtly. "We're just friends. You know that."

"Do I know that?" Eric stood up and brushed his hands off. "You're telling me the two of you haven't slept with each other again since the other night?"

"That's exactly what I'm telling you. Shannon is an amazing woman, but I'm not interested in her that way."

Eric wandered off to one corner of the basement then came storming back, waving his hands in irritation.

"Why do you insist on calling him that?" he shouted.

Curtis' eyebrows shot up in disbelief.

"Because that's her name," he said. "Shannon went through an unfathomable amount of physical and emotional anguish to become who she is today, and I have a lot of admiration for her. Whereas you …you can't even respect her enough to use the name and gender pronoun she feels she should've been born with."

"Attila will always be Attila to me," Eric said.

"So, Shannon's feelings don't apply?" Curtis asked. Then he inhaled sharply as something occurred to him.

"Fucking hell," he said. "You don't even know what your true feelings are toward her, do you?"

His face screwed up in anger when Eric looked away from him.

"Let it drop, Curtis," Shaun said, moving to intervene, but Curtis shook his head *no* and directed Shaun to stay where he was.

"You had strong feelings for Attila back in high school," Curtis continued, "and you thought those same feelings would materialize when you started seeing Shannon, didn't you?"

"You don't know what you're talking about," Eric said quietly. "I know how much I love Attila."

Curtis clicked his tongue and shook his head.

"See, there you go again," he said. "We all know you're in love with Attila. But are you in love with Shannon?"

"It's the same thing," replied Eric.

"Hm …interesting choice of words …*it*."

"Fuck off, Curtis. That's not what I meant, and you know it."

"All right, I'll back off on that one." Curtis crossed his arms, defiant. He was going to finish this.

"But tell me," he said, preparing himself. "Are you in love with a guy named Attila, or a girl named Shannon?"

Eric rushed at Curtis and pressed him into the wall.

"Let him go, Eric." Shaun raced over and shoved at Eric's arms, trying to get him to release Curtis. "He's just trying to mess with you. You know how he is."

"Shaun's right," Curtis said through strained intakes of air. "I'm just messing with you, but—" He coughed as Eric pressed him harder against the wall. "When exactly did you realize you wanted a cock between the legs of the man you love?"

Curtis closed his eyes and let his mind go blank as Eric's fist plowed into his face.

Attila rolled over, tucked himself against Eric's side, and kissed his shoulder. "What are you thinking about?"

"I was thinking I shouldn't have hit Curtis." Eric grinned and turned to face Attila. "I should've beaten the crap out of him."

"He was just looking out for me."

"I know. That's why I apologized." Eric kissed Attila's lips. "I know I've said it a million times already, but I'm so sorry for what happened between Shaun and me."

"Eric, it was a one time, drunken, impulsive thing. People make mistakes all the time. I've forgiven you. You don't need to keep telling me you're sorry. It was my fault anyway."

Eric's gut twisted. It was bad enough he'd lied about being drunk. Now Attila was blaming himself.

"How the hell do you figure that?" Eric asked.

"I shouldn't have agreed to the four of us sleeping together the other night. It opened the door for our relationship to go places we really didn't want it to go." Attila smiled at Eric and touched his lips. "You're all I need."

Eric sighed as his conscience rolled with guilt. Then he smiled, remembering what he'd been waiting to tell Attila.

"I talked to Ed while you were asleep," he said.

"About what?"

"About us having a baby—"

Eric held his index finger up to Attila's lips and grinned as tears began to form in the corners of Attila's eyes.

"You talked to her about that?" Attila asked.

"Yeah, she agrees that using her as a surrogate would be the best way for our baby to be as close to our own as possible. And she's all for it." Eric's eyes lit up as he recalled the conversation he'd had with Ed. "She's going to check out a fertility clinic here in town. She figures she's probably ovulating. They can check …so if we want …maybe I could, you know …if they can take us …I could head down there and make my donation."

Attila's face tingled with restrained excitement.

"She wants to do it now?" he asked in disbelief. "She wants to carry our child. Right now?"

Eric grinned and nodded.

"Oh, my god!" Attila exclaimed as he held Eric's face then lowered his voice to a whisper. "We're going to have a baby. You and me. We're going to be a family just like we talked about."

"We are." Eric kissed Attila's lips as convincingly as he could manage, then fought to remain focused on Attila's eyes. Because immersed in the blue depths of those eyes lay the man he loved. He whispered an, "I love you, Attila," then closed his eyes.

Mike pushed the front door open and looked out across the massive foyer and through to the view of the ocean beyond.

It had been a long trip, and he was excited to have finally arrived. The villa was everything Ming had said it would be. Unfortunately, they were the last to arrive, as everyone else had been there for a few days already, but Candace's passport had slowed things down a bit.

He set the bags down and listened out for anyone, but the house was silent.

"Everyone must be out," he said.

"Ming said our room is off the kitchen," Candace replied. "Let's take our bags down there and figure out which one it is."

She reached for her bag then pulled her hand back. Mike liked to be the one to do all the carrying of luggage or anything else he thought she shouldn't be doing. It was silly, but she enjoyed the extra attention, and it made Mike happy.

Candace had only been seeing Mike for about a year. They'd run into each other at a hockey game, and although it had initially been strange dating one of Eric's old friends, they'd gotten along so well that they'd moved in with each other after a few months. She was finding she liked having a man around the house, and her daughter Brittany had taken to Mike right away.

Mike stepped up to the door at the end of the hallway and pressed his ear against it to see if he could hear anyone inside. He smiled when he heard the familiar sound of Eric's voice and was about to knock when the sound of another voice in the room caught his attention. It was a voice he felt certain he'd heard before.

"Who did Ming say Eric was bringing with him?" he

asked Candace.

"His girlfriend, Shannon," Candace replied and stepped up to the door beside Mike, trying to hear what he'd been listening to.

She whipped around when she felt someone touch her shoulder, and found herself face to face with Kevin.

"Hey, Candace," Kevin said and then nodded at Mike. "How are you doing, Mike?"

"Good, how about you? You busy keeping the peace?" Mike shook Kevin's hand. "Brittany asks about you every day."

"She enjoys the letters and cards you send her," Candace added. "But she'd rather see you in person."

"I will as soon as I can. Maybe after we finish up here," Kevin replied unconvincingly. "How come you're standing in the hall?"

"We don't know which room is ours and I thought I heard Eric in this one," Mike answered. "Is this his room?"

"Yeah, he and Annie are in there," replied Kevin.

"Annie?" Candace exclaimed. "Like Annie, Annie?"

"I thought his girlfriend's name was Shannon," Mike interrupted. "Ming didn't say anything about him hooking up with Annie again." He sighed. "Candace really doesn't like Annie."

"Why not?" Kevin asked. "Annie's a riot." He smacked Mike's chest. "I didn't recognize her at first, and I don't know why she's going by the name Shannon, but she's got the most amazing—"

"Fucking bastard," Candace said and began hammering on Eric's door. "He just couldn't stay away."

"Candace, calm down." Mike grabbed Candace's hand to stop her from knocking, stepping back when Attila opened the door.

Candace pushed past Attila into the room and approached Eric.

"Where's Attila?" she asked.

"Attila's here? Awesome!" Mike shouted. "I haven't seen him in ages." He reached out and shook Eric's hand. "I thought I recognized his voice." He looked around. "Where is he?"

Attila turned to face the room after everyone was inside and raised his hand. He let his voice drop into its lower range.

"I'm right here," he said and looked toward Eric.

Eric nodded his head.

"Let me get this right." Kevin sunk down onto the edge of the bed and stared at Attila. "You're Annie's brother, Attila?"

"Actually, Kevin," Eric said. "Attila doesn't have a sister. Attila and Annie are the same person."

"You're one person?" Mike said to Attila then turned away in confusion, trying to wrap his head around what was being said.

Kevin remained silent, placing a hand over his mouth.

"Fuck," Mike said finally, breaking the silence. "No wonder I never saw the two of you together."

Attila smiled and raised his eyebrows. "Yeah, I kind of ran both personas past you guys in high school. I'm sorry." He looked at Candace. "Thank you for not telling anyone."

Candace sighed and rolled her eyes.

"You knew?" Mike asked Candace.

"Yes," she answered, tersely.

"But that means," Mike started. "Never mind." He turned to Attila and studied him more carefully. He let his eyes drift over the soft contours of Attila's bikini-clad body and then back up to Attila's eyes. "Jeez, buddy. What the fuck did you do to yourself?"

"It's a long story," Attila said.

Kevin scrubbed his face, deep in thought.

"Eric," he said. "We've been watching you chase after a topless Annie on the beach for days. We've had to sit through your make-out sessions, and I've personally had to listen to the two of you going at it night and day through the bedroom wall." He shuddered as the reality sunk in. "When were you planning on telling us that your girlfriend is actually Attila? A guy?"

"You were the only one over the last few days who didn't know," replied Eric.

"Thanks a lot," Kevin said. "Now I feel like a complete idiot."

"I'm sorry, Kevin," Attila said. "We should've been a bit more discreet. I wasn't thinking."

"No sweat," said Kevin. "It was fun while it lasted."

"So, Eric and Attila, together at last," Mike said, grinning. "I always knew something was going on between you two."

"How's that?" Eric crossed his arms defensively.

"You were always sitting together, whispering, and stuff," Mike answered. "And you used to look at each other all weird." He shoved Eric affectionately. "The guys all noticed, but we figured, whatever, if Eric wants to be a flaming faggot that's his deal as long as he doesn't bring it to our backdoor."

"I'm not gay," Eric said. "So, you can rest easy."

"Now I'm confused," Candace said. "If you're not gay, what's the deal with you and Attila? You are fucking him, aren't you?"

Curtis leaned against the doorframe in the hallway, listening to what was being said and decided to step in. He pushed through the door and shoved his way into the room.

"Her," he said. "Eric is fucking *her*. And *her* name is Shannon. Not Annie. And not Attila. I wish everyone would get it through their heads and stop with all this *he* crap. Shannon is a woman."

Attila's face flushed, endeared by Curtis' support. "Thank you, Curtis." He winked at him affectionately. "And, Mike, to answer your question more fully. I had a complete sex change."

"Jeez, Attila ...I mean Shannon." Mike cringed, scanning Attila's body again, and shivered. "That has to be sacrilegious or something. The sheer number of guys you went through. You were a shining example of a male libido gone amuck." He grinned and slapped his thigh, laughing. "You were an inspiration to us all."

"Attila. What the fuck?" Ming stepped in behind Curtis and pushed past him. "We were seeing each other when you were hanging out with Mike and the rest of Eric's little buddies."

"Ming, let's not do this right now," Eric said.

"No, I want to know exactly how many people Attila fucked while he was *only* sleeping with me. At first, I thought Shaun was lying to me …but then—" He tossed his hair to one side. "I knew. Deep down, I knew you were too good to be true, Attila."

"Ming, please—" Attila started.

"Stop." Ming threw his hands in the air in defeat. "I don't care. You can sleep with as many people as you want, Attila, because you and I …never going to happen again."

"That's good to hear." Shaun sidled up behind Curtis, wrapped his hands around Curtis' waist, and kissed the back of his neck. "What's the big pow-wow about?"

"We're just discussing how much of a slut Attila really is," Candace answered cuttingly. "Feel free to join in."

Eric rose to his feet. "Candace, that's enough." He looked over at Mike. "Would you rein her in please?"

"Yes, Candace, that's outrageously unfair," Shaun said then winked at Attila. "It gives us real sluts a bad name. Attila is a gem."

Candace stepped closer to where Curtis and Shaun were standing to confront Shaun, then something caught her eye.

"Is that a wedding ring?" she asked as she reached for Shaun's hand. Then she noticed the same ring on Curtis' hand.

She stared up into Curtis' face, aghast.

"We tied the knot about a month ago," Curtis said. "It was the only way to secure any kind of rights to Shaun's slutty, promiscuous ass." He directed his gaze at Eric and smirked.

Eric turned away, but Candace caught the look that had crossed Eric's face. Her head swam, and she suddenly felt the need to lay down. She scanned the room in search of Ming.

The atmosphere in the house had taken on a more relaxed and friendly vibe, partially due to the open conversations that had taken place over dinner and partly due to the amount of alcohol that had already been consumed. Ming suggested that everyone retire to the living room, and then he gathered up a platter of shot glasses and a bottle of tequila to keep things moving in an amicable direction. He motioned for Seth to pick up the game he'd brought with them and had him set it up on the large coffee table. Then insisted everyone settle in on the sofas in twos, as couples if possible so they could play the game.

"What kind of game is this, Ming?" Mike asked.

Ming sat back. "It's kind of like an ice breaker."

Ed leaped out of her seat and danced around, flailing her arms around in the air and bumping her hip into Timothy's shoulder. "It's a truth or drink game, isn't it? I love these."

"Seriously, Ming, do we have to play this?" Eric asked. "Haven't Attila and I shared enough truth for one day?"

"This will be more fun, I promise," Ming replied.

"At this point. I have nothing to hide." Attila leaned over and poured himself a shot of tequila. "I'm going to have this now because I don't expect I'll be drinking once the game starts."

Mike erupted, emitting a shrill whistle and clapped his

hands. "Go, Shannon! The bar has been set. Let's get this party started."

"All right, Mister Exuberance," Ming said, pulling open the first pack of cards and laying them out on the table. "We'll start with the easy cards and see how things go."

"Now," he said, making sure everyone was paying attention. "Each couple takes a turn picking a card, and everyone has to do what the card says. If anyone refuses to do or answer what it says on the card, they have to take a shot."

Kevin laughed. "So, the game is essentially self-correcting in terms of compliance."

"Exactly," replied Seth, feeling more relaxed around Ming's friends. "We've had a lot of fun with it." He laughed softly. "We've never actually played it with straight couples before, but—"

"They'll be fine, baby," Ming said and picked up the first card. He passed it to Seth to read aloud.

"Kiss the person in the couple closest to you," Seth said then threw the card down dramatically, laughing. "I guess I'm lucky your friend Dixie is cute, Ming."

Kevin shook his head and reached for the bottle on the table. "I'm sorry, but there's no way in hell I'm kissing Curtis freakin' Bantam. There's no telling where that boy's mouth has been."

"Wise choice," Curtis said. "We're out. Pour me one too." He took the glass Kevin handed him, toasted him, and tossed it back.

"All right, sex kitten," Timothy said to Ming. "Pucker

up," making Ming shriek with amusement as Timothy grabbed him, dipped him back, and laid a quick kiss on his lips.

Ed raised her eyebrows at Candace then shuffled over, pecking her fast on the mouth. She pulled back, snorting when Kevin started making stupid howling noises.

"Always so mature," Candace said and threw a cushion at Kevin's head.

Attila looked at Mike and tried to gauge his apprehension. "I set the bar, but that doesn't mean you have to meet me there."

"No, I'm fine," Mike said and readied himself. "I can do this."

He reached back for Candace's hand, gripping it, and closed his eyes as Attila made his way over from where he and Eric were sitting. The kiss was quick, and when he felt Attila moving away again, he released the breath he'd been holding.

"Well, that wasn't awkward," Eric said and grinned. "I'm going to pass." He motioned for Kevin to pass him the bottle.

"Hold on," Mike said. "I kissed Shannon even though my mind was screaming *Attila*. Surely you can kiss Shaun."

"Yeah, Eric," Shaun said as he moved down the sofa until he was right up next to Eric. "Don't you want to kiss me?"

"Shaun ...," Eric started, but then Shaun gripped his face, bringing their mouths together, and he found himself languishing in the taste of Shaun's mouth as he was consumed by him.

"You made your point, Eric." Mike laughed nervously when Eric and Shaun continued. "You can stop now."

Eric pulled away and wiped his hand across his mouth, fixated, his attention hesitant to stray from Shaun's face. He felt Attila's hand, which had been placed affectionately at the small of his back, retreat. Shaun just blinked at him, caught off guard, but recovered first, laughing and pounding Eric on the back.

"See," he said, his face lighting up. "We had Mike going there for a minute, Eric. We totally psyched him out."

"Real funny guys," Mike said and elbowed Candace. She just nodded her head as she studied the telling expression on Eric's face.

"Pick out the next card, Dixie, sweetheart," Ming said, trying to direct attention away from whatever was happening with Eric. It looked as if he was about to have an emotional meltdown.

Dixie followed Ming's lead and made a production out of choosing the next card and handing it to Kevin to read out.

"It's a truth card," Kevin said. "Whoever wins this one doesn't have to drink. But all the losers have to take a shot."

"What's the question?" Seth asked.

Kevin grinned. "How many people in the game have you slept with?" He flicked the card into the air. "I think Candace and I probably have this one sewn up."

"And who would be your third person?" Candace asked.

Ed hiccupped.

"You didn't?" Attila said to Ed.

"It was a moment of weakness," Ed replied sheepishly. "It's frightening what alcohol, hormones, and boredom can do to you."

"So, Candace and Kevin are both sitting at three," Ming recapped. "Can anyone else meet or beat that number?"

"Shannon and I are at three as well." Curtis leaned forward to confirm with Attila and then turned his attention on Eric.

Dixie crunched up her face in confusion.

"What about you, Eric?" Curtis coaxed sardonically. "How many people have you slept with in our little group of friends?"

"I'm going to pass," Eric replied.

"That's not how this card is played," Kevin said.

Eric slumped back in his seat. "Four. Are you happy now?"

Dixie looked around the room with curiosity. "Well, I know you never slept with me. And I'm going to rule out Kevin, Mike, and Timothy because boys that straight don't rock and roll for any reason." She tapped her chin in thought. "Ming would've told me if you'd slept with him. He's been jonesing for you since ninth grade."

"You're hilarious, Dixie," Eric said. "But you can stop now."

"Wait, I've almost got it," Dixie continued. "I think in all fairness, the winner of this card should be able to verify his or her number."

"I didn't sleep with him," Ed said. "Attila would've killed me."

"He's not my type," Seth added.

"Guys stop," Ming said, knowing where this was going to end up, having witnessed the encounter with Eric's fourth himself.

"Calm down, Ming. It's your game," Dixie said, then scanned the room as she re-evaluated who was next on the list.

Candace.

"Everyone knows Eric slept with Candace," she said.

"Who didn't?" Curtis said then stuck his tongue out at her.

"Well …Eric did Attila in high school," Candace said, shoving Mike out of the way so she could curl up in the corner of the sofa.

"You did what?" Mike asked Eric.

"Candace," Ming said, crossing his arms. "That was cruel and uncalled for. No one else needed to know about that."

"It doesn't matter," Eric said as he stared up at the ceiling. "I sleep with him all the time now. It's not a big deal."

"Her," Curtis corrected. "You sleep with *her*." He prepared to duck, but Eric remained where he was. He leaned forward. Eric was acting really strange. That comment should've set him off.

Candace pushed Mike away when he tried to restrain her from continuing. "Yes, but …," she said. "Attila was a fully equipped guy back in high school. You fucked a guy …behind my back."

"Candace, stop!" Mike said. "You've made your point."

Candace tucked her arms around a throw cushion,

bringing it to her chin as she sunk further into the sofa.

Dixie dropped her hands into her lap, regretting her decision to question Eric. She'd suspected Eric had likely been with Shaun at some point, but not Curtis, and certainly not both of them.

"So, that leaves you two oversexed hooligans," she said.

Eric groaned and tucked his head into Attila's shoulder. "I officially hate this game."

"I think we can all agree that Eric wins the slut card," Mike said. "So, let's move on and give the guy a break."

"Thank you, Mike." Eric leaned toward the table and poured everyone's shot. He hesitated and then poured one for himself. "I think I earned this …plus a few extras."

"Can I ask the four of you just one question?" said Kevin.

"No!" Eric, Attila, Curtis, and Shaun replied in unison.

"Fine," Kevin said. "It's not like I was hoping to glean some information for my upcoming *group sex for gays* book or anything." He pressed forward in his seat, poured himself another shot, and settled back into the sofa. "Hey, Ming. Out of curiosity. Could you pass me that pack of red cards?"

"Are you thinking about getting crazy, Kevin?" Ming teased as he passed the cards over to Kevin. "Keep in mind this game isn't intended for you straight folks. Especially the red cards."

Kevin read the first card, burst out laughing, and then screwed his face up in disgust at the next one. He shuffled the deck, lifted out a card, and held it up, turning it one way and then the other, trying to decipher it.

Dixie grabbed the card from Kevin, held it the right way up, and handed it back to him. "The diagram was messing him up."

"Diagrams?" Curtis asked, suddenly curious. "Can I see those?"

Shaun peered over Curtis' shoulder as he perused through the deck of cards Kevin had passed to him and shrieked with amusement as he read one that didn't contain diagrams.

"What does it say?" Curtis whispered.

"It wants you to demonstrate the most interesting position you've ever used with your partner," Shaun said. "I think we could give people a run for their money with that one."

Mike coughed in surprise. "You don't actually play this whole game, do you, Ming?"

"We have some very open friends," Seth said. "But even so, we don't tend to play the red position cards."

"And on that note," said Eric. "There's only one position I'm interested in right now, and that's the horizontal sleeping one." He covered his mouth and yawned quietly. "I've embarrassed myself enough for one night, and all this truth crap has worn me out."

"We'll see you guys in the morning," Attila said then rose to his feet, reaching for Eric's hands to help him up before they wandered off across the kitchen to their bedroom.

"We're off too," Curtis said, pulling Shaun to his feet. "We're going to hook up the swing and try a few positions of our own." Then he smacked Shaun's ass hard, chasing after Shaun when he took off for the front door, shrieking with anticipation.

Kevin shivered. "I'm sorry, but I still can't get used to Shaun being with Curtis like that. It makes my skin crawl."

"Count yourself lucky they didn't decide to demonstrate right here in the living room," Ming said. "Attila was telling me they actually do live sex shows together."

Kevin covered his ears and started singing loudly, trying to block out anything else Ming might have to say.

Dixie grinned and poured Kevin another drink.

"They're actually really good," Ed said. "It's not as weird as you might think. I thought it was hot."

"You've seen them?" Mike asked, dismayed.

"Yeah, those two can heat up a room like you wouldn't believe." Ed sighed dramatically in admiration. "You all saw them on the beach this afternoon. Imagine those hot, toned bodies sliding all over and into each other."

Ming licked his lips. "That does sound scrumptious when you put it that way. When and where are they performing next?"

"Enough!" Kevin leaped up and shoved Mike on the way past. "Can I borrow your laptop? I need beer and a plethora of *boy-on-girl* porn to clear these disturbing images from my head."

"Hold up. I'm coming with you." Mike kissed Candace and followed after Kevin.

"Wait for me," Timothy added, scrambling over the back of the sofa.

Seth watched the three men take off down the hallway.

"I'll never understand that," he said. "The beauty of the male form in the undulating throws of passion freaks them out, but they have no qualms about jacking off in front of each other."

Ming removed himself from the sofa and hung over the back of it to kiss Seth. He languished over the warmth and acceptance of Seth's mouth and moaned enticingly. "I feel like my form needs to be appreciated," he said and then headed for the staircase.

"That's my queue," Seth said. "Goodnight ladies."

Dixie stretched out and waved at Seth going up the stairs. "So, Edwina darling, why don't you tell Candace and me a bit more about this act of Curtis and Shaun's. And don't rush it. I want to get the whole hot, steamy *man-on-man* action burning in my mind."

Eric pinned Attila's hands to the pillow as he explored the heated pulse coursing just below the surface of Attila's skin. He brushed his lips along the soft indent of Attila's throat, savoring the vibrations created by the heavy sounds of passion escaping from deep within Attila's chest as he licked a line down between Attila's breasts. He inhaled the scent of the coconut tanning lotion lingering delicately on the taut, tanned skin of Attila's stomach and then paused. He laid his head on Attila's hip, thinking while letting his hand brush up and down Attila's thigh.

"What's the matter?" Attila asked as he pushed himself up on his elbows and tried to catch Eric's eye, but he was obviously deep in thought and not paying attention to him.

He lay back down and stared at the ceiling. This was the third time Eric had done this in the past couple of days. He tucked his arms across his chest and brusquely wiped away a stream of tears running down his cheeks.

"I'm sorry, Attila." Eric climbed back up the bed and dropped down beside him. "It's not you. I'm just tired." He rolled closer to Attila and kissed his cheek then rolled back away, pulling the sheet up over his shoulder.

Attila tensed, his stomach quaked, and he moved away from Eric, trying not to let on that he was on the verge of panic.

"Are you going down to the fertility clinic tomorrow?" he asked.

"We'll see. Shaun and I have a few things planned."

"Oh ...but it has to be in the next two days."

"I'm fully aware of that, Attila." Eric hauled the sheet tighter around his body and then threw it off. "Forget it. I can't sleep. I'm going to head out for a while. Don't wait up."

Attila closed his eyes and tucked himself up tighter, cringing as Eric headed out through the door.

Shaun paced the floor of the trailer, running his hand through his hair in frustration. He turned back and leaned against the edge of the bed, propped up by clenched fists, to try again.

"After what you just told me," Shaun said to Curtis. "I don't think it makes good business sense to set up a nightclub down here. I assumed you'd looked into all of this already. That everything was in order. But apparently, I should've been asking more questions." He sighed in exasperation. "Why didn't you tell me you didn't understand what the bylaws were stipulating in regards to the type of enterprise you were looking to establish?"

"Because I'm too stupid to even know what that means." Curtis shoved himself further away from the edge of the bed. "Believe it or not, some of us haven't gone to fancy business schools."

"Curtis, this is not about my education." Shaun grunted in irritation, prepared to berate Curtis once again. "This is about common sense and you refusing to let anyone help you when you don't understand something."

"I've managed well enough on my own."

"Really, you've managed all right on your own?" Shaun inhaled slowly, trying to control his rising aggravation. "You hustled your way through high school and then graduated to go-go dancing, live sex shows, and low budget porn flicks." He held up his hand to stop Curtis from speaking. "Yes, I know about the porn. Eric and I stumbled across a few of your stellar performances on the internet the other day. I can't believe you never told me."

"I didn't hear you complaining when I paid for the clinic."

"Don't you dare hold that over my head! I told you I would cover the cost of your shares in our corporation. Within a few years, your dividends should more than cover what you spent."

Curtis just stared at him.

"It's like you're speaking another fucking language," he said. "I don't even know who you are anymore. You've turned into one of those upper-class snots. All high and mighty, just like your parents."

Curtis reached across the bed for his cigarettes and lit one up.

"You don't know what you're talking about," Shaun replied.

"Give it up, Shaun. Ever since you got out of that clinic, you've been rapidly evolving into the man your tight ass little world had in store for you all along. I don't know why I even bother with you."

Shaun spun away from the bed and headed for the door.

"I'm going to sleep in the house," he said. "We'll talk more tomorrow after you've had a chance to pry your head out of your ass. Text me when the maneuver is complete." He clenched his jaw, his temper raging. "No wait," he added. "You can't do that, can you? That would require basic reading skills."

"Fuck you!" Curtis leaped off the bed, flew toward the door, and shoved Shaun out hands first onto the driveway.

Shaun picked himself up and spit in Curtis' direction.

"Fuck you too!" he shouted, brushing the gravel from his hands. "You fucking, low life …piece of trailer trash!"

Sobbing heavily, Shaun hauled the wedding band off his finger and threw it at the trailer where it hit with a click then disappeared in the underbrush lining the pavement.

He pulled his arm across his face to clear the tears from his eyes, refusing to look in Curtis' direction again, then headed down the embankment toward the beach.

Chapter Ten

Regret Overtakes Hope

Attila sat at the kitchen table, clutching the cold cup of coffee that Dixie had handed him almost forty minutes ago. He watched nervously as people moved about the house looking for any evidence that might suggest where Eric and Shaun had gone.

His head snapped up in anticipation when Curtis slid into the chair beside him.

"Shannon, sweetheart," Curtis said. "Ming just received a text from Eric ...so he's all right."

"Is Shaun with him?"

Curtis lowered his head. "Yeah, Shaun's with him."

"Where are they?" Attila gripped Curtis' arm. "Eric is supposed to go to the fertility clinic today. When are they coming back?"

Curtis' body shook as a wave of anguish flowed through him, and he dropped his head onto his arm now resting on the table.

"I'm sorry, baby," he said, "but they're not coming back."

"What do you mean they're not coming back?"

Attila stood up and scanned the room in disbelief,

looking for something that would prove Curtis wrong.

"Eric and I are going to have a baby," he said. "We're going to start a family together." He shook his head and wandered into the kitchen. "Eric loves me. He would never leave me."

"I don't understand it either." Curtis studied the faces watching them, hoping one of them would come up with an explanation, but no one spoke. "Maybe they'll come back," he said. "They'll realize they made a mistake, and they'll come back."

Attila looked down at his body and felt faint.

"It's because of this," Attila said as he ripped his shirt open, exposing his bare chest. He looked down at his breasts and cringed.

"He doesn't want me," he said, "because of all this."

"Attila, stop," Ming said. "You're not thinking straight."

"No, it is. I know it is." Attila struggled out of his shirt and tossed it on the floor, then began fighting with the buttons on his shorts. "Eric hasn't touched me in days. Ever since he had sex with Shaun. He doesn't want me, because of all this—"

He struggled with the shorts and threw them across the room, and then started hauling unsuccessfully at his underwear.

Dixie approached cautiously. "Attila, I'm sure your body has nothing to do with it. You're a beautiful woman. Something else must've been happening with Eric." She touched Attila's arm. "Why don't we sit down and talk about it?"

"Dixie's right," Mike said. "It's not about your body."

"Yes, it is!" Attila shrieked, grabbing a knife to cut the underwear from his body. "He's never accepted me as being a woman. Not ever. He's in love with a *guy* named Attila. Not me. Not Shannon. Not like this!"

He sobbed through a breath and stared down at the knife in his hand. There was only one solution.

Curtis screamed and scrambled across the surface of the table, pushing everyone aside to get to Attila. But he was too late. Attila had already used the knife to open up his chest in an attempt to remove one of the breast implants. He clutched at Attila's arm, fighting with him to release the knife, but Attila managed to take another slash at himself, digging the knife deep beneath his other breast, slicing open the silicone bag. As the fluid and blood poured down Attila's body, Curtis managed to slide the knife out of Attila's hand, drop it, and wrestle Attila to the floor, yelling for someone to throw him a towel and call for an ambulance.

Kevin stepped in with the intention of kicking the knife out of Attila's reach as Curtis pressed a towel into the large gaping wounds in Attila's chest, but Attila wrapped his fingers around the knife first, clinging to it.

Ming screamed for Curtis to stop him when he saw Attila draw the knife across his wrist.

Chapter Eleven

New Beginnings

The overhead fluorescent light buzzed to life, reminding Attila of a different time and place where anything had seemed possible. Where everything had felt like it was within his grasp. He remembered the night he and Eric had gone dancing after Candace had had her baby, and what it had felt like knowing Eric cared for him deeply, even though he was too scared to admit it.

Then he remembered he too had been too scared to tell Eric how he really felt. He sighed. If they'd just been honest with each other from the start, then things might've turned out differently.

It was morning, and now that the lights were on, it meant he would no longer be alone with his thoughts, which was fine with him. He'd done enough reflecting to last him a lifetime. They would be coming for him soon, and he was more than ready.

Attila turned his head and watched the man sleeping in the chair beside his bed. A man that was there every night when he went to sleep and every morning when he woke up. A man he'd come to rely on. The man that had saved his life.

He smiled as the man snorted and his head rocked about as the effects of the bright lights roused him.

"Good morning, sleepyhead," Attila said.

"Hey, beautiful boy." Curtis stretched out and turned his head from side to side, trying to work the kinks out of his neck. He'd been sleeping in that chair every night for three weeks now, and it was started to wear heavily on his body.

"You should be sleeping in the trailer," Attila said. "You're going to be crippled by the time I get out of here."

"Nope. If I did that, I'd have to forego seeing your beautiful face every morning when I wake up."

Curtis yawned and checked his phone.

"Anything?" Attila asked.

Curtis shook his head. "He'll call me. Shaun will call me. And everything will go back to the way it was before." He raised a hand, lifted the necklace from around his neck, and kissed the wedding band that hung from it—Shaun's wedding band. It had taken him forever to find it. Now it was safe. Safe and waiting for Shaun to return to him, and reclaim it.

He smiled when he looked up to see Attila watching him.

"So, today's the big day," he said.

"Yeah." Attila exhaled anxiously. "It'll be good to have this first surgery out of the way. Thanks again for doing this."

"Nothing but the best for you, baby."

Attila laughed and scrubbed at his hair.

"So, how much trouble are we going to be in when

Shaun finds out we've spent his trust fund money like this?" he asked.

"There's a lot more where that came from," Curtis replied. "So, let's not worry about Shaun and his family's money."

Curtis pushed himself up out of the chair and approached the bed. "Are you sure this is what you want? You can always back out. It's not too late." He placed his hand on Attila's chest. "Your face is almost a perfect match to your yearbook picture, and the boobs are already gone. Maybe you should leave it at that."

"I don't want to walk around in this body anymore," Attila said. "It's a lie. You know how I feel. If I'd just accepted who I was in high school, like Eric told me to, he might still be with me."

"You don't know that for sure."

"I know—" Attila closed his eyes. "I've been through this with the psychiatrist time and time again, and ultimately, I'm doing this for me, not Eric. Or any other guy."

Curtis leaned down and kissed Attila's head. "You understand it's not going to be the same. The doctor says your prostate is still good to go, and this new method they're using is pretty damn amazing, but it'll never be like it was."

Attila acknowledged him with a sedate nod.

"See, now, that would put me off right there," Curtis said.

"It doesn't matter. It's not about sex." Attila sighed in resignation. "I just want to be a guy again." He grinned, catching Curtis' attention. "You'll still adore me, won't you?"

"Only if you keep your hair like that. Very hot." Curtis ruffled Attila's short, bleach blond hair. "I always loved the way you used to wear it." He grabbed Attila's chin roughly and kissed his cheek. "Pity about the facial hair though. I like a good rough face on my ass in the morning. Who knew lasers could be so effective?"

Attila smiled and then blinked, in thought. "Do you really think we'll see them again? Eric and Shaun, I mean."

"You know I want nothing more than to have my husband back with me where he belongs." Curtis gripped Attila's hand, squeezing it as one of the orderlies came in through the door. "But right now …you're the person that means everything to me."

Attila's eyes filled with tears and he nodded. "Who would've guessed it? That you'd end up being the best friend I've ever had."

"Ditto, blotto," Curtis replied then smirked at Attila's expression. "You too, Attila. You too." He ducked his gaze. "I'll be waiting right here for you." He squeezed Attila's hand again, only letting go when the orderly began moving the bed away.

"You better come back as a boy," Curtis said through a smile so forced, it hurt. "Or I'll be asking for a refund." Then he sunk back into his chair as Attila was rolled out of view, and tucked his face into his hands, and began to cry. He cried for all he and Attila had lost …and for all they had gained together.

Chapter Twelve

Prodigal Son

The music reached its crescendo and then sank back into a steady rhythm, sending masses of bodies in the direction of the bar to refill the drinks they'd burned through on the dance floor.

Attila quickly checked the levels of his mixers and prepared himself for the onslaught. Every weekend it was the same thing, lots of people and lots of money to be made. If there was one thing Curtis knew how to do, it was fill a nightclub.

Attila looked out across the floor, trying to spot the familiar, black silk shirt and red suspenders that Curtis insisted on wearing while he was mingling with the crowd as the club's manager, but he couldn't see him. He briefly considered calling Curtis on his cell to ask him to send some reinforcements but decided against it when a server named Daniel stepped up to the bar.

"Hey, hot stuff. How are you holding up?" Daniel asked.

"I could use your help actually," Attila replied, thankful for the offer of assistance. He was being slammed with drink orders.

Daniel dropped his tray onto the bar and slung a towel over his shoulder. "Your wish is my command."

"Thanks. I appreciate it." Attila moved over as Daniel took a spot beside him behind the bar.

"You can show me your appreciation later." Daniel winked at Attila then discreetly let his hand drop behind the bar, where he set about caressing Attila's ass as he took the next order.

Attila's face flushed, but he managed to focus his attention and sunk back into the routine that had become part of his life for the past eight years. After being released from the hospital, Curtis had used the balance of Shaun's unclaimed trust fund money to buy a west coast apartment in Vancouver, BC for the two of them. It was a large two bedroom, tenth-floor apartment with a fantastic view of the ocean, and Attila absolutely loved it there.

They'd briefly been without work, but after a few meetings with some of Curtis' previous clients and a recommendation from Mr. Jenkins of all people, Curtis had landed a managerial position at an up and coming nightclub called *Sinders*, geared exclusively for the young urban gay population of the city, and he was thriving in the position.

Attila rechecked the floor, looking for Curtis, and spotted him chatting up a prospective business client. He nodded when Curtis looked up and smiled at him.

"So, Attila?" Daniel wiped the counter down in front of him and cleared the deck for the next set of orders. "What's the deal with you and Curtis?"

"We're friends," Attila replied. "Have been for a long

time."

"Is Curtis really as good as everyone says he is?"

Attila laughed. The number of times he'd been asked that question. "You know what they say. Fuck of a lifetime."

"So, you guys aren't partners or anything?"

"Curtis and me—" Attila laughed again. "No."

"But you two live together, don't you?"

Attila reached over and pulled a few glasses from the dishwasher, swearing at how hot they still were. He needed to remind Curtis to have someone fix the cold rinse.

"We're just roommates," he answered.

Daniel stopped and set his hands on his hips. "So, if I came back to your place, and you fucked me all night long, Curtis wouldn't have a problem with that?"

"He wouldn't have a problem, but I might." Attila grinned at Daniel and stole some of the limes from his garnish container.

"Fuck, are you serious?" Daniel stood back and took in the sleek contours of Attila's body. "Why is it every time I meet a hot guy I actually get along with, he turns out to be a bottom?"

Attila patted Daniel on the back.

"Statistics are against us," he replied then stretched out his shoulders as the last order was removed from the bar. Curtis' daily regime of exercise had done wonders for the development of his male physique, but sometimes Curtis had a tendency to push him too hard, and he was feeling the aching effects of it.

"So …do you and Curtis ever fuck around?" Daniel asked.

Attila laughed loudly. "Only when we're bored of what's on television and we've had too much to drink.

He grinned, watching Daniel's expression.

"So, yeah," he continued. "Pretty much every night."

Daniel shook his head, then stared across the crowded dance floor to where Curtis was standing.

"Some girls have all the luck," he said.

"Tell you what." Attila crossed his arms. "I like you. I'll talk to Curtis and see about taking you home with us tonight."

"Like …all three of us …together?"

"That's usually the way we do things. Curtis won't bring anyone home to play with unless he gets my approval first. And quite honestly, the chances of him picking you out of the crowd are slim to none. I'm your only hope of getting anywhere near him. And that's what you're actually looking for, isn't it? To be fucked by Curtis Bantam."

Attila turned back toward the bar and poured himself a soda. "If you're not all right with our arrangement, then there's not much else I can offer you."

Daniel moved to speak but was interrupted by a voice behind them.

"I'd definitely be up for that."

Attila's head snapped up.

It hadn't been Daniel who'd spoken. He stepped back from the bar and fought to keep his anxiety in check as it surged to overwhelm him. "What the fuck are you doing here, Shaun?"

"Nice to see you too," Shaun replied, a smug grin radiating across his face. "I'm looking for Curtis, but I saw you, *Annie* darling, standing over here, and I had to see for myself if it was really you." Shaun examined Attila's face, then sneered.

"You look almost the same as you did in high school," he said, briefly looking in Daniel's direction to ensure he was listening.

"Miraculous what a little plastic surgery will do," he continued. "Are you all boy bits now? I mean *again*?"

Attila crossed his arms, rebuttal at the ready.

"Yes, I am …thanks to you."

"What do you mean, thanks to me?" Shaun grimaced disgustedly as he realized what Attila was implying.

"Are you fucking kidding me?" he replied then motioned his hand in Attila's direction. "Curtis paid for all of this? He spent *my* money on you?"

"Yes, he did," Attila replied, smiling. "Curtis is very generous."

"Let me get this straight—" Shaun stammered in restrained anger. "He used my trust fund money to pay for *your* surgery?"

"Part of it." Attila leaned on the bar, eager to volley the next shot. It had been eight years since Shaun had absconded with Eric. In those eight years, Shaun hadn't bothered to contact Curtis even once. Now, he just shows up unannounced?

"He used the rest to buy us a really nice condo," he finished.

Shaun reached for a stool so he could sit down before he fell down. "Are you two …together?"

"Maybe." Attila grabbed a straw from a container

behind the bar and began chewing on it. "What about you and Eric?"

"Yeah, ...that only lasted about a month." Shaun sneered condescendingly, regaining the upper hand, enjoying the look of anguish on Attila's face.

"A month?" Attila turned from the bar and scrubbed a hand across his face, clutching at his stomach as a sob escaped. He looked over at Daniel, who was watching him nervously.

"Daniel, could you take over the bar for me?" he asked.

"Sure thing, Attila," Daniel said. "Should I call Curtis?"

Attila nodded his head and motioned for Shaun to follow him into the small storage room behind the bar. He sat down on the edge of a large crate, wrapped his arms around his body, and began rocking himself.

"You were only together for a month?" he asked again.

"It was a mistake." Shaun sat down across from Attila. "We thought something was happening between us, and we had fun fucking each other for a while, but honestly the sex wasn't that great, and Eric didn't like me picking up tricks when I was bored."

He paused in feigned thought.

"You know, Attila," he said. "I'm not even sure Eric's gay. I think he likes pussy better."

He cupped his hand to his mouth.

"Oops," he said, malice taking hold of his expression. He delivered the final blow. "I guess yours is gone now. Too bad."

Attila steadied his breathing, refusing to let Shaun's malevolent personality inflict any pain.

"Did he tell you why he left me?" he asked, hoping Shaun would at least extend him this small courtesy.

"No, we didn't talk much about that. We did try to find you and Curtis. But no one knew where you were."

"Bullshit ...we've been right here in Vancouver for over eight years. Every single one of our high school friends knows that."

Attila glared at Shaun.

"And," Attila added. "We're both in the fucking phone book!"

"I'm sorry, Attila. Maybe ...maybe neither one of us was ready to find you and Curtis. We probably could've tried harder."

Attila exhaled in frustration and wiped a new stream of tears from his face, and glanced toward the door.

Curtis was leaning against the doorframe, beaming.

"Hey, sport," he said to Shaun.

Shaun whipped around and rose to his feet, letting the emotions course through him. After all that time away, Curtis still wanted him. Still loved him. He could see it in his eyes.

He ran straight for Curtis' outstretched arms.

"I missed you so much," Shaun said as he buried his face into the side of Curtis' neck, inhaling the familiar cologne, and clinging desperately to him. This man truly was, the love of his life.

"I love you so much," he said. "I am so sorry for leaving you."

"I love you too, baby." Curtis kissed the side of Shaun's head. "I knew you'd come back to me." He reached into his shirt and pulled up the necklace that was hanging behind the neat row of buttons.

"Is that my ring?" Shaun stepped back and steadied his breathing. He'd been sure the ring had rolled off into the underbrush and been lost when it hit the pavement that day. The sight of it in Curtis' hands made his heart surge.

Curtis undid the clasp, removed the ring from his necklace, and pushed the necklace into his pocket. He knelt down on one knee causing Shaun to sink onto both of his.

Shaun cupped Curtis' face in his hands.

"I promise I will never leave your side again," Shaun began. "My soul has been in tatters these past few years for want of you." He dropped his head, and his shoulders shook as he sobbed.

"Curtis, sweetheart," he said. "I have never loved anyone so much as you." He held out his hand for the ring. "Please. I want to be yours again. I want to be yours forever …for all eternity."

Shaun heaved and exhaled, falling into Curtis' arms after the ring was slipped back onto his finger.

Attila smiled through his tears when Curtis looked up at him. He blew him a kiss and clasped his hands together, holding them to his lips in thanks, praising the powers that be, that his best friend had the love of his life back—even if that love was for a man who had somehow come to embody evil itself. A man that caused him and Curtis an extraordinary amount of pain.

The pub was extremely crowded and loud, but Attila usually had good luck there, so he found himself a place to stand at the bar and nodded at the bartender to catch his attention.

"Hey, Josh," he said. "Busy night tonight."

"You not working?" Josh asked.

"No, I took the night off. I wanted to see what this place looked like on a Tuesday."

Attila looked around and cringed in response when the packed bar all hollered at an apparent goal being scored in whatever asinine game they were watching on the large televisions scattered throughout the establishment.

"Can I get you something?" Josh asked.

"Pull me something light. Surprise me." Attila checked along the length of the bar, trying to see if anyone was watching him.

"Josh," he said. "The guy in the white shirt down there."

"Yeah," Josh replied. "He's a regular."

"Is he straight?"

Josh laughed and nodded his head.

"Straight as they come," he said. "You know I should hang a warning sign around your neck when you come in here." He set the beer down in front of Attila and leaned on the bar. "You seem to be a decent enough guy, so I'm not going to get too worked up." He wiped down the bar and lowered his voice. "But the first sign of trouble with your trolling scheme and I'll have to ban you."

"There won't be any trouble. I'm always subtle."

"And yet they go home with you anyway."

"I never get them to do anything they don't want to." Attila winked at Josh. "You should come home with me sometime."

"Not in your fucking life." Josh pulled a bottle from behind the bar and a couple of shot glasses. "I'm strictly a pussy connoisseur."

"Well, I wouldn't know anything about that."

"Maybe you should try it sometime." Josh filled the two shot glasses and looked down along the bar. "I could hook us up with a couple of friendly girls. Make a night of it."

"A straight buddy of mine tried that once." Attila leaned closer to Josh and touched Josh's wrist. "The night ended with me jerking off and cumming at his feet while giving him a blow job."

Josh shuddered and pulled away. "Do you want me to send these down to him?"

"No, I'll take them down myself." Attila lifted the two glasses. "He looks harmless enough. Any priors?"

"No, he's pretty quiet. He's usually here with his buddies from work, but they must be running late. He's been here for a while."

Josh sighed, impressed.

"I don't know how you do it, Attila," he added.

"It's a finely tuned skill."

Attila moved away from the bar and carefully maneuvered toward where the guy he'd been eyeing was sitting.

"Hey, I've seen you here before, haven't I?" Attila asked as he came to a sudden stop, making it look as if he'd been rushing past on his way to somewhere else. "You're usually here with a bunch of friends, aren't you? Did they stand you up?"

"Yeah, they were supposed to be here like an hour ago."

Attila set the drinks down on the bar and slid in beside him. "Do you mind if I hang with you for a minute? My friends haven't shown up either, and I hate drinking alone." He slid one of the shots over. "I'm actually here celebrating a raise, so I'll buy."

"Sure, I'm game. I had a shitty day. I could use a few extra drinks." He furrowed his brow in thought and threw the shot back.

"Do you have a name?" Attila asked.

"Sorry, …name's Mark."

"It's nice to meet you, Mark." Attila leaned against the bar and looked back to where Josh was working and indicated for him to send another round.

"My name's Attila," he said then extended his hand and shook Mark's, his becoming lost in Mark's rough, callused one.

"That's a strange name," Mark said.

"My mother is a strange woman. What can I say?" Attila pushed the second shot toward Mark and reached for the beer Josh had pulled for him, and the second prearranged succession of shots.

"What do you do for work?" Mark asked, then quickly fired back two more shots.

Attila looked Mark over, taking note of the fact he was wearing paint-spattered jeans and work boots and was keenly interested in what was happening in the game on television.

"I'm a sports columnist," he replied.

Mark pulled his eyes away from the game. "No kidding. I wouldn't have expected that." His eyes darted to the game and then back to Attila. "Shouldn't you be watching the game?"

"No, I have to review a lot of different sports every day. I have an assistant that puts together the highlights for me."

"That must be pretty cool," Mark said, beginning to slur slightly, prompting his new acquaintance to steady him. He'd been there for longer than he'd intended, waiting for his friends, and had put away a fair amount of alcohol already. The additional shots were making his head swim.

"I've got today's tape back at my place," Attila prompted as he looked around. "It doesn't look like my friends are going to show up. What about yours? Do you see anyone?"

"Nah," Mark replied. "I've been stood up."

"Tell you what." Attila pushed the last shot toward Mark and leaned against the bar. "I'm not supposed to do this. It's against regulations. But did you want to take a look at today's tape?"

"Sure. Do you live close by?"

"Just about three blocks away, actually." Attila waved to Josh and then helped Mark toward the door. "You'll be back here in no time, just in case your friends decide to show up." He opened the door and stepped out into the cool of the evening. "Do you have your cell phone with you, in case they call?"

Mark stumbled and pulled his phone out of his pocket.

"Right here," he said.

Attila lifted the phone from Mark's hands and pushed it into his own pocket. The last thing he needed was Mark calling his friends and telling them where he was. He'd had that happen once. Luckily, Curtis had been home to help him that night, or he might've ended up in the hospital. It was a dangerous game he played, picking up straight guys, but it was usually worth it.

"I'll hang on to your phone for you," Attila said. "You're a bit drunk, and I wouldn't want you dropping it."

Mark stopped, almost toppling forward, and looked at Attila.

"You're not trying to pick me up, are you?" he asked.

"Of course not." Attila patted Mark on the back, rough and buddie-like to dispel Mark's suspicions, and directed him in through the door of his apartment building.

"Good," Mark said. "Because I wouldn't be into that."

Attila observed Mark carefully for any more signs he was going to spook and then stepped into the elevator with him. Once the door opened on his floor, he walked on ahead and let Mark follow behind him. If Mark's suspicions were getting the better of him and he was going to bolt, this was the time most guys decided to run.

He unlocked his door and stepped out of the way, ushering Mark to go on in ahead of him.

"Attila? Is that you?" Curtis called from the living room.

Attila threw his keys onto the console table in the front hall and directed Mark to take his dirty boots off.

"Yeah, it's me," he said, walking into the kitchen. "Were you expecting someone else?"

"Carol said she might stop by tonight," Curtis said. "She wanted to meet Shaun."

"I talked to her earlier. She got called into work." Attila retrieved Mark from the front hall, where he'd finally managed to pull his boots off, and brought him into the living room.

"Who's your friend?" Shaun asked.

"This is Mark. I was going to show him a few sports reels from today. But if you guys are watching a movie, we can wait."

"What sports reels?" Shaun asked, then jumped when Curtis smacked him across the chest. "What?"

"Sorry, Mark," Curtis said. "Shaun just moved in a couple of days ago. He doesn't know that Attila's a sports reporter."

Shaun's eyebrows shot up in confusion as he stared at Curtis, then startled when Mark fell against the back of the sofa.

"Whoa there, big fella." Curtis jumped up to steady him. "Maybe you should lie down for a minute."

"Nah, I'm good," Mark said and stumbled into Curtis.

"Yes, Mark has to get back to the pub," Attila said and turned back toward the kitchen. "His friends might be showing up soon."

"I don't know," Curtis said. "It wouldn't hurt if he stuck around for a few minutes until he got his feet back." He patted Mark on the back. "Don't you think?"

Mark nodded his head and swayed slowly, catching his balance against the wall.

"Is it all right if he lies down in your room, Attila?"

Curtis asked.

"I guess so," Attila said. "Tell him to take those dirty pants off though. I don't want him messing up my bedspread."

Shaun shifted over to accommodate Attila as he dropped down beside him and cracked open a beer. His attention returned to Curtis, who was leading Mark down the hallway to Attila's room.

"What the fuck was that all about?" Shaun asked Attila. "Color me clueless, but that guy does not look gay."

"He's not." Attila sipped on the beer and lifted his feet onto the coffee table, relaxing into the cushions.

"So, you just pick up random straight guys in bars and bring them home with you?"

"Pretty much, yeah." Attila looked over his shoulder when he heard Curtis making his way back down the hall.

"How's he doing?" he asked.

"Well, I took him to the little boy's room, and he was very obedient, but I'd give him a couple of hours," Curtis said. "He won't be much use to you right now. He's too drunk."

"You're party to this charade?" Shaun asked Curtis.

"Attila enjoys playing with straight guys." Curtis sat down on the other side of Shaun. "He waits until they sober up, and he never pushes them too hard, do you, sweetheart?"

"No, I've had plenty of guys get up and leave." Attila finished his beer then stood up, stretching himself out. "I'm actually exhausted …and cold. I got up way too early. I think I'll climb into bed and let Mark warm me up a bit. I'll see you guys later."

Attila stepped into his bedroom, quietly closing the door, so as not to wake Mark. Then he stripped off his clothes and climbed into the bed beside him. He adjusted his pillow so he could watch Mark sleeping, and ran his fingers lightly through Mark's hair, then closed his eyes, imagining it was his husband lying beside him and fell asleep. He opened them again when Mark began to rouse and prepared himself for Mark's reaction.

Mark inhaled sharply, then swore, and shoved Attila as he scrambled away from him, almost falling off the opposite edge of the bed.

"It's all right," Attila said. "I'm not going to hurt you." He moved closer and brushed Mark's hair away from his face, and made soft shushing noises until Mark relaxed and lay back down.

Mark looked around the bedroom. "How did I get here?"

"You came home with me." Attila traced a soft line down Mark's cheek and along his throat and then shifted up onto his elbow, placing himself face to face with Mark.

He breathed gently across Mark's lips and then ran his mouth along Mark's jawline to his ear.

"I must've been drunk," Mark said but didn't pull away.

"You're not drunk now. It's almost morning." Attila licked and bit lightly at Mark's ear lobe, and when Mark didn't object, he pushed his hand under the covers, brushing it across Mark's chest, and down along his body, then smiled knowingly; Mark was already starting to go hard. He began rubbing him through the material of his underwear.

Mark's hips shot back, and he grabbed Attila's hand.

"Don't," he said. "I don't want to do this."

"You can leave if you want to," Attila said. "But no one knows you're here. So, you might as well enjoy what I can do for you."

Mark released Attila's hand, removing a finger at a time, then gasped under his breath when Attila slipped it into his underwear and started stroking him more adamantly.

He tossed his head back and clenched his eyes shut.

"I'm not gay, you know?" he said to Attila.

"That doesn't mean you can't have a little fun." Attila reached across Mark's body and lifted a flavored condom from the jar he kept on his bedside table. He ripped it open, deftly rolling it into place beneath the covers, and laid a single kiss in the center of Mark's chest as he threw the blankets off. He tented a sheet over Mark's body and went down on him. In his experience, the guys were more apt to let him start if they weren't being reminded of the fact it was a guy blowing them. But once he had them going, fully aroused, their inhibitions usually dissipated rapidly.

Before long, Mark was groaning beneath him and thrusting his hips up in desperation, so Attila pulled the sheet away, enticing Mark to watch. It was all about timing and taking it in increments. When he felt Mark touch his shoulder, objecting, he climbed up Mark's body to Mark's mouth and kissed him, abandoning his attempt. He'd need to try something different. Stress Mark's body until he couldn't resist, couldn't deny his body what it craved.

Straddling Mark's hips, Attila used his hand to press Mark's thrusting cock against the back of his ass and waited for his reaction. The fire in Mark's eyes told Attila he was definitely ready to take things further, so he rose up slightly and began sliding Mark into him, all the while keeping his eyes on Mark's face.

When Mark closed his eyes in resignation, Attila knew he had him, and let his body accept Mark the rest of the way. He moaned and swore, quenched of his need, as he completed his decent.

As Attila pumped gently above him, Mark lifted his hands and placed them on Attila's hips, assisting him as he rose and fell.

Attila dropped his head back and began to ride Mark harder, prompting an ever-increasing volume of sound to escape from Mark's throat. When he felt the tension in Mark's body increasing to its breaking point, Attila pulled himself off and fell onto the bed. There was one more step he needed Mark to take on his own. He turned his head and winked at Mark enticingly, and was rewarded when Mark hauled himself off the bed and dropped down on top of him, taking Attila's mouth and running his hands up through Attila's hair, rubbing aggressively against his body.

Holding Mark's face, Attila broke the seal of Mark's lips and gazed into his eyes. "I want you to fuck me." He ran his hands down Mark's back and grabbed at his ass. "I want to feel that big cock of yours in my ass again." He thrust his body upwards. "I want it so bad." He shifted slightly, spreading his legs. "You know you want to. You want to fuck me, don't you?"

Mark grunted and fumbled momentarily as he adjusted his position and then pushed into Attila, groaning. He shifted, lifting Attila's legs up onto his shoulders and then sunk into a steady rhythm, only breaking from it to drop himself closer so he could enjoy the warmth of Attila's mouth as he thrust into him.

He glanced down when he released Attila's mouth, noting the vicious white scars streaking across Attila's chest and an inconsistency in the color and shape of one of his nipples. Mark's mind wandered momentarily, but then Attila shuddered beneath him, bringing a rush of desire pulsing through his body. He attacked Attila's mouth again and increased his pace until he felt himself cresting. He was surprised when Attila forced him out, pulled the condom off, and directed him to cum on his chest and across the surface of his smooth, toned stomach.

Mark's stomach churned when he looked down and saw his still hardened cock resting against Attila's limp one. He wasn't sure what was more distressing, the fact he'd just had sex with a guy—or that the guy hadn't been physically aroused by it.

"What are you thinking about?" Attila asked.

"I don't know—" Mark looked down again. "Having never done this before. Is that normal for the other guy? Not to get hard?"

"Can be. Everyone is different."

"But, I'm sure …I felt you have an orgasm."

"I did …in my own way." Attila touched Mark's face.

"Trust me, you were amazing. You hit all the right spots."

Mark furrowed his brow. "I should be going." He looked over at the clock on Attila's bedside table, and his gaze fell on the large glass container of condoms and an impressive assortment of lube.

"Do you do this a lot?" he asked. "Bring guys home with you."

"It's a bad habit of mine." Attila shimmied up the bed away from Mark. He was lingering far longer than most.

"Why do you have all those scars on your chest?"

Attila swung his feet off the edge of the bed, reaching for his robe, and then rose to his feet, tying it closed.

"You have a lot of questions, don't you?" he asked.

"I'm just curious. I've never been picked up like that before. I'm trying to figure you out." Mark looked around the room and spotted his pants folded neatly, hanging over the back of a chair.

"Was there another guy in here?" he asked.

"My roommate, Curtis. He brought you into my room." Attila grinned when Mark gave him a strange look. "No, he didn't touch you. He's married to another guy Shaun that lives here."

"Did I meet him?"

"Yes, you did. On the way in."

"I don't remember any of that." Mark pulled his pants on and tucked in his shirt. "What did you say your name was again?"

Attila slid the drawer of his bedside table open and removed Mark's cell phone where he'd placed it for safekeeping.

"It's Attila," he said. "And this is my cell number." He quickly added himself as a contact in Mark's phone and handed it to him. "If you ever want to hook up again, you give me a call, all right?"

Stepping closer, Attila brought Mark's face down for a soft kiss.

"I had a lot of fun with you tonight," he whispered, then opened his door and stood back. "Curtis will still be up. He'll call you a cab if you need one." He winked at Mark and waited until he was halfway down the hall before closing his door.

Attila shrieked when he felt someone touch his shoulder, and rolled back in anticipation, elated.

"I was asleep," he said to Curtis. "You scared me."

"Sorry. Shove over."

Curtis waited until Attila moved closer to the middle of the bed and then climbed in behind him, tucking himself tightly against Attila's body. He threw his arm over Attila, embracing him, and nuzzled his face into the back of Attila's neck.

"Did Shaun go to work already?" asked Attila.

"Yeah, he left about half an hour ago." Curtis wriggled closer, making Attila laugh at the unexpected movement. "I unloaded the dishwasher and started some laundry, and considered going back to my own bed, but I was cold."

"So, you decided to bring your icy feet into my bed?"

"My feet aren't icy." Curtis lifted his legs and laid his feet on Attila's calves, making Attila scream and swat furiously at Curtis.

"You're evil," Attila said after catching his breath. "And I don't believe you for a minute. What are you really doing here?"

"I just wanted to see you. Ever since Shaun moved in, I've been so busy getting him organized that you and I haven't spent any time together. I miss hanging out with you."

"I miss you too." Attila tried to turn over, but Curtis held him in place. He sighed as Curtis' mouth brushed the back of his ear.

"Do you really miss me?" Curtis ran his hand down Attila's body to his thigh and rubbed it while pushing his hips closer.

"Curtis ...we shouldn't be doing this."

"I'm not doing anything." Curtis grinned and drew his hand back up to Attila's hip and across his stomach. He kissed the back of Attila's neck and reached further down Attila's body.

"Now I'm doing something," he teased.

Attila squirmed, overcome with emotion when Curtis' hand encased his cock and began caressing it. He closed his eyes and concentrated. The physical sensation of Curtis' touch was faint, but the caring nature by which Curtis handled him always sent chills up his spine. He rolled on to his back when Curtis slipped beneath the covers and shuffled his way down the bed.

Curtis started by kissing Attila's feet, tickling them with his tongue, and then brushed his lips along Attila's inner thigh, licking and kissing at his skin until he reached his goal. He caressed Attila's cock into his mouth, and savored the taste of him, fondling him with his tongue, and then released him. He threw the blanket off and looked up in mock irritation.

"I'm not entirely sure you're happy to see me," he said.

Attila looked down the length of his body at Curtis playing with his limp member and laughed.

"You think that's funny, hey?" Curtis grinned at Attila, then readjusted himself, so he was chest down, directly between Attila's legs, where he began inflating the penile implant, using a pump concealed in Attila's reconstructed scrotum. He ran his tongue along Attila's shaft and then took him back into his mouth as he gently worked the pump. Once Attila was fully erect, he circled his tongue around the tip, where Attila was the most sensitive, thrilling in the sounds of enjoyment coming from him.

"That feels amazing," Attila confirmed.

"Let's run with that. Where's that buzzy thingy of yours?"

Curtis pulled himself off the bed and rummaged through Attila's bedside table until he found the vibrator he was looking for and turned it on. He raised his eyebrows comically at Attila, making him laugh, and then ducked back down to the end of the bed.

"Just be careful down there," Attila said then shrieked with amusement when Curtis held the vibrator between his teeth as he hauled him closer. He exhaled, realizing he was holding his breath then brushed his hands through Curtis' hair, warmed by the affection of Curtis' actions. It was an unusual relationship they shared. They'd never been particularly attracted to each other in the past, but they'd been through a lot of heartache together, and in supporting each other, they'd formed a unique bond because. Over time, and to the surprise of them both, that bond had turned into something entirely unexpected.

Attila ruffled Curtis' hair, making him look up.

"What's up?" Curtis asked then grinned. "Besides you that is."

"I just wanted to tell you how much I love you."

"Mm …you can stop me anytime if that's the reason." Curtis smiled. "I love you too, baby."

Attila motioned for Curtis to abandon the vibrator and come up into his arms. As Curtis shifted back up his body, he let his fingers drift along the soft contours of Curtis' mouth, laughing when Curtis bit affectionately at his fingers. He waited and then encouraged Curtis to take his mouth.

When he felt Curtis' need surge, he pulled him closer, feeling the effect of their individual desires pressed between them. He slipped his hand between their bodies and began stroking them in unison.

Curtis pulled back, breathing heavily. He searched Attila's face and tracked his eyes momentarily, and then lowered his own.

"What do you need?" Attila asked.

"I need you." Curtis looked up and kissed him. "I need to feel you. I want to feel you inside me."

Attila looked away and tried to remove himself from Curtis' grasp, but found he was being held fast.

"We don't even know if I can do that," he said. "You know that."

He exhaled, almost coughing, his breath was so rapid.

"And why?" Attila asked. "Why would you ask me to do that now.... with Shaun being back and everything."

"I know. I'm sorry." Curtis released Attila but reached out to stroke his face. "I'm sorry. I really am. I just love you so much."

Attila tucked his hands up near his face, keeping his arms close to his chest. "I know, but I don't understand. Why would you want me to top you?" He blinked and watched Curtis' face. "That's not your thing—at all. You don't even let Shaun do that."

Curtis shook his head. "This isn't about being topped. Not really. We share a special bond, you and I. Until Shaun came back, I didn't realize how much I needed you ...how much I loved you."

"But why bring this into it?"

"I feel like our physical bond should be special too. Something completely different than what I have with Shaun."

Attila reached forward and cupped Curtis' face. "Curtis, it is special. You know your way around my scars, fake body parts, and equipment better than I do."

Curtis smirked. "Yeah, I kind of do, don't I?"

Attila smiled at the warmth and love in Curtis's eyes.

"I haven't let anyone else touch me the way you do," he said. "I trust you with all my ugly secrets."

"Attila, don't." Curtis kissed Attila and brought their foreheads together. "I think you're beautiful. Every bit of you. You'll always be beautiful in my eyes. Always."

Attila grinned, wanting to lighten things up.

"Well that's going to come in handy," he said, "when we're wheeling around a retirement home together trying to get a little action." He winked at Curtis and pushed him over onto his back, and lay down on top of him. He began grinding his hips against Curtis', enjoying the gasps and grins coming from him. Then took his mouth and increased his urgency. He reveled in Curtis' enjoyment and his breath caught in unison out of pure exhilaration when Curtis' body bucked up beneath him, and he felt the first warm drops of Curtis' passion wet his skin.

The club was filling up fast for a Thursday night. Even though it was still early, Attila was being run off his feet. Curtis had hired a couple of extra bartenders for him, but they were barely making a dent in things. One of the new guys, Lance, was quick and efficient, but the other one, Gary, was more concerned about picking up waiters than he was about actually working. Once the rush was over, he was going to have to speak to him.

Attila took a moment to glance up toward the stage. The reason they were so full tonight, the club was hosting a fashion show for a local men's undergarment designer — and the models the designer had picked were definitely doing his clothing justice. Attila watched a particularly toned and well-hung specimen walk down the platform, and couldn't contain his urge to whistle at him, earning him a clap on the back and a laugh from Lance.

"I wonder if any of those models are planning on sticking around after the show," Lance said as he set a row of martini glasses out on the bar, and filled each one, then nodded at the waiter to take them away.

"Which one in particular?" Attila stepped closer to Lance as they perused the next flush of guys to walk the platform. He laughed. "You know what? I'd let any of them fuck me."

"You're telling me."

Attila ruffled Lance's hair and turned away from the bar, stepping off the back step when he felt his phone vibrating.

"You'll have to fuck me first, Curtis," he said, expecting it to be a call from Curtis wanting him to run downstairs and switch over one of the beer kegs for the bar on the other side of the club.

"Um …this isn't Curtis," a quiet voice said.

Attila stepped further away from the bar and plugged one of his ears, so he could hear what was being said over the din.

"Who is this?" he asked then waited out the long pause. "Hello? If there's someone there, you need to speak up." He was just about to hang up when a subdued voice finally spoke.

"I don't know if you'll remember me. We met a few months ago in a pub down the street from your apartment."

"Well, let's start with your name," Attila replied.

"It's Mark." Then he paused. "You probably don't remember."

Attila waved at Lance to take over his station and then ducked into an alcove just outside the main office.

"No, I remember," he said. "You were the guy with all the questions." He looked around for somewhere to sit, and pulled an old stool out from under some boxes and slid onto it. "How have you been, Mark?"

"Good. What about you?"

"Busy, as usual. My roommate Curtis keeps me hopping at work. Sorry about that earlier by the way. I thought it was him looking for me to run some errands."

"Yeah, no. No problem."

Attila waited, wondering if Mark was going to get to the point of why he'd called. "Look, Mark, I'm in the middle of a rush at work here. Can I call you back or something?"

"I'm sorry. I wasn't thinking." Mark sighed anxiously, not knowing what he should be asking, but wanting to be quick about it before Attila decided to hang up on him.

"Did you want to hook up again?" Attila leaned forward and tried to see how bad the backup at the bar was getting.

"Is that why you're calling me?" he asked.

"No ..." Mark swallowed and tensed. "I was thinking more in terms of going for coffee or something."

Attila cringed, watching Gary accidentally dump an entire tray of glasses into the sink while chatting up one of the waiters; the guy was a menace. His instinct was telling him to fire Gary before he did any more damage.

"Attila?" Mark prompted.

"Sorry, Mark. I've got a jackass behind my bar that only has one thing on his mind, and it isn't work related." Attila pinched the bridge of his nose and tried to breathe through the stress.

"So, you just want to talk?" he asked.

"Yeah. Is that all right?"

"Sure. Where are you now? I could meet you in about four hours or so if you're going to be downtown."

"Tonight?"

Mark sounded surprised.

Attila sighed and got back on his feet. "Is that a problem?"

"No, I'll drive in." Mark laughed nervously. "I bought a place out in the burbs …pathetic really."

This was taking too long.

"Mark, can we talk when you get here?" Attila asked. "If I don't get back to work, the waiters are going to go mutiny on my ass." He tucked the phone tight to his ear and straightened out his belt. "There's a coffee shop across the street from the pub I picked you up in. It's a twenty-four-hour place. I don't have to close up tonight, so I'll meet you there around two."

Mark cringed as the sound of more glass breaking, and Attila swearing interrupted their conversation. Then the line went dead. He stuffed his phone back in his pocket and left the bedroom, stopping in the kitchen to grab a beer before settling in on the sofa next to his girlfriend.

"Did you get everything sorted out?" she asked.

"Yeah, but I need to go into town tonight," Mark answered. "Some of the guys left a bunch of materials lying around, and the foreman wants everything cleaned up before morning."

"So, are you going to go now?"

Mark shook his head. "No, I can't get into the building until two when the security guard shows up."

"Well, that sucks. You have to be back there again at

six."

"Yeah …I'll just stay there and sleep in the car."

"You're going to be exhausted. Maybe you should lie down for a bit before you go. I'll wake you in time."

"Yeah, thanks," Mark muttered as he pulled himself off the sofa and headed for the bedroom, knowing he wouldn't be able to sleep. The thought of seeing Attila again …made his gut flutter. Mark dismissed it. He just wanted to talk to the guy again—that's it.

Mark spun the spoon around the edge of his cup and checked the exterior of the coffee shop again. He'd been there since one forty, not wanting to be late. It was almost two-thirty now, and there was still no sign of Attila. He'd considered phoning him but didn't want to interrupt him at work again, so he'd drunk his way through five cups of coffee instead. He was about to get up and head home when he caught a glimpse of Attila's shocking blond hair jogging past the window.

Attila leaped up through the door and scanned the coffee shop, beaming with relief when he saw Mark waiting for him. He strolled up to the booth and slid in across from him.

"I'm sorry, buddy," he said. "Work was insane." He reached across the table and shook Mark's hand. "Thanks for waiting for me."

"No worries," Mark replied. "I was running a bit late myself."

Attila waved the waitress over and ordered himself an herbal tea, and asked for a coffee refill for Mark.

"Are you hungry at all?" Attila asked as he looked over the menu. "I missed dinner tonight, but I'm thinking—" He closed the menu and looked at Mark. "That anything they serve here would probably put about fifty pounds on me."

"Do you want to go somewhere else?"

"No, I'm good. I can eat when I get home." Attila leaned back in his seat and stretched his arms out on the back of the booth. "So, what have you been up to since I saw you last?"

"Working mostly." Mark sat back as the waitress refilled his coffee and slid Attila his tea. He waited until she'd returned to the counter, before leaning forward on the table.

"And I've been thinking about you a lot," he added.

"Have you really?" Attila looked around to see who was sitting close by. "Are you sure you don't want to head back to my place and investigate that thinking a little further?"

Mark shook his head.

"No, I just want to talk," he replied tersely. "I want to know more about you." Mark clasped his hands on the table and lowered his voice. "I feel like I know you already, but at the same time, I can sense there's so much more to you."

"And why does that interest you?"

"I don't know. I thought maybe we could be friends."

Attila's eyebrows shot up in amusement, and he smirked as he tried to think of an appropriate response.

"Friends?" he said. "So ...you'd invite me to your place in the burbs whenever you have a few buddies over to watch whatever mindless sports event is on television? That kind of *friends*?"

"Well …no. I wasn't thinking that."

"Wait." Attila raised his hand dramatically. "Maybe I could meet up with you and your work friends after my shift at the bar. Of course, I'd have to change out of my leather chaps and clean the makeup and glitter off my face before I showed up because that might make things awkward."

Mark furrowed his brow, annoyed at being teased.

"Why are you being like this?" he asked Attila.

Attila propped himself forward on the table and brought his face to within inches of Mark's. "Because I don't understand where you see this *friendship* going." He moved a bit closer and held Mark's arm to keep him from pulling away.

"You and I come from two very different worlds," he added.

Mark grunted.

"You didn't look at it that way when you picked me up," he said.

"That's different," Attila replied. "I was looking to get fucked by a straight guy. Mission accomplished."

Mark broke free from Attila's grasp and sunk into his seat. "See. It's that right there," he said pointing at Attila. "That attitude. Like you don't care. It's bullshit." He propped himself against the table again. "There's more to you. I know there is."

Attila stared at Mark for a second then crossed his arms.

"So, what if there is?" he asked.

"I want to know that person."

"Why on earth would you want to do that?"

"Attila, please. Just give me a chance to know you."

Attila rolled his eyes and called for the bill. So be it. He dug around in his pocket, dumped a bunch of change onto the table, and caught Mark's attention.

"All right," Attila said as he slipped out of the booth and waited for Mark to join him. "You want to know me. I'll let you in on the whole ugly truth. But you're coming back to my place because there's no way I'm spilling my guts in a coffee shop."

Then he batted his eyes dramatically. He couldn't resist.

"And after you've had your way with me," he swooned. "I do hope you'll hold me in those big strong arms of yours!"

Mark cringed when the other patrons turned to look at them, wishing Attila would keep his voice down, but at the same time admiring Attila's confidence. It was one of the things he found so fascinating about him.

He followed Attila out onto the street and up the block to his building. He was surprised when Attila's apartment only looked vaguely familiar to him. He remembered the front hall for some reason and the hallway to the bedrooms brought back some memories, but everything else was a bit of a blur.

"Do you want something to drink?" Attila asked as he took Mark's coat and hung it up in the front hall closet.

"I could go for a beer." Mark wandered off in the direction of the living room as Attila rummaged in the fridge. He was admiring the view through the massive floor to ceiling windows when Attila stepped up behind him and wrapped his arms around Mark's waist.

"What are you thinking about?" Attila asked.

"I'm thinking most friends don't hold each other like this."

Mark stepped away from Attila and turned to face him.

Attila dismissed his objection and motioned toward where he'd set Mark's beer. "You obviously don't have friends like mine." He took a seat near the window and waited for Mark to sit down.

"So," he said. "What did you want to know about the life and times of Attila Luka?"

Mark took a seat across from Attila and settled in. For exactly what, he wasn't sure. "Can you start with those scars on your chest? What happened to you? How did you get them?"

"That's kind of jumping in right in the middle, but all right."

Attila peeled his shirt off over his head, threw it down beside him, and looked down at his chest.

"These tiny scars here—" He pointed to two short faded marks. "Those are from when I got breast implants." He grinned, remembering. "I was an outrageous 'D' cup."

"You ...had boobs?" Mark asked in disbelief.

"I told you it was the middle. I had a sex change when I was twenty-two. The boobs were the first things I started with."

"Mm ...and they were luscious," Curtis said as he

wandered into the kitchen from the back hallway, looking for a glass of water. He peered out from behind the open fridge. "Quite the mouthful, if I remember correctly." He grinned and threw the fridge door closed.

Mark jumped and shielded his eyes. Curtis was completely nude, as was Shaun, who'd walked into the kitchen behind him.

"Curtis put it away," Shaun said as he pulled the dishwasher open. "You're scaring the poor little straight boy." He popped his head back up. "It's Mark, right?"

"Yeah ...nice to see—" Mark sighed and dropped his head into his hand. That had come out all wrong.

"Ditto." Curtis smirked. "Hey, Attila, we're looking for that black dong. You know ...the big one."

"I was sure I'd thrown it in with this last load," Shaun said as he sorted through the other objects in the dishwasher.

"It's in my room," Attila replied then winked at Mark, who was blushing furiously. "I haven't used it yet. So help yourself."

Curtis raced into the living room, kissed Attila on the head, and then went tearing off after Shaun.

"Sorry about that," Attila said.

"What you were saying about two different worlds," Mark said then laughed, shaking his head. "You weren't joking."

"No ...that was more of a Curtis and Shaun world thing. They used to do live sex shows together back in the day. Probably still would, given half the chance. Obscene behavior and lascivious nudity from those two is a daily occurrence around here."

Mark stared at Attila and nodded his head in acceptance. "So, those smaller scars are from breast implants. What about all the other ones? Some of those look pretty serious."

"The rest of them were self-inflicted." Attila paused and studied Mark's face; it had taken on an extremely concerned expression.

"What do you mean?"

"I tried to remove the implants myself with a kitchen knife after I found out my boyfriend had left me for another guy. I thought he'd left me because he wanted a guy with all his original parts, not some guy with a bunch of fake girl parts."

"So, your boyfriend was gay? Then why …"

"No, as it turns out, my boyfriend, Eric, is only interested in girl parts on real girls and isn't into guys at all. Or so I'm told."

"Then why did he leave you for another guy?"

"Because, apparently, he is also one of the most sexually confused people that has ever walked the earth."

Mark's brow furrowed, and he let his gaze wander over the thin white scars crisscrossing Attila's chest. His attention landed on the one nipple that looked so much different from the other. He rose to his feet and sat down beside Attila, examining it more closely.

"What happened to this one?" he asked, pointing to it.

"I managed to cut that one clean off. The surgeon had to build a new one. Not a very good one." Attila flicked at it. "I can't feel a thing."

Mark reached out and gripped the hand that Attila had raised and turned it over, revealing the thin white line across his wrist.

"Did you try to kill yourself?" he asked.

"I don't want to talk about that." Attila yanked his hand back and tucked it against his body. "Not this time anyway."

As Attila cradled his arm, Mark spotted another more sinister scar that ran all the way from Attila's armpit to his waist.

"What the hell happened there?" he asked.

Attila looked under his arm and ran his fingers along the scar.

"That," he said, "is where they collected some spare parts to supply my new penis with nerve endings and blood. They even constructed a proper urethra so I can pee through it."

Mark lowered his head and stared at the floor. So many questions answered, with just that one statement.

"Why did they have to build you a new penis?"

"The one I was born with was removed when I had my gender reassignment surgery." Attila turned his arm over so Mark could see the broad swath of scarring on the inside. He tapped it to redirect Mark's attention.

"But then," he continued, "I wanted to be a boy again, so they used this piece of flesh here to build a new shaft."

Mark fell back into the cushions of the sofa. "I didn't even know that was possible ...to change back."

"There are a few doctors around that specialize in it. It was expensive, and I had to go back a few times."

"That must have been painful. All those surgeries. I can't imagine going through all that."

"I was lucky to have Curtis with me."

"Is that why you guys are so close?" Mark asked.

"Partially. We've been through a lot of stuff together."

"Why did you want to be a girl in the first place?"

"That is an excellent question." Attila watched the unsteady intake of air making Mark's chest rise and fall hesitantly. "And I don't have a good answer for it …yet."

Mark reached out for Attila's hand and gripped it gently. "I wouldn't have known. Thank you for sharing all this with me." He looked up into Attila's eyes, searching them for any signs of the emotional pain he'd been through, but nothing. Attila had become skilled at hiding his pain.

He grinned and dropped his gaze.

"What?" Attila asked.

"Morbid curiosity. But does it work?"

Attila crossed his arms.

"Sorry," Mark said. "I didn't mean to …"

"No, it's okay. I don't mind," Attila replied waving his hand then placing it on Mark's thigh. "Put it this way …with a little help from a pump I can get it up, but there's no gas in the line." He lowered his voice to a whisper. "But I have a secret mechanic that drives me to all sorts of amazing places."

"Curtis?"

"Shh, not so loud." Attila shoved Mark over and leaned against him, tucking his feet up on the sofa. "Shaun doesn't know that Curtis and I play around."

"Then maybe you shouldn't be playing with Curtis."

"You don't know anything about us." Attila reached behind the sofa and pulled a blanket out to cover himself. "Curtis is my best friend. I love him more than my own life. Sharing our bodies is just a natural extension of that."

"But he's married to Shaun."

Attila sniffed and tucked himself further into Mark's side, trying to get comfortable. Not being satisfied with the arrangement, he pushed at Mark until Mark conceded and wrapped his arm around Attila's shoulders. Attila hummed in satisfaction.

"I have no interest in Shaun's feelings other than those that would affect Curtis' happiness," Attila replied. "Shaun was one of my dearest friends, until the day he ran off with my boyfriend."

"Shaun was the guy your boyfriend ran away with?"

"Yes." Attila sighed. It still hurt. "Do you think I was too lenient by not killing him when I had the chance?"

Mark tensed, ready to get up.

"I'll kill him now if you want," he said.

Attila shrieked with laughter, buried his face into Mark's side, and kissed his shoulder. "You're a dear, aren't you? No. Curtis is madly in love with Shaun regardless of what he did. I don't understand it, but I love Curtis too much to question him about it."

Mark brushed his hand along Attila's arm to his shoulder, and squeezed him, an action filled with affection.

"You're even more complicated than I expected," he said.

"Hey, it was your idea." Attila glanced up and kissed Mark on the cheek, then rubbed it with his fingers. "It's late.

No sense in you driving all the way home."

Mark shrugged and shook his head.

"Attila, I don't—"

"No, Mark …that's not what I meant." Attila ruffled the back of Mark's hair. "I was going to offer you a pillow and a few more blankets for the sofa."

"Right." Mark's face flushed a gorgeous shade of crimson, warming Attila's own cheeks.

"That would be great, Attila," he added. "Thanks."

"Now, I don't get up very early." Attila peeled himself off Mark's side and reluctantly got to his feet.

"So after I get you this bedding," he said. "I'm going to say good-bye. You'll call me if you want to talk again?"

"Yeah, I'll definitely do that."

Attila headed for the linen closet, but stopped at the corner of the hallway, looking back at the man sitting on his sofa. Mark was infinitely more complicated than what he'd expected as well.

Chapter Thirteen

Conundrum

Attila rechecked his phone, looking for messages, but there were none other than from Curtis, who he'd called back already, and a variety of different people he had no interest in speaking to.

It had been two weeks since Mark had called him last, and almost two months since he'd actually seen him. He was starting to wonder if Mark had moved on without him. They'd tried meeting for another round of coffee, but they'd been forced to cut things short when Mark's girlfriend had called asking him to hurry home because one of the toilets had backed up. They'd never managed to reschedule anything after that, but they'd been talking on the phone every other day. Unfortunately, Mark was almost always surrounded by people, either at work or at home, making it difficult for them to hold a proper conversation. And quite unexpectedly, the small amount of private time they'd managed to eke out had constituted some of the best conversations Attila had ever had, and he was finding himself increasingly enamored with Mark's gentle and inquisitive nature, and generally with him as a man.

Keeping his own promise of not being the one to

initiate a phone call with Mark, Attila stuffed the phone in his pocket and set back to work washing the array of pots that had accumulated in the kitchen sink. Shaun had taken to cooking gourmet meals for them, but apparently, that didn't include any responsibility on Curtis' part to help with the cleanup.

Attila set the last pot in the drying rack and went to look for the clean laundry basket so he could retrieve a tea towel. He'd just entered the laundry room when his phone rang.

He picked it up to the sound of someone sobbing.

"Hey, who is this?" Attila asked and listened intently, trying to decipher the few words that were being offered until he heard a familiar intonation. "Mark, what's wrong?"

"She left. Sandra left me," Mark finally said through sharp intakes of air as he tried to control his breathing.

"What happened? Did you have a fight?"

"No ...she's ...she's been seeing someone."

"Mark, I'm so sorry." Attila leaned against the wall and waited for Mark to quieten. "How long has it been going on?"

"She's been seeing him for almost a year."

Attila reached back to support himself against the wall. He'd known about Mark's live-in girlfriend, Sandra, for months, but he'd assumed Mark hadn't been seeing her the night he'd hooked up with him. When they talked on the phone, it was always focused more on their emotional lives and not so much on what was actually happening on a day-to-day basis. He wished now that he'd asked Mark a few more questions about his life.

"How long have you been seeing Sandra?"

"Seven and a half years."

Attila lowered his phone to his stomach and fought the urge to hang up on Mark. He hated it when people kept things from him. Especially important things. He took a deep breath and brought the phone back up to his mouth. "Why didn't you tell me?"

"I didn't think you'd be interested in hearing about my girlfriend. What difference does it make? She's gone now."

Attila closed his eyes and tried to gather his thoughts. He reminded himself that Mark viewed their relationship differently from the way he did. Mark wasn't the least bit interested in him romantically.

"Do you want to come downtown to see me?" he asked.

"No, I can't leave the house. Could you come out here?"

"What? You want me to drive all the way out to fucking suburbia to see you?" Attila looked at his phone, checking the time. It was still early enough that he could get back in time for work.

"All right, Mark," he said. "I'll do it. But if I get lost, it's on your head."

"Thanks, Attila. I owe you, buddy."

"Hold up. I just need to check something." Attila hurried to the front hall and opened the cabinet that Shaun kept all his keys in, and smiled. "I may be there faster than you think."

"It usually takes me about an hour."

"Yes, but Shaun is away for a weekend of skiing. He took his SUV and left his favorite sports car at home. What's your address?"

Mark stuffed a stack of newspapers into the already overflowing recycling bin and tried to brush some of the cookie crumbs off the cushions of the sofa. Normally, he didn't think his place was disastrous, but compared to Attila's steel and glass upscale apartment with designer furnishings, he felt like his forty-year-old split entry home with shag carpeting and wood paneling looked like a disgusting hovel.

Looking around the room, he groaned in despair. This was not how he wanted Attila to view him. His other buddies didn't care about the state of his house, but when Sandra had stormed out on him, and he'd finally calmed down enough to call someone; Attila had been the first person that had come to mind.

He stepped up to the window when he heard a car approaching, and felt his knees sink with anxiety. He leaned against the window and watched Attila literally climb out of the most gorgeous sports car he'd ever set eyes on. He grinned as the obnoxious neighbor across the road stared open-mouthed at Attila as he made his way up the driveway. Attila had done his best to dress reasonably mainstream, but the dark tan, bleach blond hair, and flashy jewelry, in addition to the expensive sports car were making it obvious he was far away from home.

Attila folded his sunglasses and tucked them into the front of his shirt. He looked around at Mark's front yard and wondered why no one had given the lawn its final cut last fall; his mother never would've stood for something like that. He raised his eyebrows and looked around at the other houses. There appeared to be a shortage of landscapers everywhere in Mark's neighborhood.

He looked up as the door opened, and then down again to see who had opened it. A chubby, shabbily dressed young girl with a massive disarray of mismatching pigtails stared up at him. She appeared to be about five years old — and had Mark's eyes.

"Hello there," Attila said and squatted down to be eye level with the girl. "And who might you be?"

"Mandy …short for Manda."

"Well, Mandy short for Manda, I think I might be looking for your daddy. Is he home?"

"He is …but my mommy's gone." Mandy sniffed and tucked a tiny fist to her face as tears began to well up in her eyes.

Attila straightened up and stepped back, looking for some kind of assistance. Realizing Mark wasn't coming to his rescue and he was on his own, he decided the best thing to do was maneuver Mandy back into the house, being mindful not to get any of the child's copious secretions on his new slacks. Once inside, he touched her lightly to get her moving up the stairs and followed behind her. He stepped into what he presumed was the living room. Although it was hard to tell with all the clutter.

"Mark?" Attila inquired as he picked his way through the room.

"I'm in the kitchen," Mark answered. "Come in through the dining room. The hinge on the kitchen door isn't exactly reliable."

He checked over his shoulder as he finished cleaning two of their nicer glasses and nodded to Attila as he stepped into the room.

"Hey, Mark. How are you doing?" Attila asked.

"I'm a bit devastated actually." Mark leaned against the counter, knocking a series of plastic plates into the sink, causing him to leap forward in surprise, followed by embarrassment. He dropped his head and tried to hide the tears he'd been stubbornly resisting.

"Jeez, Mark." Attila ducked down a bit, trying to catch Mark's attention, but ended up pulling Mark into his arms instead. He offered what few words of encouragement and sympathy he could muster and held Mark tight to his body as Mark continued to cry.

"Thanks so much," Mark said as he shuddered through a few more tears. "For coming all the way out here. I didn't know who else to call." He sighed. "You're the only person I can talk to."

"I don't know how much help I can be." Attila raised his hand to brush a few tears off Mark's cheek, but decided against it, not wanting to make Mark feel uncomfortable. "You and Sandra were together for almost eight years," he continued. "It can't be easy splitting with someone you've been with for that long."

"I feel like such an idiot. I had no idea she was unhappy with the way things were going. She never said anything."

"Maybe she just got bored."

"Thanks a lot, Attila."

"I'm sorry, Mark, but sometimes it happens. I've seen lots of couples walk away from each other because one, or sometimes both of them, have found what they perceive to be a shinier penny."

"That's really shallow."

"I know. I could never understand it," Attila replied. "When I fall ...I fall hard. And there's no pulling me back out."

"I'm not sure that's a good thing either. Look what happened when Eric left you." Mark reached out and brushed his fingers down Attila's arm. "I almost didn't get a chance to know you."

Attila tipped his head, surprised, but enamored by Mark's touch. It was the first time Mark had ever initiated any physical affection.

"Yeah, you're right," he said. "Don't be following my lead."

Mark leaned against the counter and ran a hand across his face. "My biggest concern is what this is going to do to Mandy."

"I've heard that kids are more resilient to these types of things than what most people expect." Attila scratched his head then tucked his hands into his pockets. "I was a little surprised to meet Mandy."

"Didn't I tell you about her?"

"No, I would remember something like that."

"Jeez, Attila, I'm sorry. We always get so caught up talking about other things. My whole family life just kind of drifts away on me when I'm on the phone with you."

"No, that's fine." Attila grinned. "You're not hiding anything else, are you? You're not a wizard with magical powers or anything?"

Mark laughed, embarrassed, and then scrubbed the

arm of his sleeve in thought.

"Oh, my god. I wish I were," he replied. "Then I would've known Sandra was planning on leaving me. Maybe I could've done something to change her mind before it was too late."

"You don't know that for sure."

"Yeah, I know." Mark sighed. "Hey, thanks again, for getting out here so fast."

"Lucky for you, Shaun left his speed machine behind."

Mark laughed. "That's quite the car you pulled up in. I thought you weren't supposed to touch his stuff."

"Yeah, well, he touched my stuff years ago. I'll touch his stuff all I like." Attila grinned when Mark nudged him affectionately.

"Did you want to sit in the living room?" Mark asked.

Attila looked around in confusion.

"Was that the room I came in through?" he asked playfully then wrapped his arm around Mark's neck. "I thought it was the shed."

Attila coughed and shrieked as Mark jabbed him in the ribs.

"Kidding," he said. "Just kidding."

"You think you're pretty funny, don't you?" Mark said as he led Attila through the jumble of furniture and boxes piled in what was once the dining room, finally ending up in the living room.

Attila looked down at the sofa Mark had just dropped onto and contemplated his next move. He sat down beside Mark and prayed that his dry cleaner was as talented as he touted.

"No, I just think I'm pretty," Attila replied finally.

Mark glanced over at Attila's appearance and smiled. "Well, that goes without saying."

"Really?" Attila crossed his legs and reset his posture, taking on a campy pose. "You think I'm pretty. Like man pretty or girl pretty?"

"Seriously?" Mark snorted in amusement at Attila's sudden change in demeanor. "You're a good looking guy."

"I think he's pretty." Mandy climbed up onto the sofa and tucked herself into Attila's side. She reached up and patted Attila's face lightly. "You have nice soft skin."

"Thank you, baby girl," Attila said. "Can I tell you a little secret about my skin?" He smiled, as Mandy nodded at him. "I have magic skin on my face."

Mandy's eyes and mouth popped open in surprise. "What kind of magic skin?"

"Yeah," Mark said, joining in. "What kind of magic skin?"

"Every morning when your daddy gets up, what does he have to do to his face?" Attila asked and then prompted Mandy with the answer. "He has to shave, doesn't he?"

"You don't have to shave?" Mark asked.

"Not a stitch."

"How did the hair go away?" asked Mandy.

"A man with a magic wand took it all away. It was a little painful, but worth it." Attila touched Mandy's nose. "Something to keep in mind when you're older. Even the most delicate of us require a little extra help in the grooming department."

"My mommy shaves her legs." Mandy sniffed and ran

her arm across her face under her nose, making Attila cringe.

"That's the next thing on my magic wand list."

"But that's a girl thing. Mommy says boys aren't supposed to shave their legs." Mandy nodded her head with determination, hopped off the sofa, and headed down the hall to what Attila presumed would be where her bedroom was located.

"She obviously hasn't been to my house," Attila said. "I don't think us boys have a single hair on our bodies between us."

"That's gross," Mark said.

"No, darling. It's sleek." Attila touched Mark's face playfully and winked at him. "I'll let you oil me up sometime, and we'll see how far you can slide me." He creased up when Mark looked at him in shock. He caught his breath and leaned in, tucking his face into Mark's ear. "You can slide me up and down …and around."

"Attila, don't. I hate when you do that."

"Calm down." Attila pushed away from Mark. "I'm just trying to take your mind off everything."

"I wish you wouldn't keep bringing it up." Mark looked down the hall, noting that the door to Mandy's bedroom was closed.

"Bringing what up?"

"What we did together that night."

"Mark, grow up." Attila threw his hands up in exasperation. "So, you fucked me. Big deal. It's not like it meant anything."

"You're doing it again."

"Doing what?"

"Pretending you don't care."

"Why? Did it mean something to you?"

"No, but—" Mark moved closer to Attila. "I think you pick up random guys because deep down, you want it to mean something, and you're hoping it will start with one of them."

"I do not."

"You do. And when nothing comes of it, you pretend like *who cares* …it was just meaningless sex. But that's bullshit."

"There's that word again." Attila tucked his knees up disdainfully, waiting for the next line of the lecture.

"When you picked me up and brought me home, you watched me while I slept, didn't you?" Mark waited for Attila's acknowledgment, but it didn't come. The only response he got was a raised eyebrow, so he proceeded cautiously.

"I think you pick up roughneck, straight guys like me," he continued and then paused. "Because you're trying to recreate something you lost. Something you had with Eric."

Attila pulled himself off the sofa, quaking as he tried to control his temper. "You have no idea what you're talking about! What Eric and I had together …is not something that could ever be recreated by you or any other pathetic bastard on this planet!"

Mark leaped up and chased after Attila, who'd flown down the stairs and out through the front door. He caught up with him in the driveway and leaned against the driver side door of Shaun's car to keep Attila from getting in.

"Attila wait," he said. "I didn't mean to upset you."

"Get out of my way!"

"No, I'm not moving until you tell me why you put yourself through this. Your so-called *bad habit* borders on self-destruction."

"Since you think you know me so well," Attila replied calmly. "Let me clarify a few things to correct that assumption. I've been picking up guys since I knew what it meant to do so. No ulterior motive there at all. I get horny …and I need to be fucked."

He rested his hands on his hips and clenched his teeth with annoyance then began again. "The reason I pick up roughneck, straight guys like you is because that's who I'm attracted to. Nothing more to it than that. And I'm sorry …but for the most part, sex is just sex to me. Always has been. Always will be."

Attila wiped brusquely at his face as he momentarily lost his composure. "Eric was the love of my life," he continued. "He really was. And yes …I watched you while you slept, as I do with all the guys I bring home. Not because I'm trying to recreate anything, but because after I watch you sleep, I can dream. I can dream that I'm lying beside someone who loves me for who I am inside because that is something Eric tried to do, but couldn't."

Attila paused and caught his breath. He'd never told anyone other than Curtis what he was about to disclose to Mark, but he was feeling an immense need for Mark to understand him.

"What I do isn't self-destruction," he said. "It's self-preservation. I've resigned myself to the fact I'll probably spend the rest of my life alone because of what I've done to myself. But I have a desperate human need to feel loved, and picking up random guys like you is the only way I know how to feed that need."

"Attila, that's messed up. It really is."

"Do you think I don't know that?" Attila shuddered and sobbed, allowing the tears he'd been holding release down his cheeks.

Mark was about to reach for Attila to comfort him when a couple of trucks pulled up at the end of his driveway, signifying that word must've gotten out to his friends about Sandra leaving.

"Attila, I really hate to do this to you," he said, "after you drove all the way out here and everything." Mark pulled himself away from the car door and waved nonchalantly as his friends approached. "We can talk more about this later on the phone if you want, but I think it would be best if you got going. The guys won't understand why you're here."

Attila lifted his gaze and studied the group of men approaching. He wiped the tears from his face and reset his stature.

"Are you embarrassed to have me as your friend?" he asked Mark.

"No. It's nothing like that." Mark paced about nervously as his friends came closer. He could see they were eyeing up the car and Attila's overtly feminine appearance.

"Really. Then what is it like?" Attila smiled and nodded at Mark's friends and walked right up to them.

"Hey, guys, maybe you could help me out. I was supposed to be at my grandmother's house an hour ago. My grandfather passed away, and she's having a few people over." He waved his hand in the air dismissively and fanned at his tears. "Anyway. I'm completely lost. I thought this was the right house, but silly me ...it's not."

One of Mark's friends stepped forward. "What street are you looking for?"

Attila pulled a piece of paper from his pocket and pretended to be reading it.

"South Fraser B," he answered.

"This is North Fraser A. You've gone totally the wrong way. What you want to do is head back onto the highway going south and then take the second exit. It'll take you right to it."

"Thank you so much." Attila shook Mark's friend's hand and headed back to his car. He stopped and studied Mark momentarily, attempting to read Mark's expression, then slid into the driver's seat without speaking and reversed out of the driveway.

The crowd in the pub roared as a long-awaited goal was scored, and Mark found himself being jostled unexpectedly, spilling his beer across the table. He quickly grabbed some napkins and wiped it up before any of it ran over the edge and onto his new jeans.

His friend Nick elbowed him roughly and sank back into his seat beside him. "Can you believe that goal? I thought for sure it was going to go straight over the net. But right in off the corner."

"Yeah, that keeper didn't stand a chance." Mark grinned and pounded Nick on the back. "My beer went flying in the excitement. I'm heading for the bar. Did you want me to grab you another while I'm up there?"

Nick reached across the table and punched one of their other friends, Dale, in the arm. "Hey, numbnuts. It's your turn to buy."

"Jeez, mate," Dale said as he turned around. "You know I'm fuckin' skint this week. You promised to float me."

"It's all right," Mark said. "I'll buy."

"Hey," Nick said as he shoved Mark with his arm. "Isn't that the poof that was in your driveway a few weeks ago?" He pushed Mark again. "It is. What the fuck is he doing talking to Skeezer?"

"Probably *talking* to him," Mark said, trying to sound disinterested. "Come on. I'm buying. What does everyone want?"

"Hold up there, Mark," Nick said and motioned across the room to where Attila was standing at the bar. "Do you see what he's doing? He's feeding Skeezer drinks like a fucking player."

Dale pounded the table in amusement. "Maybe he's trying to pick Skeezer up."

"Don't be ridiculous," Mark said. "Come on. Drink orders."

"Fucking hell!" Nick leaped up and tracked the movement across the room. "Skeezer's leaving with him. We've gotta stop him."

Mark stepped in front of Nick and placed his hand on

Nick's chest. He looked back over his shoulder to confirm that Attila was indeed making his way over to the door with Skeezer in tow.

"Let me talk to him," Mark said. "We had a brief conversation in my driveway. He'll remember me."

Nick nodded his head in reluctant agreement and pushed Mark in the direction of the front door, and then strained to hear what was being said, but the buzz of conversation in the pub was too loud, so he contented himself with just watching.

Mark slipped up behind Attila and tapped him lightly on the shoulder as Attila was opening the entrance door. He stepped back as Attila turned around.

"Oh, hey, Mark," Attila said. "Fancy meeting you here."

"What are you doing?" Mark asked.

"What, this?" Attila pointed to Skeezer. "We're heading back to my place to check out some old coins I found last time I went scuba diving. Skeezer here is an avid diver." He patted Skeezer's face affectionately. "Isn't that right, sweetheart."

Skeezer nodded, setting himself off balance, and fell against the doorframe.

"Fuck, Attila. He can barely stand up," said Mark.

"What's it to you?" Attila crossed his arms. "You haven't called me in weeks."

"I didn't think you'd want to talk to me again after what I said to you when the guys showed up."

"You're right. I was a bit pissed for a few days, but I was willing to forgive you once you apologized."

"You know I didn't mean to hurt you. I'm sorry. I

panicked."

Attila tipped his head in contemplation as he studied the warmth radiating from Mark's eyes.

"Apology accepted," he said. "But only because you're cute."

Mark's face flushed and he checked over his shoulder to see who might be listening to their conversation. There was no way his buddies could hear what they were saying.

"Attila," he said. "Please don't say things like that."

"God, are you serious?" Attila spun a hastened turn as Skeezer swooned, using his body to pin Skeezer to the doorframe to keep him from slipping onto the floor. "Why are you straight guys so fucking uptight all the time?"

"We're not—" Mark jumped, ready to step in when it looked as if Skeezer was about to throw Attila off balance.

"Attila, this is ridiculous," he said. "Look at him."

"I know. I better get going before legless here can't carry his own weight back to my apartment."

Mark stepped in front of the door and crossed his arms. "I don't want you doing this."

"Give me one good reason, and I'll stop."

"I work with Skeezer and so do my friends over there." Mark turned and pointed out Nick and Dale, who were maintaining tough guy stances while glaring in their direction.

"Not the reason I was looking for, but it'll do." Attila dusted his hands off theatrically. "He's all yours. But you may want to keep an eye on him. I think he's about to throw up."

As if on cue, Attila sidestepped the doorway and fled

outside just as Skeezer emptied the contents of his stomach onto the floor.

"Fucking hell!" Mark gasped in frustration and headed toward the back hallway. He leaned against the wall across from the washrooms and stared up at the ceiling, searching his mind for any sense of reason for what he was feeling.

Nick stepped up beside him and bumped his arm. "I called Skeezer a cab. Is everything all right?"

"Yeah, I hate when people throw up. It makes me queasy." Mark grinned half-heartedly, fighting to cover up the panic filling his gut.

"I just need to make a call," he said. "I'll meet you guys back out there in a minute."

"Sure thing." Nick reached out and clapped his hand into Mark's, shaking it. "Nice job getting rid of that fucking fairy by the way. You sent his perverted little ass running for the hills."

Mark sneered convincingly and saluted Nick as he walked away. His body dropped back against the wall, and he closed his eyes, trying to steady the rate of his heart. He pulled his phone out, scrolled through his contacts, and called the first number that came up on his list. Holding his breath, he waited for him to pick up.

"Hello," Attila answered, as he stopped walking and found a place out of the rain to take shelter.

"Hey, it's Mark."

"What do you want now, Mark?"

"I'm sorry about …I didn't mean to ruin your evening."

"And yet that's exactly what you accomplished." Attila waited for Mark to speak. But nothing. "Why did you call me?"

"I was just thinking." Mark paused. "I was just thinking that maybe ...maybe we could go for dinner ...or something ...sometime."

"Dinner?" Attila asked, incredulously.

"Yeah, you know. Italian ...or something."

"You know I don't eat carbs."

"Right. Of course not." Mark sighed. "You could pick someplace ...I'd pick you up ...we can go ...wherever you want ...anywhere."

Attila glanced up and down the road, trying to decide how he should answer. He didn't want to read too much into what Mark was asking him, but at the same time, there was definitely an undertone of interest beyond friendship in Mark's voice, and Mark's eyes had been telling a compelling story back at the pub.

"I'm not working next Tuesday night," Attila replied. "You could pick me up at eight. There's a little Thai place I like to go to on the other side of town."

"All right ...good ...I'll see you ...Tuesday ...at eight." Mark closed up his phone and exhaled in relief. He jumped, clutching his chest in surprise when Dale laughed beside him.

"Big date?" asked Dale.

"Fuck, you scared me," Mark said. "Don't sneak up on people like that. You almost gave me a fucking heart attack."

"It's nice to see you jumpin' right back in there. Sandra was a bitch anyway." Dale waited for Mark to offer up additional information, but gave up, impatient. "So, who's the dish?"

"Nah, it's nobody really."

"Come on. Fess up. She had you all stutterin' and stammerin' just trying to get a sentence out."

Mark laughed. "It's just someone I've been thinking about a lot recently. It's nothing. We're just friends."

"Just friends? I wish I had friends that tongue-tied me that badly." Dale grinned. "So, this friend of yours. Is it a *friend with benefits* situation?"

"Drop it." Mark laughed and shoved Dale toward the bar area. "I have a sudden urge to get very, very drunk." Then he pounded Dale's back and motioned for a server.

Mark pulled up outside Attila's apartment and set the hand brake, not wanting to have the truck roll back down the hill; he'd embarrassed himself enough for one night already. The dinner date hadn't exactly gone as planned. He glanced over at Attila watching him, unsure as to what the protocol was in these situations.

"I had a nice time tonight," Attila said.

"Oh ...good ...I wasn't sure." Mark directed his attention to the radio, fiddled with it briefly, and then fell back into his seat.

"Am I making you nervous?" Attila asked.

Mark exhaled a loud laugh and tipped his head back to look at the ceiling of his truck. "What gave you that idea?"

"Oh, little clues here and there." Attila smiled and touched Mark's arm. "Let me make it easier for you. Was this a date?"

"That's supposed to make it easier?"

"In my mind, yes. I'm not really sure what you were aiming for when you asked me out."

"That makes two of us."

"Good, so we're both as clear as mud on this."

Mark shook his head, smiling, and gathered enough courage to glimpse up at Attila again.

"I just wanted to take you out somewhere," he said. "Beyond that ...I have no idea."

"Well, that's a start."

"So, um, ...I have the day off tomorrow."

"Lucky you," Attila replied. "I have to work at nine tomorrow night."

Mark shifted uncomfortably. "Do you want to do something?"

"I'm assuming you mean with you." Attila studied Mark carefully, enjoying how nervous this exchange was making him.

"I thought maybe we could go for a drive or something."

"Like just driving around in circles?"

"No, we could head out to the valley. There's a botanical garden out there I thought you'd like."

Attila dropped his head and quelled the urge to laugh. Mark really was trying hard. But if Mark suggested going to the ballet next, he wasn't going to be able to contain himself.

"That would be lovely," he replied, deciding to cut Mark some slack. "And at what ungodly hour are we going to be setting out on this adventure?"

"I could pick you up at ten."

"That's a respectable time actually. I can be ready by ten." Attila threw the door of the truck open and shimmied over to climb out, but stopped when he felt Mark's hand on his.

"Did I forget something?" he asked.

Mark sat back and shook his head. "No, I'll see you tomorrow."

He watched Attila climb out of the truck and head into his building, and as the apartment door closed, he slammed his hand against the steering wheel and swore, cursing his cowardice.

He shoulder checked for traffic and tore out of his spot.

"I'm so sorry about this." Mark waited until Attila had his seatbelt done up before he pulled away. "Sandra didn't tell me she had a job interview this afternoon. We'll have to head back to my place and pick Mandy up. Are you sure you don't mind?"

"It's fine," Attila said. "These things happen."

"I tried to find a sitter for Mandy, but it was too short notice." Mark looked over at Attila anxiously. "I thought you'd want to reschedule. You really don't mind taking her along?"

"She's a sweetheart. We'll have fun." Attila smiled at Mark, hoping to relieve some of the stress building behind his eyes. "I always wanted to have kids, you know?"

"Really?" Mark took his eyes off the road for a second to study Attila's face, trying to determine if he was making things up to set him at ease. But Attila looked sincere.

"Eric and I were going to have a baby." Attila settled

back and watched the traffic overtaking them on all sides, and smiled. Mark wouldn't be impressed with his crazy driving habits at all.

"How were you going to do that?" Mark asked.

"My cousin was going to be the surrogate." Tucking his hands across his waist, Attila leaned against the window. "We'd gone to a fertility clinic and everything. But the day Eric was supposed to go in and make his donation, he disappeared with Shaun."

"I'm so sorry, Attila."

"I suppose it wasn't meant to be," Attila replied as he drew a few hearts on the window then scrubbed them out. "Our child would've been almost nine by now. Can you imagine that?"

Attila pulled away from his thoughts, alarmed and disoriented when he felt the truck slow and pull off onto the shoulder of the highway. Then his heart rate crept up exponentially as Mark slid closer to him across the truck's bench seat.

"I'm sorry Eric hurt you so badly," Mark said. "You deserve much better than to be treated like that." He took a deep breath and brushed his hand down the gentle curve of Attila's cheek, trembling at the warmth and softness of it. He exhaled and dropped his gaze, and then pushed himself back over behind the steering wheel.

Attila slid down in his seat as Mark pulled back out into traffic, a little confused, but encouraged by what had just taken place. He contented himself with watching the steely concentration etched on Mark's features as he drove. Then Mark looked over at him and winked, and he felt his face flush.

Uncertain, with his heart hammering, Attila undid his seatbelt and slid across the seat to tuck himself into Mark's side. He nestled his face against Mark's shoulder and hugged Mark's arm fiercely, praying he hadn't misread the signals. His emotions soared when Mark turned and laid a soft kiss on his head.

They pulled into Mark's driveway about forty minutes later and much to Attila's dismay, Mark's yard looked just as disorderly as it had the first time he'd been there. He couldn't understand how someone with a mind as concise as Mark's could stand to be surrounded by such disarray.

He reluctantly released Mark's arm and climbed out of the truck with him, in silence, following Mark into the house. Once inside, Mark took off for the bedrooms to put together some stuff for Mandy, leaving Attila standing on the upstairs landing.

Stepping through into the kitchen, Attila was pleased to see that Mark had taken down the non-functioning door at least. He checked through a few cupboards looking for a clean glass to get a drink of water but then decided against it after concluding the water was going to have to be drawn straight from the kitchen sink.

He leaned against the counter, bracing himself when he heard someone come in through the front door.

Mandy came flying up the stairs first, dragging a doll in her wake and latched herself onto his legs.

"Hey, Mandy short for Manda," Attila said as he lifted her up into his arms at her insistence.

"Daddy says I'm supposed to call you Uncle Attie,"

Mandy said.

"Does he really?" Attila said as he deeked to avoid the piece of cereal Mandy was attempting to feed him.

"I don't eat cereal, sweetheart," he said.

"Why not?"

"Because it makes me fat."

"You could never be fat." Mandy giggled and pulled at Attila's nose. "My daddy says you always look nice because you live with boys." She shrieked with laughter and patted Attila's face affectionately when his eyebrows shot up.

"Why on earth would anyone want to look nice for boys?" Attila asked teasingly then grinned at Mandy's animated reaction.

"Ew …no. They smell bad," Mandy replied as she wrinkled up her nose. She wrapped her arms around Attila's neck and sniffed his shoulder. "You smell nice for a boy."

"I'm a different kind of boy."

"And what kind of boy would that be exactly?" A woman Attila assumed was Sandra asked, as she leaned against the doorframe of the kitchen and crossed her arms.

She chewed obnoxiously on a piece of gum and motioned for Mandy to climb down out of Attila's arms.

Attila extended his hand. "Hi, I'm Attila."

Sandra waved him off and stepped into the hallway. "Mark? Where the fuck are you? I'm going to be late."

Attila looked down at Mandy and made a silly face at her in response to her mother's bad language, making Mandy giggle.

"What the fuck do you think you're doing?" Sandra

asked Attila as she pulled Mandy away from him, and shoved her out into the living room. "And who the fuck are you, anyway?"

"My name is Attila Luka." Attila held out his hand again. "I'm a friend of Mark's."

Sandra looked at Attila cautiously and shook his hand. "Mark's never mentioned you. I'm Sandra. Mandy's our daughter."

"She's quite the inquisitive little thing, isn't she?"

"I hope she wasn't bothering you."

"No, not at all." Attila ran his hand up his sleeve, his anxiety building, wondering what was taking Mark so long.

"What are you and Mark planning on doing today?" Sandra asked.

"I don't think we'd really decided on that yet."

Sandra pulled the fridge open and lifted out a couple of juice boxes for Mandy to take with her. "Do you live around here?"

"No, I live downtown."

Sandra closed the fridge door. "I didn't see your car out front?"

"Sandra," Mark interrupted as he stepped into the kitchen. "Cool it with the twenty questions. I picked him up, all right?"

"All the way from downtown?"

"Yes, all the way from downtown. That's where he lives."

Sandra rolled her eyes and shoved the juice boxes at Mark. "Fine, whatever," she said. "Make sure Mandy has something to eat. She hasn't had breakfast yet."

Mark's entire countenance changed. He'd been annoyed before. Now he was mad. Attila clutched the counter behind him.

"It's after eleven," Mark said. "Why haven't you fed her?"

"I've been busy getting ready for my interview."

"And you couldn't take two seconds to set down a bowl of cereal in front of her?"

Sandra just shrugged and popped her gum.

Mark decided to drop it.

"Never mind," he said. "We'll pick up something on the way."

"I know a little place," Attila said. "My roommates always head for it when they're out this way. It's got breakfast all day."

Mark grinned. "Great. But what are you going to eat?"

"I'm sure they'll have a fruit plate or something I can suffer through." Attila sighed emphatically. "Or I could just have tea."

"Tea?" Mark laughed and gripped Attila's shoulder then let his hand drift down Attila's arm, pulling affectionately at the fabric of his sleeve. He let it drop from his fingers. "You can't just have tea for lunch. We'll find somewhere else to eat."

"Thank you, darling." Attila patted Mark's cheek. "I wasn't sure how I was going to dig myself out of that one. I don't honestly know how Curtis and Shaun can eat food like that and keep their bodies so toned. Good genetics, I suppose."

"Yeah, they're both in pretty good shape."

Attila barely contained a shriek of amusement then poked Mark in the chest instead. "So, you were looking. The plot thickens."

He let his fingers linger over one of the buttons on Mark's shirt as he studied Mark watching him.

"So um …where do you two know each other from?" Sandra asked, as she threw her gum in the garbage and slammed the cupboard door to get their attention; the two men appeared to be in their own little world at the moment.

"I met Attila at a pub downtown." Mark motioned for Attila to follow him as he made his way down the stairs and out through the front door. "Sandra, do you have Mandy's car seat?"

"I put it in your truck already," Sandra replied, chasing after them. "What pub?"

"Just a pub the guys and I go to sometimes." Mark lifted Mandy into his arms and opened the truck door. "Attila, you'll need to get in first and sit beside me."

Mark blushed, as Attila made a soft mewling sound. "Stop it," he said, grinning. "Mandy's car seat has to be on the outside."

"Fine, but I sincerely hope your heater's broken," Attila said as he climbed into the truck. "Because I'm feeling chilly."

"We could bring blankets." Mandy twisted in Mark's arms to face Sandra. "Couldn't we, Mommy?" She turned back and held Mark's face. "I don't want Uncle Attie to be cold."

"Uncle Attie?" Sandra jammed her hands onto her hips. "What the fuck is that about?"

"Uncle Attie will be just fine," Mark said to Mandy. "Daddy will make sure he stays nice and toasty warm."

Attila shrieked happily and drummed on the dash, exuberant, sending Mark into a wave of subdued laughter as he strapped Mandy into her seat.

Sandra surged up to the side of the truck.

"What the fuck is going on between you two?" she asked, as Mark closed the passenger door. She shoved him against the truck then followed after him when he forced his way past her.

"If you must know ..." Mark opened the driver's side door and slid into his seat. "Attila and I went on a date last night, and we had another one planned for today." He pushed Sandra back, so he could close his door, then rolled his window down.

"You're dating him?" Sandra laughed nervously and checked around to make sure none of the neighbors were listening. "Just you wait until the guys hear about this." She slammed her hands against his door. "Give me Mandy back! Right now!"

Mark started up the truck and locked the doors. "No. We're taking Mandy to the wild animal park. You can pick her up at five, no later. I have to get Attila back home in time to get ready for work." He motioned for her to step back so he could back out of the driveway and then took off down the street.

Attila waited until they were on the highway before speaking.

"It's entirely your choice," he said to Mark. "But you didn't have to do that. This is only our second date. We don't know for sure how things are going to turn out."

"So, you think it would've been better if I'd lied?"

"I just think you could've waited."

Mark grunted and clenched his jaw.

"I hate all this gender crap," he said. "I like you, Attila, and I don't know why everyone has to make such a big fucking deal about it."

"Daddy!" Mandy banged on her window. "No bad words."

"Sorry, honey. Daddy's upset." Mark reached over and brushed his hand along Attila's leg, glancing up when Attila grasped it. "I guess I've done it now, haven't I?"

"That you have. And I'm honored you feel strongly enough about me to do something like that." Attila nestled himself closer to Mark and lay his head on Mark's shoulder.

"I have a good feeling about us," Mark said.

"You better, because you just burned some seriously large bridges back there."

Mandy tapped Attila on the shoulder and dropped her voice.

"Did daddy start a fire?" she whispered.

"No, baby girl," Attila whispered back. "Your daddy is a very good man. He wouldn't do something like that." He gripped the little hand that was extended to him and kissed her fingers. "And you, my dear, are daddy's bright little star."

"I'm a star?"

"Mm …," Attila replied. "I was my daddy's star when I was your age, so I'm an expert on star children."

"How did you know you were a star?"

"Well ...my daddy would hold me on his knee, and he would tell me all the things he loved about me ...and then he'd get me to look deep into his eyes ...and see the glistening sparkle."

"That was you shining back?"

"That's right." Attila touched Mandy's nose and tucked himself back into Mark's side. "I'm sure you would sparkle just as brightly as I once did."

Mandy sighed in fascination.

"Where's your dad now?" asked Mark.

"He died when I was eleven." Attila shivered at the memory then brushed his cheek against Mark's shoulder.

"How did he die?"

"He was working a log jam and got pulled under."

"God, that's horrible." Mark released his arm from where it was wedged against Attila's, wrapped it around Attila's shoulders, and kissed his head.

"Daddy?" Mandy whispered, not wanting to interrupt. "Is Uncle Attie your boyfriend?"

"Um ...yeah," Mark replied. "I guess you could say that."

"Cool," she answered.

Attila looked up at Mark and raised his eyebrows. "Did you hear that? We've been given the thumbs up *cool* seal of approval."

"And from the only critic that matters to me."

"Pretty cool." Attila grinned and bit playfully at Mark's shoulder as they pulled into the parking lot of the wild animal park. Thrilled didn't even come close to how he was feeling. "Oh, my goodness. If these animals are sending out a randy vibe, I'm in trouble."

"Just hold it together until I get you home."

"Really?" Attila sat up straight and looked at Mark. He hadn't even considered bringing up the subject of them sleeping together again. He had been prepared to wait things out, to see how their relationship developed over time.

"Does that surprise you?" Mark asked.

"Uh …yeah, a little."

Mark winked at Attila and waited for his reaction, beaming widely when a flush rose in Attila's face.

"Like I said before," he said. "I really like you, Attila."

Attila blinked as he watched Mark's eyes studying him intently, then dropped his head, looking away.

He wasn't very good at this.

"Uncle Attie …," Mandy prompted. "You're supposed to say it back when you like someone."

Attila laughed and lifted his head. "I like you too, Mark."

"There …see," Mandy said, showing her approval by clapping her little hands together. The acceptance was overwhelming.

After climbing out of the truck, Attila waited until Mark lifted Mandy down, and then wrapped his arm around Mark's waist when Mark unexpectedly dropped an arm around his shoulders.

"This is really the way you want to do things," Attila said as Mark hugged him closer, making it obvious they were together.

Mark leaned into Attila's ear and dropped his voice to

a whisper. "No, I can think of a few other ways I'd like to be *doing* things, but this is the only one I can do with you in public."

"Lord have mercy!" Attila swooned and fanned his face dramatically, then caught himself on, remembering he was in a public place in the middle of an agricultural community where it was probably unwise to draw any additional attention to their already unconventional party. But his outburst had amused Mandy.

"You're silly," Mandy said.

"I've been told that by more than a few people." Slipping his hand into Mark's, Attila clung to Mark's arm, attempting to stay warm. "I don't have to be at work until nine tonight, maybe even ten." He sighed happily, as he ran the plan through his head. "If we drop Miss Muffet off at five, we could get back to my place by six. We'd have about three hours to ourselves."

Attila looked up at Mark gazing down at him with the warmth of desire in his eyes and felt his knees buckle.

"Fuck it," he said. "I'm taking the night off."

"Uncle Attie. No bad words!"

"Sorry, baby girl. My bad." Attila slapped his wrist and shrieked in mock agony, sending Mandy into fits of giggles.

Mark caught Attila's attention. "Since you're not going to work …do you want to skip the drive and stay at my place?"

"I don't know." Attila lowered his voice, not wanting Mandy to hear what they were discussing. "Are your sheets clean?"

"Relatively." Mark dropped his gaze, embarrassed that

Attila had felt the need to ask. "I could change them."

Attila pulled Mark away from the fence they were standing beside, keeping Mandy in sight as she watched the giraffes.

"Supplies?" he asked.

"Um …I don't know," Mark replied. "Sandra and I never used anything."

"That's all right. We can stop at a drugstore on the way home." Attila looked up and waved at Mandy. "Are you sure you want to do this with me?" He turned his attention back to Mark. "It would mean something this time. For both of us."

"I want it to mean something." Mark stroked his fingers along Attila's cheek. "You mean so much to me already." Then he brushed the front of Attila's jacket and checked over his shoulder to make sure Mandy was still where they'd left her. "I know we haven't spent much time hanging out together, but we've spent hours talking on the phone. I feel like we've really connected."

"We definitely have something happening between us. But we're talking about having sex." Attila paused as he tried to collect his thoughts. "Mark …picking you up and encouraging you to fuck me was one thing, but what we're considering is completely different. You're not in the habit of sleeping with guys."

"Maybe I view sex differently than you. To me, it's about two people amplifying an emotional bond through physical touch. And an absolute desire to devour one another." Mark grinned when Attila squeaked quietly. "I want to share that with you."

"And you're definitely attracted to me that way?"

"I wouldn't be having this discussion if I wasn't."

Attila studied Mark's face and then redirected his gaze. Everything Mark was saying was exactly what he wanted to hear, which was why it was scaring him. The thought of having his heart torn apart again was a frightening barrier to cross, but his feelings for Mark were succeeding in removing the shrouds his heart had been hiding behind. He felt safe with Mark, even cherished.

And it felt good.

"Then I can't wait to feel your arms around me again," Attila said as he looked up into Mark's eyes.

"Fuck, this is brutal." Mark looked around at the people wandering through the different enclosures and gave Mandy a *thumbs up* when she pointed to the baby giraffe.

"Don't you like the zoo?" Attila asked teasingly.

"No, it's not that. I just want to kiss you so bad right now, it's killing me."

"Then kiss me. No one will blink if you keep it brief." Attila ran his hands up Mark's chest and wrapped them around his neck. "Get all sloppy and gropey though, and someone will call the cops."

"Can you see Mandy?"

"Yeah, she's still watching the gaffers."

"God, I can't believe I'm doing this."

"Live a little. It's good for you." Attila grinned. "Gets the heart rate up. Better than a treadmill."

Mark smiled at Attila. "You're impossible."

"It's part of my charm. Now kiss me already."

Mark took Attila's face in his hands and laid a soft kiss on his lips, then pulled away and groaned emphatically.

"What's the matter?" Attila asked, laughing.

"That only served to whet my appetite." Mark looked around. "And earn me a few nasty stares."

"Forget the stares. The haters of the world will hate. They can't help themselves." Attila reached for Mark's hand and led him back over to where Mandy was standing.

"I want to see the elephants next," Mandy said.

"Elephants it is then." Attila accepted the little hand extended to him and navigated his way through the enclosures, leaving Mark to follow behind watching them with contentment.

The drive back was quiet. After they'd stopped at the drugstore and Mark had bought Mandy enough coloring books to last her a lifetime so Attila could shop in private, she'd passed out in her car seat, leaving Attila to enjoy the warmth of Mark's body in silence as the winter sun sank down behind the mountains.

Attila closed his eyes, savoring the musky scent of Mark's skin and imagined what it would be like to be married to him. He opened his eyes and chastised his imagination for getting ahead of the current situation, and sat up as they pulled into Mark's driveway. Sandra's car was already there, and so was a large truck.

"Who do you think is here?" asked Attila.

"That's Nick's truck." Mark jumped down from the truck first then helped Attila out. "Can you grab Mandy?"

"Yeah, sure."

Attila checked over his shoulder as he rounded the truck to the passenger side, watching Mark step in through his front door. The necessity of Mark doing so made him feel uneasy. The last time he'd encountered Nick, Nick had been glaring at him, ready to pull him to pieces over encouraging Skeezer to leave the pub with him.

He unclipped the belts of Mandy's car seat and lifted her sleeping form into his arms.

The sound of a heated discussion erupted from the kitchen as Attila stepped in through the front door. It was predictably revolving around Mark's current choice of companion. He crept up the stairs as quietly as possible, wanting to lay Mandy down on her bed and close her door before the loud voices woke her up.

Unfortunately, as he passed the open kitchen doorway, Sandra spotted him.

"What are you doing with my daughter?" she asked, exhibiting an aggressive tone and stance that made Attila step back.

"I was going to lay Mandy down on her bed," Attila replied. "She's completely worn out, and I didn't want you waking her up."

"So, now you know what's best for my kid?"

"No ...I was just—"

"Sandra, leave him alone," Mark said as he stepped into the hall. "I'll take her, Attila." He lifted Mandy into his arms and leaned in close to Attila, whispering, "Come with me, all right?"

Attila followed Mark down the hall into Mandy's room and closed the door behind him.

"Mark," he said. "Maybe you should take me home."

"No, I want you to stay."

Mark lay Mandy down then unzipped her coat and covered her with a thin blanket.

"I refuse to be bullied in my own home," he said, "by a bunch of pathetic bigots."

He pulled the door open and took Attila's hand, leading him back down the hallway to the kitchen. He released Attila's hand as they walked in amongst the small group gathered there.

"Attila, this is my buddy Nick and his wife Cheryl," he said, motioning to the couple leaning against the kitchen counter.

"Pleasure," Attila said and crossed his arms, feeling uncomfortable in the obviously hostile environment. He eased slightly when Mark began rubbing small circles on his back.

"So, you weren't really lost," Nick said to Attila.

Attila looked up. "No, I knew exactly where I was." He glanced over at Mark, catching his eye. "Could you get me a drink of something? Preferably vodka or gin." He instantly regretted his request when Mark nodded and headed out of the kitchen, leaving him to fend for himself.

"Did you pick up Mark the same way I saw you making a play for Skeezer?" Nick asked. "That's what you do, isn't it? Get guys all liquored up and take advantage of them."

"I never took advantage of Mark," Attila replied.

"So, you admit you picked him up?"

"We've moved past that obviously." Attila directed his

full attention on Nick. He'd never been one to back down from a confrontation, but Nick was a very large man and more than a little intimidating. He sighed, relieved when Mark stepped up behind him and handed him his drink.

"Sorry. I don't have any ice," Mark said.

"That's all right, hon." Attila leaned into the comfort of Mark's chest, enjoying the feel of Mark's possessive hold on his hip.

"Oh, for fuck's sake, Mark." Nick stepped forward. "What the fuck are you doing with this flaming faggot?"

Attila's face pinched up in aggravation, but he remained silent. This was Mark's fight, and he didn't want to get involved. He reminded himself that his own world was waiting for him if things didn't work out. He pulled away from Mark and went to find the bottle of vodka. He vaguely remembered spotting it in the dining room when he'd been in the house earlier. He grabbed it and went to sit down on the sofa in the living room, groaning in exasperation when Sandra and Cheryl decided to join him.

"What exactly does Mark see in you?" Sandra asked.

"I can't honestly tell if you're a boy or a girl," Cheryl added. "From where I sit, you're some kind of perverted mix."

The women waited for a response from Attila, but when he didn't offer any, they huffed off back to the kitchen.

Attila filled his glass with what he estimated to be about four shots and threw it back. He reclined into the cushions and closed his eyes, wanting the nightmare to end, and retrieved his phone, speed dialing Curtis' number.

"Hey, sweet stuff," he said when Curtis picked up. "I need you to launch a rescue operation."

"Where are you?" Curtis asked.

"I'm at Mark's. The address is in Shaun's GPS unit." Attila sighed. "Mark is getting raked over the coals for dating a beautiful and multi-talented boy such as moi by a bunch of narrow-minded twits. And by the sound of things, he's not faring well."

"I'm sorry, baby. I know you'd set your hopes on this one."

Curtis paused to catch his breath.

"It's going to take me a while to get out to Mark's place," he said. "Are you going to be all right until I get there?"

"I'll be fine. I've found myself a bottle and a glass."

"Hang in there. I'll be there as soon as I can, and we'll take the night off. Shaun is still away on business. So we can run around in our skins and practice our wrestling moves if you want."

"Sounds glorious. I'll see you soon. Love you."

"Love you too, baby."

Attila ended the call, straightened up, and opened his eyes.

"Who were you talking to?" Mark stood across from the coffee table with his hands stuffed in his pockets.

"Curtis. He's coming to get me."

"I thought you were going to stay here with me?"

"Are you kidding me? With all this negative energy whipping around? I'm sorry, Mark, but my mojo has vacated this space and escaped back to where it belongs."

"Then let's go back to your place." Mark stepped around the coffee table and sat down beside Attila, brushing Attila's face with his fingers. "I want to *be* with you tonight."

"I don't know, Mark. On second consideration, I don't think this is going to work between us." Attila stood, moved away from Mark, and opened a search on his phone.

"We can talk more on the phone," he added. "I'm going to call a cab instead of wait for Curtis, so I can get out of your way."

"Please don't go," Mark said, his voice betraying the sense of panic setting in. "You have no idea how badly I want this to work between us. I haven't been able to get you out of my mind since that night we slept together."

"You slept with him?" Sandra stepped into the living room and threw her hands onto her hips. "Are you fucking kidding me?" She looked over her shoulder as Nick and Cheryl pushed into the room behind her. "He actually slept with this freak."

"Have you lost your fucking mind, Mark?" Nick said.

"That's it!" Mark shouted, standing up. "Everyone get the fuck out of my house. Sandra …Mandy's car seat is still in my truck. The doors are unlocked. Please try not to wake her. Attila ran her off her feet today." He rushed across the room and began pushing Nick and Cheryl toward the front door, only relenting when they jogged down the stairs of their own accord.

He stood at the top of the landing and waited until Sandra joined them with Mandy in her arms.

"I will not," Mark stated emphatically. "Have the three

of you ruin what may well be the best thing that has ever happened to me. I want Attila in my life, and there is nothing any of you can say that will convince me otherwise."

Attila tucked his arms across his chest and smiled behind the hand he'd been holding to his mouth. He leaned against the railing and watched the front entry clear of people.

"You certainly told them," he said as he turned to meet Mark, who'd stepped up behind him.

"What can I say?" Mark said as he cozied up closer. "When it comes to you, my motto is going to be, if you burn one bridge, you may as well burn them all."

"You're a regular pyromaniac," Attila teased when Mark swept him up in his arms.

"And I have an out of control fire burning for you that is going to need some serious attention."

"Hold that thought for one second." Attila pulled his phone out and hit the speed dial. "I have to call Curtis off."

"Just text him."

"No, it's best if I speak to him." Attila tucked himself into Mark's arms as he waited for Curtis to pick up.

"Are you all right, sweetheart?" Curtis asked.

"Yeah, everything's peachy. You can abort the mission. Mark tossed the belligerents out on their duffs."

"So, are you staying the night?"

"That's the plan." Attila waited out the long pause. "Curtis, you knew this was going to happen eventually."

"I know. I am happy to see you moving forward with someone. I really am." Curtis pulled the car onto the side of the road and turned the engine off. "Call me if he misbehaves."

"I will. I'll see you tomorrow."

Curtis dropped his head into his hand, praying he could control his emotions until he was off the phone.

"I love you, my sweet boy," he said.

"I love you too." Attila ended the call and tossed the phone onto the sofa, and turned back into Mark's arms.

"There," he said. "I'm all yours for the night."

Mark pulled away from Attila, tentative.

"Are you sure there isn't more going on between you and Curtis than what you're telling me?" he asked.

"Not at all. Curtis is crazy about Shaun. And I'm here with you."

Attila placed both his hands onto Mark's chest and pressed him up against the wall. He let his fingers run up over Mark's shoulders and down his arms, and then lifted Mark's hands and draped them around his waist. Stepping closer, Attila gyrated his hips then brought his mouth to within a hair's breadth of Mark's lips and let his arms drape provocatively atop his own head.

The feel of Mark's breath on his lips drove Attila closer, and he closed the gap between them, diving into the warmth and desire he found waiting for him.

Mark resurfaced and pulled away, his breath escaping in short, frantic gasps. He became engrossed in the sleepy and seductive quality of Attila's appearance and almost stumbled as heady desire took over.

"Do you want to head to the bedroom?" he asked.

"Bedrooms are overrated." Attila grinned and slid

down Mark's body to undo his pants. He let them drop to the floor and settled himself on his knees, licking delicately at Mark's cock then taking him into his mouth.

"What if Sandra comes back?" Mark asked, peering anxiously toward the front door.

"Won't she be surprised—" Attila readjusted his position to give himself better access but stopped to smile when Mark gasped and slammed his hands against the wall, trying to steady himself.

Standing up, Attila licked his lips and latched on to Mark's mouth again, using his hand to stroke Mark even firmer.

He backed off slightly and breathed across Mark's lips.

"Did we remember to bring the condoms in with us?" he asked.

Mark laughed softly. "They're in my room."

"Thank God! Run and get them …and the lube."

"You want to do it out here?" Mark asked.

Attila hummed against Mark's shoulder, teasing him with his teeth. Then grasped onto Mark's arm.

"Mark, I swear to all that is righteous," he said. "If you don't start fucking me in the next five seconds, I'm going to explode."

"So much for romance." Mark smacked Attila's ass then headed down the hallway to his room. By the time he got back, Attila had removed all of his clothing and was waiting for him.

"We can do romance later." Attila set one foot on the arm of the sofa and looked back at Mark. "Right now, I need to feel that hard cock of yours tearing up my insides."

Mark stepped up behind Attila, laughing, and kissed the soft skin between Attila's shoulder blades as he positioned himself.

"You're a bit of an enigma," he said.

"Take it slow like last time." Attila gasped and gripped tighter to the sofa cushions. "Yeah, like that. An enigma? How so?"

"You're so delicate in your appearance and everything." Mark brushed his hand up and down Attila's back and then gripped his hip again. "But when it comes down to something like sex, your masculinity comes out full force."

"I can do soft and feminine too, you know?" Attila dropped his head and grunted as Mark closed in against him. "Oh, fuck yeah! That feels so good." He reached back and used his hand to help set Mark's pace. "Ride me hard and fast, and I'll be doe-eyed for the rest of the night, I promise."

"I never said I wanted you doe-eyed."

Mark gripped onto Attila's shoulder and wrapped his other arm around Attila's chest, increasing the force of his thrusts until Attila was crying out in waves and clawing at the back of the sofa as he tried to retain a futile grasp on reality.

He rode through Attila's staggeringly arousing sounds of enjoyment without losing his stride until he couldn't hold back any longer. He dropped his hands to Attila's hips to haul him closer as his own body shuddered and pulsed, releasing the pent up desire he'd been holding.

Mark collapsed against Attila and kissed a line along

Attila's spine to his neck, and laughed softly in his ear.

Attila coughed out his own laugh and took a deep breath, pulling himself away from Mark and staggering across the room, sighing with exhilaration.

"Well, I'm glad we got that out of the way," he said. "Now we can go to the bedroom and have a little fun."

"Hang on. I need something to drink." Mark smacked at Attila and motioned for him to follow him into the kitchen.

"Do you have any juice?" Attila bent over in front of the fridge and rummaged through what little was in it. He lifted a juice box and cocked an eyebrow at it before removing the straw and puncturing the seal. Leaning against the wall, he sucked noisily on the tiny box until it was done, far sooner than he'd expected.

"I didn't think you'd be into juice." Mark finished the glass of water he'd poured for himself, and set the glass by the sink.

"I find I need the sugar for stamina." Attila set the box on top of the fridge and danced his way across the kitchen, using some of the moves Curtis had taught him.

Mark was mesmerized by the seductive undulations of Attila's body as he moved. Then his gaze strayed across the soft, unresponsive reconstruction of Attila's manhood, and he felt his heart crush in on itself.

Reaching out, Mark pulled Attila into his arms as he attempted to control his emotions. It proved impossible. His insides melted away, and he broke down, releasing tears onto Attila's shoulder.

"What's wrong?" asked Attila, completely confused.

"I swear to God ...if I ever find him."

"Find who, sweetheart?" Attila lifted Mark's face from his shoulder and looked into his face.

"Eric ..." Mark sobbed. "I'll kill him, I swear. I'll kill him for what he did to you. For what he made you do to yourself."

Attila ran his hand down along Mark's arm, clasped Mark's hand, and led him down the hall toward the bedroom. He navigated the clutter on the floor and removed a few piles of laundry from the bed before stretching out and inviting Mark into his arms. He tucked Mark's head onto his chest and brushed his fingers through Mark's hair as he contemplated Mark's declaration.

"Don't blame Eric," Attila began. "My issues with gender started long before I met him. I've always been effeminate, and I assumed I was like that because I was supposed to have been a girl. The whole gender identity crisis thing ...I thought I'd found the answer to why I was feeling so lost." He closed his eyes and settled in as he felt Mark relax against him. "The internet has a wealth of information ...but no counseling to go along with it." He sighed and kissed Mark's head. "I learned the hard way, because ultimately, for me, the only reason I wanted to be a girl was that I thought the guys I was attracted to would want me to be one."

"The last time I asked you, you weren't sure why."

"I've been giving it a lot of thought since then."

"Well, I don't want you to be a girl." Mark looked up at Attila watching him, and then looked away. "I like your gentle mannerisms and the way you bat your eyes and everything." He smiled when Attila poked him playfully. "But there's also a fierce masculinity about you that is absolutely primal. I wouldn't be attracted to you without it." He rolled back on the bed and studied Attila's gentle but confident countenance. "I feel safe with you. Like you'd protect me if anything went wrong."

"Boyfriend," Attila said, grinning. "You're talking like a bottom. And that just won't do if this is going to work between us."

"You're going to have to explain when you say stuff like that." Mark sat up and gathered the sheets around his waist. "I know nothing about all this …" He waved his hand around. "Stuff."

"Simplified," Attila replied. "I like to receive, not give. I assumed you'd be all right with that."

Mark swiped his hand across his face then crossed his arms.

"What do you and Curtis do?" he asked.

"We're really doing this?" Attila asked as he sat up. "You're going to play the jealous boyfriend card on me already?"

"No, I'm just curious because you two are so close."

"I guess that's fair enough." Attila pursed his lips. "Let's just say there's very little Curtis and I haven't done. And leave it at that."

"Did you ever have sex with Curtis when you were a girl?"

"Yeah, the first time I ever had sex with him actually. It was about ten years ago, and Eric and Shaun were with us." Attila snorted and rolled over onto Mark's chest and began stroking the dark hairs that ran the length of his torso. "The four of us were pretty close at one time."

"You guys all slept together?"

"Just the once."

"Why would Eric agree to something like that?"

"Because he thought it would make me happy."

"Did it?"

"Sweetheart, Curtis is the most skilled and attentive man I've ever been with. He made me immensely happy."

"Can I play the jealous boyfriend card now?"

"No. There's more to a relationship than great sex."

"But you and Curtis have more than that. And Shaun was out of the picture for years." Mark shifted slightly. "How come the two of you never ended up together?"

Attila let his hand drift back up Mark's chest.

"I'm going to tell you the truth," he said. "I want this to work between us, so I don't want to keep secrets from you."

"You're in love with each other, aren't you?" Mark guessed. "Like actually, really *in love* with each other."

Attila laid his head on Mark's shoulder. "Yes. But we're also inextricably bound by suffering ...and you can't build a relationship on pain."

"That's why you're not together?"

"That ...and Curtis loves Shaun, more than he loves me."

Mark closed his eyes and just thought for a moment, trying to decide if Attila's baggage was becoming too heavy for him to bear. Attila was still in love with two very different men, both of which didn't want him for two very different reasons, and the last thing he wanted to do was see Attila hurt again. He needed to be sure about his feelings before he pulled Attila in any deeper.

His eyes snapped open when he felt Attila's lips kiss his chest.

"I hope I haven't scared you," Attila said. "You're the first person I've ever shared all my secrets with. Even Curtis doesn't know everything I've told you since we met."

Mark smiled, feeling secure in his decision. "You haven't scared me." He stroked his fingers through Attila's hair, enjoying the short, stiff feel of it.

"Everything you're telling me," Mark said, "reminds me of why I fell in love with you in the first place."

Attila sat straight up. "You did what?"

Mark snorted with amusement at Attila's expression. "Don't be so surprised. You're an amazing person with an amazing amount of resilience, and you have so much love in you to give. How could I not fall in love with you?"

"But when did you know?"

"Right after Skeezer threw up on my shoes." Mark grinned and then shifted his position so he'd be facing Attila as he sat up.

"Nice."

"Hey, don't knock it. It brought on an epiphany."

Attila cradled Mark's face, kissed his lips, and lingered, soaking up the love being exuded from them.

"Let's keep that little anecdote to ourselves," Attila said when he finally tore himself away. "There are some things the grandchildren don't need to hear about."

Mark smiled, content with Attila's overzealous acceptance of his proclamation.

"I agree," he replied. "Love and puke shall never be mentioned in the same sentence again."

When Attila gazed up at him, his brilliant blue eyes beaming with happiness, Mark felt himself being swept away by Attila's desire for him. Feeling Attila's body pressed to his, Mark realized the scariest part of entering into this relationship with Attila hadn't been that Attila was a man, but the uncertainty, the uncertainty as to whether or not Attila would accept his love.

Chapter Fourteen

Mismatches

Mark turned up his collar to protect himself from the light rain that had started falling and glanced around nervously as small groups of people and a steady stream of couples passed by him on the street on their way home from whatever entertainment they'd partaken of for the evening. He checked his phone to see what time it was and was surprised to see it was almost eleven thirty. He'd been waiting in the line outside Attila's club for nearly an hour.

He'd dropped Attila off at his apartment early that morning on his way to work with the intention of not seeing Attila again until the weekend. But when he'd been sitting at home, eating his dinner, he'd realized he couldn't wait that long to see him, and had decided to surprise him at work, and then hopefully stay over at his place. They'd had the most incredible night making love and talking, and he was looking forward to doing it all again.

Laughing to himself, Mark looked along the line of people waiting to get into the club. If someone had suggested a few days ago that he'd be queuing up outside a gay bar so he could see his boyfriend, he probably would've decked them.

"Miserable night to be standing outside isn't it?" a voice asked over his shoulder.

The guy standing behind Mark had been hovering increasingly closer and was now resting his hand on Mark's shoulder, attempting to make a marginally forward version of small talk.

"Par for the course in Vancouver," Mark answered and turned to face the guy, not wanting to be rude.

"I don't think I've ever seen you here before."

"It's my first time…. I'm actually here to see my boyfriend. He's working tonight."

"Maybe I know him. I'm pretty much a regular."

"He's a bartender. His name is Attila."

"You're seeing Curtis Bantam's boy?" He extended his hand to Mark and shook it heartily. "Good on you. My name's Scott."

"Mark."

"Nice to meet you, Mark." Scott shook his head in amusement. "I had no idea Attila was into bears."

"I'm sorry. I'm not familiar with the lingo."

Scott looked Mark over. Then met his eyes again.

"Well that would explain a lot," he said. "So, do you identify as gay? Or are you clinging onto your bisexuality?"

Mark cleared his throat in confusion, not sure how he should answer something like that. "I have no idea how all that works. I just know I'm in love with Attila."

"Oh, wow. Things are serious between you two. And here I thought Attila was a perpetual player." Scott crunched up his face in thought. "How come you're not on the guest list?"

"There's a list?"

"Man, you really are new to this." Scott motioned for Mark to follow him up to the head of the line to speak to the bouncer.

Mark followed along, but hesitated, unsure as to whether or not Attila would've bothered adding him.

"Hey," Mark said to the bouncer. "I think I might be on your list…. Mark Stedman?"

"Plus one," Scott said over Mark's shoulder.

The bouncer reached back, pulled a clipboard off a table just inside the door, and quickly flipped through it.

"Yeah," he said and stepped out of the way. "Go ahead."

Mark groaned, chastising himself for not being familiar with how nightclubs worked; waiting in the rain, getting soaked instead.

"Hey, I'll see you later, Mark." Scott clapped Mark on the back and then took off into the pulsating crowd, leaving Mark on his own to navigate his way through the throngs of men, some of which were wearing very little in the form of clothing.

Mark slowed midway across the floor, mesmerized by the scantily clad dancers gyrating to the music atop a series of performance pedestals. Complete shock set in as he realized how incredibly turned on he was by what he was seeing.

He needed to find Attila.

Pulling his attention away from the dancers, Mark scanned the numerous bars set up on the various levels and sections that made up the club. It wasn't long until he spotted Attila working front and center at the main bar, his very own spotlight illuminating him as he laughed and chatted with the various customers waiting to get their drink orders filled, entirely at ease in his role.

Mark stepped through a few people and began walking toward the bar but stopped short when Attila started dancing to the music, putting on a show by juggling and spinning bottles in the air, creating an intricate spectacle while making each drink.

He grasped a railing to support himself. He'd never witnessed anything so incredibly hot before in his life.

That was *his* boyfriend.

The man he was in love with.

As Mark waded closer, he became far more interested in Attila's attire and makeup than what Attila was doing. The only pieces of clothing on Attila's upper body were a black leather vest, snapped closed to cover the scars on his chest, and a thick armband strategically placed to hide the massive scar located there. His eyes were done up with sparkly, copper-colored eyeshadow and thick black lines, making his already intense eyes stand out dramatically.

He'd never seen anything so beautiful.

Mark pushed his way past a few more people, so he'd be standing right at the bar, and just about stumbled into it when he saw what Attila was wearing on his lower body. He'd only ever seen the clothing Attila was wearing on his biker friends—and they always wore a pair of jeans under theirs. Mark remembered Attila's comment about having to change out of his leather chaps before meeting up with his friends. He'd assumed Attila was joking.

While studying Attila's attire, Mark became fixated on the shimmery, black material that was barely covering the space between Attila's thighs. Then Attila turned around to retrieve something off the back shelf, and Mark's heart shimmered explosively, leaping from his chest with enthusiasm and dismay. The material from the front formed the more significant part of a G-string, the back leaving Attila's ass wholly exposed.

Mark refocused when Attila turned around and spotted him.

"Hey there, baby," Attila said as he stepped up on a riser behind the bar, propelling himself up so he could lean across the bar's counter. He reached forward, brought Mark's face closer, and gave him a long, sensuous kiss that had the other two bartenders whistling and erupting in loud, raucous noises.

"I wasn't expecting to see you until Saturday," Attila said as he dropped back down onto the floor.

"I couldn't stay away," Mark said. "And after seeing you in that outfit, I'm glad I made the decision to come and see you."

"You like?" Attila spun around then swayed his hips as he ran his hands up through his hair seductively, prompting a whole new round of whistling.

Mark laughed huskily as he watched Attila.

"I definitely like," he said.

Attila leaned against the bar and brushed his fingers along Mark's arm. "Are you planning on staying the night? I've been giving a lot of thought to that *thing* you asked me last night ...and I want to work out the details with you."

"Really?" Mark beamed, excited. He hadn't been sure. "I am so happy to hear that."

"I'll be happier once I'm spending every night with you." Attila stepped back and checked up and down the bar to make sure the other two bartenders weren't being overloaded.

"I wasn't sure what your answer would be," Mark said. "But I went and bought all new bedding …just in case."

"Mm …well, aren't I just the luckiest girl ever." Attila winked at Mark then set to work cutting up some limes. "I'm not off until two thirty …maybe three. Do you want the keys to my apartment? You could hang out there until I'm done. Or you could stay here. Your choice. Drinks are on the house."

"I'll stay here for a bit and watch you work. Then I'll head over to your place."

"Sounds good. What would you like to drink?"

"Gin and tonic on ice would be great."

Mark turned when someone touched his shoulder.

"Hey, Mark," Curtis said, extending his hand. "I hadn't expected you'd be brave enough to venture in here all by yourself."

"It was a last minute impulse." Mark shook Curtis's hand and set his stance. He wasn't going to let Curtis intimidate him.

"I just can't get enough of Attila," he added.

"Yeah, he's a gem all right." Curtis clapped his hands together then drummed them on the bar surface. "Just wanted to say *hey*, but I've got to get back to work. It was nice running into you, Mark." Then he cocked his head, lips pursed, and whistled, as his gaze wandered over Attila's body. "Aren't you a delightful vision this evening?" he said to Attila. "I'll see you back at home, sweet cheeks. We've got the place to ourselves tonight."

"Actually," Attila replied, "Mark's staying the night."

"Oh ...but I thought you and I had plans," Curtis said. "It's not often Shaun is away like this." He leaned against the counter. "I went shopping today. Picked out some of your favorite things."

Attila stepped up onto the riser so he'd be closer to the two men, and lowered his voice. "Curtis, we can't be doing all that anymore."

"Doing what?" Curtis answered coyly.

"You know what I'm talking about. I'm with Mark now. We can't be getting each other off anymore." Attila brushed at Curtis' arm with his fingers when Curtis cringed, ready to draw back. "I've told him everything about us. It just wouldn't be right."

Curtis dropped his gaze as he clung to the bar.

"Like everything ...everything?" he asked.

"Yeah. Everything." Attila reached up and touched Curtis' face, trying to get him to lift his eyes, but Curtis pulled away.

"Why would you do something like that?" Curtis asked. "Tell Mark stuff about you and me? I thought that was between us."

"Because I want to be honest with Mark about what's been happening between you and me. The open relationship thing between you and Shaun works for the two of you, but Mark doesn't want me to be seeing you like that anymore."

Curtis glanced up, and Attila was shocked to see tears streaming down Curtis' face. In all the years he'd known Curtis, he'd never seen him cry before.

"Jeez, Curtis...." Attila jumped back off the riser, motioning for the two men to make their way around to the office behind the bar.

As they stepped into the room, Mark closed the door, and Curtis broke down completely, pulling Attila into his arms, sobbing.

Attila stepped back and lifted Curtis' face to look at him. "I'll always love you, sweetheart. Always. But I'm with Mark now."

Curtis shook his head aggressively and rushed his hands through his hair. "Attila ...please ...no."

"Curtis, Mark is offering me everything I've been looking for. Everything you and I talked about. He's asked me to move in with him, to be part of his family ...he loves me, baby."

Curtis fixed his attention on Mark, who was hovering near the door. "Is that true? Do you love Attila?"

"I do," Mark replied and shivered at what the meaning of those two simple words under different circumstances would signify.

Curtis lifted his hand to brush his fingers along Attila's face. "It's different with us, you know?" He pulled his hand away and brusquely wiped at his face, trying to compose himself. "With Shaun, it was an instant thing. I woke up that first morning ...and I was struck down by my love for him. It enveloped me. But with you—" He reached for Attila's face again, tracing his lips. "Our love grew over a long period of time."

"And it's been incredible, but ..."

Curtis clutched his chest, shaking his head.

"No," he said. "The love I have for you, Attila, is so much more intense. It's permeated my flesh right down to my bones." His breath caught. "I could never love Shaun the way I love you."

"Why didn't you say anything?" Attila sobbed through a sharp intake of air as he tried to comprehend what Curtis had revealed to him. "You've had all these years to tell me how you felt, and you waited until I found someone. Why would you do that?"

Curtis cradled both of Attila's hands to his lips and kissed them, lingering over the familiar feel of them. "I was too scared to say anything before. But now ..." He pressed Attila's hands to his forehead. "Please, baby ...I could make you so happy."

Attila pulled his hands away and stepped back, gasping for breath, prompting Mark to rush to his side to support him, but he pushed Mark away and reached for Curtis.

"Curtis, what are you saying?" Attila asked.

Sinking down onto his knees, Curtis wrapped his arms around his waist as he tried to quell the panic that was rising in his gut.

"I'm saying I would leave Shaun for you," he whispered, then gasped through a breath. "I would divorce Shaun in a second if I thought you would have me."

A sharp intake of breath coming from the vicinity of

the doorway caught Attila's attention, and he looked up to find Shaun standing there, hands cupped over his mouth. The look on Shaun's face was the most painful thing Attila had ever seen.

Curtis spun around and fell onto his hands.

"Shaun, no!"

He attempted to scramble to his feet as Shaun bolted from the room, but crumpled into a ball instead, twitching. His shoulder rolling in its socket of its own accord, his gut clenching, unclenching. He couldn't get up. Shaun was gone, and he couldn't go after him. He dissolved into a fit of screaming tears on the floor.

Chapter Fifteen

Unexpected Expectations

Attila rolled over and tried to adjust the massive boxer shorts Lance had lent him, and almost launched himself onto the floor beside the sofa. He finally managed to straighten them out, and then flipped back the other way, jamming the pillow under his head.

He'd barely slept. Each time he'd begun to drift off, the image of Curtis sobbing and crawling toward the door after Shaun, caught in one of his unrelenting episodes, screamed through his mind and sent his heart pounding in his ears, making it impossible to sleep. He'd attempted to lull himself to sleep by keeping the image of Mark rushing to Curtis' aide in his mind, thinking it would be gentler on him, but remembering the two men together like that, both devastated—heartbroken, had only served to bring on a whole new wave of turmoil, destroying his sleep.

Attila rolled onto his back and stared at the ceiling, wondering if Mark had made it home okay. He'd texted him, but hadn't received an answer. Understandable, considering he'd told Mark he needed to be alone and had asked Mark to give him some time to think about everything. He wrapped his arms around his chest. Mark had been fully expecting to leave the club with him.

Attila reined in his emotions as Lance came into the room.

"How'd you sleep?" Lance asked.

"I didn't."

"Can I make you some coffee?"

"That would be great. And thanks for letting me crash at your place." Attila pushed himself up and swung his feet onto the floor, marveling at the texture of the faux animal skin stretched across the floor of Lance's living room. It wasn't something he would've chosen, but it suited Lance to a tee.

"No problem. Any time." Lance turned and headed toward the kitchen, flicking on a few lights along the way.

Attila was about to head for the bathroom when his phone rang.

He groaned with resignation, expecting it to be either Mark or Curtis. But he didn't recognize the number.

"Hello?"

"Uh ...hey," the voice said. "Is this Attila?"

Attila dropped his head into his hand.

"You've got to be fucking kidding me." He raked his fingers up through his hair in amazement.

"Did I catch you at a bad time?"

"Eric, sweetheart ...there couldn't be a worse time."

"I'm sorry. I'll call you some other time."

"No, wait." Attila sank back into the cushions and nodded at Lance as he set a cup of coffee down in front of him and headed back toward the kitchen.

"I haven't spoken to you in almost ten years," Attila

continued. "I can set my miserable life aside for a few minutes." He reached for the coffee and took a short sip. "It's nice to hear your voice."

"Yours too." Eric cleared his throat and flipped through a map of the city, trying to figure out where Attila was living.

"How did you get my cell phone number?"

"Kevin found it for me."

"Ah …I'm glad to hear he's still making good use of police resources. How have you been?"

"Good. Really good. I'm working for a big accounting firm as their office manager …and I got married."

Eric contemplated whether or not to disclose more, but decided against it, knowing it would be too painful for Attila to hear.

"Do you have any kids?" Attila asked.

Eric fell back on the bed. The mention of kids was exactly what he'd planned on avoiding. "Three. Two boys and a girl. They're seven, five, and two."

"You've been busy."

"Yeah, my wife …she's great with them. They're really fantastic kids. My eldest started playing hockey this year. You should see the way he whips around on the ice."

"You sound happy. That's good." Attila tucked his knees up and drained the rest of the coffee from his cup.

"Attila, do you mind if I ask why this was a bad time for me to be phoning you?"

"It's nothing new, I'm afraid. I swear if someone ever writes a story about my life, it'll be titled *Love Sucks*."

"What happened?"

"Well …I've been seeing this wonderful man. And, he really loves me. He has a five-year-old daughter, who is absolutely adorable. I just love her to bits."

Eric laughed nervously. "That doesn't sound sucky, Attila."

"Yes, but see …I'm not in love with him."

"You're not?" Eric paused and took a deep breath. "How long have you been seeing each other?"

"Three days—but that's not the point."

"He fell in love with you after three days?"

"No silly. I've known him for almost a year."

"Do you think you could love him?"

"I don't know. Mark is amazing. I know he and I would be happy together, and he's offering me everything I've ever wanted. A home. A family. Everything."

"I don't understand why you wouldn't want to be with him."

"Because complications abound in my life."

"That's nothing new. What's the complication?"

"Last night, Curtis effectively split up with Shaun."

Attila rolled into the sofa and attempted to hide his face in case Lance made his way back through the room. He'd already embarrassed himself enough last night by bawling uncontrollably in front of a very bewildered and seemingly uninitiated Lance.

"I didn't know Curtis and Shaun were back together."

"Yeah, Shaun showed up about a year ago, and they just picked up where they'd left off. No questions asked." Attila hesitated. "Problem is—while Shaun was off gallivanting around hell knows where, doing who knows what with thousands of people, Curtis and I fell in love with each other."

"You're in love with Curtis?"

"I know. Crazy right. But it's your fault, you know."

Eric sat up and stared out through the hotel window. "How do you figure that?"

"When you took off, it was Curtis that *literally* held me together as I was falling apart. He picked up the broken pieces of my heart and helped me put my life back together. If it hadn't been for him, I wouldn't be around at all." Attila waited out the silence on the other end of the line. He hadn't meant to be so harsh, but Eric needed to know what he'd put him through.

"I'm so sorry, Attila," Eric said finally. "Kevin told me what happened in the kitchen at the villa."

"Yes, well …apparently, performing surgery isn't my forte."

"I never meant to hurt you like that."

"You should've thought of that before you took off for a month-long *fuck fest* with our best friend's husband."

"Attila, don't …it wasn't like that."

"Eric …I don't want to know what it was *like*. I've moved past all that, and I don't want to talk about it anymore."

Eric scraped his finger along the edge of the bedside table, picking at the glossy finish, steadying his breathing.

"So, why did Curtis take Shaun back?"

"Because Shaun was the love of his life, Eric. You know that. Curtis waited for Shaun to come back to him for all those years."

"Then why is Curtis splitting up with him?"

"Because he wants to be with me."

"Christ, Attila."

Eric scrubbed the back of his neck to relieve the anxiety building. He'd flown all the way to Vancouver specifically to see Attila. But now that he was actually talking to him, his nerves were getting the better of him.

"Have you made any decisions yet?" Eric asked, not sure if he really wanted to know the answer.

"No. I need some more time to think about things."

"I'd like to see you. I'm in town on business for a few days. I thought we could grab a drink or something."

"Eric, I have enough on my plate right now. I don't need to be throwing you into the mix."

"I just want to talk."

"I don't know. My emotions are a mess right now."

"Attila, please. I need to see you."

"Eric, I—" Attila studied the oddly shaped button stitched onto the back of the sofa. It wasn't like any of the other buttons in the row. He pulled brusquely on it until it popped off, and then realized what he'd done; he was as bad as the rest of them. It had been different from the rest, and he'd instinctively wanted to discard it as being wrong.

"Where are you staying?" he asked.

"Four Seasons. Downtown."

"I'll meet you in the lounge tonight at nine. I'm supposed to be working …but I'm not really in the mood."

"Thank you. I'll see you tonight."

Attila ended the call and flipped onto his stomach, and screamed as loud as he could into the cushions, sending

Lance dashing out of the kitchen in absolute shock.

Attila stood just inside the entrance of the lounge as Eric checked his phone for what was probably the twentieth time since Attila had snuck into the room to watch him. He'd briefly considered going in and actually sitting down with Eric but had decided against it. The plan had been to show up, and from a safe distance, determine whether he still had feelings for Eric. The idea of actually sitting across from Eric as he tried to explain why he'd run away with Shaun was too painful to even contemplate.

He froze, unprepared, when Eric looked up, spotting him. The look on Eric's face confirmed his suspicion. Eric hadn't known he was no longer Shannon. Kevin hadn't been very thorough in his research after all. After watching Eric studying him undecidedly for longer than he should have, Attila turned and left the room.

There was somewhere else he needed to be tonight.

Attila raced for the doors, excited to spend his life with a man who had accepted him for who he was, inside and out, good and bad—completely. He was about to step out into the night air when someone grabbed his arm.

"Attila, wait!" Eric hung on desperately until Attila turned around. Then released him.

"What do you want?" Attila straightened out his coat sleeve and crossed his arms. "I'm obviously *not* who you were expecting."

"God, Attila. You're right …you're not who I was expecting. But you're exactly who I was waiting for …who I was hoping to see." Eric reached out for Attila and pulled him into his arms, hugging him tight to his chest. "I've never been happier to see anyone."

"But the way you looked at me—"

Attila buried his face in Eric's neck, and let the tears he hadn't realized were hiding beneath the surface, spill out.

"You took me by surprise, that's all." Eric stepped back and held Attila's face in his hands. "Kevin needs to think about a different profession. He sucks at sleuthing." He felt slightly better when Attila laughed. "I never thought I'd see this face again." He brushed Attila's cheeks to clear the tear stains. "I missed this face."

Throwing his arms back around Eric's neck, Attila inhaled the familiar and comforting scent of him.

"And I missed yours," he said. "More than you can imagine."

"So, can I buy you that drink?"

"Absolutely." Attila released Eric and let himself be guided to the lounge. He settled into the booth, anxious about the delay in his plans, but thrilled to be spending time with Eric after all.

"It's so good to see you …like this." Eric leaned back in his seat and let his eyes wander over Attila's features. There were slight differences in his face, but they were practically imperceptible.

"I felt like I needed the old Attila back." Attila stirred his drink, spinning the ice. "I guess I finally accepted myself."

"For the amazing person you are."

A flush of color rose in Attila's face. "I guess so."

Eric grunted softly, trying to think of what to say next.

"Where have you been working? Kevin said you went back to university and finished your MBA."

Attila grinned. "I've been working at *Sinders*."

"Is that an accounting firm?"

"No." Attila finished his drink and motioned for the waiter. "It's one of the nightclubs Curtis manages." He reached for Eric's hand. "And before you ask me if I do the books for him …no. I'm the head bartender …and I wear ass-less leather chaps to work."

Eric's eyebrows rose slightly. "I think I'd like to see that." He grinned. "When do you work next?"

"Very funny." Attila turned and thanked the waiter for his drink.

"So, Curtis did all right after all."

"Yeah, he's really fallen on his feet. It takes a special kind of depravity and sense of imagination to run those clubs the way he does. He's earned quite the name for himself in the industry. Two of his clubs rate in the top twenty worldwide." Attila leaned forward. "And get this …he finally let me enroll him in a literacy program at the college. And I am pleased to say that Curtis is now reading as well as you and me. Maybe even better."

"You're proud of him."

Attila smiled shyly. "Immensely."

"You really love him, don't you?"

"So much it's painful." Attila set his glass down as the pain welled up inside him, and he broke down in tears.

Eric leaped up and pushed into the seat beside him.

"Jeez, Attila, I'm sorry. The way you were talking …I assumed you'd made your decision. That you'd decided you wanted to be with Curtis."

Attila shook his head as more tears erupted. "Can you get me out of here, please? I'm a mess."

Eric paid the bill and bundled Attila out of the lounge, up to his hotel room. He sat Attila down at the small table in his room and ordered some coffee from room service.

"Do you want me to call Mark for you?" he asked.

"No, not Mark." Attila looked up. "I can't do it."

"Can't do what?" Eric reached for Attila's hands and held them in his own, hoping to catch his attention.

"I can't go to Mark tonight. I was going to ...but I can't. It wouldn't be right." Attila shook his head. "I don't love him."

"Then don't." Eric paused in thought, trying to decipher where Attila's mind was taking him. "If Mark is as amazing as what you say ...he'll find someone."

Attila nodded his head in agreement then launched out of the chair onto his feet. "I should get going." He rolled his shoulders, his decision made. Life would go on.... "If I leave now, I can still get to work before the rush hits."

"Are you sure you should be going to work?"

"I'm fine. I should be there in case ...Curtis needs me."

"Do you want me to call you a cab?"

"No, I'll get ...Curtis ...to pick me up." Attila dropped his face into his hand and fought to regain his composure. "I'll have the concierge call me a cab from downstairs."

"Why don't you just go to him? To Curtis?"

"No, Eric. Do you have any idea what it would be like, being the life partner of the great Curtis, fuck of a lifetime, Bantam? Guys literally line up around the block to ride him." Attila swatted at Eric's arm. "Count yourself as one of the lucky ones. You actually lost your virginity to him. He doesn't do that for just anyone."

"You'll have to excuse me if I'd rather forget."

"Easy for you, but not so easy for Curtis. It's part of who he is. His whole life revolves around the world he's created with those nightclubs ...and the sex that comes out of it. I could never live like that long term. It's pointless even considering it."

Eric followed Attila over to the door and held it open for him.

"Will I see you again?" he asked.

Attila leaned against the doorframe and traced his finger down the side of Eric's face. "Do you want to see me again?"

Eric tipped his head and moved closer to Attila, wrapping one arm around Attila's waist. "More than anything."

He brushed his thumb across Attila's lips then raked his hand up into Attila's hair, taking his mouth softly at first, but as Attila responded with his own desire, Eric let himself sink into the passion and dove deeper.

The door clicked shut and locked as Attila busied himself undoing the multitude of buttons down the front of Eric's shirt. He quickly became frustrated with the pace and simply ripped the shirt open the rest of the way, discarding it—then dropped to his knees to undo Eric's belt and rid him of his pants.

Eric braced himself, knowing what was to come, and flung his head back in exhilaration as Attila took him in.

There was so much familiarity there. Like they'd never missed a day.

But they had.

He lowered his chin to his chest, prepared to step away, when Attila looked up at him, his piercing, blue eyes, alight. The sight filled him with joy. That was definitely the face he'd been missing.

Attila rose to his feet and led Eric over to the bed, pushing him down onto it. He slipped off his shoes and climbed on with Eric, positioning himself astride Eric's waist to tower over him.

Flicking open each buckle of his leather jacket with deliberation, Attila took his time removing it. Eric was stroking his legs, heavy with arousal by the time Attila pulled his jacket off and threw it onto a chair beside the bed.

"I don't want you touching me," Attila said.

"Why not?"

"Shh. Just do as you're told."

Bending forward, Attila let his lips hover a hair's breadth away from Eric's, and then he licked them and pulled away. He reached back behind him and started stroking Eric's cock lightly, riding the thrill as Eric arched up beneath him in response.

Attila's hands snapped back fast, clamping on to Eric's arms as he attempted to lift Attila's shirt away from his body.

"I said *not* to touch me!"

He challenged Eric with his eyes, but then looked away. Eric had broken his concentration. Now he just needed to get out of there. He never should have followed

Eric up to his room. Distraught or not …it never should have happened. He shuffled down the bed, taking Eric's cock into his mouth, and finished him, savoring every familiar drop.

Then he climbed off the bed …and went looking for his shoes.

Eric caught his arm, restraining him.

"Don't you dare," he said to Attila. "Don't you dare treat me like one of your fucking tricks."

Attila spun around. "And how would you have me treat you?" He pulled Eric's hand off his arm. "You got what you wanted from me. Now go home to your wife."

"Goddammit, Attila. That's not why I came here."

"Bullshit! You haven't tried to contact me in ten years. Suddenly you're here, alone in the city, calling me up under the guise of a friendly drink. And low and behold, you make a move on me." Attila settled his breathing. "What the fuck am I supposed to think? That you actually want me?"

"Attila—"

"Don't. I'm tired, Eric. I'm tired of the drama and the pain that seems to permeate my life, and I don't need you adding your own layer of bullshit. I've got enough of my own to shovel around."

"Attila—"

"You're living the life you've always wanted. You have a wife …kids. So, go back to it …and leave me the fuck alone."

"Are you finished?"

"No! Go fuck yourself!"

Eric grinned. "Now are you finished?"

"Maybe." Attila sat down on the edge of the bed and leaned his head against Eric's shoulder. "I'm sorry. I know why you're here."

"I figured as much after that routine."

"I'm still in love with you too, you know."

Eric tipped Attila's face up and kissed him.

"I figured as much," he said then attacked Attila's mouth with more urgency. Sinking fast, he pried himself away.

"Can we try this again?" he asked Attila.

"What did you have in mind?"

"I was thinking of starting the evening by eating an entire menu of desserts off your naked body."

"Why, Mr. Templeton, you're making me blush." Attila rose to his feet, undid his buckle, and let his pants slip to the floor.

Eric fell back onto the bed and invited Attila into his arms.

"And then—" He stroked Attila's lips with his finger. "And this is your favorite part."

Attila rolled onto his stomach, comfortably settling himself on the bed, and stretched his arms up over his head in anticipation as Eric moved up behind him and started kissing the back of his neck.

"What's my favorite part?" Attila gasped softly when Eric manipulated his underwear off his body and used his tongue to excite his senses into a rush of familiar desire.

He reached forward and curled his fingers into the pillows, spreading his legs wider as Eric brushed back along his body, pinned him still, and thrust into him.

"The part where I fuck you all night long," Eric answered.

"Definitely my favorite part."

Attila moaned, enthralled by Eric's touch, encouraging him to increase his pace. Reaching back for him, Attila pushed himself up onto his knees and used his own power to force Eric deeper. He shook his head in exhilaration, letting the overwhelming euphoria caress his entire system. The thought of having Eric back inside him was something he hadn't even considered in years.

Eric brushed his hands along Attila's body, taking in the familiar contours of Attila's shoulders and waist, then pushed Attila's shirt up and over his head, removing it.

He leaned down, kissing the soft skin between Attila's shoulder blades as he pulled out of him, urging Attila to roll over.

Attila hesitated. "Eric, I don't know."

"Attila, I want to make love to you." Eric stroked his hand down Attila's back. "To every part of you."

Attila lowered himself onto his stomach and rolled over, covering his chest with his arms. He blinked up at Eric watching him, waiting. "I don't want you to feel guilty. Please …I did this to myself because of my own insecurities." He waited for Eric to nod his agreement then removed his arms from his chest.

"Fuck, Attila—" Eric touched the skin of Attila's chest and traced his fingers along some of the scars, lingering over what must've been the wound that almost killed him. He leaned over and kissed it softly, thankful that it had been unsuccessful. Then the guilt did wash over him, and he broke down in tears.

This *had* been his fault.

Eric moved to get off the bed, but Attila stopped him.

"Eric, you promised. Please, don't do this to me. I don't want to lose you again …not because of this."

"You're not going to lose me. I just need a second."

Eric held his head in his hand and breathed deeply, attempting to quell the nausea that was rising in his throat.

Attila's hand brushed across Eric's shoulder.

"Eric?"

"I'm right here, baby. I'm not going anywhere."

Eric turned back to Attila and pushed him onto the bed, and brought his mouth down along Attila's throat and across his chest, kissing each scar as if doing so would remove the guilt somehow. He stopped momentarily to catch his breath and then turned his attention to the familiar taste of the skin leading him down the center of Attila's stomach. He slowed at the soft curve of Attila's inner thigh, intrigued by what he found there, and ever so carefully pulled Attila's soft member into his mouth, sending Attila gasping and calling his name. His curiosity piqued, Eric released him and pressed a soft kiss to Attila's stomach, and caught his eye.

"How do I work this?" he asked.

"Sugar, you're working it just fine."

Eric grinned. "That not what I meant."

Attila reached down, depressed the pump a couple of times, and then let Eric take over. As Attila's erection increased, Eric's tongue wandered over the tip, prompting a sharp exhalation of air from Attila. Eric chuckled and licked the spot again, then sucked gently. Attila moaned and gripped onto the sheets, so he played Attila with his tongue for a while longer then kissed his way back up, taking Attila's mouth as he pushed into him again, reveling in the symphony of sound it elicited.

When Attila's body bucked up beneath him and shuddered in ecstasy, the world as Eric knew it was brought back into alignment.

Attila fussed about, getting comfortable beneath the covers as he layered his body against Eric's. His hand drifted across Eric's chest as he found the niche in Eric's shoulder he was looking for and tucked his head into it. "So, what happens now? How often do you think you can come to see me?"

He gazed up at Eric, waiting for an answer.

"I'm hoping every day," Eric answered.

"What do you mean?" Attila lifted his head, confusion clouding his features. "Eric, we don't even live in the same city."

"I mean, I want to do what I should've done ten years ago." Eric shifted over and brushed Attila's cheek with his fingers. "Even after all these years, I never stopped loving you." He lowered his eyes. "I know you've been through a lot of pain because of me—"

Eric's hand wandered down across the worst of the scarring on Attila's chest, and he felt his breath catch—it had all been his fault.

He'd never forgive himself for that.

He refocused on the brilliant blue eyes watching him.

"I love you, Attila. I want to spend the rest of my life with you."

"Eric, I—"

Eric laid a finger on Attila's lips so he could finish. "My wife and I were never legally married, so there's nothing to stop you and me from finally tying the knot."

"Eric, I can't ask you to leave your family."

"You wouldn't be. Sharon and I haven't been together for almost two years now." Eric brushed his fingers up and down Attila's arm and pulled him closer. "My relationship with my wife was always a bit strained. I was never fully committed …and I made a lot of excuses for that. But the truth is …I never got over you."

"Eric, I don't know what to say."

"Don't say anything for a second." Eric scurried off the bed and rooted around in his luggage, and then leaped back onto the bed. He arranged himself in front of Attila and opened a small box.

"Attila Luka …will you marry me?"

Attila fingered the ring delicately. It was beautiful.

"You came prepared."

"I came hopeful. I've never loved anyone as much as I love you. Since we first met, on that first day of school, not a single day has gone by that I haven't thought of you …wanted to be with you."

Attila let his attention drift along the covers of the bed and around the room as he tried to sort through what Eric was asking of him. Marrying Eric would be a dream come true, but he couldn't help but feel tentative about accepting. Eric had let him down before. There was nothing to guarantee he wouldn't do it again.

He looked up into Eric's eyes, saw the love radiating from them, and realized he was willing to take the risk if it meant he could spend even one beautiful, solitary day as Eric's husband.

"Yes, Eric."

"What?" Eric shuffled closer and cradled Attila's face.

"I'll marry you ...on two conditions."

Attila fumbled with the keys in his haste as he tried to unlock the door to get inside as soon as possible. He finally worked the lock and pulled Eric into the apartment, tripping briefly on the motorcycle boots Curtis had left lying in the front hall.

"Just hang your coat over there, and I'll show you the way down to my ...I mean *our* bedroom." Attila giggled quietly, accepting Eric's mouth on his, then shrieked when Eric tipped him backward, swooning uncontrollably as Eric deepened the kiss.

"Hey, you two. Leave a little for me." Curtis peered around the corner of the hallway, hanging back a little. Then he rushed into the front hall to take Attila into his arms.

"How's my beautiful boy?" he said, only just loud enough for Eric to hear, while scooping Attila closer to him.

"I'm good. I wasn't expecting you to be home yet."

"I took the night off. I wanted to be here to welcome you and Eric home." Curtis released Attila, stepping around him with purpose to offer Eric his hand. "Eric...."

"Hey, Curtis." Eric gave Curtis' hand a firm shake and

let himself be pulled into a hug. "So good to see you."

"Cut the crap," Curtis whispered as he pulled Eric closer, tucking his mouth against Eric's ear. "This is your warning. If you do anything to make Attila shed one single tear, I will personally hunt you down and rip you a new asshole with my bare hands."

Stepping back, Curtis pounded Eric's back a few times then wrapped his arm around Attila's shoulders, hauling him close, possessive, and kissed him on the cheek.

"Congratulations you two crazy kids. When's the wedding?"

Attila held out his hand so Curtis could see his ring. "We went down to the government office first thing this morning to get our marriage license. I told Eric I didn't want to wait. The lady of uncertainty has had her way with us in the past, and I wasn't about to let that happen again."

"Wow. So, it's a done deal then."

"Almost," Eric said as he lifted his bag onto his shoulder. "Which room should I be headed for?"

"First one on the left, sweetheart."

Attila sighed with contentment as he watched Eric head down the hallway and then turned his attention back to Curtis.

"Are you all right?" he asked.

"Um …when you texted me to say you were meeting with Eric," Curtis replied. "I was not expecting to hear from you a few hours later saying he'd asked you to marry him."

"It was all very sudden," Attila replied. "But our feelings for each other haven't changed a bit since we were together."

"But he ran off on you."

"Yeah, with Shaun. And you took Shaun back?"

Curtis lowered his head. "Shaun came to see me today right after you texted me about your engagement." He sighed quietly, remembering. "He was as beautiful and angelic looking as ever." He scrubbed his face. "And just as deceptive and conniving."

"What did he want?"

"He wanted to come home. He offered to forgive me for loving you. As long as I never saw you again."

"What did you say?"

"I asked him where he'd been for those eight years. And reminded him that I'd been prepared to wait for him forever because I loved him. And that I'd put my life on hold waiting for him to come home to me." Curtis shuddered and shook out his hand, it was twitching badly. "He refused to tell me. Said it was none of my *fucking* business. So I told him he didn't need to forgive me for loving you because I had no intention of stopping." He raised his head. "And then I told him to fuck off."

"You didn't?"

"I did. And I was very proud of myself for doing it." Curtis grinned and reached for Attila's hands. "I never should've taken him back. It wasn't until he was back in my life that I realized I loved you so much more than I ever loved him."

"And all this time, I thought I'd lost you to him." Attila cradled Curtis' face and gently took his mouth, letting the emotions swell in him, urging him to continue. He pushed Curtis up against the wall and fervently devoured him, his hands searching for a way into Curtis' clothing.

Curtis grabbed Attila's hands and stopped him. "What are you doing? Eric might come out and see us."

"And that wouldn't be a problem." Attila shoved Curtis against the wall, pinning him there. "He knows how much we love each other, and he doesn't want to stand in the way of that. Eric and I going to be married, and he expects certain things from me, but monogamy, in regards to you anyway, doesn't happen to be one of them."

Curtis pushed Attila away after grappling to free himself.

"And you thought I wouldn't have a problem with that?"

"You never did when you were together with Shaun. You spent just as much time in my bed as you did in your own."

"That's because I wanted to be with you and not Shaun."

Curtis inhaled as if to continue, but then turned away from Attila and paced down the hallway toward his own room. He paused for a moment and then backtracked to Attila's door and hammered on it to the point of the door shuddering. He waited for Eric to appear, and when he did, Curtis shoved Eric hard in the chest.

"Maybe I don't want to share Attila. Did you think of that?" Curtis shoved Eric again, pushing him further into Attila's room.

"Maybe I want to fight you for him," he added.

Eric held up his hands, not wanting a confrontation.

"Whoa, Curtis, Attila loves you. He can't imagine

living life without you, and I suspect you feel the same way. Who am I to step in and break that up?"

"You idiot ...that's because he's supposed to be with me. Attila should be marrying me, not you!" Curtis threw his hands up in exasperation, his body threatening to convulse as a slow burn extended up his left leg, weakening it. There was no way to stop the progression now. He reached for the post of Attila's bed.

"How could you two think I'd be all right with this?" he asked.

Attila stepped into the room and leaned against the dresser.

"Curtis, think about what you're saying," he said. "You don't want to be married to me. We don't even want the same things."

"How do you know that?" Curtis replied. "When have we *ever* sat down and discussed what *I* want? We have spent countless hours talking about what you want. The husband, the kids, the fucking white picket fence—but never once did you ask me what I wanted."

"I assumed you were living the life you wanted. You've worked so hard to get where you are, and you love what you do."

"You assumed wrong, Attila. Every minute I spend working is a means to an end, nothing more." Curtis hurried from the room as best he could, using the wall for support, and came back with a stack of papers and thrust them at Attila. They contained pictures and specifications for a new housing development very near to where Tekla Senior High was located, nearly five hours away from the coast—and the nightclubs Curtis had been nurturing for years.

"What is this?" Attila scanned through the pages, making special note of the ones containing Curtis' unwieldy scrawl.

"It's a house I bought." Curtis moved closer to Attila and turned over a few pages. "It's almost finished. I was going to wait, to let you pick out the paint colors." He pointed to a room on the floor plan. "I thought this could be the nursery because it would be close to our room—" He brushed his finger along the paper. "Ours was going to be this room here because I know how much you love being able to see the mountains when you wake up."

Attila scanned over the pages again, shocked at the detail and thought behind some of Curtis' notes. "When did you do this?"

"I put a deposit down about two years ago. It was supposed to be a surprise. Kind of like a wedding present. I was planning on retiring from the club business and heading back home with you." Curtis scratched his head and adjusted his position, crossing his arms to contain his rising anguish. "I guess I made some assumptions of my own. I assumed you and I were destined to be together. I'd made the decision to move on without Shaun, to stop waiting for him because I knew deep down I only wanted to be with you.

Then Shaun came back, and things got really confusing. I knew what I wanted ...for you to be my husband, but I was too damn scared and fucked up to do anything about it."

"You were too scared to propose, but you bought me a house?"

Attila sunk down onto the edge of his bed and covered his mouth with his hand.

"Yeah ...I even made sure it had the exposure you wanted for your garden because I know how much you want to grow your own vegetables and everything." Curtis dropped down at Attila's feet and rested his forehead on Attila's knees. "I know I'm an idiot for not telling you what I was thinking, or what I was planning, but I wanted everything to be perfect so you'd say *yes*."

Curtis involuntarily slipped away from Attila as his body began twitching violently. He tried to contain the movement of his arms and legs, but they had no intention of behaving. He groaned as his shoulder rotated back, sending a sharp pain across his chest.

"Fuck ...Attila."

Attila lowered himself down onto the floor and began rubbing small circles on Curtis' back, attempting to slow the stress reaction down. "Did you forget to take your medication this morning?"

"I might have ...I was a bit ...pre—" Curtis grunted through a breath. "Fuck ...and then Shaun ...and everythi—" He shuddered forward as his shoulder jammed itself back.

He clung to Attila's legs.

"Sweetie, I need you to breathe with me." Attila tucked Curtis into his chest and then turned and caught Eric's attention. "Eric, could you go into Curtis' bathroom. There's a special cabinet on the wall with all his meds in it. On the bottom shelf, over to the far right, is a short blue bottle with very tiny white pills in it. Could you grab it for me? I need about three of them."

"Sure ...yeah." Eric stepped out of the room but glanced back at the way Attila was cradling Curtis against him, whispering to him, and coaching him through his breathing. He felt a twinge of regret shiver down his spine. The two men were close in ways he hadn't expected. Their intense love for each other was undeniable.

The medicine cabinet was easy to find, but Eric was stunned by the number of prescription bottles in it. He lifted a few, recognizing some of the names as drugs used for a multitude of mental issues, plus some other ones, possibly seizure medications. He set them back to examine the chart taped to the inside of the door. It was written entirely in Attila's hand and included color-coded sections that referred to certain bottles in the cabinet. He figured Attila must've designed it before Curtis learned how to read.

Eric retrieved the bottle he'd been sent for and returned to Attila's room, expecting to be acknowledged, but found himself marveling at the efficiency by which Attila dispensed the pills and placed them under Curtis' tongue. They'd been together for a long time, and it showed; they were truly like an old married couple.

As Curtis gripped onto Attila's arm, tucking into him for comfort, and Attila leaned over and kissed Curtis' head, lingering just long enough to inhale the scent of his hair, Eric knew that marrying Attila would be a huge mistake.

He approached Attila and ran his hand over Attila's head.

"Could I talk to you for a second ...alone?"

Attila nodded his head, turned his attention back to Curtis and maneuvered him onto the bed, removing his pants and tucking him securely under the covers. He bent down, kissed Curtis on the lips, and told him he'd be back in a second.

Chapter Sixteen

Home

The sun streamed in through the elegant panel of drapery that hung delicately across their bedroom window. Attila pulled it aside so he could take in the breathtaking view of the mountains beyond. He purred contentedly as Curtis stepped up behind him and wrapped him up in his arms.

"Did you manage to get Sarah back to sleep?" he asked.

"She's all tucked in snug as a bug." Curtis shifted the hair away from the back of Attila's neck and kissed it. Attila had been growing his hair out, and it was already gracing his waist.

"It's hard to put her down when she looks up at you with those gorgeous blue eyes," he added.

"I wonder which side of the family she got them from?"

"Definitely yours. Mine aren't quite that brilliant."

"Mm …so, is Ed coming over to take Sarah out tomorrow?"

"That's what she said. I think your mom mentioned coming around as well. Something about canning jars?" Curtis turned Attila to face him. "You're still in your dressing gown." He peered down inside the front of the silk fabric and returned his gaze to Attila's face. "And absolutely nothing else."

"It's our first anniversary, so I'm having a lazy day." Attila kissed Curtis soundly and headed off across the room. "And besides... pink suits me."

Curtis followed Attila downstairs into the kitchen. "I think after we have lunch, we should spend some time celebrating our nuptials by reliving the honeymoon."

"Who says we have to wait until after lunch."

Attila untied the knot in his dressing gown and let it fall open as he wandered over and ran his hands up Curtis' chest. He sighed as he began rubbing Curtis through the fabric of his jeans, prompting an immediate response. That was one of the things he loved about Curtis. He was always ready.

Curtis groaned his disappointment when someone rang the doorbell, triggering Sarah to start crying again.

"I'll get the door if you grab Sarah," he said as he bustled off toward the front door, trying to adjust himself, eventually opting to pull his shirt out of his pants to cover up what Attila had started with his seduction routine. He pulled open the door to a very flustered looking woman.

"Hi, I'm so sorry to bother you," the woman said. "My name's Linda. We just moved in next door, and for some reason, our electricity hasn't been turned on yet. Would you mind terribly if we plugged into your house? Just until the power company shows up."

"Sure, go right ahead. There's an outlet right next to the gate leading into our backyard." Curtis turned when he heard Attila making his way down the stairs talking to Sarah. "Hey, sweet, this is our new neighbor, Linda."

Attila bumped up beside Curtis affectionately. "Please tell me those lovely teenaged girls of yours babysit."

"I'm sure they would." Linda reached out for Sarah's little hand and cooed softly at her. "How old is she?"

Curtis grabbed Sarah's foot playfully. "Almost six months now. It's amazing how fast she's growing."

"They have a tendency to do that." Linda smiled shyly at the couple standing before her. It wasn't often you moved in next door to a couple who looked like a male supermodel and his gorgeous wife. She studied the man's face carefully; he seemed vaguely familiar.

"Are you Curtis Bantam?" she asked.

"Guilty. Do we know each other from somewhere?"

"We went to school together at Tekla. You probably wouldn't remember me. I was a short mousy thing."

Linda paused, in thought, as she recalled some of the things she'd heard about Curtis.

Attila juggled Sarah into a secure crook in his arm. "I think you and I might've been in the same algebra class."

"You went to Tekla as well?" Linda asked.

"Just for a few months. I created a bit of a scandal, so I had to leave *post haste*." Attila handed Sarah to Curtis so he could adjust his robe from falling open.

"Right. Annie, isn't it? I heard a lot of rumors about you after you left." Linda laughed, dismissing the very idea. "Some people even thought you were a guy. Can you imagine?"

"Well, that has got to be one of the funniest things I've ever heard," Curtis said and kissed Attila on the cheek.

Attila smacked him in the arm in jest. "Ignore him,

Linda." He extended his hand. "I'm Curtis' husband, Attila …Annie was my alter ego back in high school."

"So, you are—" Linda stuttered.

"A guy, yeah …through and through."

"I'm so sorry." Linda's gaze floated briefly over Attila's face and attire. "I just assumed—"

"No, that's perfectly all right." Attila grinned. "Here I am with my hair down, wearing my pink robe and high heel slippers, standing beside my adorable husband and baby. It was an honest mistake."

Linda looked around, not sure what to say next. "Well. I better run …but once I get the house organized, I'm planning on having a barbeque. I'd love for you both to come."

"We wouldn't miss it." Attila closed the door after Linda turned and hurried down the steps, and then leaned against it, completely creasing up in hysterics.

Curtis bounced Sarah in his arms while trying to contain himself, but the tears were rolling down his cheeks.

"Oh, that was priceless," he said. "Did you see her face?"

"Which time? When she figured out I was a guy, or when it dawned on her who Curtis Bantam was? I don't think we'll be seeing her again, except over the fence." Attila fussed with the collar of his dressing gown, smoothing out the inconsistencies. "I suppose I'll have to do some damage control. Obviously, most of our new friends aren't going to believe you were a hustler. And if they do, I doubt they'll hold it against you."

"I'll leave it in your capable hands."

"Oh, and you know they are *very* capable," Attila replied, and then winked at him.

"On that note, my lovely bride, Sarah's passed out, so I'm going to put her back in her crib. I expect you to be naked and waiting by the time I get back down here."

Attila undid the tie on his dressing gown and let the entire thing fall to the floor, fixating Curtis in place.

"I'm ready," Attila said as he raked his hands up into his hair and then combed it out, letting the soft, blond tresses fan out over his bare chest. "What's taking you so long?"

He pouted seductively at Curtis then strutted over to the sofa and arranged himself on it as he worked the pump, quickly achieving his erection. He let his slippers drop onto the floor and reached behind him for a condom that he rolled onto himself.

Curtis took a couple of steps toward Attila, enthralled by the implications of what Attila was doing. They'd talked about it and cleared it with the doctor, and Attila had said he'd consider it and maybe surprise him someday.

Apparently, today was that day.

"Curtis, sweetheart," Attila said. "The baby …she goes upstairs. And then you can come back down and let me fuck you senseless." He grinned contentedly. "Happy anniversary, baby."

"Attila, my beautiful boy." Curtis blew him a soft kiss. "I love you so much." He grinned, remembering a phrase Attila often used. "You're just simply marvelous."

About the Author

Leigh Jarrett (she/he/they) is an unabashedly queer, quirky, and passionate author of Contemporary MM+ Romantic Fiction. Their published contemporary works include warm and sweet HEA romances as well as dark romances filled with grit, trauma, and angst.

In their hometown of Victoria, BC, Canada, Leigh can be found nestled up with their fabulously supportive wife and trusty laptop or enjoying the wondrous Vancouver Island outdoors.

Please consider joining Leigh's mailing list:
http://eepurl.com/xuhej

To connect with Leigh Jarrett:
Email: leigh@leighjarrett.com
Website: www.leighjarrett.com

You can also find Leigh on Facebook, Twitter, and Instagram

THE STARS ON MY ARM

TEKLA SERIES

Joel Carrigan and his girlfriend, Erica, are excited about starting their graduating year at Tekla Senior High. The long hot summer is drawing to a close, and their plans for a promising future together are on track. But their carefully laid plans are about to be disrupted by a dark and seductive force neither one of them anticipated.

That force is named Ethan Cooke. His gothic persona, covered in tattoos, piercings, and reckless abandon, set Joel's heart racing—but not out of fear.

TWO NIGHTS A WEEK

TEKLA SERIES

Chad Parker, the privileged son of a wealthy hotelier, has made the decision to transfer to Tekla Senior High for his graduating year. Events during the summer have made it far too dangerous for him to remain at his old school.

But on the very first day, he meets Derek Steeple, and finds himself in precisely the same situation, except this time, the consequences of his actions will forever change the lives of those he loves.